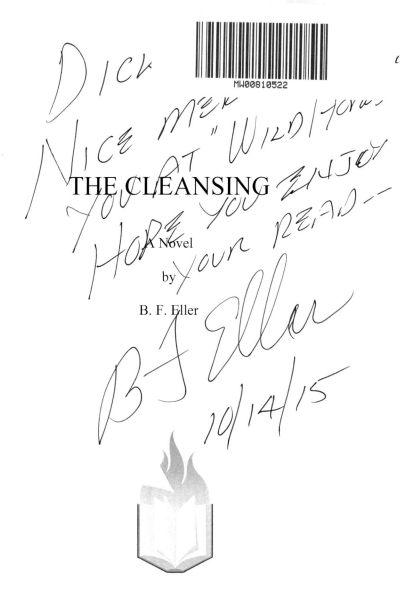

THE CLEANSING

A Novel

by

B. F. Eller

Fireside Publications
Lady Lake, Florida, 32159

This is a work of fiction. All of the characters, organizations and events portrayed in this novel are either products of the author's imagination, or are used fictitiously and are not based on any persons, living or dead.

FIRESIDE PUBLICATIONS
1004 San Felipe Lane
Lady Lake, Florida 32159

www.firesidepubs.com

Printed in the United States of America

First Edition: September 2009

ISBN: 978-1-935517-02-3

To Brenda, our children and grandson.

Words Of Praise For: *THE CLEANSING*

Congratulations to Dr. Ben F. Eller, runner-up in Fireside Publishing's 2008 Novel Writing Contest. His skill and insight in developing this "science-fiction bordering near-reality" story will become apparent as it keeps you clinging to the edge of your seat while reading his imaginative novel.

THE CLEANSING.
Don't read it alone in the dark!

Lois Bennett, Editor /Co-publisher
Fireside Publications

Ben Eller's science-fiction novel, "The Cleansing" is a response to our current global dilemma. At the point where our planet seems poised on the brink of apocalypse due to environmental pollution, escalating crime and raging warfare in the Middle East, suddenly our problems are resolved—not by leaders, but an unknown "Power." As governments struggle to adjust to a world in which violence is in 'remission,' Eller's protagonists, Josh Jones, and Sarah Trent launch a search to determine the true nature of the Power—are they Saviors or Enslavers? Most importantly, do we have a choice? Now, this is what I call a white-knuckled, page-turner!

Gary Carden, 2003 North Carolina Arts Council Playwright's award and The Appalachian Writers Association Book of the Year Award for "Mason Jars in the Flood."

We are not alone. In Ben Eller's new science fiction thriller, *"THE CLEANSING,"* the sordid, ugly and evil among us are under cool observation. The terrorist villain, moving toward mayhem with the radiation-tainted fuel he plans to feed American gas-guzzlers, does not proceed unnoticed. Child-battering dope dealers only THINK their unspeakable badness is beyond retribution.

Mysterious spacecraft, and their awesome cargo, keep track of who the wicked are, and where they do their trash. The Cleansing is at hand. Ethnicity has nothing to do with violence, blood-lust and cruelty—the crimes and dark habits that attract the 'Blue Light' of instant oblivion.

Oh, what a welcome flash and glow, as another miscreant is gone without a grease-spot! Can peace be far behind?

Dot Jackson, National Conservation writer of the year and winner of the Appalachian Writers Association Fiction book of the year and The Weatherford Award in Fiction for her 2006 novel, *REFUGE*

INTRODUCTION

Terrorism, violence, war and the ravishing of our environment are the nightmares of our troubled times and the theme of "The Cleansing". But what if "peace on earth" and living in harmony with ourselves our environment became a reality—the capacity for war, terrorism and violence stripped from human experience? The book asks and answers how this could be, and more intriguing what then?

The novel begins with a mysterious anomaly, the systematic disappearance of the most despicably violent humans on the planet. Privilege, power and wealth grant them no refuge. Child predators, serial killers, the perpetrators of violence, terrorism, genocide and war suddenly begin to vanish.

The world is plunged into an abyss of peace and harmony— the dream of billions but is it a dream or a nightmare? What is happening to the most despicable among us?

The world's fate hangs in the balance as the U.S. President, protagonist Josh Jones (genius graduate student haunted by demons of his own) and his girlfriend, Sarah Trent, (daughter of the U.S. UN ambassador) race to find the truth confronting a world never experienced by the human species.

Man, with all of his noble qualities...with his God-like intellect which has penetrated into the movements and constitution of the solar system still bears in his bodily frame the indelible stamp of his lowly origin.

Charles Darwin

CHAPTER ONE

Innocence

In wind-chilled darkness, Sarah stood naked and trembling and he didn't care. He yanked at the rope tied and twisted about her raw, chaffed wrists. Her eyes and mouth bound with duct-tape, she lunged forward, arms extended, unable to grope.

He grunted as he tried to hurry, forcing movement of his left leg, which seemed bigger than his right. Its stiff awkward gait rolled forward, trying to follow the normal steps of the other.

His voice was guttural, hoarse, "Gotta get you rooted. Best done at night when they's restin'."

Her feet were numb and bleeding, causing her to stumble and fall to her knees.

He jerked the rope again, scraping her legs across the frozen earth as her upper body lurched to the ground.

"Git up!" he yelled. "Wanna go back in the seasoning barrel? Do you?"

She slowly shook her head.

He moved to within an inch of her ear and whispered. "Then git up."

Sarah rose to her feet and stood shivering, more from his whisper than the cold biting at her bare skin.

In his office, Dr. Jason Maxwell, head of Homeland Security, sipped coffee and watched as Kate Dockery, Chief of Staff to the President, sat on the couch to the left of his desk reading the report. He enjoyed watching Kate. Her attractiveness was irrelevant at the moment. It was her devouring of information. In cold-sweat encounters with the most powerful leaders on the planet, she could focus her photographic mind with laser intensity and this was the fireplace warmth of his office. He expected the report to burst into flames.

"Think it's time to brief the President?"

Kate read for a few more seconds, laid the report in her lap and looked at Maxwell, "I don't know. It's too bizarre, and this thing with the 'Viper,' I saw the tapes. They had his house surrounded shoulder to shoulder—waited for him to go in. Had agents waiting in the house and in broad daylight the man still gets away. There were no hidden doors, no tunnel. They disassembled that house. It was on a concrete slab. That blue flash and the man's gone. Kills a woman every Tuesday for fourteen weeks, taunts us, then gets away from fifty agents. He's not human—how many more corpses with fang marks do we..." Kate slapped the report against her thigh.

Maxwell took off his reading glasses, "Been three weeks and we're covered up with reports from all over the country, FBI to county deputies. Check the last two pages."

Kate flipped to the back pages, "What's all that about people being attacked? Oh, any word from Bishop?'

Maxwell's phone interrupted, "Yes, Rachelle. Good, send him in."

Maxwell hung up the phone, "No word from Bishop, but Paul's here."

Five minutes later agent Paul Rantell, Associate Director FBI, paused in his briefing when Maxwell asked, "Heard anything from Bishop?"

"Said he'd call as soon as he landed, which was supposed to be twenty minutes ago, but you know how it is at Dulles."

The underbrush lashed Sarah's legs until she fell hard against the base of a tree. He yanked her to her feet, the ropes twisting deeper into her wrists. Stones tore at her feet as she waded through a stream and fell again. The freezing darkness and water paralyzed her as he bellowed, pulling her body across the rocks. She hit the bank, dug her bound hands into the mud to get leverage and was jerked forward again.

"Got to git you rooted."

A helicopter sounded overhead. He stopped and she blindly ran into him. Her scream muffled through duct tape as she stumbled backward. His mouth gaped and drooled as he looked up. The helicopter roared closer. Large, white, emboldened "FBI" letters gleaned on its side as the scanning search light from the chopper passed over them. He lurched forward, tying the rope around his waist. "Git you rooted then climb you forever."

Dr. Maxwell looked from the Citron projection screen to Rantell, "Let me be sure we're on the same page. The past ten days you've had over six hundred reports of hardcore criminals disappearing?"

"Actually, sir, it began about three weeks ago. Takes time for this kind of info to make its way up through the bureau. Initially, we didn't think too much of it—the good ole boys of law enforcement doing their thing. But Quarrels followed up..."

"Quarrels?" asked Maxwell.

"Yes sir, one of our egghead types. Brilliant guy—Ph.D. in Philosophy; anyway he followed up and his report, sir, we've never seen—well, sir, Ms. Dockery, this is more than off the chart. There's no chart for this."

Rantell left the computer screen and sat down in an easy chair to the side of Dr. Maxwell's desk facing Ms. Dockery. He stared at the floor and spoke softly.

"And this new report I'm giving you, there's stuff that defies..." Rantell shrugged then continued, "Man in Oregon, lived like a hermit, worked the night shift at Sears cleaning floors. Never missed a night of work for eleven years then didn't show up for three days straight. His boss got worried, called the sheriff's office. Went to his house, broke in, found his wife and three children chained to the wall in the basement, almost starved to death—been chained for two years. You can't imagine the filth. Wife told us he was beating her and the kids. Then a blue flash and he was gone. Remember the blurb in the news about the Judge Abrams, the Federal Judge in Toledo, disappearing?"

"Yeah, I remember getting something on that from your office," Kate answered.

"Exactly—another one that lived by himself—bachelor. Yesterday, we found four bodies buried under the floor of his crawl space. Killed four of his neighbors, and planned to kill more. How many, God only knows. Found their names on his computer. Had the grave dug for the fifth, his next-door-neighbor. Had him bound and gagged. Killed 'em in his bathtub with a pickaxe, starting at their feet. The neighbor said he wore a hood and robe like the KKK, only the robe was black. Said he raised the axe—a blue warmth flashed in the room and he was gone. His fingerprints was on the axe lying beside the tub, his car still in his garage. Found his billfold with all his credit cards on his nightstand. His bank account hasn't been touched.

"Had the Angel Rats, bunch of punk gang-bangers, had 'em cornered in Boston, all six of 'em. They'd kidnapped another eleven-year old girl—we figure she was at least the tenth one. She was on her way home from school. Her cell phone was in her coat pocket. Thank God it was on. Traced it to their apartment, heard the girl screaming. Found her alone tied down on a bed. Said they were dancing around her naked, one started to—then a flash and they were gone."

Rantell stopped, took a long drink of coffee and continued.

"Arrested three security guards and two custom officials at Bush International in Houston after three child slave traders running out of Mexico and one of their 'Johns' disappeared. The traders were flying children into Juarez smuggled out of the Ukraine and Latin America. Had their system canned. Landed them in Houston, skipped customs loaded them in vans and fanned them out all over the country. RV child brothels, coast to coast—kept them moving—stayed no longer than two weeks in any one place. They charged according to what you wanted to do. And if you had the money you could do anything you wanted."

His voice grew softer. "They had a menu, make you sick to read it. Any perversity you can name, if you had the money." Rantell hesitated and looked to the floor again, "Four days ago in Southside Chicago, a John disappeared. He liked the sound of a child screaming—was about to start on a six-year-old girl, blue flash and he was gone. The woman traveling with the children, who booked the Johns, and the RV driver started beating the girl, wanted to know what happened. Another flash and they're gone. This same thing, the exact same thing happened in LA, New Orleans, Beverly Hills and Paint Lick, Kentucky. Found children wandering around all over the place—said they were looking for the blue light."

He looked up from the floor, "I said there were hundreds, but there's more and we haven't found a one."

Maxwell retrieved his reading glasses and shook his head, "How've you kept this out of the news?"

"Good question, but in a way, we haven't. You know the beating we took when 'The Viper' got away." Rantell hooked his fingers in the air when he said *got away.*

"Think any of our guys are going to say, *'there was a warm fuzzy blue flash and then he was gone?'* Press would love that. There were a couple of minutes on SNN about Abrams and the bodies and him missing. The Angel Rats, according to the press, are still at large. But we came out okay on that one. We rescued the girl. She told us, and fortunately not the press, about the blue light. The high profile guys make the news at six, but so far, they're just missing. But a gang-banger in a project on the west side that disappears when he's about to ice pick his mother for drug money, nothing new, lucky to make the blotter. This thing is going to blow, getting to be too many, way too many."

Maxwell shook his head, and picked up his phone, "Rachelle, any word from Bishop?" Silence as he waited for her reply. "Yeah thanks, but as soon as you do let me know, we're going to be awhile." He hung up the phone and muttered, "Where the hell is he?"

He stopped and again Sarah ran into him. His right arm locked around her neck, dangling her feet off the ground. She felt the heavy black edge of unconsciousness losing the drone of the chopper in the distance. She trembled and felt his fingers digging in her head. The ripping away of the duct-tape about her eyes tore at her hair and face. She moaned through the tape until he whispered in her ear again.

"Gonna root you right here then I can climb you whenever I want and you can hold me way up high. Gonna root you right here with the big tree."

The last loop of tape ripped at her eyebrows. Sarah blinked and convulsed in the darkness. He released her and hypothermia dropped her to the ground. Her face hit fresh dirt. She tried to focus in the blackness then the light of the moon showed her the pit with mounds of dirt piled about it. The wind creaked the limbs of a large elm. He ripped away the duct tape from her mouth and she felt him pushing her.

Kate leaned forward in her chair and asked, "Was Abhar Ohim the same story?"

Rantell looked up from the floor, "He's was one of the first. Had him nailed to the barn. Thirty agents, round the clock. We knew when he peed. Believe it, or not, he was going for the Vietnam Memorial. Thought it was a soft target, national symbol, lots of tourists on Sundays. We waited until the last minute. Wanted to squeeze as much as we could—his contacts, explosive connections, communications, the whole nine yards. Had his apartment so wired he was tripping over 'em. Hell, we put him to sleep and tucked him in and he was clueless.

"Then he acquired a taste for hookers. Two days before he was going to hit he had two in his apartment. Four a.m. he put a gun to the head of one of them and threatened to blow her head off if the other didn't give him what he wanted. Building surrounded, all exits sealed, fifteen agents went in."

Rantell hesitated and looked away then back to Maxwell and Kate, "Now here's the thing. The man pulls the trigger and the gun fires at the same instant of the flash—the blue thing, got it on tape, and he was gone, vanished. The hooker walks away. The gun was two inches away from her head, it fires and she walks away."

There was silence before Kate asked, "What did the tape show about the flash."

"Remember those old flash bulb cameras, like that, a blinding blue flash. We had our best try to filter it out—couldn't. He was there, then the flash, and he was gone."

"Did you get the others, the co-conspirators?" asked Maxwell.

"Nope. Same story."

Maxwell stood unexpectedly, "Unbelievable, anybody want some water?" He retrieved three bottles of water from the office cooler without waiting for a response.

"So, what can we reasonably assume?" Rantell leaned forward, "They ran, escaped, got away. Okay, we send out missing persons, APB on their make and model of car. Data bank their credit cards, bank withdrawals, crosscheck airlines, bus lines, taxis, motels, hotels and flophouses for a hundred-mile radius, did that and nothing. Like I said, they're not taking their cars, withdrawing cash from their accounts, using their credit cards. They leave everything, clothes, personal items; they take nothing, none of 'em. And when we talk to their families, friends, lovers, acquaintances, even ones who have a grudge, even hate 'em—to a person, they swear they haven't seen or heard from them and they're telling the truth.

"We rewrote the 'Patriot Act' tapping lines and we don't have a clue as to where these people are. Remember, I'm talking hundreds. Hell, maybe thousands. Haven't had time to verify them all, but the ones we have, same story. That's the weird part; they're not missing, they're gone. Law enforcement loves it, calls it *'The Cleansing.'*"

"Anything like this ever happen before?" asked Kate.

Rantell fish-eyed the floor.

He pushed her toward the hole. Sarah screamed and tried to turn to dig her feet into the ground, but he was too strong. She fell forward, the lower half of her body struggling not to fall into the pit. She felt his hands on her back—pushing. The sound of the chopper was loud. A blue light flowed over her and she felt warm, falling asleep then she jerked awake. She lay beside the pit. *"Oh, God where is he?"* The roar was deafening. She struggled to her knees and frantically gnawed at the ropes about her wrists. The arm around her shoulders froze her. Her scream was muted, hoarse then she heard a different voice.

"Miss Trent you're safe now. I'm Lieutenant Josh Jones, FBI. Sarah, you're safe. I've got you. Can you hear me? You're safe."

She felt a blanket about her. As she slumped toward the ground, he pulled her into his arms.

The phone rang in Dr. Maxwell's office.

"Yes, Rachelle. Great, send him in."

Maxwell turned to the others, "Bishop is finally here."

The door of his office opened. A paunchy, graying, rain drenched Dr. Bishop, European office, FBI, stood in the door.

"Sorry I'm late. My cell phone went dead and I didn't want to take the time to…"

"What'd you find out?" Maxwell interrupted.

"Sir, it's worldwide. It's everywhere—they're disappearing *everywhere.*"

Rantell whispered, "My God."

The room was quiet until Ms. Dockery turned to Dr. Maxwell, "Yes."

"Yes, what?" asked Maxwell.

"Yes, it's time to brief the President."

CHAPTER TWO

Perplexity

Three months later, Oval Office, the White House.

"He'll be here in less than an hour and he's got questions so I want details. You know how he's been about this. He'll want details."

Kate focused on the information Dr. Bishop had power-pointed onto a screen. Dr. Maxwell sat to her right.

Bishop began.

"It lasted a month and it was global. In the U.S., as best we can determine somewhere between seven and twelve thousand."

Kate interrupted, "Why can't you pinpoint the figures?"

"So many individual accounts. The seven thousand are those we have more than one person reporting on an incident and there are many, maybe thousands who just don't report anything. Can't say that I blame them. You're about to be chain-sawed and your attacker disappears in front of you. You're fine, no injuries, no evidence anything ever happened. Some psychopath is about to attack you and disappears. Would you report something like that?"

"How about the Mideast, the bloodbaths in Abaya, Ethiopia, Albania, Krygyzstan, the purge in the Qaidam Basin ... "

"Nothing in the last three months."

CHAPTER THREE

Ugly

One Month Later

Josh Jones's voice came in short breaths. Muscle burned in his arms and chest. It was his third set of pushups. "Seven, eight, nine, forty...hun, two, three, four, five, six, seven, eight, nine... fifty."

Five minutes later he sat on the edge of his bed, the latex rubber tubing tied around his forearm. He thumped at a bulging vein then lit the candle. He picked up the syringe as the phone interrupted. His sister's words were slurred.

"Josh, I think they're hurting Cindy. They're not hurting Cindy, are they, Josh?"

"Donna, what's wrong? Whose hurting Cindy?"

"I have to go. I have to go."

The phone went dead in Josh's ear. Two minutes later Josh was in his old rusting Ford-pickup. It was the third week in October. He weaved through the "leaf lookers" on the James H. Quillen Parkway into Tennessee. The weather was clear, crisp, the sky crystalline after the hard rain. The sun was eating the fog from the mountains. It should have felt good. He should have called, kept in contact. She'd been working at Pal-mart, taking night classes at Walther Junior College. He'd seen his niece, Cindy, only once. That was over two years ago.

He passed a semi. The last of the rain mist from the pavement filtered through the broken front passenger window. His leg quivered, and the roar in his ears became gray. He was doing eighty.

Ninety minutes later, Josh eased his pickup beside the two muddy Kawaisakis parked by his sister's trailer. It was midday and the heat blended with sticky sweat. Sachem butterflies flitted about a damp tire track. The front tire of Josh's truck crushed one. He never knew.

10

The Cleansing

A loud TV blared out of the trailer spilling noise of dirt-bike racing. Mud, patched with stunted weeds, surrounded the trailer. Crabgrass flourished in the middle of an old tire making a nest for a banded yellowing newspaper. A wrecked and rusting tricycle lay in a mud puddle.

Josh knocked on a screenless metal door, pocked with heavy dents and slightly ajar. Broken glass lay beside it. A high-pitched male voice, slurred with beer, giggled and answered, "If you're selling beer or pussy, come in, huh Mace?"

Josh entered. Two wind burned men, one bearded, sat on a green vinyl couch laced with white splits. Biker helmets lay to their right. The immense one who answered was sitting on half the couch. His bucket face was cherubic, childlike and pink like his eyes that constantly moved to his brother. He had no hair, no eyebrows. He wore a heavy, greasy coat, sleeves extending beyond his fingers. His cap had three flaps. One covered his forehead, the other two dangled about his ears. His grin was silly and green-stained.

His brother sat beside him peering through sunglasses at the TV. His sunburn, flecked with white scabby patches, disappeared at the edge of his beard. A basketball rested in his lap. He was shirtless under a black leather vest, bare arms heavy, muscled and tattooed. The smell of cigarettes, beer and urine defiled the air penetrating the open door. Cigarette butts, beer cans, and wads of paper from junk food littered the room.

Josh's three year-old niece sat in a high chair next to the kitchenette, dressed in a gray and yellow-stained T-shirt. A baby bottle lay on the tray beside her, half full of coagulated milk, while a drying yellow puddle attracted flies at the base of her highchair. Her head wobbled from side to side.

Josh stared at her.

Her eyes crossed then corrected, focusing on nothing.

Josh's jaw gritted as he looked back to the two men.

The large simple one alternated his eager grinning between Josh and his brother.

"Hey Mace, hey Mace. He come in, he come in, so he must be selling beer or pussy. Hope it's beer cause we already got plenty of pussy, huh Mace?" His giggle was false, and high pitched.

The Cleansing

Mace's eyes never left the TV.

"I'm here to see my sister, Donna—Donna Jones," Josh said, looking back to his niece.

Mace moved his eyes from the TV and picked up a beer can, slowly shook it from side to side, spit in it and dropped it. Its contents oozed onto the floor. His grin exposed brown gums.

"Well, how about this? The man selling beer and pussy is her brother. Terrell, we've got to learn to be more polite. Hey, brother man, I'm Mace. Brother here is Terrell, and last time we checked your sister was in the bedroom."

The brothers laughed and high-fived. Mace's eyes locked on Josh.

Josh hesitated then headed toward the bedroom.

The voice of Terrell followed him.

"Wouldn't be going in there if I'z you, huh Mace?"

Josh opened the bedroom door. The sole of his boot crushed a syringe. The smell was worse.

His sister lay on the bed on her stomach, spread eagle, naked. She snored through matted hair stuck to the side of her face and forehead.

Josh put a blanket over her, then tried to wake her.

"Donna, it's me, Josh. Donna, wake up, it's Josh."

Donna moaned then opened her eyes, "Is that you, Terrell?" Mace? Did you get some more? Have all you want for some."

Josh dropped his head, "Come on, Donna. You're getting dressed. You and Cindy are coming with me."

Josh looked for clothes among the filth. The dry wail of Cindy from the next room made Josh shiver. He spun around to see a grinning Terrell picking up Cindy from her high chair. Josh started toward Terrell as the gray began to roar in his ears. His left leg twitched and he moaned, "*Parate quieto, las minas.*"

Terrell's mouth gaped, "God Mace, what's wrong with him? He like me? Huh Mace?"

The brothers stared as Josh's eyes focused. What they heard was primal.

"Put her down."

Very deliberately, Mace pulled fingerless black leather gloves from his back pocket and put them on, repeatedly clinching his fists. Clamping Cindy between his legs, Terrell imitated his brother pulling gloves from the right pocket of his brown coat.

Mace smiled at Josh, "Oh, come on brother, beer, pussy man. Me and Terrells just havin' a little fun. You'll get a kick out of this."

Terrell stood facing Mace pinning Cindy's arms to her sides.

"Your turn, Mace—huh Mace? Then we cut her like the other'n?"

Mace picked up the basketball from his lap.

Terrell giggled and smacked his lips, "Watch her eyes beer, pussy man, watch her eyes. Huh, Mace?"

Cindy whined and struggled.

"Now, don't you be moving or we'll burn your ass. Huh Mace?"

Josh stepped forward, "Let her go and get out."

Mace jerked with surprise then gritted his jaw. He picked up the remote and turned up the volume, fist-clinching his gloves.

"Well, would you listen, Terrell? Brother, beer, pussy man wants us to leave. And after all we've done for his little family."

Mace stared at Josh, "Ever see your bones exposed? What we do before we stomp em'. Terrell likes that."

Terrell whined, "My turn to stomp first. My turn to stomp first. Huh, Mace?"

Mace ignored him, eyes fixed, "No hard feelings, brother. Watch, you'll like this, watch her eyes."

Mace picked up the basketball from his lap. Terrell braced Cindy. With his right hand, he grabbed her hair and yanked her head upward. Mace bounced the basketball off Cindy's forehead. The thick splat brought bile to Josh's throat. Cindy's eyes crossed as she uttered a guttural, dying moan. Terrell giggled, and jerked Cindy's head toward Josh.

"Did ya see her eyes, did you see em'? Usually takes hitting her four or…"

Terrell didn't finish. Josh cut forward and punted his right foot into Terrell's groin then spun and smashed his palm into the bridge of Mace's nose. A blue blaze filled the room, snuffing out Terrell's and Mace's screams. Josh fell backward. He tried to get up but his body resisted.

The Cleansing

The next thing he remembered he was standing. The room was empty except for Cindy who was lying on the couch. He stumbled to Donna's bedroom with Cindy in his arms. Donna hadn't moved.

Two hours later Josh checked his sister into Quallen Rehab Center in Johnson City, Tennessee and then headed to Chapel Hill Children's Hospital with Cindy.

CHAPTER FOUR

The Script

Two months later

Dr. Gayle B. Trent, the U.S. ambassador to the UN, arose at 6:30a.m. She had a breakfast meeting with the ambassadors from France, Germany, Japan and Russia in two hours.

"*For five years we've been trying to convert Russia to the Euro—maybe today.*"

Dr. Trent showered, dressed, left her Manhattan condo, waved at Phil as he opened the electronic security gate, and headed east toward the eighteen acres that was her life. Gayle Trent was fifty, matronly trim, attractive, brown eyes and auburn hair. She looked younger when she tinted away the streaks of white, but she didn't. Aging was an asset with UN peers. Her position was wearing on her and she knew it. She relished time for walking and aerobics when her schedule permitted, but it rarely did. Traffic was moderate and the Mercedes XL made good time. A Tractor-trailer, with screaming horn, roared past to her left. She cringed with raw memories.

"*See you Monday*" she had said to her husband Lincoln.
"*Okay, call me when you get there. Love you.*"
"*Love you, call you tonight.*"
"*I'm calling for Ms. Trent.*"
"*This is she.*"
"*Ms. Trent, this is Sergeant Buckles of the Kentucky State Patrol. I'm sorry to be the one to tell you but there's been an accident…*"
"*Sarah, you need to come home.*"
"*God, did you hear about Adam and Lincoln? What on earth will she do?*"

The Cleansing

"If it's any comfort, Dr. Trent our investigation, suggests it was instant."

"Gayle, we love you. If there's anything we can do."

"Our prayers are with you."

"Ladies and gentlemen, we're gathered here to honor and pay respect to the family..."

"Mother this can't be. This can't be."

"The Trent family lost a father, a son, a husband,, our country lost a great ambassador and the world lost..."

"After this is over we want you and Sarah to come stay with us for a while. We'll go to the beach house and ..."

She thought she would know if something like this ever happened. She didn't until the call. Lincoln, her husband, and Adam, her son, were dead and it was forever. She would wake herself up screaming then sit for hours in a stupor. The blackness of her bedroom became a refuge.

Two days later, hundreds attended the funeral including the President and Vice-President, foreign dignitaries, congressmen, judges, businessmen and friends. Contributions from the public to UN children's fund quadrupled over the next few weeks before returning to normal. A week later, everyone was gone.

"I'm going to drop out. I can't go back. I just can't."

The call came from the President two weeks later. He was gracious and sincere asking about her and Sarah." Gayle admired the President, although she knew he had asked her husband to be the UN ambassador as a political maneuver, but then as Lincoln reminded her, "That's the way it is and in my case that's just fine."

The President gauged his conversation. When he was confident she was ready, he asked. "Gayle, I have another reason for calling, and I will depend on you to be honest about the timing. I know it has only been two weeks but our country needs a UN ambassador, and our country would be fortunate and I would be honored if you would consider taking the post."

She must have been quiet for some time when she heard the President say.

"Gayle, are you there?"

"Yes, Mr. President, I'm still here. I just don't..."

The Cleansing

The President interrupted, "I don't expect an answer now. I know you have a lot to consider. Talk it over with Sarah and yourself. Take the time you need. But I want you to know my entire cabinet and the majority and minority leaders in both houses would support your nomination. And, Gayle, that just doesn't happen around here."

"Mr. President, I didn't even vote for you in the last election."

The President laughed, "Well, since I'm in my second term you know I'm not lobbying for your vote. Truth is, Gayle, our country needs a UN ambassador."

Gayle knew when she hung up what her answer would be.

A horn from another semi jarred her from her thoughts into today, two years later.

At precisely 7:30a.m., Gayle walked through the outer offices of her staff toward the UN office door labeled *"U.S. AMBASSADOR - Dr. Gayle Trent."* The office bustled and "good mornings" were exchanged. Brenda Spencer, her chief administrative assistant, rose and followed Gayle to the Espresso machine.

"The assembly meeting has been postponed until next Tuesday. That conflicts with your commencement address at Duke."

Gayle sipped coffee as she continued toward her office. "Confirm the Duke commencement. They'll postpone the assembly again. Middle East." She said the last two words like they explained everything—and they did.

Gayle entered her office as Brenda turned to leave then stopped.

"Oh, Sarah is on line two."

"Thank you, Brenda. Let Maurice know the Russian ambassador will be joining us for lunch."

Gayle answered the flashing light and read messages on her desk as she talked. "Hey, how's my someday Ph.D. daughter?"

"Great, just calling to tell you I'll be a little late getting home for Christmas."

"And why's that?"

"Ever heard of Dr. Charles Bellamy?"

She thought for a moment. "No, can't say that..."

17

The Cleansing

"Big name in astronomy at UCLA—up for the Nobel."

"Oh, sounds impressive."

"For his work on black holes—the top five Nobel candidates were given time on our Terrestrial-Planet-Finder. Dr. Bellamy is scheduled at 4a.m. Christmas morning."

"Four a.m. Christmas morning?"

"Sure, the TPF is scheduled 24/7, months in advance. They postponed maintenance for the Nobel wannabes."

Gayle stopped reading her messages, "So, let me guess. You volunteered to stay and set up the TPF for Dr. Bellamy."

"Along with fifty other graduate students. Lassiter, Drake and I were selected. Can you imagine me, a lowly graduate student, loading software on the most advanced planet finder in the history of the world?"

"Chip off the old block. That's great, hon, when do you think you'll be able to get home?"

"Oh, Christmas day, early afternoon, can't wait. Hey, what's going on in your world?"

"Terrorism, famine, the four horsemen of the apocalypse, we need to pay our dues, same ole, same ole."

There was a pause.

"Sarah, are you...?"

"Yes mother, every Monday, Wednesday and Friday. Dr. Witt is great, and I'm fine if I could ever get rid of this rash. That fertilizer really liked me."

Gayle couldn't help but smile, "You are unbelievable."

A red light flashed on Gayle's phone.

"Sarah, got a hot line here. Love you hon, see you soon."

Gayle pushed the red light button and heard the familiar voice of Dr. Brad Chissom.

Dr. Chissom led the IBM team that designed the computer-communication-security system after the terrorist breach three years ago. Ambassador Trent chaired the UN committee charged with overseeing the project. CRAY and NEC were hired to hack into the system after it was put on-line by IBM. It took three years of brain-wrenching, fun to watch competition, before the system was cleared for service but since, the system had been invincible.

"Ambassador, this is Brad. You turn on your computer yet?"

"No, just walked in." She paused before asking, "Why, got a glitch?"

"Yeah, a big one. Appreciate it if you'd turn it on and read what your terminal displays."

"Okay, give me a sec." Gayle turned on her computer and frowned. "Brad, instead of our logo there's a message titled "*THE SCRIPT.*"

"Yeah, I was afraid of that. Could you read me what it says?"

"Sure." Gayle read the following:

THE SCRIPT
Preservation of earth's habitat and species requires the following:

- *Cessation of wars and violence among Homo sapiens.*
- *Disabling the weapons of Homo sapiens conflict.*
- *Discontinuance of planet destruction and extinction of species.*
- *Cessation of the reproduction of Homo sapiens.*

The above will be implemented in two years.

"Well, at least our first hackers are creative." Gayle chuckled into the phone, "I must admit I'm a bit anxious to know how they plan to pull it off in two years."

"Good question but every ambassador we've checked with got the same message and we've contacted all but ten. UN security, the FBI and the state department are having a hissy."

Gayle laughed again, "The FBI and state department? Seems more like a prank than a security break. Brad, you guys wired this thing for sound—retina check, fingerprint confirmation, and DNA analysis. Have you asked Ambassador Neheran about this? He's always..."

"He was the second ambassador to call me about the message."

There was a pause before Gayle asked, "What do you think? Frat boys at MIT and Cal Tech bet a keg of beer who could hack us first?"

"Gayle, if CRAY and NEC can't hack us then—hell, I don't have a clue. That script message was delivered in every ambassador's native language, over a hundred languages—Mandarin, Japanese, German, and English, just to name a few. There are no Mandarin or Japanese characters on your keyboards."

"But software could have been used to…"

"Could've, but that message was delivered to African ambassadors from Mali, Chad and Mauritania in their native dialects. No software exists that translates those languages much less their specific dialects. I know. I'm working with the team here to do just that and we're at least two, three years tops, away from it. But, that's not the hard part. We've checked your email data banks. There's no file on these messages—none. Our system is telling us you've never received that message. And this couldn't have been done internally. To convert that many languages and dialects, then somehow fool the fingerprint, retina and DNA ID for every UN member, then crash individually secured computers—and while you're doing this avoid security guards and staff not to mention three hundred surveillance cameras. We don't know whether to handcuff whoever pulled this off or hire them."

A soft knock pulled Ambassador Trent's eyes to her door as it opened. Brenda leaned in.

"Sorry, but Ms. Dockery is here. Just walked in. Says it's urgent."

"Thanks Brenda. Brad, I have to go. Keep me posted."

"Will do."

Gayle heard the click and put down her phone. *The Chief of Staff to the President, Kate Dockery is here?"* When Lincoln and Adam were killed, Kate Dockery was the one who came and would not leave until Gayle came out of the bedroom, three days later. Their friendship flourished and defied frenzied political careers and the commute between Washington and New York. *But why is she here? Surely, the White House is not…*

Her door opened and Kate Dockery entered. They embraced.

"Kate, good to see you. Happy holidays and you're supposed to be at my house Christmas eve.

"I'll be there. It's so good to see you too. How's Sarah?"

The Cleansing

"Believe it or not, she's great." Gayle shrugged and smiled, "I'm still a basket case, but she seems to be just fine. Like her dad, tough as nails. You'd think nothing ever happened. Didn't miss a beat in graduate school. Dr. Witt, her therapist, says she amazes him."

"Thank God. She is something." Kate shook her head. "I'd be in a fetal position, drooling for the next twenty years. Did he really bury her in a barrel of fertilizer?"

"Yes, well, up to her neck. Sarah said he kept saying something about 'seasoning her'. They found traces of fertilizer on the other girls. Can you imagine, burying five girls alive under trees? We got his history, did you hear?"

"No, I didn't."

"Goes without saying he was deranged. Use to climb trees to get away from the abusive aunt who raised him. Fell climbing one when he was six. Severe brain injury, almost died, steel plate and he got worse as he grew older. His aunt disappeared when he was sixteen. Never found her. They think he buried her somewhere."

"And he really picked her up in a taxi?"

"Yeah, she was visiting me here, went shopping. Car broke down. Battery if you can imagine. She waited ten minutes for her security but they were blocked in traffic. She was in a hurry to get home to get ready for a party. Got careless, hailed a cab, and he just happened to pick her up."

"He got all the girls that way?" Disbelief filled Kate's voice.

"Yes, stole a taxi. Would ride around until he spotted a girl alone hailing a cab and pick her up. Took them to his pit, miles from nowhere in the Adirondacks. Buried them up to their necks in fertilizer then at night took them to one of his trees where he buried them around the roots."

Gayle turned from Kate, "And, he's still missing."

Kate touched her friend's arm, "I know."

The ambassador faced Kate, "If that hiker hadn't reported what he saw—but that's enough of that."

Gayle stopped and cleared her throat.

"Update me on our blue light that probably saved my daughter's life. Whatever that is."

The Cleansing

"Nothing much since our last memo. As best we can tell, the reports have dissipated since last month. Hard to sift through fifty thousand disappearances every month to find the ones that reported a blue light. What we know is that over a four to six week period somewhere between five- and twelve-thousand of our worst citizens disappeared and I'm talking bad, scary people. Casting crew for nightmares. We have no clue on any of them, not one." She tilted her head toward Gayle. "What's the scuttle in your neck of the woods? All we've heard is that they're scared."

"You're right about that, scared and hiding. Hamas, Hizballah, PLF, the Kahane Chai all suddenly underground. And the Libyan National Front who thought genocide was the thing in Koro—nowhere to be seen. UN relief workers and the Red Cross are moving in and out with no problems. Same thing in Abaya, Bela and you know what happened in Jadhpur? Oh, you won't believe—Ambassador Taell, he..."

"Taell, Liberian ambassador, right?"

Gayle nodded, "Yes, unbelievable story, witnessed, according to him, by hundreds of children. Remnants of the old Charles Taylor regime trying to gain power again."

Gayle mumbled, "God, won't that man's ghost ever die? Anyway, they were back to their old habits..."

"Stealing children out of Sierra Leone, Ivory Coast even Mali," Kate interrupted, "drugging them and forcing them to join their war against the Liberian government. Spaced out ten-year-olds with AK-48s."

"Exactly."

"You're going to tell me the kidnappers started disappearing."

"Yes, and Ambassador Taell said the reason is the blue. Patrols raid a village, start off with the children—the blue and the kidnappers are gone. Same thing is happening in Kosovo, Sri Lanka, and Uganda. But Taell added something I hadn't heard. The child soldiers who tried to kill didn't disappear but their weapons quit working, wouldn't fire."

That was news to Kate. "What?"

"Got so bad with the Taylor wannabes they gave up and went home. Ran out of Ak-48s and soldiers."

"Yeah, that's something different. Will check with intel on that. Anything else?"

"Well, the ones that are talking—same MO, some monster starts to commit an atrocity and they're gone. Some say hundreds, some thousands. Is it true about Amon in Kindu?"

"The word we got from agents out of Tanzania is that his men from his Red Guard were disappearing. He thought they were deserting so he decided to chop off the hands of one of his officers and *'poof'* he's gone. Did it in front of two hundred of his men, wanted to set an example. His Red Guard disbanded after that little incident. Some even volunteered to help the UN workers. Got the bad boys pulling back all over the place. Not as bad in Europe, well, got remnants of the IRA, skinheads, a few Nazi's—yeah, it's everywhere."

"But you say it is dissipating?"

"Yes, for the past month. And violent crime in the good ole US of A is down eighty percent?"

Gayle arched an eyebrow. "You're joking. I haven't seen any reports..."

"We didn't report eighty percent. We reported a slight drop."

"A slight drop? But why would—of course, can't rile the masses."

"Yeah, they suspect something ain't quite right. They're right and we don't have a clue."

"But our blue terminator is not why you're here."

Kate returned Gayle's wry smile. "You're a wise lady. It's about your breech. I'll explain in the limo."

"Our communications breech? You can't be serious." Gayle shook her head, refusing to accept it as anything more than a prank.

"Yes, got a briefing in six hours with Dickenson and Stewart plus the President wants you there. Our limo is waiting."

In the Limo Kate explained, "There's more to your breech, quite a bit more. The joint chiefs and the Vice-President are in a twit and frankly it has me feeling a little creepy."

"Creepy? The Vice-President and the joint chiefs make me creepy, but you? Kate, what are you talking about?"

The limo hummed toward the airport as Kate pushed the button that closed the window behind the driver.

"Six months ago your script turned up on the computer terminals of the President, the English prime minister, President Surakov of Russia and the Prime Minister Yow Ping of China. Well, it wasn't exactly the same message. The last line read, 'In two and one-half years', and the rest was identical."

Gayle turned in her seat and faced Kate, "The same message?"

"Yes, and nobody knows anything. During the last six months the CIA and the FBI have violated every national and international privacy law on this planet trying to find out who did this and to paraphrase Dr. Chissom, *'they don't have a clue'*."

"How'd you know about Brad?"

"Oh, we've had him working on this for months. After Interpol was penetrated I bet him twenty bucks they'd get to the UN. Interpol had a damn good system. And like the blue buzz, we have no idea. Getting to be SOP."

"How about the English, Russians and Chinese?" Gayle asked.

"Scotland Yard is befuddled as usual. The Russians and Chinese aren't talking, and that means they don't have a clue either. And the French are sulking because their President didn't get a message."

"Any repercussions?"

"None so far, or if there have been we don't know it yet."

"Kate, there has to be an explanation. Somebody or some clever bunch of Ivy League fraternity boys are probably drinking beer and high-fiving as we speak."

"That's what we thought, and frankly hoped, but there's more. You've heard of Dr. Jane Thrower's work with African chimpanzees?"

"Of course, who hasn't but…"

"Exactly one year ago she was handed a tablet that contained the same message except the last line read 'In three years.'"

"Well, that's it! Who handed it to her? Surely, you followed that lead."

Kate shook her head, "Dr. Thrower was ten miles deep in the Gombia Stream game reserve in Tanzania when a three month old Chimp dropped the tablet at her feet and the message was in Swahili. That same day, whale hunters from Iceland found an identical tablet, transcribed in Icelandic, in the innards of a whale they had just slaughtered—threw it at a *Green Peace* boat that was harassing them. And on that same day, a Tibetan monk found the same tablet, written in Sanskrit, lying on his prayer altar."

Gayle starred at Kate, "How'd you find out all this?"

"*ABS* and *SNN*."

"Are you serious?"

"Dead serious. *ABS* funds Dr. Thrower, and *SNN, just happened to have a* Satellite Network on assignment in Tibet getting a story on the monastic life of monks, or some such, and *Green Peace* came up with the tablet. *ABS* put it together and ran it a month ago, Monday night, 9:00 p.m. prime time and Gretchen happened to be watching."

"Gretchen? President Meyer's daughter?"

"The same."

"This is…" Gayle's words drifted off. "What are the tablets made of?"

"The tablets were sent to Oak Ridge National Laboratories for analysis. But so far they haven't been able to tell us a thing—nothing."

CHAPTER FIVE

Power

Gayle and Kate entered the outer office of the President. Ann Stophel, the President's personal secretary, greeted them. It was Christmas Eve and, except for security, the staff was off.

Gayle quipped to Kate, "So deserted it's eerie."

Ann came from around her desk and hugged both, "Gayle, Kate, good to see both of you back, especially you, Gayle. We see Kate all the time. Hope you had a good flight."

"It's good to be back. How's Tom?" Gayle responded.

"Oh, grumpy as ever, still trying to get his book published. I'll talk to you later." She pointed toward the door to the Oval office, "He said for you two to come right in when you arrived."

Gayle and Kate entered the Oval office. Gayle had been in the office probably more than a hundred times since becoming the UN ambassador, and each time she felt like a first grader the first day of school. It took three visits before she quit whispering.

President Gerald R. Meyer rose and greeted them. He served two terms in the Senate before becoming the minority whip, then majority leader. He ran for President at the urging of his party and after the cleanest campaign in decades beat republican Dana George of California in a close election, his home state of Oregon tipping the scales. He won his second term in a landslide.

The President was an anomaly. He was intelligent but few suggested brilliant except when it came to political skill. In that arena he had few equals. He was average in height and features but not in appearance. His slender body and thinning, gray hair matched a sharp chin and nose that always held teetering reading glasses. All nondescript individually, but it was his eyes—gray, alert, peering comfortably over his glasses, always focused on the individual but never challenging or threatening even when provoked. His demeanor could change with a whisper—

26

attentiveness, compassion, understanding, anger or forgiveness and always perceived as genuine.

He gave the common voter the benevolent neighbor or relative who evoked their absolute trust. To the more sophisticated, he was the English Lit professor who had extolled the virtues of Poe and Dickens. Even his enemies admitted they liked him. He was honest but didn't let that get in his way of being a good politician.

He smiled and extended his hand, "Before either of you say a word, I apologize. I know it is Christmas, and I know about your workloads lately, but I promise this won't take long and I don't know—it may be important. But before I forget, Gayle how's Sarah?"

"Fine. Actually she's amazing. Doing well in school. Graduating soon, at least that's what she tells me."

"That's so good to hear. You be sure and tell her I asked."

"Will do Mr. President. How are Hanna and Gretchen?

"Oh, Gretchen's getting ready for college. She applied at UCLA, Arizona and you will be pleased to know—Duke." He gave her a grin. "And Hanna's in South America, due back tomorrow, has to get her daughter ready for college. Oh, excuse me ladies, but would either of you like something to drink, coffee, anything? Roswall, Tom and Annabelle are going to join us in a few minutes. Oh, and I've asked Dr. Maxwell to join us."

Gayle noted the President's half-second too long glance at Kate. One year after the death of Lincoln, at a reception at the White House, Kate had introduced Dr. Maxwell to Gayle. This led to a few discreet dinners, concerts and then speculation in the tabloids. The truth was, they were two friends who enjoyed each other's company. Unfortunately, or as Gayle thought, perhaps fortunately, they rarely saw each other. Washington and New York were worlds apart. Dr. Maxwell was ten years younger than Gayle, and Gayle liked that.

The Center for Strategic and Budgetary Assessments in Washington, Behavioral Sciences in Quantico, military intelligence and even the research portion of the CIA, was the first to feel the wrath of President. The duplication of resources and competitive bickering came to a head during the Sudanese campaign. The continued inability of the various Intelligence branches to share information cost the US military an extra two billion dollars and 1500 causalities. The President cleaned house and HS was recipient to the most advanced technology, resources and minds in the world. Dr. Maxwell was appointed head of HS and was given three directives by the President; *"Number one, Do your job, Number two, share everything or Number three, I'll find someone who will."*

Jason Maxwell's companionship was good for Gayle and she knew it. He had never married and eventually polite dinner conversation got around to asking why.

"Very protected childhood. Both my parents were musicians, mother taught violin, dad was a clarinetist for the New York Philharmonic. I attended private school, entered high school when I was ten, graduated when I was twelve, immediately entered Princeton and graduated two and half years later. Entered graduate school at the ripe old age of fifteen—Penn University. Not much chance to date in college when your peers are just entering high school. Both my parents are deceased. I have a sister, married, lives with her husband and two children in LA. She teaches physiology at Cal. State. We're close but the distance and our jobs—you know what that does to priorities, so it's just me, Sandy and Molly."

"Sandy and Molly?" She had asked

"Yeah, my two spoiled girls. Found them at the pound. One's a lab, the other a pointer, well, as close as they can get. Their fathers didn't hang around long enough to establish a family pedigree. Like dogs?"

"Love dogs. Have a couple at home in Chapel Hill. They came with the farm. When we started to build they arrived one day, checked us out, and decided we'd be okay to live with. Both old hounds, but they're part of the family and as you say, spoiled rotten. You entered graduate school when you were fifteen?"

"Yep."

"And you have two doctorates, Chemistry and Genetics?"

"Well, Organic Chemistry and Nuclear Genetics."

"Oh, so you're 'way smart'?"

"'Way smart'? That would be Goodwill Hunting, 1998, right?"

"Right! You're pretty good."

They smiled, sipped wine, and he asked another question about the UN.

"Now, what do you know about us building power plants in the Middle East?"

Ambassador Trent jarred back to the President's office. She looked to Kate, then the President. "Dr. Maxwell is going to be here?"

"Yes," Meyer responded.

"HS has some ideas on the breach, and I wanted Roswall, Tom and Annabelle to hear what Jason has to say." General Roswall F. Dickenson was head of the Joint Chiefs, Tom S. Stewart was Vice President and Annabelle E. Royer was Secretary of State.

The President gestured toward a table that contained pastries and drinks before pouring three coffees. "Now, ladies, I would appreciate it if you would give me the executive summary on this breach."

Gayle and Kate filled in the President on the day's happenings. The President listened as he sipped coffee. When they finished he turned his chair a bit to one side.

"If it's not some blue flash, it's somebody crashing the most secured systems—whatever happened to old fashion budget deficits, educational reform and partisan bickering?"

"Oh, Kate being in New York, you haven't heard the latest on the blue buzz. Gayle, we call it the blue buzz around here. Happened two days ago. Just got the report from our embassy in Ukraine. We've been trying to break up the 'Balkan Runners' for a decade. Branch of their Mafia that lures women out of Russia, Poland, Turkey, Hungary—promise of jobs. I say women. Most are teenage girls. Get them to Belgrade. There's no jobs then they're told they owe thousands for the service. Forced into prostitution, locked up in houses, no communication with families, nobody. Twenty, thirty customers a day and it costs their families a fortune to get them back, if they ever find them. Suicides—well you've read the reports."

Meyer stopped and adjusted his glasses before continuing. "Well, it seems one of the girls tried to escape. They caught her, tied her up and start to break two of her fingers in front of the others. Their way of keeping control. Two men start to do it—the blue buzz and they're gone. The girls just walked out with five 'runners' watching, not one did a thing. Now, here's the good part. Three days later the ones that escaped liberated girls from three other houses. Just walked in got the girls and walked out. Not one runner tried a thing. Word got around."

The President shook his head, "We've been trying to close those damn hell houses for six years—couldn't. Too damn much money greasing too many pockets. Took this blue..."

President Meyer's intercom buzzed. A few seconds later Dr. Maxwell, General Dickenson, Vice President Stewart and Secretary Royer entered.

Gayle liked the surprised smile on Jason's face when he saw her. Secretary Annabelle Royer was the last to enter. Gayle hugged her. Secretary Royer was the great granddaughter of former Senator Everett K. Dietz. She'd been exposed to political life since birth. She was known by her fiery red hair and the gravely voice of her great grandfather. In political circles, she was revered and feared for her blunt honesty, dirty jokes and acid wit.

Neither Kate nor Gayle had ever trusted General Dickenson or Vice President Stewart. Both were career military men through and through. Roswall Dickenson was a short toad of a man, small darting alert eyes within a massive head, small thin ears and a short neck etched with buttermilk streaked acne scars. His hair could be attractive, a soft premature gray white, but it was always a slick mayonnaise yellow.

Vice-President Stewart was on President Meyer's ticket during the first election to deliver Texas and he did. He was sharp, lean, very striking and a consummate politician. Stewart was the Texas cowboy who'd been educated yet both Gayle and Kate had noticed that underneath the political savvy was an indifference that was numbing.

Gayle had been in the middle of briefing the President's staff on the atrocities committed in the coup in Namibia, Africa when Vice-President Stewart interrupted with a question. "Dr. Trent, do you have any idea why only three to five hundred?"

Dr. Trent, puzzled by the question, had asked, "Three to five hundred?"

"Yes, according to your report, page six, item four, only three to five hundred women were raped during the two week coup. You'd think the rebels would've taken more advantage of their victory."

The meeting began with Kate briefing on the UN security breach.

President Meyer asked, "We haven't talked with Wells yet and you say UN security hasn't uncovered anything?" Edward Wells headed the FBI.

Kate responded to the question, "Sir, they don't know a thing."

"Hell, they never do," General Dickenson scoffed. "This is a job for military intelligence. You can't tell me this is not a threat to national security. What do these bastards have to do, stamp this script on somebody's—excuse me ladies, but you get my drift. If the bastards can get into the communication systems of national leaders and the UN, God knows what else they can do. We can't be dicking around with UN security. The FBI and CIA haven't done squat. Give my boys the green light, and we'll find the bastards—period."

Dickenson was ignored until the Vice-President spoke up, "General Dickenson has a point. We have to find out who's behind this. The CIA is checking out what they call the *'message trail.'* They have a couple of professor types analyzing the script's message. They're looking at militant and pro-choice groups. Something about the message theme of disarming and no more reproduction point to those types."

"Jason, you might want to fill us in on what HS is doing" stated President Meyer.

"Well, our people are analyzing at ORNL but they haven't been able to ID the tablets and China and England aren't doing any better. Russia sent their tablet to us. Their people said they have no idea, but they did confirm that the tablets are deteriorating, despite anything we do—sealing in a vacuum, varying temperature, humidity, nothing has worked yet." Jason hesitated, his voice taking on even more of a perplexed tone. "One very interesting tidbit, the dust from their deterioration resembles the dust brought back by Vulcan II from the last Mar's probe. We're checking more on that. Cal Tech and MIT want a crack at the tablets and I think we should give them a shot. Whatever we do, we have about two years. The tablets are deteriorating that fast."

General Dickenson boomed, "Hell's bells, Martian dust . . . Martian dust! Damn, Dr. Maxwell, you don't buy that horse hockey, do you?"

Annabelle, who had been silent until now spoke. "Well, if he was in the business of buying horse shit, you'd be a mighty rich man wouldn't you Dickenson."

General Dickenson bellowed laughter, "Hell, Annabelle, I am a rich man. What's that tell you?"

Like the others, Annabelle, knew military intelligence had been working on the breach for months and hadn't uncovered a single thing, and Dickenson knew they knew.

The President raised his hand, "Gentlemen, ladies, it's late and it's Christmas. Tom, keep the CIA and FBI on this and Jason, I agree with you—let Cal Tech and MIT have a look at those tablets. When you have something, let me know."

"Yes sir, Mr. President. "

Again Gayle was surprised, "*Jason had been working on the tablets? He hadn't mentioned that.*"

The President continued, "Roswall, keep your boys on it too and if anything breaks, and I mean anything, everyone is to know and I mean everyone. Do your people have any problem with that, General?"

"No sir, Mr. President, no problem at all."

"Good. Ladies and gentlemen, let's have some Christmas cheer."

Ninety minutes later—Vice-President Stewart's office.

The Vice-President and General Dickenson sat smoking cigars.

"Well, General, your boys come up with anything yet?"

"Nothing yet, but by God they will. Shit, Tom, they have to. This is damn serious."

Stewart nodded, "Your boys need anything? I could pull in Los Alamos or..."

32

The Cleansing

"No, I'd rather we handle this. Whoever cracks this will be able to make hay for the next two years and I want it to be us. Best keep this one in the family."

The Vice-President slanted his eyes toward the General, "Thought you had no problem sharing information."

The General pulled on his cigar, "No need to push that button right now—Alabama cornbread in New York buttermilk. Hell, have to give him credit though, that sharing information crap did cost us in the Sudan."

"Well, filter everything through me. I'll keep the President informed of what he thinks he needs to know. But you're right, this is serious; so don't hold out on me with this. I have to know. If we screw up, somebody will have our goodies. So dammit, keep me posted."

The General smiled, "I will, I will. But you know what really pisses me off—these fucking Democrats. Every one of the bastards gets cramps every month."

CHAPTER SIX

Seeds of Vengeance

The same day

Despite the animals, the lab was eerily quiet, immaculate, sterile, except for the faint smell of exhaust fumes. The corridors of stainless steel shelving were lined with plants and caged animals. The hundreds of plants were labeled by hemisphere, country, and species. Most were from Western Europe and the U.S. and were planted in soil from native habitats.

Technology from the West automatically watered and organically fertilized the plants in accordance with the requirements of their species. Artificial sunlight was measured to insure the best of growing and reproduction conditions. Yet, most of the plants were dead and decaying, exhibiting their agony with gross distortions and mutant deformities. A few of the plants resisted, but the brown and gray on their stems and leaves stated it was only a matter of time.

The animals were mice, rats, cats, dogs, rabbits and chimps. In the two largest pens, two horses and two goats pressed as close to each other as they could. They licked at each other's lesion wounds through the bars. Like the plants, the animals were meticulously cared for. Their cages were large and contained the shelter and sleeping space they required and were cleaned twice daily. They were fed the diet required by their species. Nutrients were scientifically measured for optimum growth and health. Lighting insured sleeping and opportunity for mating was given every opportunity. But all were silenced with lesions and the festering of burnt flesh.

Most of the mice were dead. The birds had lost their feathers, revealing bloated purple bodies. They would be dead within the day. The water did not protect the marine life. Fish, turtles and coral covered with warty contusions floated motionless on the surface of pristine tanks.

The Cleansing

Six randomly dispersed red lights suddenly flashed, followed five seconds later by a bleating repetitive horn. None of the animals flinched. Two men dressed in white rubber suits, plastic helmets with shielded faces entered the lab through large metallic, electronically controlled doors. They examined and probed a random selection of the dead and dying plants and animals.

One of the men, Ishmael Zolef, asked, "Are there any exceptions?"

"None, all of the plants and animals are dying."

Zolef smiled, "God is great. It is time for the prisoners. Check the provisions again. Everything, enough for two years."

"Yes sir."

At 2 a.m. the next morning, thirty shackled men and ten women entered an adjacent lab to the plants and animals. They were placed in large jail cages in pairs. The women were paired with a man of their choosing. They did not know of the plants and animals next door.

Zolef and his assistants stood outside the lab. They drew on cigarettes and looked out over the Persian Gulf toward the lights of Kharg Island where endless oil pipelines from the oil fields of Iran carried crude to Jazireh-ye Khark terminal. Here they mated with the giant tankers from the west, daily loading eight million barrels into their bellies. Then, pregnant with oil, the tankers snailed through the Persian Gulf to the Gulf of Oman out to the Arabian Sea. Ishmael dropped his cigarette, stared at its glow before pressing it into the sand. He rubbed his mustache, lit another cigarette and gestured toward the pipelines.

"Look at it, six years and the proverb was always there."

One of Zolef's assistants glanced to the other one, "Proverb?"

Zolef took a long draw, "'The greed of your enemy is your sword'."

"It was your genius, Ishmael. No one believed you could do it. I beg you forgive my doubting you."

The burn of Zolef's cigarette pointed toward the tankers. He thought of the years spent determining the effects of emissions on the plant and animal life of Europe and the West. The lab had been stocked with the plants and animals native to the infidel's homeland. Emissions from automobile engines and simulated

The Cleansing

factory pollutants spewed into the ventilation systems of the lab. The emissions were calculated precisely to the emissions of the forty largest cities in the United States and Western Europe. Now, two years later the results were better than he could possibly have hoped. The genocide would be complete.

The prisons of Iraq were scoured. Forty of the worst were chosen. Women were purposely placed with men to determine the poisonous effects on unborn children. The tests started today. In two years, he would know.

CHAPTER SEVEN

Family

The University of North Carolina at Chapel Hill

The small astronomy auditorium overflowed with seated faculty and students lining the walls. The less crowded podium provided comfortable seating for two senators, the University Provost and a five-million-dollar donor. Dr. Nockari, chair of the Astronomy department, stood to dedicate the installation of the Terrestrial Planet-Finder known to the scientists as the TPF.

"In 1996, Dr. Daniel Greene, head of NASA, addressed the American Astronomical Society. He told them of his plan to get detailed pictures of other 'earths,' and these detailed pictures would include continents, oceans and clouds. His audience was shocked. They looked at each other, smirking. A listener questioned him.

"'With all due respect Dr. Greene, to see features the size of California on a planet just ten light years away would require a telescope 200 miles wide operating in space. But continents, oceans and clouds . . . not in our lifetime, Dr. Greene.'

"Well, ladies and gentlemen, you know the history. In 2016, a year ahead of schedule, NASA launched four terrestrial planet-finders. The four crafts flew in formation, were 300 meters in length and each was equipped with four separate telescopes and four-meter mirrors designed to search the universe for life. The four telescopes provided the power and focus of a single telescope 300 feet wide. They had the capacity to beam light to a fifth spacecraft that assembled the images and beamed them to earth. Now the world's planet hunters have a tool to search for the brothers and sisters of planet earth.

"And due to the tireless work of Senators Hays and Fuller, our Provost Dr. Stillwell and the generosity of Mr. Dick Striker." Dr. Nockari turned to the men seated on the podium. "The University of North Carolina is privileged and honored to be one of only four installations in the world to house a TPF. Ladies and gentlemen, a round of thanks for the individuals primarily responsible for making the University of North Caroline a leader in the world in the search for new planets."

The audience stood in applause.

The following semester

It was 2:30 a.m. as Sarah Trent walked alone in ten degree cold toward Franklin Street on the Chapel Hill campus. She walked fast, head down. The hooded-down Parka did its job, but she should've worn her sweats over her jeans. The streets were lined with student cars but there was no traffic. Stoplights swung aimlessly, waiting for an audience. It was a wet snow falling off shivering maples, landing in startling plops. She was alone, cold, but she knew they were there, in the shadows, seconds away. They had doubled since the incident and the bracelet never left her arm. Her mother no longer trusted the FBI. The new shadows were special-ops and despite her front, she was glad they were there. She'd never ditch them again. Her mother assured her she couldn't. "*So, don't even try.*" Her mother, not anyone would ever know of the nightmares, not even Dr. Witt.

She knew how lucky she was to survive and how fortunate she was to be a graduate research assistant at one of the universities picked to monitor the TPF. *But, it wasn't all luck, 3.86 GPA in Physics from the University of Tennessee, Who's Who, Cum Laude, and a sorority list of other university activities.*

Sarah knew her application was solid, more than solid, less than spectacular. But she was the daughter of the U.S. UN ambassador. She hurried her step and turned at Henderson noting the memorial.

Special treatment? Maybe. Maybe not. This is Chapel Hill and the selection process for graduate students is competitive as hell. So, if being the UN ambassador's daughter greased a little consideration I'll take it.

Only three other locations in the world were privy to the TPF, one in the Keys with NASA, one at Cal Tech, another at

Edinburgh, and the final one at the University of North Carolina at Chapel Hill.

With the TPF you could explore the surface of Mars like the back of your hands. The wizardry of the TPF computer system identified the mineral contaminants in the ice in the outer rings of Saturn, and it was predicted, it would solve the mystery of the missing matter in the ghost galaxies.

The grad students joked, "*The TPF and Hubble II converse like phone sex.*"

Dr. Nockari, her major professor, stated, "*The TPF is the most remarkable piece of technology since the microprocessor, as signified by its primary goal, the search for 'new earths'*".

Sarah was in the second year of her doctoral program in astronomy, fortunate in family background, fortunate in her place at one of the selected schools. She'd seen the excesses of the privileged, money, drugs, alcohol and abuse of power. She had seen it, but not in her family. Then on a Tuesday traveling south on *Interstate 75* at 2:14 in the afternoon the caffeine pills of a tractor-trailer driver lost their effectiveness and his truck crossed the median and smashed into the car driven by her father Dr. Trent. He and her brother Adam were killed.

Sarah remembered how her mother refused to let her retreat from life after the accident. She would ask Sarah, "*What would your father and Adam want us to do? After we cry and hurt, what would they want us to do? After we cry and hurt, I'm going to be the next U.S. UN ambassador and you're going to graduate school.*"

It was December 20th, time for Christmas break. The semester projects had been turned in. The cramming for finals was over. "*Two 'A's' two 'B's, maybe three 'A's.*" She didn't care, it was over and the thought of home tasted like hot chocolate. Her mother had time off, but Sarah had heard that before.

Then Dr. Nockari, Sarah's major professor, posted the announcement about Dr. Bellamy. Bellamy was in the running for the Nobel in Physics for his theories on Black Holes. He'd been granted a block of time on the TPF, 4:00a.m. to 7:00a.m., Dec. 24th and needed three graduate assistants. God, how she looked forward to Christmas, but found herself, along with two other graduate students, volunteering, actually begging, to assist Dr. Lawrence B. Bellamy.

It would require staying at the University over the Christmas break but working with the TPF was an opportunity an Astronomy graduate student didn't pass up. Fate and nine inches of snow gave Sarah more than an opportunity. Dr. Bellamy was snowed in at O'Hare and the three graduate students had the TPF all to themselves for three precious hours. Sarah called her mother at 1a.m.

"What you doing girl? Yes, I know what time it is but you got to hear this. Your daughter is going to be one of the first in the history of this planet to seek out new earths. Just the TPF and me. Well, me, Drake and Lassiter. Loading the software that receives the signals real trekky stuff and..."

Her mother interrupted, "How in the world did you wrangle that, hon?"

Sarah explained about Dr. Bellamy getting snowed in.

"Isn't he the one you told me about?"

"Yep, same guy."

"Sarah, I'm glad for you, but that's a shame about Dr. Bellamy. On the verge of a Nobel and sitting in an airport stranded by weather but it is an opportunity for you, so take advantage. Will you make it home for Christmas?"

Sarah felt bad for Dr. Bellamy but she lusted after this opportunity. The TPF was booked for months. The opportunity for Dr. Bellamy was gone. Sarah had received word from Dr. Nockari around midnight. Dr. Bellamy wasn't going to make it. Sarah asked, trying to sound sympathetic but knew one of those opportunities of a lifetime was going down the drain.

"That's terrible. Can he be scheduled later?" She asked

"Sure, but he needed this time for his Nobel work. Has to have everything submitted next week. MIT and Cal Tech are scheduled over the holidays and no way they'll give up their slot. Got Nobel ideas of their own. I know Bellamy, decent guy, bright as hell. Damn shame."

There was an awkward pause. Sarah strained not to beg. "Dr. Nockari, would it be possible for Drake, Lassiter and myself

40

to get on in and load the software? I think it would be good practice to…"

Nockari stopped her with the news, "Oh, you haven't heard from them? They're snowed in worse than I am, car slid into a ditch 100 feet out of their driveway. Wrecker can get to em' sometime late tomorrow afternoon."

Drake and Lassiter lived off campus. Sarah was quiet. She felt nauseous. Her chance was slipping away with a snowstorm. She heard Dr. Nockari in the distance.

"Sarah, if I could I'd get there I would, but damn, I'm fifteen miles from campus and 23 is closed, got a semi lying across the road. State patrol said it would be noon before they get it cleared. I called Dr. Henry. He's just three blocks from the observatory but no answer and Fred and Pat are gone for the holidays, so, that leaves you. Now, if I were a graduate student on campus, hell freezing over wouldn't keep me from that observatory. Please tell me you have the keys."

Sarah couldn't believe her ears. She had picked up the keys from an irritated secretary who had to come in on Christmas Eve. "Yes sir, I have the keys and hell hasn't frozen over yet."

"Well, when you get to the lab, call me. Hope the power doesn't go out." Sarah tasted acid in her throat. Nothing worked without power. Again the words of Dr. Nockari soothed. "Might want to turn on auxiliary when you get there. If main power goes out, you won't even notice. Just be sure you turn it off when you leave."

Sarah contained herself, "I will, and thanks Dr. Nockari."

"If you can get there, you've earned it. Call me if you have any problems loading. Nah, call me as soon as you get there."

Sarah giggled like a seventh grader and Dr. Nockari joined her.

"I'll call you before I start. I promise."

Sarah couldn't sleep and at 2:30a.m. found herself headed to the observatory, grinning. The cold had taken over, and it was blowing raw and sharp and she was starving. She crossed the street and tailing two hardhats headed for *"The Waysider"*. Two blocks later she smelled coffee, crossed the street following the smell and a flickering humming neon light. She walked into a toasty warm, hardhat crowded grill whose aroma perfumed you for the day and that was fine.

The diner had survived since the 50s and smelled of coffee and bacon, mixed with maple syrup and hot cakes. Red and white checkered the tile floor. Six drooping ceiling fans turned in slow motion. Country Christmas music came from the jukebox. There were twelve tables, each squared with four chairs and a Formica counter lined with stools. Stainless steel shelving, behind the counter, bristled with business through a long glassless window to the kitchen. Elvis and Marilyn graced one wall, Dean and Bogart the other. A glass case of truck driver belt buckles grinned silver beside the cash register.

Waitresses in red aprons, with stitched labeled names of Nell, Glenda, Mabel and Lynn on their breasts served large plates of ham, bacon, sausage, and eggs, sided with hash browns, gravy, hot cakes and biscuits all fore-played with steaming coffee.

The waitresses teased the men they served who wore hooded work cloths, hard hats and baseball caps. They hunkered over their coffee while they waited for a breakfast that would sustain labor, on buildings, trucks and diesels, in weather so bad they had to ignore it.

They took their usual places. Some around tables slid together to make room for friends of years. In half-finger gloves, they wrapped their hands around hot thick ceramic coffee cups and sipped until they felt the warmth enter their bones. They talked about football, hunting, and fishing. They spoke of foremen they respected but mostly of those they didn't and of the strength and foolishness of the younger men. They were vulgar with each other and about women they'd like to have for a night or so but always distant about those they cared about.

"Jim told me his girlfriend mentioned to him that she thought it was about time they were getting married. He said he thought about it then told her he thought, "that was a great idea—but hell, who'd have us?"

"Hell son, I'm closing in on sixty years and I agree with Willie Nelson—the only thing in life I know for damn sure is that 'money makes women horny.'"

When the men left, they took large warm thermoses of coffee and white paper bags stacked with tin-foil wrapped sandwiches.

The Cleansing

Sarah was too young and too privileged to understand the sanctity of such a place. Only two other women were there other than the waitresses. One, a coed, with her boyfriend. They sat in a corner glued to each other and no one paid any attention. The other was a woman in her thirties dressed in a business suit. She sipped black coffee and munched wheat toast and grilled her laptop. She worked in a "good old boy" accounting firm and knew it. She drew a few glances.

The menu was a board on the wall. This morning all tables were taken. Lynn hurried by with plates of incredible looking food and glanced toward Sarah. "Just have a seat when you can, hon—be right with you."

Sarah had time to simmer in the aroma of *Waysider* the essences of coffee, bacon, and hotcakes. No way to leave without eating. Sarah spotted a table with only one customer. He was slouched, reading an astronomy book, sipping coffee. He fit in the *Waysider* like it was his home. He wore a four-day maroon beard, faded jeans that fit and a disheveled dark blue hooded sweatshirt that capped a red toboggan emitting a four-inch pony tail. The graduate level astronomy book was an invitation.

"Mind if I take a seat?"

He didn't look up as his right leg pushed out a chair.

Sarah sat down and asked, "Astronomy major?" She pointed to herself then to the book he was reading, "Astronomy grad student. I noticed your book."

He eyed Sarah and slowly pulled the hood and toboggan from his head, and extended his hand, "Do I know you?" He asked, curiously, "You look familiar. Sorry, name's Josh—Josh Jones."

They shook hands, then she remembered, "Wait a minute, I read about you in the Tar Hill. Josh Jones, you're the guy, you're 'Goodwill'."

On Friday of the past week the student newspaper, *"The Daily Tar Hill"*, had run an article entitled *"Goodwill is Alive and Well at Chapel Hill."* The story was about the student who now sat next to Sarah. Josh T. Jones, nicknamed *'Goodwill'* by the newspaper, broke all the academic rules. He enrolled as a freshman, and attempted to sign up for advanced graduate courses in a variety of disciplines, computer science, music,

The Cleansing

psychology, math, English literature and astronomy. Mr. Jones was informed that, as a freshman, he couldn't enroll in graduate courses. When he asked "*Why not?*" rules were patronizingly explained.

Mr. Jones responded by camping out in the offices of professors who taught the courses he wanted. They repeated the same rules replacing patronization with condescension until two professors relented; one in psychology and one in English lit. In the two courses, he earned the highest grades in the class. He did the same the next semester with four courses.

His reputation spread, and he continued to enroll in courses of his interest. Numerous professors dismissed him, confused by his notion of "*Not interested in a major—just want to learn.*" A few were intrigued and allowed him to enroll ignoring the "*can't do's*" of university rules.

Josh was in his second year at the university and in the courses he was allowed to enroll he had a 4.0 average. The undergraduate courses he took were language courses. After four semesters he spoke three languages—fluently. Professors began to brag to peers that "*Goodwill*" had asked to enroll in their class. Twice he was asked to lecture when professors were away, and was offered a stipend to assist in research for academic publications.

Sarah smiled, "Can't believe I've met Goodwill."

"Yeah, heard about that article."

His smile was honest, his eyes somewhere else then at once on you. Sarah summed him up as a seven. Date bait, maybe. He had an angular face with large ears that accented with the growth of the beard, a little taller than average. "*Body? Hard to tell with him sitting. But what's with the rubber band ponytail?*" His smile was disarming causing Sarah to look long enough for him to notice. "*Maybe a little better than seven. It's his voice. How does he measure his words like that without hesitating? So seduct...*"

Josh interrupted her thoughts, "Didn't get your name?"

Sarah extended her hand, "Name's Sarah—Sarah Trent. Nice to meet you."

Josh stiffened as his eyes widened, "You're Sarah Trent?"

"Yes, why?"

44

"Sarah Trent, as in Ambassador Trent's daughter?"

"Yeah, I get that a lot."

Josh looked about the diner, "Are you here looking for me? Because if you are you don't have…"

"What're you talking about? Why would I be looking for you?"

Josh studied Sarah, "You don't know? No, you're messing with me. There's no way we'd…"

"You're beginning to creep me out. What are you talking about?"

Josh knew by her expression she didn't know, "I wondered why there were agents on campus. Oh, are you okay? The news says you're doing great but sometimes that doesn't mean much."

"If you're talking about my kidnapping, I'm fine. How did you know about the agents, they're invis…"

Sarah interrupted herself, it was his voice singeing her memory, "*Miss Trent, you're safe now.*" She froze stiff-backed in her chair and stuttered her words, "You're the…you're the one, the FBI guy that…"

"Yeah, I was the first one to you."

Sarah sat mesmerized, "*No way this is happening.*"

"Oh, I get it, you're one of mine. I just didn't think, it just never occurred to me that you'd be one—you'd still be assigned to me."

"Miss Trent, I'm not assigned to you. I was special-ops when we found you. We work with the FBI when someone like you is involved."

Sarah slowly shook her head, "I never had a chance to thank . . . I woke up in the hospital, never met any of you guys. I did send a letter to a Mr. Burton who headed the search but I never…I just can't believe this."

Lynn, a whiskey tenor waitress, with breasts that teased large tips from the men was suddenly at the table. She leaned toward Josh and refilled his mug. "Coffee all you having for breakfast?"

"Yes, I'm fine. Thanks. Sarah, you want some breakfast, it's really…"

"I know." She said slowly. "I'll have coffee, blackberry pancakes and cheese grits."

"Coffee, blackberry pancakes and cheese grits," repeated Lynn. She leaned closer to Josh, her right breast pressing against his arm, "If you need anything else, you let me know."

As she walked away, Sarah muttered, "Nothing like being obvious."

Josh grinned and leaned toward Sarah, "So, you're a grad student in astronomy?"

"Yes, and you?"

"Pediatrics."

"Pediatrics?" Sarah exclaimed,. "You're already in med school? How can—what's with the astronomy book?"

"Helps with CLEP courses. Astronomy is just a course I wanted to—are you sure you're not…"

Sarah giggled, "I'm just as dumbfounded as you are. By the way are you guys any closer to catching that creep?"

Josh shook his head. "Believe me, I'm not involved in any way. You're the U.S. ambassador's daughter, if anyone should know… "

"She won't tell me a thing except I won't be ditching my security anymore and I will carry mace and I won't be needing the cute little button on my watch anymore." She pointed to her left arm. "All implanted in the two, not one but two chips in my arm."

"Wouldn't be smart to mess with you."

"Right about that. Seconds away. Do you know which one in here?"

"Yeah, guy in the last booth on your left, facing you. Don't look. Tells them they've been ID'd. They hate that."

Josh took a long drink of coffee and was the recipient of another rub from Lynn's breasts as she delivered Sarah's breakfast. She glanced at Sarah then locked on Josh. "Here you are honey. Let me know if y'all need anything."

Josh leaned to the next table and got some cream for Sarah's coffee. "What does your mother have to say about that blue thing?"

"She's really closed mouth about that too. Says it's something there're working on which tells me there's something to it."

"She's right. There's no way your creep gets away. I've had two instances where…" Josh's voice trailed off.

Minutes later, Sarah swirled her last bite of pancakes in syrup and grits. "That was good, oh, that was good." She stood and took a last sip of coffee. "Still can't believe we met this way. I owe you big time. Nice meeting you, but I gotta get going. Got a date with the TPF. Maybe we can…"

Josh jerked his head toward Sarah, "The TPF? How'd you manage that?"

She quickly explained what had happened with Dr. Bellamy. Josh sat starring at Sarah. Sarah smiled again. He was easy to read and she owed him and liked him. "Hey, I could use a hand, wanna check it out?"

An innocent grin crossed his face, "Seven billion people on the planet and she sits down beside me in a café, 3a.m. Christmas morning and has access to the universe."

As they started to leave Josh stopped, "Just a sec." He put his left boot on the edge of a chair. He untied then tied his shoelaces. He checked his right boot but didn't retie. "Okay, I'm ready."

CHAPTER EIGHT

The Blue

Later that morning, Josh and Sarah visually walked on the moon—the earth's and three of Saturn's. They took pictures of former lakes of Mars and the five satellites of Uranus. They were photographing the satellites of Saturn when Sarah looked up from her viewing station. Josh was immersed. "God, what Schiaparelli must have felt."

"Who?"

When Josh didn't answer Sarah stood, "Hey, this is undergraduate stuff. Let's do something."

He didn't move from his viewer, "What'd you have in mind?"

"If you can set the coordinates as I call 'em out I'll code in Hubble II. See what's really out there tonight. Oh Jesus, I forgot to call Dr. Nockari."

Sarah hurried to the phone as Josh asked, "We can access Hubble II?"

Sarah turned, phone pinched between shoulder and chin, "Like we're hard-wired right to its mirror. But the pictures are fuzzy again. NASA's going back up next fall. Hope she can make it till then."

She turned away from Josh, "Hello, Dr. Nockari, I made it. So excited I almost forgot to call." Sarah filled in Dr. Nockari and returned to her station after promising to call him every twenty minutes.

Josh swung out of his viewing station and headed for the central computer. Sarah coded without looking up.

"You're not going to believe these pictures. They'll be fuzzy but still off the charts. I'll code. All you have to do is set coordinates. Just gotta upload a little software."

"How about me giving the computer a go and you setting coordinates?"

Sarah looked at Josh, "You sure?"

48

Josh smiled, "The universe, computers, pretty ladies and blackberry pancakes. I'd like a shot."

"Pretty ladies? Okay Huckleberry, code sequences are always on the upper screen, all it's used for. It's set, just code what it says and tell me the coordinates. You can do it on the stations, but it's faster if you call it out and let me code to the mainframe, saves downloading time."

Ten minutes later Sarah and Josh were gawking at pictures from Hubble II on their computer screens, picking the best to print. Josh was mesmerized.

"Look at this, happened years ago and we have pictures of it. Is that a star constellation?"

Josh was poring over a picture and pointing to a cluster of blurred light points. "Are they always this fuzzy?"

"Well, like I said, Hubble has the pip."

"Anybody tried refocusing from this end?"

Sarah didn't look up, "Whadda you mean?"

"Well, the images are just pixels. So clear up the pixels from this end before you print out the images."

"Can't, the pictures are digital. Hubbel II is different, takes the pictures, runs them through its computer then to TPF, then here. No pixels."

Josh was quiet for a moment, "Does the central computer have Visual Comp 4 and Fuzzy Logic?"

"Yeah, it's got em' all. Why?"

"Okay if I fiddle with it a while?"

"Sure. I'll try the constellation again. Might get a better shot."

During the next hour Josh coded and Sarah took more pictures. Every fifteen minutes or so Josh would ask Sarah to recapture picture six, the star constellation. Josh would get the picture, study it, and continue coding. Sarah looked up from her station.

"Josh, we've only got another hour. Get on a viewer. You're missing it."

"Just finishing up. Print picture six one more time."

Sarah typed a line of code, "You got it."

49

The Cleansing

Josh walked to the printer and studied the picture. "That be much better and yes, Miss Cheese Grits, that is a star constellation."

Josh straddled a viewer as he handed this last picture to Sarah. Sarah glanced at the picture from the side of her viewer. She couldn't believe what she saw. The picture was perfectly clear. "How the hell did you do that?"

"Computers and the universe, kinda my..."

"Josh, how'd you do that? Can you do that with the other pictures?"

"Yeah, just a conversion program. Converted the digital images to pixel format, filled in the pixels that were jagged, then reconverted back to digital and printed it out."

Sarah stammered, "That...that would work on any scope. Do you know what this could save?"

Josh turned back to the computer, "Visual Comp 5 coming out in a couple of months has a smaller pixel configuration. Should be a little better but interfacing VC with Fuzzy Logic is a little dicey."

Sarah stared at him then returned to her station. Her head suddenly pulled away then back to the scope viewer.

"What the hell is that? Josh, get on your station."

"What'cha got?"

"Don't know. Looks like blue shooting stars. God, there are hundreds of them."

"Tardy Leonids?" offered Josh.

"Too late for Leonids, and no way that many. Josh, forget the computer. Get on a station." As Josh locked in to a viewer Sarah whispered, "They're so beautiful and they're bursting into a blue haze or something."

Josh focused and took a sudden breath, "What is that?"

"I have no idea. God, there are hundreds, thousands of them. Josh, get on number four now! Need to get back up on tracking and video." Sarah punched at her keyboard, "When the words 'Kodak moment' comes up on your screen, double click it."

"Kodak moment?"

"They made a contribution. Double click it. Yeah, that's it. Got back up now. What am I forgetting? Don't panic, just think, Sarah, think."

Sarah frantically looked about the conservatory as Josh locked into the station-four viewer.

Josh whispered, "Cheese Grits, this may be the night." Then he was silent. What he saw was thousands then tens of thousands of Sarah's "shooting stars." Then there were hundreds of thousands. Sarah locked into station one and both were silent till Sarah yelled, "Josh, your back up, check disk space, it might be…"

"How do I do that?"

Sarah realized what she was doing. As bright as Josh was, tonight was the first time he had ever seen the TPF. "Never mind, I'll get it." She scrambled to Josh's station and frantically typed at the keyboard.

"Good, plenty of space. Josh, I have to call Nockari. Oh God, you don't think these things can take out satellites do you? We've got to get Dr. Nockari down here."

She forced herself away from the station, returned to station one and started keyboarding software, locking in back up.

"We got it right—now!" Sarah yelled, "She's on line with everything she's got. Oh, shit, sound."

Sarah hit three keys, "If they're making any noise we'll get it." She raced for a phone looking backward toward Josh, "What's it doing? What's it doing?"

"They're breaking up. Look at that," Josh whispered.

Sarah dropped the phone and sprinted back to station one. She viewed millions of "shooting stars" as they hit the earth's atmosphere and burst into a blue florescent crystalline haze. First the haze was intermittent and sparse, but like fog it began to expand and the blueness grew. The color glowed with a florescent blueness, and it was beautiful. Sarah knew, through any telescope, especially the TPF, what human vision sees is space as in a bottle that balloons at the end. But what astronomers know is that this confined space is hundreds or thousands of square miles, and this blue haze was encompassing it as if it were blowing smoke into a Coke bottle. Sarah forced herself to look at the TPF parameter readings, and they were still recording.

"This stuff is circling hundreds of miles."

"The whole earth, Miss Trent. The whole Mother Earth."

The Cleansing

The remainder of the night was a blur. A frantic call to Dr. Nockari started him walking in fourteen inches of snow. One mile into his trip he was picked up by a chained-tired state patrolman and driven to the observatory. Sarah, Josh and Dr. Nockari studied data for hours. They reviewed the videodisk four times resulting in calls to every prominent astronomer Dr. Nockari knew. The blue haze had lasted two minutes and 37 seconds.

After fourteen hours, the three made their way to *Waysider*. The food and coffee made exhaustion and sleep trivial, and they talked for another four hours.

When Sarah got back to her room, the adrenaline and caffeine had given her all it could. She fell on her bed and was almost gone when she forced herself to reach for the phone. She and Josh had traded phone numbers.

"Hey, where are you? I need to know something. If our future dates are going to be like the first two we need to talk." She smiled as she hung up the phone and as she sank into her bed, she bolted upright. "*Oh my God, he's seen me naked.*"

The next morning her answering machine was blinking when she got out of the shower. It was her mother.

"*Sarah, something has come up. I'll be late. Kate and I will see you around midnight Christmas day. Can't wait to get caught up. Lots of interesting stuff to tell you. Be careful, love you.*"

Sarah smiled, "*You think you got interesting stuff?*"

An hour later she, Dr. Nockari and Josh were back at the Observatory. They worked for hours trying to contact other Observatories to verify their sighting. All were closed for Christmas. Four more hours of work netted two amateur astronomers in North America. One in Montreal and one in Henry, Illinois, were reporting over the Internet the observance of a 'strange blue fog' on Christmas Eve. Other faculty who observed the disk were astounded but could offer no explanation.

Thirty-six hours later, Dr. Nockari received a call from the CIA wanting to review the disks. How they knew about the disks was not offered. Sarah had made a dozen copies of the disk and backed it up on four computers. The CIA informed Dr. Nockari they would be there in two hours. They did not ask directions to the lab. Ninety minutes later, two men in dark suits arrived. They were polite and explained that NIH scientists wanted to view the aberration for atmospheric contamination. They asked a few questions which were recorded. They provided a receipt for the disk, promised to return it within three months, and did not ask if there were copies.

The next week, Sarah showed the pictures Josh had reconfigured from Hubble II to Dr. Nockari. Two days later, Josh was offered a research assistantship, designing software for the TPF. He turned down the offer stating he had to concentrate on med school.

CHAPTER NINE

Sex

Sarah was not promiscuous but there'd been men. One serious, Ted. They were engaged when her father and Adam were killed. He was there for her—through the aftermath of the news, funeral, and for a month afterwards. When he broke it off, he was honest—no dramatics, no other woman, no pettiness. He didn't think it would work, and he told her. Sarah felt it was the spotlight, daughter of a UN ambassador, the media and all the trappings. Difficult to be the fiancé of a UN ambassador's daughter when your ambition is to be a dentist. They stayed in touch until it didn't matter.

Josh was different. Her notoriety didn't seem to matter to him. After the sighting, they went out, although Sarah wasn't sure if it could be called dating—student and faculty functions, the library, and an occasional movie and pizza. He was attentive, said little, and consequently she often found herself uncharacteristically babbling about her studies, her teachers, her day. He'd listen, smile, offer nods until she realized what she was doing. There would be silence, but it wasn't awkward. Odd to Sarah, that it was never awkward but she liked it…

They would be talking, studying in the library or at a movie, and she would glance at him or touch his arm and it would rise in her body, the flush the warmth. It was sexual, very sexual and she liked that too. And that distance in his demeanor made him even more appealing. He listened mostly but she noticed others, even faculty, waiting for him to speak, express his opinion and when he did, they'd smile and nod.

Women flirted. Oh God, how they flirted and they didn't care that she noticed. The subtle asking of where he was, or would he be at the party. If so, their dress would be a little nicer, sexier. She saw the touches, the signals. They flirted but what made her want to jump his bones was that he was oblivious.

54

The Cleansing

Jenny tried her best. She was the one with the slim butt, long legs, flowing blonde hair and breasts. God, those breasts! They turned *"B's"* into *"A's"* with male faculty, and grinning fools out of frat boys and an All American linebacker. Sarah was secure about her looks; she was attractive, very attractive with raven dark hair, fall sky blue eyes, a taut athletic body and a nose made perfect by just a hint of surgery. But Jenny was the test. She wore a cut-away t-shirt and the edge of too tight shorts to the cookout. She'd asked if Josh would be there with an "*oh, by the way*", and the linebacker was playing in Raleigh. She had them on display and she was despised, and adored, by gender.

Sarah was talking with Dr. Nockari as he grilled barbecue chicken. She glanced at Josh ten yards away and Jenny had him. She was within inches, locking her eyes on his, her conversation the excuse for smiles, gushes and inadvertent brushes of her breasts. Sarah exhaled, "*How could he not notice? Any man would notice.*"

He glanced toward Sarah, found her, and his eyes and smile said she was Christmas morning. He turned to Jenny, said something, turned and walked to Sarah and Dr. Nockari, leaving Jenny with hands on hips, glaring. He hugged Sarah. "Need some help? Sure smells good."

Afterwards they rode his bike. It moved with subdued power, teasing that there was more—much more. She held on, pressing against him, eyes closed. The wind whipped cold but she was warm.

She melted. That night was not like a first time. The candles shadowed a tanned lean swimmer's body except his arms and legs were too muscular—almost. But the warmth, how could he be so warm? When his muscles tensed they were hard and cut. But he was lost in her and his body felt fleshy firm and so warm that nothing mattered except the moment. She arched without knowing it as her nipples raisined. Then the moment was minutes and still he moved with her. She moaned. It was too soon. The foreplay had been since she had known him, now she had his warmth and it took her.

He must know, how could he not…then he did. But he didn't stop. It was almost painful, then again she felt herself rising . . .

55

she had never, not ever. She felt him shudder against her and she went with him. She couldn't help it, and it wouldn't have mattered if she did.

The night was time. Time used for moments of sleep to give reprieve to bodies desiring more. They murmured softly in the dark until the warmth of legs, breasts, bodies and mouths said—again.

It was daybreak, and she was awake. She could sleep forever yet she was awake spooned to him as he slept. The cotton-soft quilting smelled of cinnamon and sex. Her thoughts drifted with the morning light. Her mother and father would emerge from their bedroom on slow Saturday mornings or afternoons, smiling, silly, teasing, grabbing at her robe, never taking their eyes off each other. She and Adam were too young to know but they sensed something, something good that made them feel safe and loved.

She was eight when she figured it out. It was during Saturday morning cartoons. She walked to the kitchen to raid the fridge for orange juice. Her father with his back to her had her mother against the kitchen sink kissing her. Sarah giggled and asked.

"Ewe, what'cha doin?"

Her father turned smiling as her mother hastily closed her robe and answered. "Morning hon, just fixing some coffee. You and Adam bout ready for break...?"

Her father interrupted. "Well, that's not entirely true. I was kissing your mother."

And with that he kissed her again and untied her robe. Sarah giggled again, as her mother doing the same, tried to get away from her husband.

"Why did lying beside Josh at five in the morning make me think of...?" She almost said aloud, *"Oh God, Oh, my God—I'm in—aw, shit, I don't have time, I don't even know him. Two more years of graduate school—landing a teaching position—a career? God, he's only starting med school. Older. Okay older and smart. God, he's smart but he's still just a first year grad student. And how does he feel? No, it's infatuation, a first time thing and he's good. No, admit it girl, he's unbelievable."*

She wondered if this was how her mother felt in the kitchen seventeen years ago. He stirred.

"About time," she whispered. Still spooned to him, she kissed his shoulder, moved closer to him and teased. He turned to her, smiled, and was suddenly out of bed. "Where're you going?"

He didn't answer. Thirty seconds later she heard the shower running. He returned to the bed, scooped her up and carried her to the shower. She squealed as water, soap, and shampoo became toys. While they were drying each other, she noticed and for a moment froze. Twenty minutes later, he lay in the bed dead asleep. She was beside him, but awake. Naked, in the light of the morning, she saw the scars in his left leg and arm, and the long one down his back.

"*God, what happened to him?*"

She knew he'd been a SEAL. But the scars were not what froze her. It was the needle tracks. She'd seen such before. Her father told her once, "T*he difference between the rich and poor ends with vices. Both lie, cheat, steal, commit adultery and do drugs the same way with the same results. Remember that.*"

She'd experienced the vices privilege, power, and money offered. Sarah was no saint but it could have been worse. The public eye was no picnic. When a county deputy busted Adam, Sarah swore that she drew the line with drugs. She'd seen the hurt and pain in her mother and father's tears at two in the morning in a jail in Jackson County.

The scars were out of character. He didn't smoke or drink, and worked out like a fanatic but she knew little of his past. "*SEALs? But that was years ago.*"

Past lives had not yet been shared and it didn't matter until tonight and he already knew about her mother. He never talked of his past and she never asked. "*Is it important now? Yes, yes it is, at least the needle tracks were. Yeah, that's important.*"

He stirred. He had an eight o'clock class. He thought she was asleep. He got up and dressed quickly. She sat up and he looked at her, smiled, walked to the bed, leaned over and kissed her on the forehead. She cocked her head.

"The forehead is where you kiss your sister, your grandmother or a one nighter."

He spoke without looking at her, "'People's Players' tonight at Wolfe auditorium. Wanna go?"

"Okay."

"Pick you up at seven?"

"Sounds good. But we do…need to talk?"

Josh stopped at the door, hesitated, turned and looked at her for a long time. She sat up with pillows to her back and faced him. He looked at her but spoke from somewhere else.

"In the forests of Eastern Europe, there's an ant, the Myrmica sabuleti, that's unique to the area. The ants live in large colonies burrowed around the base of wild thyme. The natives call the ants 'The Shepherds of the Thyme.' Every spring, large blue butterflies migrate to the thyme, mate, and lay their eggs on the leaves. Two weeks later, the eggs hatch. The thyme leaves provide the larvae food. When the larvae grow into caterpillars, they signal the ants, who then carry them to their nests. The ants stroke the caterpillars, milking them and use the milk to feed their young. In return, the caterpillars are allowed to feed on the eggs of the ants. They do this every evening.

When morning comes, the ants herd the caterpillars back into the tops of the thyme so the caterpillars can feed. They do this for four weeks until the caterpillars evolve into blue butterflies. Do you know what the ants do with the butterflies when this happens?"

Sarah shook her head and wasn't sure she wanted to know.

"They take the butterflies to the top of the thyme bushes and set them free."

Josh looked away from Sarah then back to her and asked her like a third grader would ask his teacher, "Do you think that's intelligence?"

Sarah studied this brilliant third grader and thought, "*God, I don't have a chance.*"

"No, I think that's symbiotic—much more than intelligence and you're weird."

Josh smiled and looked away again, "Yeah, you're right, we need to talk." He kissed her gently on the forehead again and left.

The *"Famous People's Players"* performed to a packed house. Sarah lost herself twice in the performance because her mind was rehearsing "the talk". "*Maybe I'm wrong. Maybe he had to take shots for something. Something the SEALs...maybe he got sick and had to take...*"

The ending of the performance interrupted and she was standing, applauding. They left and walked to her apartment, a half-mile off campus.

"I'm starved. Wanna make some pancakes at my place? And coffee. Gotta have coffee with pancakes."

He looked at her and she knew he knew this was foreplay for the talk. His mouth smiled. His eyes didn't. "Sounds good. I'd invite you to my place, but your shadows might not approve."

"Sorry, hope it's okay. You knew coming in. Come to think of it, they haven't intruded once since we—you guys got signals or something?"

Josh smiled, "Tie the left shoe first, always the left first, check the right but don't tie. They've cleared me through three agencies by now. They know the kind of toothpaste I use. We'll be fine."

"I knew it, I knew it."

Sarah stopped and put her hands on her hips, "God, they probably took bets on how long it'd take you to score."

As Josh skipped backwards facing Sarah he grinned, "Yeah, Eric won the pool, split it with me."

Sarah caught him and hit him as he laughed and tickled her.

In her apartment, she made pancakes while he made coffee. The syrup was heated, and the butter melted and it was good. They ate and made small talk about the performance. They scanned the fine arts program and agreed on two others. This reassured Sarah. She took a sip of coffee. It was time.

"Josh, last night—was, I felt..." Sarah stopped and looked at him. He was listening, but looking down and away from her. "Josh, who are you? What do you..."

"Just ask, Sarah. What you feel or need to know, just ask."

He turned and looked at her. She thought, "*Why was he so easy to...*"

"Josh, this is not one of those silly coed, next level...relationship..." Sarah stopped again and took a deep breath. "Josh, the scars and your arm. Are those? I've seen that before."

She looked down then back to him. "Josh, last night mattered to me. But if you're into drugs—well, that's what I need to know."

There was a pause before he answered, "The scar on my back is from a burn—train wrecking in India—the scar on my upper arm is a bullet wound. The tracks on my arm are from needles—heroin."

He looked away. Sarah looked to him and there was silence. "I had to know Jos…"

Again, he interrupted, "About last night." His voice drifted till she could barely hear him. "I forgot, for a few moments and it was more than that."

His head dropped.

"Forgot? What did you forget?"

There was a silence but unlike the others, it was awkward.

"Sarah, I killed children and maybe their…" He spoke deep, and his voice broke. He looked through her. His eyes glistened.

She was paralyzed by his words. She heard her voice as if it were in the distance.

"Josh?"

He still didn't face her, "We were training in Colombia off the coast of Cartagena, basic routine training. They dropped Stu, myself and Deke, five miles off the coast and told us to get to shore before dawn. It was midnight. We did the drill, swam together, and at four in the morning we were five hundred yards from the coast. Stu and Deke were great swimmers, swam in college. They'd bet a six-pack and were on shore laughing about 'Bac Lager' or 'DaChutes'. I was still a hundred yards out. It was pitch black but I could hear them."

His voice trailed, "Then I heard the zip of the silencer and looked up to see the flash of the next shot. Stu and Deke didn't make a sound. There was a pause, then two more flashes. A truck was leaving as I got to shore. Stu and Deke had been shot twice, once in the chest and a kill shot to the head. They'd stumbled into a drug deal and I was in the ocean, helpless. Hadn't been for that bet…"

Josh stopped then continued, "Took us a year to track them down. You don't kill *SEALs*. The runners didn't know who they'd murdered. Thought Stu and Deke were competition. Didn't matter—you don't kill *SEALs*. Found them in Columbia running drugs to Jamacia. They came at night in their boat and met buyers from Jamacia on the beach. We watched them for two months before we hit. We set mines at the edge of the beach, triangled the dropping point and waited. At 3:00 in the morning the boat from Columbia beached. Just had to wait for the Jamaicans."

Josh voice trailed to silence as he remembered.

Four kilometers east of Montego bay, a drone from the ocean drew twelve pairs of PVS -14 night vision eyes. It was the drug runner's boat. It hummed with power, skimming the water like liquid light. The boat held its breath and beached. Eight shadows exited, all with automatic weapons, four with black satchels. The eight fanned and moved fifty meters down the beach. Forty-five seconds later, the two remaining on the boat were dead, their necks wrenched from their spines and the bomb was planted.

The headlights of the vehicle loomed four hundred meters west of the boat runners. Forty meters from the beach, in dunes and thicket, Josh stirred without moving and his PVS night vision clicked three times.

"Always a different vehicle. Professionals."

The lights kept coming. It was a bus. The bus grumbled with age. It breached the zone and stopped twenty meters from the hidden runners. A metallic voice crackled in Josh's earpiece.

"Mines activated, sir."

To the left of Josh, Captain Pierce acknowledged, "Roger mines."

The right front door of the bus hissed and lurched open. Giggling children burst from the bus followed by several adults and a Spaniel. The Spaniel ran to a hidden shadow and began barking. Squealing children ran toward the water. The frantic staccato words of Captain Pierce crackled in the earpieces of the SEALS. "O Jesus, civilians. Abort! Abort! Straley, deactivate your bomb. Straley, the bus!"

The Cleansing

"Sir, the timer is set. I don't have ti..."

The crouched shadow took one-step backwards away from the Spaniel. A mine exploded with a muffled thump. The shadow screamed and his automatic rifle sprayed the air. There was two seconds of paralyzed silence before the screams of adults and children mingled with the gunfire of the runners.

The children and adults spilled and ran in every direction. Two children and two parents crumpled and lay still. Josh heard Captain Pierce again, "Mines engaged, focus on runners, mines engaged, focus on runners. Take them out!"

Josh chilled in the heat and hesitated, "Sir, there are children..."

The runner's boat exploded and laser-guided fire began. Ten seconds later, four of the eight runners were dead. Two more fell and were silent. Frantic parents and teachers grabbed at running children. A teacher lunged backward, fell and lay scarecrow contorted in the sand.

A child ran toward the mine perimeter and kept running. Josh, twenty-five meters away, screamed and discarded his weapon. He ran toward the child, ignoring orders.

"Jones, no! Cease fire! Cease fire!"

Briars and thickets tore at Josh's legs until he hit sand. One of the two remaining runners detonated a smoke bomb as three bullets ripped away his chest. The smoke obliterated Josh's night vision, but he kept running toward his last sight of the child. His left arm wind-milled, rotating three times before he could stop it. It felt like a bee sting. He knew it was a graze or the arm would be gone. The child was five meters in front of him. He screamed, "Stop! Jalto! Stop!"

She stopped but not from his scream. An arm swept her up and the last runner held her with an automatic pistol to her head. Josh froze and slowly raised his right arm. His left dangled and felt sticky. Josh spoke calmly, "Stand still, the mines. Parate quieto, las minas."

The runner dropped to his knees, shielding more of his body with the girl. His eyes bulged as he spoke in grinning terror, "Your friends will have the puta candy and the money. You will not. You and I, and the little girl are going to die. First you then the little girl then me." He pointed his pistol at Josh's chest.

The Cleansing

Josh looked up at Sarah, "I've thought about that second every day since—it was his weapon, only a runner would be carrying a Beretta 687. I wasn't afraid—tasted sulfur. He was too close. My vest couldn't protect me. Then I heard the zip of a silencer behind me. The runner twitched and fell backward, still holding the girl. He fell on a mine. I remember blood on my face and chest. My legs flew up and I was on my back. Shrapnel hit my left leg. The runner and girl didn't move. The last thing I remember was Captain Pierce standing over me yelling. Funny, but in the distance, I could hear the Spaniel whimpering."

Josh put his palms to his eyes, "School had just ended and the children were being treated to a sunrise. For making good grades, their teachers and parents were treating them to a sunrise on the beach and for that they were…"

There was silence as Sarah stared at the man she had made love to twenty-four hours ago.

"The bullet wound in your arm, is that…?"

He looked at her, "Stu, Deke, children, teachers, parents dead and me, I followed orders, sixteen rounds." Josh's voice trailed, "Just like Stubin and Clter at Auschwitz."

Her question registered with him, "Yeah, caught a round from Delker trying to cover me." Josh's voice was ironic, "Friendly fire in the midst of children."

Sarah asked before she thought, "How do you know you shot one of the…?"

"Only SEAL Intelligence knows."

"But you said Delker shot you, how do you know it was Delker?'

"Our ammunition is marked. After a mission, we're able to check. Gives us efficiency ratings. They gave us the hits on the runners and Delker's hit on me. Hits on civilians are always sealed. Teachers, parents and children and we sealed it as collateral damage."

Sarah took Josh's hand, "But I don't remember anything in the news. This would have made, would have been a mess politically, this would have…"

"Used ammunition made in Libya. They took the hit. Ops call it, 'rat fucking,' borrowed from Nixon."

The Cleansing

Sarah remembered the headlines, the denial by the Libyans, and their condemnation in the UN. "Did you hit any of the runners?"

"Yes."

Again, there was silence.

"I can't believe they ordered you to fire on...and at night, how could...?"

"Oh, we could see. With the night vision they have now—night, day, distance doesn't matter. Night is like noon and you scope with them, just fire at what you see and you hit it."

"Did you see the...?"

"I don't know but I fired."

Sarah whispered, "Do you want to know?

Josh didn't respond.

The Cleansing

CHAPTER TEN

Christmas

Two years later

Sarah sat before her doctoral committee. She had studied, rehearsed and pestered her committee members for three months preparing for this last hurdle of her doctorate—the dissertation oral exam.

The members sipped coffee and munched on the doughnuts Sarah had provided as they leafed through her dissertation, checking the changes they had recommended. Her Chair, Dr. Nockari, took a large bite and mumbled through soft pleasure.

"Sarah, if you're trying to soften us up with these, it's working. How'd you keep 'em warm?"

The committee members all nodded save one and Sarah noticed. It was Dr. Abrams, a statistics guru, known to rip hide from graduate students lacking statistical skills.

"Oh God, I've missed something."

Dr. Nockari interrupted her fear, "Sarah, your committee knows your dissertation inside and out, but we're here today to determine if you do. To begin, I think it would be appropriate to give us an overview of what has transpired since your sighting."

The committee members' nodded agreement and two reached for another doughnut.

Sarah's dissertation topic was "*An Empirical Analysis of a Witnessed Astronomical Event - The Blue Phenomenon.*" Sarah took a last sip of coffee.

"Well, gentlemen as you know, Josh's and my observations caused quite a stir in the academic community. This 'stir' ranged from *'one of the most mysterious unsolved observations of the new millennium'* to *'a malfunction of the TPF'* to *'a hoax initiated by students.'* Public reaction was pretty much nonexistent despite the SNN five-minute segment they ran. I'm sure you remember their cute little title *'Angel Dust'*.

65

The Cleansing

"Three months after the sighting, a copy of our disk was borrowed by the FBI and later returned, by mail, to Dr. Nockari. No explanation accompanied the disk."

Dr. Abrams interrupted with a question, "Miss Trent, since this was an incredible sighting, in your opinion, why do you suppose interest within the academic community dissipated so quickly?"

Sarah did not hesitate, "I think it was because there were no other academic sightings to confirm our observation. We had a few hobbyists with anecdotal reports and we were compared with reports of flying saucers and Santa Claus. In the scientific community, especially astronomy, we're pretty uptight about confirmation and validity."

The committee members managed a smile, which relieved Sarah. "Also, new information about the universe began pouring in from the other TPF stations. We became old news fast, had our fifteen seconds.

To date, NIH environmental scientists monitoring global precipitation contaminants report nothing abnormal other than the fact that acid rain is increasing faster than government models predicted.

Dr. Nockari, commented, "Sarah, you might want to mention the testing in the Northern Brazilian rainforest."

"Yes, thank you Dr. Nockari, almost slipped my mind. A team was testing where precipitation is the heaviest in the world and found a blue tinted enzyme in rainwater. Four different labs confirmed the blue tint but couldn't identify what it was. Tests on animals and plants in the area revealed no adverse effects. In fact, no effects at all."

Sarah stopped and again sipped coffee, "Josh showed me an article he ran across just day before yesterday. Dr. Nockari, I didn't get a chance to discuss it with you before today but I think it's worth mentioning. As you know Josh is in Med School and 'The New England Journal of Medicine' is required reading. In the last issue an article related reports by a number of coroners and medical examiners throughout the Western Hemisphere of a perplexing phenomenon. Recent brain autopsies were revealing the inner layers of the cerebellum and the core of the hypothalamus had a slight blue tint.

"The article hasn't made much of a splash in the medical community because of the few patients involved and the fact the reports came primarily from coroners and examiners—not very high on the medical academic hierarchy. At least, that's the scoop from Josh. The article stated that *'there are no medical procedures or surgery'* that reveal the inner parts of the cerebellum and hypothalamus. They are observed in *'medical procedures only when radical autopsies of the brain are required as in cases of fatal head trauma, most notable in crimes and accidents.'*

"The *'blue tint'* is being explained away, by the few interested medical academicians as a result of *'a blow to the head'* or *'a lack of oxygen at death'*. Whether or not this has anything to do with *'the blue'*, I have no idea. I sure hope not."

The committee members sat quiet until two reached for another doughnut.

CHAPTER ELEVEN

Joy

Despite a postgraduate fellowship, fall semester had fatigued with age and Sarah looked forward to the holidays. Her mother had promised, UN business be damned, she would be home December 20th. Kate was coming, arriving the day after Christmas and Josh was coming if she had to drag him. She couldn't wait to show him off.

He was finishing a practicum in the children's ward at University Hospital. She hadn't seen him in three days, as she headed for his trailer. He'd invited her to dinner. She arrived early and found him in the field above his trailer helping his landlord-farmer with his tractor.

Josh looked up from his work and smiled, "Sorry, but we've got to move some hay. Have to finish today, rain predicted tomorrow."

Sarah waved him off, "Take your time, I'll start dinner."

"Thanks, won't take too long. Tilapia and salad in fridge, potatoes already in microwave. Not going to tell you about the strawberry shortcake," Josh retorted as he bent to the hay-baler.

Sarah went in, put on a Marian McPortland CD then went to Josh's bedroom kneeled and petted the Spaniel. It slept under his bed. She stood, and was heading toward the hallway to the kitchen when she noticed the picture on the right bedroom wall. Had it been earlier in the day, she wouldn't have seen it, maybe the reason she'd not noticed before. The angle of the sun caught its glass and flash-bulbed her eyes. It was small, inconspicuous. The open door to the bathroom obscured half the picture, a simple 8 by 11 wood frame.

She moved to it expecting family, SEAL buddies, maybe a former girl friend. *Better be a former girlfriend!*

She stopped, her right hand moved involuntarily to her mouth catching her breath. It was children, two hideously deformed children. She made out one to be a girl. She assumed she was a girl because the child had on a dress. She was black but not with race—she was black with death. Her skin was pitted tar, rotting with some insidious disease. It covered all of her exposed body; hands, arms, legs, neck and face. Only strands of hair remained and it appeared bleached.

Sarah shivered, *"God what's wrong with her?"*

She'd seen the advanced stages of syphilis from her mother's UN reports. *"But a child that young? Maybe radiation exposure or Ebola. Yet those were red and festering and the girl was not the worst. It was the boy—yes, it is boy."*

He sat with the girl in the woman's lap. He was smaller, much smaller. His head was no bigger than her thumb. There was no neck, his eyes were too far apart and long straight teeth overlapped his lower lip. His body was stunted and wrapped with his clawed hands and feet. Both the girl and the boy were reaching forward.

And the woman, she seemed so serene. Sarah moved closer to the picture. The woman, her face, *"She looks like Mother Teresa."*

She had the children in her lap and she had a puckered smile on her lips.

"What's that in her hand? What's she doing?"

Sarah moved to within inches, *"My God, she's blowing soap bubbles. Those children in her lap and she's blowing soap bubbles."*

The little girl's hideously deformed mouth and the boy's long bare teeth were smiling. And what Sarah thought were tiny round stains on the picture, weren't stains. They were bubbles, pictures of bubbles. The children were trying to reach for the bubbles and they were smiling.

"No, they're laughing. You can almost hear…."

Sarah moved back without knowing it and saw the carved word on the top of the frame - 'JOY'. .

She heard his pickup pulling up to the trailer. Two hours later, they were naked in bed.

Sarah giggled, "No, no, first you have to promise to go home with me for Christmas."

"Really want me to abandon sick children on Christmas?"

The Cleansing

"You're not abandoning anyone. It'll be fun—food, presents, lots of presents, a jillion people, my crazy friends; all the foreign students who can't get home are invited. A lot of faculty will be there and of course, you'll meet my mother and her UN friends. Lots of food and decorations, a real down-homer, only way you're going to get your gift. And New Years, I love New Years. There'll be a big party. If you want to be my date, and I only date hotties, have to get your bid in early."

"Sure you want to introduce me to your mother?"

"Oh, I can't wait. My God, it's been years, how long you think—I'll pick you up Christmas Eve. "

"No need to do that. I'll just..."

"I'll pick you up Christmas Eve, 6:00 sharp. Bring a tie. On Christmas day, dawn church services. That's a have to, UN ambassador, with daughter, attending church on Christmas day—good press. I promise I'll get you back to the children by Jan. 2nd."

Sarah smiled. She was getting her way and she liked that when they were both naked. "Now, come here."

Josh did as he was told. Sarah never mentioned the picture.

Christmas Eve, Sarah pulled into *'Racetrac Gas'* just east of Chapel Hill. She turned to Josh, "If you fill it up, I'll pay."

"Sounds like a deal to me."

Josh opened the door and slid out. Sarah did the same and whispered over the top of the car, "I gotta go pee."

"I'll be right here. Regular?"

"Yeah."

Five minutes later Sarah returned to the car, "Feel much better, ready to go."

He didn't move and when Sarah looked up he was motionless. His eyes were that of a manikin. Then she heard the man.

"God damn it, you forgot the money? How the hell we supposed to get gas without money?"
The voice was coming from the pickup parked at the pump in front of her. The man was holding the nozzle of the pump, glaring at a woman standing by the pickup door. The man was short but his girth was immense, bulging overalls over a t-shirt.

The Cleansing

His face was flat and red, etched by a black, two-day old beard. A three-year-old boy stood beside the woman clutching her leg. She was dressed in a faded, thin, short-sleeved dress. Her thin arms and legs were blotched purple from the forty-degree cold. The woman said nothing as she put both hands on the head of the boy and pulled him to her. The passenger side of the pick-up opened and another man got out. He was the only one of the four that had on a jacket.

"Dammit Nick, don't start. We can…"

Nick slammed the gas nozzle back onto the pump, "You got any fucking money, Pete? Huh? You got any fucking money?"

"I got three bucks, but…"

"You don't have any fucking money so shut your mouth. Just shut your mouth. Dumb bitch can't even remember to bring money." Nick moved toward the woman and child, screaming, "Get'n the fucking truck. Get the fuck in."

As the woman turned to open the truck door Nick grabbed the handle and jerked it open. The door slammed into her and she stumbled backward and fell on pavement. The boy fell with her and began to wail.

Nick raged, "God damn it, what the hell is wrong with you? He grabbed the woman by her arm and slung her toward the open door. She whimpered as her legs banged into the running board. Blood trickled down the shin of her right leg. A rip in her dress exposed an oozing rash on her thigh.

"Nick don't."

Sarah heard Josh. It was almost a moan, "Stand still, the mines. Sarah, stay here, stay here."

Sarah saw Josh's eye's roll then focus. He moved toward them.

"Josh, you shouldn't, don't…"

Nick raved, "Get in the fucking truck. Stupid cunt."

The three-year-old boy whimpered. Nick turned on him, "Don't you start." Nick grabbed the boy by the arm, "God damn it, I said shut up."

Josh flashed in Sarah's vision.

Nick stood the boy on the pavement and raised his hand to slap him. Josh caught Nick's arm, spun him and smashed his right palm into his chest. Nick sprawled on his back.

71

Josh picked up the boy and took him to his mother. She took the boy, sat on the running board of the truck and with frozen eyes glared at Josh. He looked to his right and left.

"Stay here, the mines."

Pete started around the truck, "Who the fuck?"

Nick got on his feet, bellowed, and hog sprinted toward Josh.

"Josh!" Sarah screamed.

Josh spun, whipped his right leg and smashed his foot into Nick's solar plexus. Nick emitted an air escaping 'huh' and fell to his knees.

Pete, now behind Josh, whipped lashed a chain as Sarah screamed again. Josh moved but the chain caught him across the left shoulder. He yelled with pain and wrapped his left hand around the chain, jerked Pete forward and smashed his palm into the bridge of his nose. Pete went careening backward, blood spurting from his face. The woman stood from the running board, screamed and attacked Josh. Josh held her at arm's length. His glaze focused.

Two black sedans came from nowhere and screeched beside and in front of Sarah, blocking her from the fight. Two men and a woman in black suits approached her. The woman held a shield toward Sarah.

"Miss Trent, I'm special agent Bower, we're part of your security team. Please get in the car. Get in now, please."

A county sheriff's car pulled in next to the fight and three deputies exited. The largest with his right hand on his weapon yelled.

"Hold it right there. Freeze. On your knees! On your knees, hands behind your head! Now!"

Agent Bower was pushing Sarah into the sedan. She resisted. "They're not trying to get at me. That man hit the woman. Josh is trying to help."

"Sarah, listen to me. Listen. I know you're right, but you can't be part of this. You're the UN ambassador's daughter. Get in and I'll straighten it out. You have to get in and you have to trust me. Your mother, Sarah, think of your mother."

Sarah looked at agent Bower then to a kneeling Josh being handcuffed. Pete was sitting, holding a towel on his face. The spots of blood on the towel were getting bigger. Nick sat on his haunches still trying to breathe. Sarah got in the sedan.

"Thank you, Miss Trent."

Agent Bower turned and walked toward the deputies holding up her ID. She approached and talked with the deputy in charge. He nodded and walked to his cruiser, leaned through the window and retrieved the mouthpiece to his radio. He talked, waited thirty seconds, nodded once then tossed the mouthpiece back into the cruiser. He came back to Agent Bower. They talked then shook hands. Bower returned to the sedan and got in beside Sarah. She spoke toward the driver.

"Okay, let's move before news at six gets here."

The sedans whipped out of *Racetrac*. Another agent was on their bumper in Sarah's car. Sarah grabbed agent Bower by the arm. "Wait, we can't leave Josh. Go back, I can't...."

"Sarah, Mr. Jones will be fine. Pretty obvious he can take care of himself."

Sarah looked out the back window, "He'll go to jail. That man was beating up on that woman and that little boy. We can't just leave him."

Agent Bower looked straight ahead, "I'll check on Mr. Jones. But we have to clear this area before the press gets here."

Sarah turned toward Bower, "I would like to borrow your phone, please."

Agent Bower hesitated then handed Sarah a cell phone. She punched numbers and waited. "Mother…" Ninety seconds later Sarah handed the phone to Bower, "She wants to talk with you."

Bower took the phone, "Ambassador Trent, Agent Bower." Bower listened for half a minute, "Yes, ambassador. Yes, ma'am. We'll take care of it. Oh, you're welcome, have a nice holiday."

Agent Bower punched the phone once then ten times.

"Charlie, Miss Trent is clear and we have a code-4. No, I can take it as soon as I deliver Miss Trent. Okay, you too."

Bower punched the phone once and dropped it in the seat between her and Sarah. She looked straight ahead. Five minutes later Sarah asked, "How do you know Josh won't say something?"

Agent Bower's smile was ever so faint, "JJ's a good boy."

The Cleansing

Twenty miles later the sedan pulled in front of the Trent home, an elegant Tudor surrounded by a hundred wooded acres. Cars were parked everywhere. The Christmas party had begun. An agent exited and opened Sarah's door. The one that drove her car handed her car keys and her purse. She started up the brick sidewalk leading to the front door then turned back to the sedan. The black window descended. Sarah leaned in.

"Look, I'm sorry. I know you guys are just doing your job. I…"

Bower interrupted her, "Miss Trent, I appreciate what you're saying, have a nice Christmas."

Sarah stuck her hand through the window and shook hands with Bower. "Thanks, sorry for all the trouble."

She turned toward the house. Agent Bower's voice stopped her, "I'll check on JJ."

Sarah turned and agent Bower smiled at Sarah, "Have a nice holiday."

Before Sarah could respond, the black window was going up and the sedans were speeding away.

Twenty minutes later at the county jail, the sheriff entered his office, taking off his coat. He was dressed in slacks and heavy red sweater.

"You'd think a man could take off Christmas Eve to watch his daughter's play but hell no, got to deal with politics." He started to hang his coat on the hall tree in the corner but stopped when he saw Agent Bower standing to the left.

"You're right, Sheriff, you should be home with your family on Christmas Eve. Your government appreciates your assistance in this matter."

Fifteen minutes later the sheriff stood with Josh beside a deputy cruiser, "Son, I don't know who the hell you are, but you sure know somebody. If you'll sign this, you're outta here."

The sheriff put papers on top of the cruiser and handed Josh a pen. Josh signed and the sheriff handed him a copy, "But boy, do me a favor—don't come back. I get testy when outsiders assault citizens of my county and get away with it. Real testy."

The Cleansing

The sheriff opened the back door of the cruiser, "Deputy Barnes is going to escort you and agent Bower anywhere you want to go—across the county line."

The Trent family home was bedlam with friends and Christmas. The home was built for comfort and entertaining, a rambling New England Tudor with large spacious rooms that opened into each other, each with its own roaring fireplace. Visitors were greeted by an *1880 R. J. Horner Carved Partner's Oak Desk* that sat to the right as one entered the foyer. A *Nelson Marshmallow Love Seat* sat to the left.

The soft elegance of expensive antiques, pewter and stained glass blended with Christmas decorations smelling of spice, hot cider and candles. The living area easily accommodated two large couches and an assortment of comfortable recliners, large throw rugs and had warm wooden floors. Bookshelves lined the walls and immense windows framed views of mountains and woods. Two large Christmas trees nesting presents stood on both sides of a huge flaming warm fireplace.

In the dining room, a *Rosewood Round Table* and a *Frankl Cream Cork Top Table* were both laden with food along with a *Jelly Pine Cupboard*. The tables were ringed with *Chippendale Pierced Splat Back Chairs*. A large hound greeted the guests with a wagging tail and wet nose. Another one stretched lazily on the couch closest to the fireplace, unperturbed by the hubbub.

Guests greeted Sarah with squeals, hugs and kisses of friends and cordial handshakes by faculty and dignitaries. She tried to hurry without the effort being noticed; yet it took her an hour to get to her mother. She and her mother slipped into the basement kitchen under the guise of a phone call. They took pork cake and coffee with them, hugged for longer than usual then settled into kitchen chairs.

"Well, Dr. Sarah Trent, have any days last semester that you would like to live over?"

"Quite a few—today's not one of them. Mother I'm sorry, I..."

"Well, it is a little disconcerting when your daughter rings in a level four. Not exactly a festive greeting." Gayle joked.

"Mother, I am sorry. I had no idea, but you've got to help Josh. I don't ask…"

"Josh is fine and I know you don't ask, but the UN ambassador's daughter was out with a man who assaulted two people. Sarah that cannot happen, that simply cannot…"

Dr. Gayle Trent stopped, grabbed her daughter's hands and squeezed them. "I've missed you. It's good to have everybody here. Your father and Stewart would have …"

Her daughter interrupted, "What do you mean assaulted. He was helping that poor woman and her little boy. That guy was a redneck goon. He was cursing and beating up on, I guess it was his wife, and the little boy, that Neanderthal was about to hit him. Are you sure Josh's okay?"

"Yes, he'll be arriving any time now. How bad did he lose it?"

"Well, pretty bad, but the one that really lost it was that red neck."

Sarah stopped and looked away, "We've been seeing each other for two years and he's never… he's the most gentle…he's never done anything like this. Mother tell me, you have to tell me."

Gayle looked at Sarah like a mother who knows her daughter's secrets, "No, I think you should tell me first."

Sarah relented. "Well, I suppose you've guessed by now that he's different."

"No guess to it. What do you like about this man who is so different?"

"Everything, his personality, his honesty and the way—let's just say he's clean sheets. Would you just tell me please?"

"Clean sheets?"

"Yes mom, clean sheets. You know guys you want to be around, you just want to curl up and—you really need to get out."

"So, the cute guys are clean sheets now?"

"Oh, yeah. Okay, your turn. And you have to tell me everything. I mean everything."

"I thought you didn't like for your friends, much less yourself, to be put under a microscope."

"Well, I don't, but this time…" Sarah adjusted her eyes, away from her mother's gaze. She smiled, but after her abduction, she wanted the security even the the implanted chips she still didn't believe in. She'd read the research, how they could tell when she was afraid or in pain, and the chips capacity to determine degrees of pain and fear. Kevin Warwick's research, Department of Cybernetics at the University of Reading, was so advanced that few believed him until he used it on himself and his wife.

"You sure you want to hear this?"

"Yes, now tell me. Tell me before I scream."

"Well, Sarah, surely by now you know quite a bit about his past."

"All I know is that he's a former SEAL. His only family is a sister and her daughter, whom I know nothing about, and you probably know about Jamaica. He's traveled a lot but I'm not sure where, he mentioned India. He doesn't talk about himself. Oh, and he's smart. God is he smart."

Gayle stared at her daughter for a few seconds, "You really care for this one, don't you?"

Sarah held her mother's eyes, "Yes, yes I do."

"Then it might be best if Josh told you."

Sarah looked down, "Yes, I guess you're right. It probably would be best if he told me."

Sarah grabbed her mother's hands, "If you don't tell me right now I'm going to pee."

Gayle laughed, "I can't blame you. I'd want to know too. Dr. Sarah B. Trent, you are involved with one remarkable man and you're right, he is smart. He's a former SEAL and I do know about Jamaica. God, what a mess. You know he resigned his commission after that?"

Sarah nodded as her mother continued, "He left the states. Worked at some of the most grueling jobs you can imagine, probably punishing himself—*'train wrecking'* in India, coal mining in Siberia, and you won't believe this, he worked in the 'dead zone' in the Gulf of Mexico. Left there and went to Calcutta then to Haiti where he worked with 'Restavek' children".

Sarah asked, "Restavek children? That's the slave children, parents sell them, right?"

The Cleansing

"Yes, so much for our WTO treaty. Still being sold and worse. He worked with a Jean-Robert Cadet until he was kicked out of Haiti for stealing an eight-year-old girl away from a wealthy family. The rich family's sixteen-year-old son was using her as a prostitute for himself and his rich friends. Josh was exported back to the states and he enrolled at Chapel Hill."

Sarah got up, poured their cold coffee into the sink and refilled with hot, "My God, I'm in love with a guilt-ridden Saint."

"Oh, he's far from a Saint."

Sarah handed her mother coffee and sat down, "What? What do you mean?"

"Sure you want to hear this?"

"I know he did drugs, if that is what you're talking about, but that's in the past—at least—yes, I want to hear."

"As best we can tell, the drugs began in Russia while he was coal mining, and some while he was train wrecking in India. None since."

Sarah breathed relief and her mother knowing she would, paused. Sarah asked. "How do you know? How do you find out all this?" Gayle didn't answer. Sarah sipped her coffee. "That's not so bad, especially after Jamaica. God, mother, we've got friends who'd put him to shame."

"I agree, I agree, but I haven't told you about his sister and her daughter."

"What about his sister and her daughter?"

"Well, his sister is dead."

Sarah's face withered, "What happened?"

"Died of alcohol poisoning. Apparently, she became an alcoholic while Josh was out of the states. From what we learned, Josh didn't know. He'd been at Chapel Hill two months when she called him. He went to see her then caught two men abusing her and her daughter."

Sarah's eyes widened, "Oh God, he killed them?"

"No, he didn't kill them. At least we don't think he did. We have no idea what happened to them. They just disappeared."

They were quiet for a moment as Gayle let her daughter digest.

"Jesus, that just doesn't sound like, what happened to the little girl, his niece?"

78

"He checked his sister into a rehab clinic. Took his niece to Children's Hospital at Chapel Hill. She suffered brain trauma from the abuse. May be visually and mentally impaired. She's improving, but they're not sure. A week later, his sister checked herself out of the clinic, and three days later she died of alcohol poisoning."

Sarah looked away. Gayle moved to the chair next to her daughter and embraced her. "You're dating a remarkable man, but he's been through it. Just watch yourself."

"Mom, how do you do it?"

"Do what?"

Sarah sat up and wiped her eyes, "Well, I haven't seen you in months, and all I can talk about is this man I'm involved with. Haven't asked a thing about you." Sarah paused then continued, "How're you doing? What's going on in your world? And with all you have to deal with you have to listen to a spoiled, self-centered, daughter. I'm sorry, I should… "

Gayle took her daughter's hands in hers again, "Oh Sarah, you don't how good it feels to just be a mom. What's going in my world? Well, just multiply what Josh has been through by a thousand. No, make that seven billion. But, being a mom, I need that. I really need that." She pinched her daughter's nose, "Although every once in a while you can be a pain in the butt."

A knock interrupted. Ambassador Trent smiled and took a large sip of coffee, "Wonder who that could be?"

Sarah stifled a giggle and went to the door. It was Josh. His left arm was in a sling. He held a book in his right hand. His clothes were scuffed and dirty. Sarah embraced him. She held him and then turned to her mother.

"Mother, I'd like you to meet Josh Jones."

Ambassador Trent extended her hand "Yes, I know. Good to finally meet you, Mr. Jones."

Josh put the book in his hand under his arm and shook her hand. "The pleasure is mine, Dr. Trent. I'm honored and I want to offer an apology to you and Sarah."

"Apology accepted with the understanding you're on your own if it happens again," Gayle said.

"I understand."

The Cleansing

Dr. Trent pressed, "Will there be a next time Mr. Jones?" Josh's brow wrinkled, "Probably. There's a lot of bad stuff out there and I'm still working on how to respond."

"I don't think adding more bad stuff is the answer. Med school is much better."

Sarah tried to change the subject, "Where'd you get the book?"

Josh took the book from under his arm and smiled, "Was in the jail library, very extensive collection. Filled two metal shelves. The sheriff wanted me to leave and never come back. I said okay if I could have this book. It's my peace offering to you."

Josh extended the book past Sarah to her mother. Gayle took the book noticing the stained cover.

"You found *'Expressions of Man's Self-Understanding'* by Tillich in a county jail?"

"Sure did."

"We have a signed copy in our library. He was on campus for a lecture series some years ago. So you like Paul Tillich?"

"I admire those who try to make sense of what we're about."

Gayle raised an eyebrow, "Do you agree with his explanation?"

"I agree with him about Schelling. Have you read Annie Dillard?"

Gayle's face lit up, "You've read Annie Dillard? I've read everything she's written—twice. Have Brother Carl Porter's words on my office wall at the UN."

Josh smiled and Sarah knew this was good, but she was out of the loop. "Not familiar with Anne Dillard and who's Carl Porter?"

Gayle looked to Josh and Josh grinning said, "I can do the 'Amen, thank God,' part."

She laughed, "That's the easy part."

Sarah was befuddled, "What are you two talking about?"

"Remember, Sarah, you asked."

With that, the U.S. UN Ambassador launched into a primitive preacher's rendition of Brother Carl Porter's words. Josh followed her every line with 'Amen, thank God'.

The Cleansing

"God ain't no white-bearded old man up in the sky somewhere. He's a spirit."

"Amen. Thank God."

"He's a spirit. He ain't got no body."

"Amen. Thank God."

"The only body He's got—is US!"

Josh concluded with a resounding, "Amen. Thank God!"

Gayle laughed as she pointed at the expression on her daughter's face, "Straight from Brother Carl Porter preaching in Scottsboro, Alabama. Compliments of Annie Dillard, well, actually Dennis Covington. So, Josh you've read Annie Dillard's *'For the Time Being'?* That's a search."

Sarah asked before she thought, "I haven't read it. What's it about?"

Josh responded, "Well, Ms. Dillard poses questions about life, herself, but mostly about God—begins with her eagerness to hear God's explanation of 'bird-headed dwarfs.' She also has questions about the bubonic plague killing 13 million people, Stalin killing 25 million and the 100 million children on the planet who live on the streets."

The picture in Josh's trailer flashed in Sarah mind, "Bird headed dwarfs?"

"Yes, babies born dwarfed and retarded, with displaced legs and arms, joints are contorted—faces the length of your thumb. At age six they're the size of your hand. If they live, and some do, they grow to be about three feet tall if they get their hips fixed so they can stand. But they're friendly, pleasant, can love and are loved and as Ms. Dillard points out, if anyone have souls they do."

There was silence before Sarah asked, "You've seen them?"

"Yes."

Again there was quiet until Sarah asked, "Ms. Dillard, offer an answer?"

Josh looked to Dr. Trent, "She talks of many—religions, beliefs, philosophy, but only one that made sense to her. It's hanging on your mother's wall at the UN."

Gayle's eyes narrowed, "Are you a religious man, Mr. Jones?"

The Cleansing

"To quote your guest lecturer, '*Being religious means asking passionately the question of the meaning of our existence and being willing to receive answers, even if the answers hurt.*' So no, I'm not a religious man."

Gayle looked at Josh with a hint of admiration, "You like Tillich, even quote him, but in fairness you should finish the passage. '*Such an idea of religion makes religion universally human, but it certainly differs from what is usually called religion.*'"

Sarah smiled because she knew it was going very well.

Gayle asked, "So you haven't found your Carl Porter?"

"No, but caught a glimpse in a picture once." Josh looked back to Gayle, then at Sarah, "There's a home in Calcutta, the 'Mirmal Hriday,' founded by Mother Teresa. It's a place you can go if you're poor and dying. I worked there for a while as an orderly. A picture hung on the wall at the entrance. It was of Mother Teresa, a six-year-old girl and a younger boy. The girl is black with leprosy, found her locked in a shed, and the boy has no neck, clawed hands and feet—'Hurler syndrome'. They sit in Mother Teresa lap. The picture is titled '*JOY.*'"

"Why 'JOY'?" asks Sarah.

"In the picture Mother Teresa is blowing soap bubbles. The children are laughing. Just two children in her lap—laughing. Closest I've ever come to Carl Porter. I think Annie Dillard and Tillich would like that picture."

"Are the children still there…at the home in Calcutta?" Sarah asked.

Josh looked at Sarah for a time, and then answered, "No."

Feeling the tension, Gayle broke the mood, "Josh, I'm rude. Would you like some coffee and I bet you've never tasted pork cake?"

Sarah jumped up, "I'll get it."

As Sarah got the coffee and cake Gayle saw in Josh's eyes that he went away for a few seconds, returned, and looked at her. "The insistence of religion and nature that some are born just to suffer and die is morally corrupt." Josh looked at the floor, "'*Obles oblea*', which, too often the world takes for a fool."

"Think Tillich would have liked Carl Porter?"

The Cleansing

Before Josh could answer, a repetitive beeping sounded from Ambassador Trent's waist. It was sudden, out of place taking the moment to something else. Sarah saw an expression form on her mother's face that scared her. This was a beeper that Sarah or Gayle had never heard. The one that said the United States had gone to Def-Con-One. Gayle hurried to the red phone in the basement and talked, in hushed tones, for less than 30 seconds.

CHAPTER TWELVE

The Coming

Out in the darkness of the universe, where sunlight is almost nonexistent, there's a world that Galileo and Newton never imagined. Both knew of Mars, Venus, Jupiter, Mercury even Saturn, but they did not know of Uranus, Neptune and Pluto. If there is to be a future recorded history of earth, many say it will note they came a hundred light years beyond the knowledge of Galileo and Newton.

The first human sighting was in Amundsen-Scott Station, Antarctica where the National Science Foundation and the U.S. were in a joint venture constructing a Scientific Outpost. Perhaps it was fitting this was the first sighting. The South Pole is the most arduous place this side of outer space. The temperature had climbed to –25F this brilliant December morning. The first human to see them was David Phelps, an engineer assigned to the first shift.

The gale was whipping across the glacier with a wind chill that could freeze eyelids. Mr. Phelps was inside the cab of a frozen caterpillar, trying to get it started, a half-hour before his shift began. He'd been out too long, fifteen minutes. He thought he was hallucinating. Four bronze tubular ships hovered about 100 meters from the edge of the construction site and then settled into the snow and ice of the glacier.

According to Phelps, *"something,"* or several *"somethings,"* exited each craft and slowly moved about in the snow for at least a minute. He could not make out their appearance or shape. Fogging goggles and blowing snow prevented a clear view. Then they reentered the crafts and disappeared not into the sky but underneath the glacier.

Thirty minutes earlier

A Homeland Security team member left the funeral of his grandmother; another, a sixth grade soccer game; another, church; another, the bed of a lover; another, vacation with family. Dr. Jason Maxwell's limo was speeding toward the White House. He glanced at his watch. It was 7:31p.m. He was fifteen minutes away.

At first he thought it was the sound of the shower. He turned the shower off, and the sound was unmistakable. One long, two short—only the third time his beeper had signaled *"Protocol Six."*

Naked and dripping wet, he coiled the speaker around his face as he read from the screen of laptop iMac Citron III. He dressed, without drying, as he read.

"PROTOCOL SIX - TWENTY MINUTES"

The second line read.

"Beginning in 129 seconds…128…127…126."

The HS team had three minutes to respond to 'Protocol Six' before 'protocol' began. Jason hit the return key. Seven members were already on-line. *"TWENTY MINUTES"* meant there would be five minutes to review the brief, five minutes for brainstorming and five minutes for suggestions and solutions. The last five minutes would be used to finalize the report to the President. The eight members now on-line, now ten, had additional precious seconds to review as the Citron counted and waited for the others.

"PROTOCOL SIX" had been initiated only twice, the Russian Chinese border dispute and the kidnapping of the Canadian Prime Minister's daughter. Two minutes later he was in the limo scanning the brief displayed on the Citron iMac.

The top line in red stated *"PROTOCOL SIX."* It was followed by:

"NATURE: International and national - violation of air space, four continents, ninety countries. U.S. at 'Defense Condition - 1."

"CONFLICT: '07:34:44…45…46…47 - None."

"CASUALTIES: '07:34:44…45…46…47 - [Civilian - None] [Military - None]."

The Cleansing

"SOURCE: Unknown aircraft from outside earth's atmosphere."

"NUMBER: Hundreds."

"DESCRIPTION: Tubular, 40 X 10 meters, bronze in color."

"COMPARISONS: Guided or manned missiles, rockets."

"SEVERITY: Unknown."

"DURATION: Unknown."

"SIMULATIONS: None."

Dr. Maxwell looked up from his iMac and thought, *"My God, they'll think this is a drill."* He slid the glass window between himself and the driver, "Malcolm, step on it."

"Yes sir, Dr. Maxwell."

Jason scanned the brief again and spoke into his mouthpiece linked to data banks. Verification was confirmed, and the Russian-Chinese border was the only comparison. It happened three years earlier. Both countries had violated each other's borders with troops and artillery, and planes had been scrambled. For the first time in three generations, a conflict with the potential for escalating into a nuclear war had been a reality.

There had been less than an hour before warplanes carrying nuclear weapons would have violated borders. HS had anticipated the dispute and proactively suggested a UN force of Russian and Chinese peacekeeping troops train together for the sole purpose of diffusing such an occurrence. The UN had taken Homeland Security's advice. The UN Russian Chinese force had parachuted between the borders and warring factions. With their troops in harm's way, both sides blinked, and time was bought for a diplomatic solution.

But this was different, very different.

"Where the hell did they come from?" Jason said to himself.

A message from the Citron ended his thoughts and the first five minutes of PROTOCOL SIX.

"REVIEW COMPLETE."

Fifteen minutes later the President and the Joint Chiefs were reading the report from HS's computer screens.

Three hours later Dr. Trent entered the White House Situation Room. A White House deserted just hours ago for the holidays, now bustled with activity. The President, Vice-President, Secretary of State, Secretary of Army, Navy and Air Force, Kate

Dockery, General Dickenson and three of his staff were assembled.

Major General John. T. Wayland, Air Force Chief of Staff, was briefing. General Wayland was a product of the Air Force Academy. He was intelligent, articulate and had the demeanor of a lanky bent grandfather. He was a veteran of the Iraqi and Sudanese wars, known for his competence and candor. The men and women under his command revered him.

Gayle was concerned that General Wayland was briefing. This meant the situation was serious, and she had never seen him this stoic and grim.

"Ladies and gentlemen, at 1400 hours Christmas day, NORAD, our space surveillance radar in Maui and two of our Strategic Response Satellites intercepted unknown aircraft entering U.S. airspace." He stood before the group. "Simultaneously, according to NATO reports, similar forces entered the air space of the following."

General Wayland gestured to a first lieutenant who flashed a global map on an iMAC screen-wall. The map was dotted with numbers. "Examination of GPS information shows the crafts have entered the airways of the regions numbered on the map. You will note this includes every continent on the planet; the Polar Regions, North and Central America, South America, Africa, Europe and Asia including Southeast Asia and Australia. The total number of invading aircraft is as yet unknown but we do know they number in the hundreds.

"Advance warning time was diminished by the fact that the aircraft did not come from the direction of any country or countries on the planet. Our GPS and radar, as well as those of other countries, are directed toward each other and the force did not come in an east-west direction."

The general paused, looking about the room, hesitant about speaking his next words, "The invading craft appear to have come from a northerly direction outside our atmosphere."

The hush about the room grew quieter.

"John, what the hell are you saying?" A raspy General Dickenson asked.

"General, we're not sure but there's more. By 1415 hours, interceptor aircraft had been scrambled in seven different countries: the U.S., England, France, Germany, Russia, Canada and China. Five of these countries, including the U.S., have engaged the invaders. All of the reports are identical. The invading force was slow moving, methodical, as if deliberate. Their craft are bronze in color, cigar in shape, and the size of a medium sized commercial jetliner. They fly in a 'V' pattern, similar to Canadian geese, with nine craft in each formation.

"Engagement, at least by our planes, the British and the French, was by the book, with various communications attempted on all military and commercial flight frequencies. Requests for identification were ignored and met with silence. Escort brought no reaction. Repeated warnings were seemingly ignored. THADD locked on with Heras as the invaders approached within fifty thousand feet of the earth's surface.

The President gave the order to engage by firing warning missiles. This was attempted by four of our Stealth II interceptors, and their missiles failed to fire. The order was given to ten additional interceptors with the same result. Finally, our entire interceptor force was given the order to fire and all four hundred and twenty failed. THADD then tried with their ground missiles and they failed to launch."

His words came slower and more pronounced, "As bizarre as it sounds, it appears sabotage on an unbelievable scale has disabled the combat capability of our planes and missile defenses. And, this is not isolated. Our planes were scrambled from five different military bases; Langley, Destin, D.C., Salt Lake and Riley as well as THADD in White Sands and Kennedy. We disengaged and gave orders to our pilots to shadow the invaders until we could get additional interceptors air born.

"During the next five minutes, we contacted the Brits and the French and they reported their interceptors were also disabled, and they confirmed the same with the Canadians and the Russians."

Vice-President Stewart interrupted, "Good God, how many planes have we lost?"

"None, Mr. Vice-President. All of our planes as well as the interceptors of the other countries returned safely to their bases."

"Returned to their bases? I don't understand. They had orders to shadow the invaders."

"Yes and they did as long as they could, sir."

"What do you mean?" The Vice-President whispered.

"The invaders have landed, sir."

"Landed? Judas Priest, where?" Stewart exclaimed

"Our planes and the planes of the other countries tailed the invaders until fuel depletion forced their return to base. By that time our Global Positioning Satellites, as well as satellites of NATO, had a lock on their location and tracked them until they landed. In the U.S., they have landed in the Everglades in Florida and in the Denali Park in Alaska. We have them locked in with GPS.

"We've also confirmed they've landed in the following sites; the Morne Trois Pitons on the island of Dominica, the Manu Biosphere Reserve on the eastern slopes of the Peruvian Andes, the Pamirs in Asia in the eastern half of the Republic of Tadzhikistan, the Tepuis rock towers in southern Venezuela, the Okavango Delta in Africa, and the Pacific Ocean. There are other landing sites, and we'll have their locations within the next hour."

Again there was silence around the room, until General Dickenson spoke.

"John, I know a little about the terrain of the Peruvian Andes and the Tepius rock towers. A greased corkscrew couldn't land in those places. And the Everglades and Denali Park?"

The general scoffed, "Hell, they're the most God-forsaken places in our country, if you consider Denali Park, Alaska part of our country. Take us days…hell, weeks to get troops in there."

General Wayland nodded agreement, "Yes, sir. The invading craft appear to have incredible maneuverability and seem to be targeting the remotest places on the planet to land. This makes a lot of sense militarily if they know the limitations of our planes and military forces. Our planes can't follow and I agree, general, it'll take weeks to get significant ground forces to those areas."

The Vice-President asked, "But you said some landed in the Pacific. If they are floating around out there, we can get our planes and naval personnel…"

"Yes sir, but they're not floating around, sir. They didn't land on the ocean surface. They submerged, and according to sonar information from the Nautilus and the U.S.S. Oklahoma, nine of their craft are eight miles beneath the surface of the ocean."

"You mean they crashed and sank?"

"No sir, they're moving about, sir, as if exploring and there's more, sir. "General Wayland hesitated yet again.

The President who had remained silent until now finally spoke.

"John, they need to know."

General Wayland looked about the room, "We have not been able to determine why our planes could not fire on the invaders. Simultaneous to launching interceptors, we mobilized ground troops and Special Forces. Like the missiles of our interceptors, our ground troop and special force weapons have been immobilized."

"Immobilized? John, what the hell are you talking about?" General Dickenson roared.

"General, none of our weapons will fire—none."

Wayland looked to the President.

The President nodded.

"Ladies and gentlemen, if you'll permit me."

General Wayland again gestured toward his lieutenant.

The lieutenant left the oval office and reentered with a capital security guard armed with the issue of capital guards, a standard sidearm Remington 38 pistol.

"Officer, we need your assistance," General Wayland said firmly.

"Yes, sir."

"Did you load your firearm prior to your shift?"

"Yes, sir."

"Officer, when was the last time you fired your weapon?"

"Last Thursday." He answered quickly. "We're required to practice small arms fire once per week, sir."

"Did you practice last Thursday with the sidearm you are carrying now?"

"Yes, sir."

"And it fired?"

The officer looked puzzled. "Yes, sir," he replied.

"Where did you get the ammunition to load your firearm this morning, officer?" Wayland inquired.

"Issue. We're issued ammunition through central command at the Pentagon, sir."

"Thank you for your cooperation, officer. We would like now for you to fire your sidearm into the pillows on the chair directly behind you."

While General Wayland and the security guard had been conversing, the lieutenant had placed several pillows on the chair. The security guard hesitated.

"It's all right, officer. This is just a demonstration."

The security guard snapped to attention, "I have strict orders never to expose my weapon in the presence of the President, Vice President, staff member, congressman, cabinet member, or civilian unless they are overtly threatened with harm, sir."

"I understand, officer, but…"

The President interrupted, "Frank, it's all right. We're not testing you. You can do as General Wayland asks."

Frank looked to the President, then about the room. He turned and approached the chair. He turned again and surveyed the room.

"How many rounds, sir?"

"As many as you can," General Wayland answered.

The guard looked to the President one last time before facing the chair, pulling his sidearm, pointed it to within a foot of the pillows, and pulling the trigger. His weapon did not fire. He snapped the trigger four times. He opened his .38 and checked the ammunition. He holstered his weapon and turned to General Wayland.

"It's okay Frank, we were pretty sure your weapon wouldn't fire. Now, if you'll reload and attempt to fire the shells from each of these boxes."

The lieutenant handed Frank three boxes of shells. The three boxes were different brands. Frank looked to the President and the President gestured approval. Frank tried shells from each box and none fired. General Wayland stopped the attempts.

"Thank you, officer. We appreciate your cooperation."

With a "yes, sir" Frank turned to leave as the President commented, "Frank, we'd appreciate it if you would not repeat what…"

"Understood, Mr. President."

91

The Cleansing

Wayland surveyed the room, "Ladies and gentlemen, the three boxes of shells that Frank attempted to fire were purchased this morning at Mall-Mart, and a local firearms store."

"John, I'm smarter than the average poke of turkeys but I have no idea what the hell is going on," stated Dickenson.

General Wayland hesitated for a few seconds before speaking, "Simply this. We cannot find any shells or ammunition that will fire—military or civilian. We've checked munitions at twelve of our military bases and shells purchased at civilian stores in at least two-dozen cities, and we have been unable to find any that will fire. Our weapons are in perfect mechanical shape; small arms, artillery, missiles, rockets but nothing will fire. Something, somehow, someway has contaminated munitions throughout our armed forces and in the civilian population."

Dickenson stood up, put his hands on the table and leaned forward. His voice was hoarse, "How in God's name is that possible? This—that means we're totally defenseless. I thought I'd heard everything, but this is the biggest bunch of horse— excuse me, Mr. President, but could I use your phone?"

The President pushed his phone to General Dickenson. Dickenson, mumbled and glared around the table, jabbing the phone buttons then yelled, "Marge, this is me. Yeah—yeah I know. Marge, I don't have time and this is important. Get one of the, no get both, get both of the automatics out of the case and go to the target room and fire off a few rounds."

There was a pause, "Yes, Marge, I'm serious, dead serious. No, I'm not joking. Marge this is important. Do as I say. Dammit Marge! Okay, okay, I'm sorry, but this is important. Please take both the automatics and fire a few rounds. Either one! Hon, I'll explain later. Please do it, and come back to the phone. I'm going to wait on you. Good. Yeah, I know but I'll wait."

The room waited for four minutes before General Dickenson responded.

"Yeah, I'm here."

There was a long silence.

"Both of them? And the pistols? Did you try with the new box of…yeah, thanks punkin. No, that's it. Yeah, I got it…milk, dog food and shells. As soon as I can, but I'll be a while. I have to go. Yeah, me too—bye." General Dickenson hung up the phone and stared at the table.

The room was quiet until the Vice-President spoke, "This is not possible. There is no technology that can disable every last one of our weapons."

Wayland responded at once, "Sir, you're partially correct. Our planes can still fly and all ground-mechanized vehicles can still move. That means we can still transport, observe and track and as I speak, we have chemists working on munitions."

General Dickenson whispered, struggling with panic in his voice, "My God, do those damned Arabs, or North Koreans know about this? If they find out about this they'll be kicking our asses before nightfall. My God, you don't suppose they're behind this, do you?"

"General, so far everyone has been tight-lipped about their military. And believe me, General, nobody on this planet has this kind of technology. I've communicated with some of our allies and our contacts with our adversaries. Those that would share information have the same problem. And sir, we have ways of confirming and it's been confirmed."

The Vice-President whispered as well, his voice hoarse, "Are you saying this may be global?"

General Wayland looked to the President and again the President gestured for him to respond.

"Yes."

The Vice President leaned back in his chair and shrugged. "Anything else?"

"Yes, if you consider the ramifications of this, whatever this is, it affects more than just our military. A lot more, sir."

"What *'more'* General?" The Vice-President realized he was still whispering tried to sound louder and his voice cracked.

"Civilian law enforcement, sir."

The room grew silent as the ramifications of the disarming information began to take form. "Do you mean that none of the weapons of law enforcement or civilians work?"

"Yes sir, but neither does the weapons of criminals, at least, not so far."

93

The Cleansing

"Thank you General Wayland," The President said, sensing the bewilderment affecting the group. "People, we're getting ahead of ourselves a bit here. We have two major concerns: the invading force and restoring our armed forces with weapons that work. Until we can get a handle on those two things, here's what we will do. John, you coordinate everything through General Dickenson. I want an update every ten minutes. Use the red line. If there are more landings, let me know. If there is any aggression on their part let me know. Anything unusual, anything, let me know."

General Dickenson protested, "Mr. President, we have to confront these invaders. This is war. Let's mobilize everything we have, get our M88s on the move and declare a state of..."

The President again interrupted, "General Wayland, are you sure there's no one on this planet who could do this? How about the Japanese? That guidance technology they've been experimenting with is..."

"They were the first ones we checked, sir. The technology you speak of is for public transportation and the auto industry. NATO is their military. And sir, no one could hide that many craft from us. To launch craft by the hundreds, without detection, then re-enter the earth's atmosphere and land the way they did, no sir, that's not possible, not on this planet."

The President looked about the room, "Everyone listen up, this is important." He looked straight at General Wayland, "General, have we suffered any military or civilian casualties?"

"No, sir."

"Have any of our allies or any country suffered any casualties?"

"Not that we know of, sir."

"And no country is being occupied or attacked?"

"Well, air space has been violated, all over the world, but so far the landings have been in the remotest spots on the planet and our tracking tells us there are no forces other than the craft, sir."

The President again looked about the room, "Thank you, General. Everyone hear what he said? In view of that and the fact we can't defend ourselves, we'll track and observe. Hopefully, we have the time to...John start with the factories. Maybe new munitions will work. General Dickenson, get your men on the move. How soon can you get to the craft in the Everglades?"

"Sir, we'll be on the move in the next three hours. Contained? Without weapons, that's another issue. They're in the most remote part and it's wet. Water two to six feet deep. Take weeks to get the number of forces we need there. Logistics, supplies—there's no place to setup. We'll have to assemble pontoons—and sir, we've scrambled our 'NEST' teams, just in case."

The Vice-President asked, "You think we're going to need to disarm nuclear weapons?"

"Well, we don't know and that's the point, sir."

The President shook his head, "Hope they're as good as whoever disarmed ours." The General didn't respond. The President looked to the floor. "Okay, we'll have to live with contained. Report to me every fifteen—ten minutes. I repeat, if there are more landings, or anything starts to move that has already landed I want to know. Stewart, check with Special Forces. When they get within twenty miles, secure and have them stand down. Then let me know. Under no circumstance is anyone to get closer than twenty miles. Have to give HS time to check on biohazards. Report in to the command center at the Pentagon. We'll set up there until—until we get a handle on this.

"And ladies, gentlemen I hope I don't have to tell you that no one is to talk to anyone about invaders from space. The public will know soon enough, if they don't already. The origin of the craft is unknown and until we know, it's unknown. No one is to speak to anyone about this until I address the nation. Ladies and gentlemen. That's an order. Clear?"

Most everyone in the room mumbled, "Yes, sir."

The President stopped. "I didn't hear that."

There was a resounding, "Yes, sir."

"What if we're attacked, Mr. President?"

"I want your answer to that question in my hands in fifteen minutes, General," the President said as he grabbed his coat and turned as he headed for the door. "Kate, tell Sue to get the boys on the line. I need to talk with all of them but start with Prime Ministers Roy and Yelve. Roy should be in London. Yelve was supposed to leave for the Black Sea yesterday, so check there first. Gayle, Annabelle, get hold of your colleagues, those you

95

trust, and find out who has weapons that work. If you find any—yell."

"Mr. President, you need to address the nation as soon as you can," Annabelle reminded him. We have word that SNN is going to break the news anytime now.

"Yeah, you're right. Kate, we need to hold up the report from SNN. Tell them they can report anything they want after I address the nation."

As the briefing began to break up, the President stopped and tossed his coat over a chair-back.

"Kate, Gayle and Annabelle, I'd like you to remain here for a few minutes." They all heard the President whisper to General Wayland, "John, you're sure about our nukes?"

"Yes sir, we're sure."

Three minutes later the President, Gayle, Kate and Annabelle were in a small office adjoining the situation room. The President picked up a phone, covered the speaker end with his hand and looked toward Gayle.

"Gayle, is Sarah home for Christmas?"

"Yes, sir."

"Chapel Hill or Hilton Head?"

"Chapel Hill."

The President punched three numbers. He listened, said "Chapel Hill" and hung up.

"Gayle, I want you to call home and tell Sarah that agents from the CIA will be picking her up within the hour. Do you suppose she can contact the fellow that was with her the night of that blue haze, what's his name? Yes, yes, Mr. Joshua Jones. And the professor, a Dr. somebody. They just might be able to help us on this. God, I hope they can."

Gayle was stunned, "Yes sir, how did you know? How can they…"

"Gayle, it's an interesting story but let's wait 'till they get here. All of you need to make your calls. Join me at the Pentagon as soon as you can."

Gayle, confused, watched the President leave.

Annabelle shrugged, "All I know is the NRA is going to be defecating building material."

CHAPTER THIRTEEN

Revenge

One hour earlier

Red lights flashed, in unison with bleating horns as Ishmar Zolef and four assistants entered the lab. Their "Level - 4" biohazard suits fluoresced with the red lighting. They moved quickly, as quickly as their suits allowed. The cells were silent. The sobbing ended last week, the moaning, two days ago. They'd survived longer than the plants. It took twenty-four months for all of them to die. Eighty percent lasted until last month then they died at a geometric rate.

The assistants entered the cells and examined mummy-like bodies. The bodies were wrapped with layers of clothes and bedding, an attempt to shield. Sharp metallic probes brought no responses. The assistants peeled back clothing clinging to flesh and with distorted expressions confirmed death.

Zolef and the assistants filed out of the lab through the metallic doors. They stood in their suits for six minutes as the chemical showers sprayed them then walked to the next room and stripped. In the next room, their bodies were scanned for radiation. Traces were detected and they showered again naked. The traces were fainter but still detectable. Zolef disdained another shower and he and his assistants entered the next room to dress. They exited the building. Two diesel dozers and a halftrack waited at the entrance. Zolef pointed to the drivers of the dozers.

"Crush it then bury it. No trace. When you finish there will be nothing here but sand."

Zolef and his assistants climbed into the halftrack and headed toward the Persian Gulf and Kharg Island. They arrived two hours later and entered a small lab near the hub of the largest pumps where giant 900-millimeter pipelines from the vast oil reserves of Iran's oil fields fed the Jazireh-ye terminal. Zolef checked instruments in the lab and smiled when one read "ACTIVE."

"Bring them in!"

Four Iranian soldiers entered with two blindfolded gaunt gray men of western origin. The two men had been reported "MIA" during the invasion of Iraq. Then, they were in their late-twenties but now approaching forty. After removing their blindfolds, Zolef took a dagger from one of the guards and touched the blade to the throat of the tallest man. He stared hard at the shorter, scrawny prisoner and nodded toward a lever.

"Pull the lever, or I will kill your friend," he growled.

The man hesitated, quickly glancing toward his buddy. Zolef razored a one-inch slit on his prisoner's throat. The injured man gasped, his hands grasping the cut. Blood oozed between his fingers. He didn't moan as he struggled to breathe. Zolef leaned forward and nodded toward the lever.

"Pull the lever."

The prisoner didn't hesitate. He pulled the lever, and the "ACTIVE" light glowed red.

Zolef smiled, "In two years I will show what you have done to your family, your friends and your country. Then I will kill you."

Zolef watched as one prisoner was led away, the other dragged along behind, leaving a trail of blood.

"God is great."

CHAPTER FOURTEEN

Crisis

Three hours later.
Intelligent, starched shirted men and women hurried everywhere. Orders and action were brisk, efficient and crisp, the Pentagon at its best, what it was designed for. They had trained for such a day and for many it was a rush. They scrutinized the theatre-sized monitor screens on the 40-foot walls of the war room, and punched at keyboards then scrutinized again. GPS systems and the new KH-13 SRGs (Strategic Response Satellites) along with their older sisters, the KH-12s, were doing their job.

Printers spewed out data that had been analyzed, detailed and painstakingly made into understandable information. The reports were hand-carried by double timing couriers to majors and colonels in sealed envelopes that were black-lettered "TOP SECRET." The reports were studied and executive summaries ordered until generations of technological evolution and billions in expenditures were boiled down into three page reports that politicians and generals could understand.

Twelve HS members gathered in a sterile room in the Pentagon and with speakers connected to their Citrons communicating with HS members around the globe. *"PROTOCOL SIX - No comparable simulations"* mocked them from their computer screens, the first time this had happened. HS had not simulated an intrusion from space. Simulations for asteroid collision, space shuttle, and space resource mining crises were useless.

The brief had been updated and continued to list unknowns: origin, reason, motive, threat, and duration. What was known was defined; continents violated, landings in identified remote areas, as of 8:14p.m. no known ramifications, violent or otherwise, public reaction as yet non-existent. Estimated time public reaction would become evident - two hours. The President wanted the next report in fifteen minutes.

As HS staff communicated with each other, their computers recorded and analyzed everything said. Software and the Citron compiled, analyzed and provided probabilities.

PROTOCOL SIX dictated that members were entitled to three comments, but each comment was limited to thirty words. The thirty-word rule was for crisis dictated by time and maximizing diversity of participants. This rule had taken HS six months to determine. In normal conversation, the average person speaks three words per second. An intelligent individual, purposely speaking fast, can legibly articulate four to five words per second. Factoring hesitation between comments, in five minutes, team members would speak and hear one thousand words. In short, HS had three thousand words between them to draw conclusions. The updated brief had been read. The second five minutes would be brainstorming and the last five, compilation of the report.

The first was from Dr. Terrell a psychologist, "Two primary factors; one - how or should we encounter and two - the severity of national and international ramifications of no arms."

Other members commented in rapid order;

"Primary concern is potential danger."

"We're getting ahead of ourselves. The factors depend on where the craft originated. We should have two agendas. One assuming the craft originated on earth; the other, they originated somewhere other than earth."

The citron beeped. This was a signal of protocol violation and counted as two comments by the offender. There was no interruption of comments.

"Do you believe they're from outer space?"

"From the report, the speeds they entered the earth's atmosphere, the places they landed, disarming the planet—yes, I believe they are from somewhere other than earth."

"I don't. We'll know their origin when a country steps forward with weapons that work, and we'll have the new and only super power."

The Cleansing

"We have surveillance systems in place that signals significant military activity. No one on this planet could have built or launched that many craft without us knowing it. We'd know about such technology."

The Citron beeped again. This is what Dr. Maxwell feared, protocol violation.

"Obviously, we didn't. Maybe whoever's technology is so advanced they can avoid detection."

"We cannot assume the craft are manned. This is critical in terms of how or whether to encounter."

"Doesn't matter. If they are not manned, they are guided. Both require technology." Another countered.

"And the craft were made by someone or something. It flies. It lands. It's here and required very advanced technology."

"Should we assume they're all the same? Externally, from the information we have, yes, but internally, we don't know."

"If the craft are potentially harmful, why are they landing in the remotest areas on the planet? If they are meant to do harm wouldn't they have landed in communication, population and military centers?"

There was no beep from Citron.

"Maybe, they're avoiding us because of fear."

"Fear? They've disarmed us. What's to fear?"

"The reason for disarming is fear." One pointed out.

"Are the invaders responsible for the disarming? And we should consider…there is nothing for us to fear?"

"Invasion of air space, failure to communicate, disarming the planet, regardless of how it was done. Yes, fear is a reasonable response."

"How to engage the invaders, public reaction to the invaders and the realization of no arms, those are the issues."

"Diversity…diversity is the issue. This is an international crisis as well as national. That means diverse national, religious and political reactions. The reaction will be all over the page."

"We have to be the first to engage." A soft-spoken member stated.

"Why?"

"We can design how best to do it. We have the best chance at doing it right."

101

"Can we convince other countries of that?"

"No, another reason we have to be first."

"Protect them from themselves."

"Yes, soon someone will be chopping at one of the craft with a pick axe."

"Can we prevent that?"

"We should try. No, we must."

Five hundred and ten words later Citron interrupted.

"Discussion complete."

Twenty five hundred and eighty four words later HS gave their second report to the President and the Joint Chiefs

The Secretary of Defense and staff, Gayle, Kate, Annabelle, and the President had established central command in the pentagon war room. Couriers filed in and out as they pored over incoming reports. One of the couriers reported that Sarah and Josh had arrived. The President picked up a red line.

"They're here. We'll be ready in three minutes. General Wayland first, then Dr. Maxwell and McLean."

Gayle's eyes and ears perked at the name of Dr. Maxwell. Sarah, Josh and Dr. Nockari entered the war room escorted by three CIA agents. Josh and Dr. Nockari were introduced to the President and the Secretary of State. Annabelle felt kindred spirits and hugged all three. Ninety seconds later, the group sat attentively around an oval table watching the monitors still trained on bronze cigar-shaped craft—craft that had not moved since landing.

General Wayland entered with the President and again General Wayland briefed.

"During the last hour we've had additional landings; the Taymyr Peninsula in Siberia, the Cairnogorms in the Scottish Highlands and the Kimberley Plateau in Northwest Australia. Like the other landings, they are remote and inaccessible to aircraft, naval and ground forces and like the other landings, they have not moved since landing. In addition, approximately 100 more craft of the same description have entered the earth's atmosphere and according to their path and speed will land in the next hour. They slow considerably as they approach the earth's surface.

102

"We've had four casualties, but they were not attributable to aggression by the invaders. One of our Apache IIs crashed off the USS Alabama attempting to land. As of," the General checked his watch, "as of four minutes ago, there had been no reported aggressive acts by the invaders. In fact, we have yet to see the pilots or occupants of the invading aircraft. We have some in NSA and SOD suggesting that the craft are some sort of probe, void of life forms. However, their flying patterns and landing capabilities are a result of piloting, or a guidance system technology that is advanced beyond anything we know." He stopped and breathed deeply before continuing.

"Now as to our defenses. None of our weaponry will fire except for," he paused slightly, "water cannon. We've tried new weapons and munitions with no success. Planes, ships and our other mechanized equipment continue to be fully functional. We can and are transporting Special Forces, the second and fifth army divisions to the perimeters of their landing sites in the Everglades and Denali in Alaska. However, as of this hour our forces are armed with weapons that won't fire. This is also true of arms in the private sector including law enforcement. We've mobilized the National Guard and they are reinforcing law enforcement agencies throughout the country. I'm happy to report that, so far, crime has not been a problem.

"We have reports from our embassies in 63 other countries, and they are experiencing the same with their weapons. Obviously, many countries are refusing to discuss their situation. However, we're averaging five calls per hour from countries begging for our protection. Concerning your earlier orders, Mr. President, we will be within fifty miles of the landings in Florida and Alaska within the next hour. We have advised other countries to maintain parameters and all are complying except the Aussies. They are attempting to parachute troops to within two miles of the craft in the Kimberly Plateau."

A tired President looked up and took a long draw from a mug. "General, is there any way of determining what's inside those craft?"

"Our CH-54 Stallion choppers just came on line, sir. If we can get within a thousand yards we can detect sound and life forms."

"inside the craft?"

"With the equipment on the CH-54s, yes sir, we can. But we have to get within a thousand yards."

"Well, we'll have to wait on that. Do we have pictures yet?"

General Wayland gestured toward the large screens, "Lieutenant, could you bring up Denali?" Fuzzy pictures of the craft displayed on the screens.

"Sir, the KH-13s will be giving us detailed close-ups soon and we have hard pictures."

General Wayland nodded toward a captain. The captain handed President Meyer a brown envelope. The President pulled 8 X 11s from the envelope. General Wayland continued, "Mr. President, you'll note the outer surface of the craft is bronze in color and is perfectly smooth. There's nothing that suggests viewing, such as a window or portal, not a door or hatch, nothing. We've not been able to examine their underbellies. Several of our interceptor pilots reported seeing what they thought was a small tube emitting a faint jet stream vapor on their bellies. This suggests some sort of rocket engine but we haven't confirmed that."

"So these things could be ticking time bombs?"

"Yes sir, they could be but Intelligence doesn't believe they are, and I agree. But every NEST team we have is on its way to Florida and Alaska."

"How many teams do we have?"

"Six, sir."

"Then please convince me they're not bombs."

"Sir, what we know for sure is that these invaders can fly and maneuver better than any aircraft known. They enter the atmosphere at speeds we haven't been able to measure. At the speeds and angles they enter, they should burn to a cinder. Then, as they approach the earth's surface, they slow to speeds of less than two hundred miles per hour, and land at less than five miles per hour. They maneuver like humming birds. Bad weather conditions, the most severe terrain on the planet, oceans, swamps, and glaciers are nothing to them and, as you know, their landing sites to date. And, they seem to know exactly where they're going.

"As they approach the earth's surface, their formations separate, always into three groups of three craft. We've calculated their entry into our atmosphere to their landing locations, and it is always the shortest possible route. With such precise technology, if they are bombs meant to destroy, why aren't they landing in our cities—around our military installations?"

General Wayland finally paused before meeting his superior's eyes directly, "Mr. President, there is something that needs to be said. If these invaders are bombs, and they have our nuclear capability, there are enough of them on the planet to destroy the earth ten times over."

The President looked about the table, "Thanks, John. Ladies and gentlemen, General Wayland has been working with HS the last few hours. Dr. Maxwell is here to bring us up to speed on civilian impact so far."

The President pushed an intercom button, "Has Dr. Maxwell arrived yet? Good, send him in."

Ambassador Trent's eyes locked on Jason when he entered until she realized what she was doing. He headed HS but briefing the President as well as the military on what could be the most serious crisis ever to confront the U. S. and the world was much more than she...

Her thoughts were interrupted by Jason, who began to speak as he opened his briefcase.

"Ladies and gentlemen, we're time sensitive, going to move fast, lot to cover, please save your questions. First, the President is scheduled to address the nation in 15 minutes. We've advised the President to be brief and to the point. This first communication is critical." Dr. Maxwell handed reports to a first lieutenant who passed them around the table.

"Our first report to the President detailed economic and social impact, international consequences, even political ramifications. We've outlined this in the report. A few examples; following his speech the stock market, nationally and internationally, will plummet, suicide rates will quadruple and the President's approval rating will increase 12 points.

"Now to the crisis at hand. Ms. Sarah Trent, Mr. Joshua Jones and Dr. Nockari's star gazing caused our government a great deal of concern, work and money."

Sarah and Dr. Nockari looked at each other perplexed.

Josh stared straight ahead as Dr. Maxwell continued

"As a result of your observation, we've had ten teams of environmental biologists checking water, plant and soil samples on every continent of this planet for the past two years. Appreciate you loaning FBI a copy of the videodisk.

"As you know, the blue haze you observed and recorded encircled the entire planet. To our knowledge, that anomaly was a first. Our concern was twofold. One, what was this blue haze and two, what environmental impact would it have on the planet as it settled on the earth's surface? No cause for alarm has been suggested by analysis of plant, water, and soil samples over the past two years, but to date we haven't been able to determine the source or composition of the haze. However, water samples from Angel Falls near the rain forests of Nuyan-tepui and Lake Baikal in Russia had contaminates of a blue protein enzyme that we haven't yet been able to identify.

"What we know for sure is that this contamination has permeated the water and soil of the entire planet. We're talking about plant life, drinking water, the growing of crops, animal life, seas, oceans . . . in short, all life forms and life sustaining sources."

Jason paused, and looked directly at Sarah. "Miss Trent, you, Dr. Nockari and Mr. Jones were the only people on the planet that recorded the 'shooting stars' that burst into the blue haze. Do either of you recall what color the shooting stars were, before they burst into the blue haze?"

"Yes, I do."

"What color were they?"

"Brown no, more of a bronze color, like the pictures on the table."

Sarah pointed to blown up slide pictures of cigar shaped craft lying in front of the President.

"Thank you, Ms. Trent. Now, where we are headed with this and what does this have to do with our current situation?"

106

The Cleansing

Jason turned to Gayle, "Dr. Trent, I'm sure you recall the security communications breach at the UN two years ago?"

"Of course."

"Thank you Ambassador. Now the quantum leap. Ladies and gentlemen, we had the blue haze, the UN breach with the script, and the tablets all in the same week exactly two years ago. Not to mention the period of time we had thousands of reports of violent people disappearing. We're still working on that one, but to date we don't have a clue. And now, two years later, to the day, we have craft on our planet of unknown origin, and as the script stated, we have no violence. Can we start connecting the dots?"

Dr. Maxwell did not wait for a response.. "On page four of the report you have, we've listed what we've learned the past two years. Note item three, *'the tablets were made of a humus rock substance that is not found on this planet.'* It is similar to the humus composition of rocks brought back from the last two Mars expeditions. I say *'were made of a humus rock'* because the tablets began deteriorating on discovery and despite our efforts to preserve them, as of yesterday they have completely decomposed.

"We've had several at Homeland Security working on the content of the script. One of the messages stated *'weapons of homo sapiens conflict disabled.'* That's now a reality.

So, is the script some sort of communication, warning, prophecy, or as it appears, a decree? Simulations are inconclusive. A very simple way to test that possibility is by checking the remaining script messages. Specifically, I'm talking about the *'reproduction of Homo sapiens will cease'* and *'cessation of wars and violence among Homo sapiens.'*

We're happy to announce that babies are still being born, but we have some interesting preliminary reports on violence. In New York, Chicago and Atlanta where we have teams, there has not been one reported homicide in the past twelve hours. We have checked Los Angeles, Detroit and, of course, Washington DC as well as a dozen smaller cities and towns. The report is the same."

There was a shocked silence about the room. Jason moved on, "Initially, we attributed this to immobilized firearms but

107

thirty percent of homicides do not involve firearms. But more important, and almost unbelievable, there have been no murders, no assaults, no rapes, no reports of domestic violence. In fact, there have been no reported crimes of violence of any kind, if I may quote, *'cessation of wars and violence among Homo sapiens.'*

"The rate of nonviolent crimes, theft, drugs, prostitution, misdemeanors hasn't changed. Law enforcement agencies are at a loss to explain, but they're a happy bunch of campers since they don't have weapons that work either. Something that's very interesting that we're following up on is that we have numerous anecdotal reports from individuals who claim muggers attempting to assault somehow became immobilized, and the intended victims walked away unharmed. What that's all about, we have no idea.

"Social ramifications? A loaded question. Once the public learns that we don't know the origin of invading craft there will be panic. The severity and form it will take—we should have a report within the hour. It could be ugly."

The room remained silent, "We can provide a laundry list of national and international ramifications of no firearms, but our focus has to be on the craft. Our recommendations are in the report in front of you. Please note the item we feel is most important, *'no aggressive acts on our part.'* "

The Secretary of Defense threw up his hands, "What do you mean *'no aggressive acts?'* We have no weapons."

"You're correct, Mr. Secretary. It sounds trite in view of our lack of weapons. Another concern is that we don't know what action or movement on our part that might be interpreted as hostile. Second, we must determine if the areas where they have landed are safe for humans. Can't approach the way they did in *'Close Encounters.'* Wish we could. What sort of germs, microbes, viruses, radiation, or God knows what, have they brought with them? We don't know. They may not know. We don't even know if there is a *'they.'*

"Our people from NIAID (National institute of Allergy and Infectious Diseases) and ACDC (Atlanta Center for Disease Control) are coordinating with AMRI (Army's Medical Research institute of Infectious Diseases). They're providing equipment for data gathering. The plan is to approach the Denali National Park site with CH-54 choppers equipped with biosafety measuring probes. They'll approach circling on a one hundred mile perimeter. Air samples will be taken one hundred miles out, and if the area is clean, clean in terms of biohazards, one chopper will land and a team will collect soil, plant, and insect samples. The samples will be tested, and if they're clear, equipment teams will be dropped to establish the first base camp. We will continue to circle and approach, testing at ten-mile increments at random points on a circumference. It's important to mention that satellite observations have shown that animal, insect and plant life about their landing sites have not yet demonstrated any visible side effects. I repeat; any visible side effects. But there may be other problems such as radiation or viruses that haven't been observed yet, or can't be observed.

"We will continue to circle until we're with our first contact forces, within twenty miles of their craft. At that point, we'll start testing at quarter mile intervals. When we're within five miles we'll begin testing every tenth of mile until we are within one mile of the craft. At this point we're going to seal the area at *Biosafety Level 4.'* Level 4 is the highest degree of laboratory containment for isolating microbiological organisms. This means all personnel entering this area will be equipped to work with the most dangerous agents known to humankind such as Ebola, and the hunta viruses.

We'll keep the number of personnel approaching to a minimum in case something goes nuclear. Teams and equipment are assembled and on their way. They'll begin testing within the next two hours. The teams have orders to abort if there's any sign of aggression or movement on their part. Obviously, we'll abort if we discover contaminants. We're monitoring the movement of the teams with our KH-12s and the invading craft with KH-13s and GPS. And our UAVS, that's our predator spy planes, will be airborne today."

There was a pause.

"If any of you have any questions or suggestions—now's the time."

The Cleansing

The President stood, "Jason, if they've brought some new virus or germ with them, something we've never seen, will you be able to detect it?"

"Good question, sir." A negligible shrug raised his shoulders. "If it's detectable using the best equipment in the world, we'll find it. But, if it's new, we might not know what it is, or if it's dangerous and sir, that scares us to death."

A mesmerized Sarah looked to Josh, who whispered, "We unlearn and learn anew what we thought we knew before."

Dr. Maxwell looked at Josh and smiled, "We do want Ms. Trent, Dr. Nockari and the man who recites Thoreau to hang around. Want to pick their brains a bit more."

The President spoke quickly, "Thank you, gentlemen, ladies. I want an update as soon as I finish my address."

On cue, an aide stuck his head in the door, "Mr. President, your address is in four minutes."

He grabbed his suit coat and headed for the door, "Kate, contact Dickenson and tell him to be damn sure the areas in Florida and Alaska are sealed. The press and some of our more patriotic citizens will try anything to get to those craft."

Three minutes later the President addressed the nation.

"Fellow citizens, as your Commander and Chief, I am regretfully reporting to you that United States air space has been breached by a number of aircraft. We have tracked the invaders on radar, satellite and with interceptor aircraft since their intrusion. The invading craft landed in isolated areas, many miles from civilian habitat. I've been in constant contact with our armed forces that have isolated and contained the invaders.

"The invading craft have not yet engaged in any hostile action. I repeat, the invading aircraft have not engaged in any hostile action toward our armed forces or our citizens. There have been no casualties, no loss of life and no conflict. And I repeat our Air Force and ground forces have the invaders encircled in an isolated area many miles from civilian habitat. For security reasons, I will not divulge their location. I urge each of you to remain calm. I'll be reporting to you as needed. Thank you and God bless America."

The President returned to the war room.

"Brief and to the point, sir." Kate remarked.

"I know, I know, but my God the panic is going to be bad enough as it is. Anything new?"

General Wayland sat glued to the monitors, "Contamination and NEST crews are air-borne, sir. Our visitors are still dormant, haven't moved a muscle. The Vice-President is briefing senators. General Dickenson has moved the Third and Fourth Armies and Seventh Marine Divisions into combat readiness. Well, as much as you can have without firepower. Eighty-six countries have now admitted they are without weapons, and are pleading for our help."

Ambassador Trent commented, "Most of the others are still posturing, but according to their UN ambassadors they can't light a firecracker."

The President shrugged and asked, "What's your read on the home front? Agree with Jason?"

"It's unbelievable, Mr. President. We're getting reports from all over the country. Towns, cities, rural and urban areas are confirming what he said, *'no violent crime.'* It's true, sir. In fact, sir, the ambassadors we've contacted are saying the same thing."

"Are you telling me that crime has ceased worldwide?"

"Yes sir."

"My God, no violence, and we're defenseless. Define irony."

General Wayland didn't look away from the monitors as he answered, "We don't know, sir but maybe our visitors do."

The President shook his head, "What about the Australians in the Kimberley Plateau? How close are they?"

His general picked up a report and handed it to the President as he spoke, "They've set up a base camp at the end of Gibb River Road. That's the only road into the northern part of the Plateau and it peters out at Mount Elizabeth. From there they're planning on parachuting Special Forces to within five hundred yards."

"That's confirmed by their ambassador," Gayle offered.

"Damn! Kate, get Minister Wells on the red line. What the hell do they think they're doing?"

A Major knocked and entered the room. "Sorry to interrupt Mr. President but Prime Minister Wells is on red line 2 and Ambassador Trent has a green alert from the UN."

111

The Major started to leave but the monitors focusing on the invading craft stopped him. He froze and as his eyes widened, he stammered, "Mr. President, the monitors, they're moving. They're coming out."

The major pointed toward the monitors and all eyes in the room followed his. The top half of the craft that had landed in the Denali Park had slid backward about five meters, and figures were emerging from the opening. The President grabbed a red phone.

"Minister Wells, are your boys still closing on the craft in the Plateau? Well, get them out of there! Get them out now! Yes, someone or something is emerging from ours in Denali Park. Yes, now. Get'm out!"

The President kept the phone to his ear and punched three buttons, "Are you watching? You're on your way? Good!"

The figures were blurred, but the GPS focused and they became clearer. The figures were large, at least seven feet tall. Nine figures emerged from both the craft. Voice communication from the Nautilus crackled in the background.

"This is Admiral Herzog from the Nautilus. We have movement here. Nine small tube like craft have exited from one of the craft. They are identical in shape and color as their mother ship, just smaller. Advise."

General Wayland responded, "Read your message, Nautilus. Continue to observe and track. Do not approach. I repeat do not approach. Any hostility, get the hell out of there and let us know."

"Yes sir".

The General's eyes never left the figures on the screen. It was impossible to see their features. They appeared to have on large hooded robes that extended below their feet, if they had feet. They moved in threes, deliberately, almost gliding.

McLean and Maxwell followed by Sarah and Josh burst into the room. The figures on the screens froze them.

After ninety seconds the President spoke. "Talk to me, people, talk to me. What's happening here?"

Dr. Stillman spoke her thoughts aloud. "I see no breathing apparatus. So, no breathing apparatus on land and the ones in the Pacific are in tubes. Apparently, they breathe our air. No sign of any weapons—see anything on their movement, Lois?" She glanced at the others in the room. "Oh, I'm sorry ladies and gentlemen, I'm Pat Stillman one of our anthropologists and to my right is Dr. Lois Pulo our linguist."

No one took their eyes off the monitors as Dr. Stillman continued, "They're human-like, sir. Their size would suggest evolution of millions of years, and they must come from a similar environment. Breathing our atmosphere and gravity affects them as is does us, unless—they appear to have vision similar to ours, and being in groups, suggests language, socialization—communication. They show no sign of fear. They appear to be exploring which implies reasoning and thinking skills similar to ours. My God, do you believe…"

Stillman interrupted herself pointing, "Look, the second monitor, the one that's touching the tree, is that an arm? It's hard to make out and the one to the right is bending over as if feeling the ground. I think he, she or whatever just picked up something. So, we got tactile stimulation. Okay, we see signs of reasoning, curiosity, size, vision but what about hearing and language, the ability to communicate, with symbols? Oh, and the eyes, if they have eyes, are forward. Don't suppose we have sound on this do we?"

A lieutenant manning a monitor answered, "No sir—ma'am".

"Dr. Stillman will do just fine lieutenant. Damn, we have to know if, or how they're communicating. Notice they're staying in groups of threes. Uh, oh that group is moving away. They're already past that clearing. How do they move like that? They're gone. Can we track them? Can we track them?"

"Only when they're in sight, ma'am—er, Dr. Stillman."

Dr. Stillman continued, "The second group is headed into that gorge. They move so deliberately. There's no fear in their actions. How do they move like that? I think they're checking out the place. God, this is incredible."

Dr. Stillman moved closer to the screen, her nose within an inch, "Can you focus on the spot where it touched the tree? Yeah, it was that one, a little lower, yes about there. Can you focus in closer?"

The screen focused on tree bark as if viewing inches away.

The Cleansing

"Wow! I say you can. Amazing, and this is from a satellite three hundred miles in space?"

"Yes, uh, Dr. Stillman."

"Notice there's no damage to the bark, no marks at all. That's good. Can you focus on the ground?"

"On the ground?"

"Yes, the ground. Focus directly on the area where they walked or levitated or whatever."

"Yes, Doctor."

"Yes, that's it. That's perfect. We're looking for two things, footprints and something alive, a bug, an ant—anything."

The monitor picture moved about on the ground finally focusing out ants.

"There's what I'm looking for—life. That's a good sign. Plant and insect life alive and well. That's good, very good. But where are their footprints?"

Dr. Stillman whispered, "Think of it, we are the first humans to ever observe, we need...we're not alone. We have to send someone in there."

Dr. Stillman glanced to the President and back to the screen, "It has to be a team from HS."

The President did not move from the screen, "I know, I read your report. Dr. Stillman, why did you say, *'eyes forward'* was important?"

Dr. Stillman answered without taking her eyes off the monitor, "Sign of a predator, for measuring distance to prey, may or may not be relevant here. Nothing I just said may be relevant here." She turned toward him and said, "Mr. President, someone is eventually going to get to them. The Australians are in their laps. Sir, they or whoever, will be defenseless just as we are. We should send our very best. If we can communicate, the ramifications, sir, I can't even begin to imagine and sir, it may be our only hope."

Jason shook his head, "Ladies, gentlemen, let Biosafety do their job. We have to test before we expose anybody. The risk is too..."

The President interrupted, "Jason, how long is it going to take to determine if the area is safe?"

Jason checked his watch, "In three hours we will have base camp set up at the 100 mile perimeter. In eight hours we can be within a mile and geared for Level 4. Now, all that assumes everything is clean."

There was silence until Jason added, "Mr. President, in three hours we'll have a team ready to approach as close as the data allows and I agree with Dr. Stillman. We need to send someone in. Sir, whoever we send, we have to bring back. We have to test not only going in, but also when they come back. God knows what they could bring back with them. We have to test, sir."

The President turned to General Wayland, "General, we'll need a few of your best to escort. How long do you need?"

"Sir, we can fly equipment out of Atlanta to Anchorage. Move them in with choppers from there. We have Special Forces with the Bio teams. We're ready when you are."

While the men were talking, Gayle had returned the call to the UN. She cupped the phone in her hand, "Excuse me— excuse me, ladies and gentlemen, Mr. President we have another security breach at the UN and it is exactly like the one two years ago but with a different message. I have the Secretary Generals executive assistant on the phone with the message."

Everyone in the room stared at Gayle as she put the phone on the speaker. "Go ahead Omer."

As Omer spoke a copy printed in triplicate, "Dr. Trent, the message on all our computers is as follows: First Line, all caps, reads:

'COMMUNION'
Second line reads,
'Jeston Mehra, history'
Third line reads,
'Laku Rumula - a child who sees'
Fourth line reads,
'Tesh Dupree - a child of music'
Fifth line reads,
'45 23 18.'

Mr. Omer hesitated, "That's all, Dr. Trent. That's the entire message. You got copies?"

"Yes. There was nothing else?"

"No. Nothing, and it is the same as before. Every ambassador received the message on their communication terminal in their native language."

"Even those numbers?"

"Yes."

"When did this happen?'

"Seven minutes ago."

The room was silent.

"Thank you, Omer."

In slow motion, Gayle hung up the phone.

The President looked to the group, "Ladies and gentlemen, you have my attention."

Kate Dockery spoke first, "I've heard the name Jeston Mehra. But where, where have I heard that name?"

"Jason, could this be related to what's going on here?" asked the President.

"Another good question, Mr. President. Best way to find out is locate one of those three people if they exist. But is the message related to our universal guests?"

Jason shrugs as he asks, "Kate, are you sure you've heard the name Jeston Mehra?"

"Yes, but I can't..."

Dr. Lois Palo, the linguist, advised, "The name suggests someone from India, maybe Tibet. Tesh Dupree could be English, North American or Australian. Laku Munum—Indian, maybe Tibetian. Should get hold of Trefe. She's our linguist from India one of the best. And of course the WEB."

"What about the descriptions, 'history, a child who sees, and a child of music', if those terms are descriptions, and what do those numbers mean?"

Maxwell hung up a phone, "Ladies and gentlemen, UH-60s out of Quantico can get you in. The U.S.S. Arleigh Burke is on maneuvers in the Gulf of Alaska. The Burke is a guided missile destroyer. They can provide communication and support. Four Apache IIs from Burke are on their way to Anchorage, an hour away from Denali. Dr. Maxwell, you're correct. Denali gives us time and the distance and terrain is good. Where they landed in the Everglades, they chose the worst terrain—the swamp makes getting in and out difficult. We're dropping probes. The

Canadians know we're on the way. We have a jet waiting at LaGuardia. A UH-60 will be waiting when you land. If we leave now we can be on the Burke in less than three hours. You'll literally follow the contamination crews."

HS members looked at each other until Dr. Palo spoke, "I need to go. We're going in for the purpose of communicating and that's my thing."

Jason disagreed, "Doctor, with your heart condition I don't think that's a good idea. I think I should go, and I think Dr. Taylor should go. Genetics and psychology might come in handy."

Josh, along with Sarah had been quiet, watching and forgotten until Josh interrupted. "I should go."

All eyes turned to Josh surprised by the intrusion.

"Mr. President, General, I'm a logical choice. I'm young, in shape, speak five languages, am currently in Med school, and I've had military training. I spent four years as a Navy SE…'

General Wayland protested, "Son, we appreciate your spunk, but we need experienced men with special skills for this one."

Josh continued, "General, you're right about men with special skills but correct me if I'm wrong on what hasn't been said here today. As we speak, you're trying to figure out where to point your missiles. You've got enough ICBMs, Minutemen and Tridents but they don't work. Even if they did, you couldn't hit that many places and you would destroy the planet. And pointing them toward every continent on earth, that's violating every UN agreement and international treaty of the past four decades.

"So you have unmanned aircraft, UAVS, arsenal ships and stealth barges deployed to get close as they can. They are loaded with AGMs, GBUs, and A-Tac-Missiles Systems along your M88s and M89s. The 88s and 89s are impotent, but they're small, and they are nuclear weapons and if the tech boys can find a way, you'll be ready. The unmanned aircraft and small crews of the arsenals and barges are not the best for gathering info but unmanned means, no casualties.

"C4 has location data and has assigned targets. Intelligence figures the invaders made a mistake landing in remote places. Backing them up, Navy's *'Coop Engagement'* is on-line engaging the radar of every warship in our arsenal and coordinated with Globemasters, loaded with troops, movement is global. Hell of a time to be overhauling Nimitz, and too bad U.S.S. Carter won't be on-line for another two years.

"SARA, in Huntington Beach, has already checked out Vortex, Microwave and Laser weapons and they don't work. You would've informed the President if they did. And since they don't work, you're deploying SOGs and SEALs to parachute into the Everglades. They're equipped with everything that could possibly be used as a weapon, canisters of toxins, gases, everything from acids to viruses to flammables.

"They'll use *'paint ball'* if they have to. But before you can get anyone close you have to clear the area at Biosafety Level 4. And that's going to take time, maybe too much. If our visitors have brought Biohazards with them, a few hours may be too long. And that's not the problem. The problem is that the invaders have landed in too many different places. All the satellites in space can't provide surveillance on a hundred remote locations. Not even with GPS, UAVS and the new KH-13s and NATO air. And, containment in such areas, a dozen, yes, two dozen you can still count their freckles, but a hundred without weapons? You've got Intelligence all over the world working on that one."

Josh paused then continued, "And what have the simulations the Pentagon, SARA, MIT and Cal Tech said about the potential weapons systems of our celestial visitors? If HS simulations agree with theirs, based on the performance of their aircraft and disabling our weapons, they're off the chart. I doubt if they've ever heard of the Star Trek's *'Prime Directive.'* General, we have our worst nightmare, an enemy, if they are our enemy; our own intelligence says we can't beat. I have the training and the skills and I don't have a family. I should go, sir."

General Wayland looked at Josh for a long time, then turned toward the President while keeping his eyes on Josh, "Mr. President, I don't know much about this young man but I think we should add him to our team." He forced his gaze away from Josh to Jason, "Dr. Maxwell, who else do you recommend?"

"Well, I'm going and our group recommends Dr. Taylor. You might be familiar with his work. He led the team that won a

118

Nobel two years ago for developing enzymes that can be used in vaccines for the Ebola and Hanta viruses. We had a bunch of people volunteer and we do need them, but sir, three people are enough to risk."

"Does Dr. Taylor have family?" asked the President.

"Yes sir, wife and three children."

Two minutes later the three men left with a Major, but not before one called home, one hugged Sarah, and one hugged Gayle.

The President turned to Sarah, Annabelle and Gayle, "Ladies, you all right?"

All three nodded.

"Good. Gayle, Annabelle, check in with your colleagues again and find out if anybody, anybody on this planet has found weapons that work. Kate, get hold of General Dickenson and tell him to let me know where the hell he is. Kate, do you remember where you know this Jeston Mehra?"

"We're checking on the internet, sir."

The President turned to Wayland "Any word from the contamination crews?"

"Yes sir, both air and ground samples are clear at the ninety mile perimeter and they're proceeding, sir."

Just as Kate and Gayle went to the phones, everyone in the room froze as they saw what was occurring on the screens. The figures were reentering their craft. The crafts on the Pacific Ocean floor were the first to take off. The others left within seconds. The President picked up a phone and punched numbers.

"Tell them to abort. Yes, I want escorts but stay a mile away from the craft. And no communication—nothing. That's right, we don't know how it might be interpreted. Keep the satellites on them. If you get a read on where they're headed let me know."

The President hung up the phone and watched the monitors, "What're they doing?"

Eyes fixed on the monitors as the invading craft became airborne. Initially, they moved deliberately in their 'V' formation. The spy satellites and intercepting aircraft were able to track. Then the bronze cigar craft left their interceptors and spies and

119

disappeared at speeds that left the Pentagon monitors blurred. The President turned to Kate, "Kate, get NORAD."

As he spoke, the bronze craft reappeared on the monitors. Hundreds of cigar craft hovered three miles above the earth's surface over South America allowing the satellites to assume tracking. They hovered for fifteen seconds, then at unrecorded speeds, they flew toward earth, slowing as they approached. A phone signaled. The President answered, listened and hung up.

"NORAD and DSP have a track on where they're headed. They are going back to the same places they were before."

Dr. Palo spoke, "Mr. President, I think I know what they're doing or at least what they did. They've changed positions. They rendezvoused, communicated, and changed positions."

"Any ideas on why they would do that?" asked the President.

"No sir, unless they just compared notes and now are going to check out each other's places? Curiosity?"

"You think they just changed places?"

"Yes, sir."

"Do you think it's safe for the team to continue?"

"I'm not sure it's safe either way, sir."

The President picked up a phone.

CHAPTER FIFTEEN

The Chosen

For forty years, Jeston Mehra has lived and labored within the sloping, thick-based walls of Rwa-sgren. He studies, builds Studas and prays, yet his love is the Sam-ya history he teaches the younger monks of his sect, Nying-ma-pa (*The Ancient Ones*), the oldest sect of Lamaism. Since Atisa, a Buddhist monk, journeyed from India in 1057 A.D. and built Rwa-sgen Monestary in central Tibet, *The Ancient Ones* have revered the life of discipline, temperance, and celibacy.

For generations Jeston has explored the mysterious writings of the ancient Lamas, the *"Master Teachers."* He knows of Master Dromton's writings, *"The Dromton Itinerary,"* which details the routes of Atisa's travels. Jeston Mehra admires the work of Master Dromton, but agrees with the route of an earlier record, "Diparnkara Srijnana." Jeston Mehra can recount from memory the evolutionary history of Sanskrit, the spoken word of the *"Masters."*

The "blue" awoke him. Jeston had studied until sleep came with crumpled arms on open books. He flinches as his eyes open. A blue sun played about him and his books.

"It was a dream but the dream has left a tablet in the language of 'The Ancient Ones.' "

Five years ago in the slums of Moti Jheel

How does one explain Victorian palaces shadowing "Bastis" (shanty towns)? How does one justify opulence that requires servile destitution damning races and classes to desire such for each other? Those who live there know the explanation lies in the capital of West Bengal . . . Calcutta.

Oshish Rumula stood twitching in gritty rain next to the bin. He held his son of two hours. Despite the saintly work of Mother Teresa the slums of Moti Jheel still thrived next to St.

121

The Cleansing

Mary's, the school where she taught. Despite Shishu Bhavan, Mother Teresa's missionary hospital, and her Mirmal Hriday Home for Dying Destitutes, in Calcutta's early morning, dead bodies still were carried out of shanties for collection. Premature babies, too weak to suckle, are tossed into overflowing garbage bins. Kali, the Goddess of destruction and death, still thrived in the slums of Moti Jheel, Calcutta.

One hour earlier, in crippled numbness, Oshish had carried out his wife of twenty years from their dirt-floored tin shack and laid her in the street for collection. She died giving birth to their fourteenth child. Muted glances and quickened steps greeted her body. Her only mourning came from the tears of six children who survived her.

Oshish looked at his newborn son, blind with leprosy, and the fifth he had carried to the bins. He stood in the stench of death. His son was still, maybe already mercifully dead. But the baby cried and the blue came and warmed both of their shivering, and the goddess of destruction and death was denied. In his shanty, Oshish told his other children the baby's name would be *"Laku"* and he was blessed

New York City

"If only it had rained."

The words seared the consciousness of Tesh as the four boys dragged her deeper into the alley. Patent leather scraped against concrete. The largest of the boys flashed the razor that glinted in the darkness.

"Don't scream, won't cut you so much."

Tesh's terror fixated on the one who licked at the white powder about the corners of his mouth. His eyes glared and rolled back into his head, returned, glared and rolled again. Tesh was fourteen and she knew what they were going to do. The one with white eyes and mouth knew what else.

Tesh's mother couldn't afford voice lessons for Tesh, but her school concert displayed a voice that traversed the bleakness of the inner city. Her mother told her, *"You child will have lessons."*

The Cleansing

But this night, Tesh disobeyed her mother. After her voice lessons, to save two dollars, she walked. If it had rained, she would have taken the subway...if it had rained.

They held her down and the boy with the powered mouth picked up a bottle and stood over her. His eyes focused and widened as if seeing her for the first time. He grinned and his eyes became white again. Tesh screamed through a hand. The razor moved to her face. Time passed and Tesh felt nothing. Then her father was holding her as he did years before he died. The blue lights felt warm and he smiled then faded, but the blue lights remained. She opened her eyes. She was standing in the alley buoyed by the crystalline lights. The boys were gone. A broken bottle lay to the side. Her father's voice said she could go home. That night when Tesh told her mother what had happened, her mother wept.

CHAPTER SIXTEEN

Welcome Wagon

Present

General Wayland reported to the President, "Sir, Bio-camp will be operational in two hours. So far, readings are normal. *'Welcome Wagon'* is within ten miles of Burke and awaiting your orders."

"Welcome Wagon?"

"The tag we put on our team, sir."

The President gestured and General Wayland gave orders on the phone, then picked up another line, "You have six minutes until Welcome Wagon arrives."

Kate jerked toward the President, "Mr. President, I remember who Jeston Mehra is. The monitor, the TV, ABS—he's the monk who found the tablet at his prayer alter. Gayle, remember the ABS program I told you about two years ago during the UN security break? He was the Tibetan monk on the program."

"Kate, are you sure?"

"Yes, sir."

"General, have Welcome Wagon stand down. We have to find this Mehra. How do we get hold of ABS?"

CHAPTER SEVENTEEN

The General

In his cigar smoke filled office the Vice-President sat alone. The room was dark. His thoughts drifted. She was naked and blindfolded. He warmed as she struggled. He moaned reassurance but it was taking too long.

"*I told them no hair, no hair, dammit.*"

He grimaced. The heat drained away. He opened his eyes.

"*And how did the voice find out? One hundred thousand, and nothing since. A million couldn't find it.*"

He closed his eyes. She moved again, soft, helpless, he breathed heavy—a knock at his door caused him to twitch and shiver. He leaned and turned on a desk lamp. His voice was wet and hoarse, "Yes."

General Dickenson entered and slumped into a large soft black leather chair and eyed the Vice-President, "You getting a cold?"

The Vice-President cleared his throat, "Aren't you supposed to be getting troops deployed or something?"

"Delegated to good men. Secret to success and long life."

"Any of these 'good men' got fire power?"

"Not yet. Not a damn weapon in our fucking military will fire. We have people running all over the country trying to find a civilian weapon that'll kill something. But what are you doing here? Shouldn't you be with the President? Pass me one of those cigars."

The Vice-President opened the box and slid it toward the General.

"Yeah, he and Wayland and their girlfriends are over there trying to play soldier without weapons. You'd think a man would know when he's been castrated."

The Vice-President watched the General bite the tip of a cigar, spit it on the floor and light up.

125

The Cleansing

"What about chemical weapons?"

"Chemical weapons my ass. We can't kill mosquitoes with what we've got. Hell, when your nukes can't get a hard on, you're in trouble. You know what really galls me about this? If we had gone ahead with 'Star Wars' like Reagan wanted us to back in the eighties we might not be in this mess. If the world comes to an end, those fucking Democrats are going to pay."

"Robotics?" The Vice-President's expression didn't change.

"We're assembling a team—on line in eight hours."

"We may be dust in eight hours."

General Dickenson squinted at the amber end of his cigar,

"Hell, you may be right. We should go in with our boys and hand to hand if we have to. Invaders from outer space—shit! This is fucking nuts, and if we listen to those pussies in the White House, we'll sit on our asses till they take over." He chuckled at himself, "Damn Tom, I'm getting too old for this. But hell, I've earned it. Fought in all of em' since Nam. Did you know I fought in Nam?

"No General, I didn't know that."

"Yeah, that was our last real war. They called those wussy Iraqi incursions wars. Shit, they weren't wars, they were slaughters, same thing in Sudan. Push the buttons and they died, by the thousands, shit, they heard a whistle and they were dead. But in Nam we fought gooks, in their jungles, nose to nose. Now that's war. Sixteen years old, forged a birth certificate, landed right in the middle of the Danang. God, it was awful—Jesus! Saw men die…"

The General paused and drew hard on his cigar, "And God help me, I loved it. But Danang was hunting Easter eggs compared to Ashau Valley. Went in with the Eighty Second Airborne. If ever there was a hell on earth—forest so damn thick it blocked out the sun, always dark, always. You drop Napalm in that place and the bombs never hit the ground. Just singed the edges. That's how dense it was. A week later, you couldn't tell you'd dropped anything. Trees as big around as houses. I mean bigger than fucking houses. Families would dig out huge bunkers in the base of the trees and live in 'em. I swear to God, they'd carve out a cave in a damn tree and live in it. Fire at us from knotholes.

126

The Cleansing

"They infiltrated our camp. Knew every square inch of it. Hell, knew it better than we did. We hadn't been there a week, when they opened up with their mortars. Mortar shells exploded in single file and marched straight to the 'Big Top.' If the Colonel hadn't been in the latrine taking a shit, they'd a blown him to hell."

The General let the ashes of his cigar drop on the floor.

"Ever scared?" the Vice-President asked.

Dickenson settled back in leather, "We circled our camp with rolls of razor wire. Rolls taller than your head. Stacked three on top of each other, moved out twenty feet and stacked 'em again, moved out twenty feet and stacked em' again. Planted Claymore mines thicker'n fleas. No way them bastards could get in.

"It was two in the morning. I was on perimeter watch. Thought I was a soldier, night vision on an M-16. Before we went on watch, we'd take Darvon pills and cut em' open, take out those little yellow centers. Half a dozen of those babies and you'd kill your mother and never know it. Two in the morning and God here they came. Hundreds, waves of 'em, gooks, old men, women, children fucked up on heroin, screaming, beating pots and pans, sticks. Half the bastards didn't even have weapons. The first wave hit the razor wire and laid down on it. The next wave climbed their bodies. Like human caterpillars coming over that damn wire. They laid on that wire and bleed to death so the next one could get over—God!'"

The General looked at the floor, "They hit the mines and those behind them just kept coming. Followed the path of body parts in front of them, screaming, beating those damn pans. We opened up with everything we had. M-14s, 16s, M-50 machine guns. You could see puffs of dust around holes in their cloths where the bullets were hitting 'em and they'd just keep coming. Had to hit 'em in the head or blow their damn legs off to stop 'em—on that fucking heroin. I saw one of the bastard's left arm fly off and he kept coming, couldn't have been more than twelve years old. Yeah, that scared me. When it was all over I volunteered to go in that damn jungle after 'em. Came back with an M-69 round stuck in my neck. Son-of-a-bitch was long as your hand, stuck in three inches."

The Cleansing

The General pulled down his collar. The scar was the size of the bottom of a coffee cup, grizzled and white. The General laughed, "Had the son-of-a-bitch rotated again—blew my damn head off."

The General contemplated his cigar again, "Shit, we unleashed the hounds of hell on those bastards; bombs, napalm, agent orange and stuff no one will ever know about. And they still kicked our ass. Those bastards were warriors. After that, all I thought we had to worry about was these piss ant wannabe dictators who put on a beret and a khaki shirt and brainwash a few idiots to be suicide bombers. Damn, at least we can pretend to have some security against these damn wannabes, but space aliens? Fuck, aren't we supposed to be hit by some damned asteroid? And why ain't these damned aliens destroying our cities and taking over the world, or turning us into pods, or doing whatever the hell they're supposed to do?"

He paused and chuckled at himself, quiet for a moment. "Tom, this is second time in my military career, hell in my life, I've been scared. The first was a twelve-year-old with his arm blown off. Now, fucking space aliens who've disarmed the fucking world. Shit, how'd they do that?"

The General rubbed his right hand through his hair, "The only reason we're the super power of this planet is because we have the smartest egghead scientists. Hell, that's how you define war now. Who has the eggheads to build the best technology? All it would take for one of the wannabes to become a super power is one, just one, fucking genius smarter than our fucking geniuses. And that fucking genius and thousands just like him may have just landed in our backyard and they can do anything they want. But you know what I think? I think they just don't give a shit. They're that good or smart or something, and that scares the piss out of me."

"General, I have to get back over to the pussy White House." The Vice-President stood up,

General Dickenson grinned, "I know that, Mr. Vice-President, and I also know you like pussy. Know what making love is?"

"What's that General?"

"What a woman does while some guy is screwing her."

The Cleansing

The Vice-President looked away and shook his head, "Get that Robotics team going. I have to get to the Pentagon and see if us pussies can save the planet."

CHAPTER EIGHTEEN

The Empty Quarter

Thirty minutes later, the Vice-President entered a humming war room. Giant monitors imaged bronze cigar craft. Banks of phones blinked. Unless they were red, they went unanswered. Unraveled computer paper carpeted the floor. Couriers came and went with messages that were mostly ignored. The President wore a headphone and read from a printout that strung to the floor. Annabelle and Kate were engaged on red lines. Gayle and General Wayland were glued to the monitors. When the President saw the Vice-President, he pushed his mouthpiece to his forehead.

"Come in, Tom. You're missing all the fun. How do you like your pizza?"

The Vice-President tilted his head, "Onions and green peppers. Why?"

The President flipped down his mouthpiece, "And one large with onions and green peppers and plenty of cokes and coffee."

"You're ordering pizza? The President of the United States is ordering pizza?"

"Well actually, I'm giving Sue the order. It's been a long day and we're hungry. How'd it go on the hill?"

"How it always goes. Some are fine, going home, some are mad as hell, want our heads on a platter and some could care less. But, that group is getting smaller, a lot smaller. Any more movement?"

"No, but they're spread out all over the globe. Eighty locations so far, and all are in some isolated wilderness, swamp, ocean, mountain range, glacier or desert. Have you heard from Dickenson? I haven't heard from him in over an hour."

"Talked with him bout thirty minutes ago, he's got more divisions on the move and still looking for weapons." The Vice-

President shrugged, "Mr. President, you need to address the nation again. It's getting out that we don't have weapons."

"You're right, and I was hoping you..."

Kate put down her phone and interrupted, "Excuse me, Mr. President, but we have Jeston Mehra. He walked into our embassy in Tibet...just walked in. Informed them that he had to be taken to the Rub al-Khali desert in Arabia. He claims he can communicate with them."

The President stared at Kate, "The Rub al-Khali desert of Arabia? Six of their craft are there."

"Yes sir, and sir, he says it's essential that Laku Rumula and Tesh Dupree join him."

"How in God's name does he know Laku Rumula and Tesh Dupree?"

"I have no idea, sir."

The President turned to General Wayland, "John, our team?"

"Still on the Burke, sir."

The President looked to Gayle, "Gayle, get HS and tell them I want a briefing in fifteen, in five minutes on the Rub al-Khaliub desert in Arabia. Tell them Rub al-Khaliub means 'Empty Quarter' in Arabic. The desert borders Oman and Yemen off the coast of the Gulf of Aden. But, I guess they'll know that. I want all they can give me; terrain, closest civilians, everything and I want it on one page. Kate, call the CIA and find out if they've made any headway in finding Laku Rumula and Tesh Dupree."

Kate interrupted again, "Mr. President, Mr. Mehra told our embassy where to find Laku Rumula and Tesh Dupree."

For the first time in the seven years Kate had worked with the President, she witnessed him turn pale. He sat down in a heap and spoke softly, "Kate, tell our embassy in Tibet to fax everything they can on Jeston Mehra, everything."

"Yes, sir but I can tell you, until three hours ago he hadn't left his monastery in forty years. He's their historian. And sir, there's little communication with the outside world with his sect. They allow few visitors, no mail, no phones, no electricity, nothing, not even running water. ABS tried for eight years to get a story on their order. The only reason they finally did was because of the tablet. Mr. Mehra gave the tablet to one of the ABS correspondents, told him it would be 'our history,' and returned to his sect. That was two years ago."

The President exhaled and asked, "Where did he say we could find Laku Rumula and Tesh Dupree?"

"Our embassy is faxing that information now, sir."

The President again turned to General Wayland who was on the phone, "General, while Kate has our embassy on the phone, see if you can help them with transporting Mr. Jeston Mehra, and get transportation ready from here."

"Mr. President, do you believe he—they can communicate with whatever is out there?"

The President flopped his hands in the air, "General, how long would it take to get Biosafety out of Denali Park and into the 'Empty Desert' "?

"Better to leave the boys in Denali; easier to put a new crew in 'Empty Desert.' Can coordinate through our fleet in the gulf." General Wayland thought aloud, "Encircling and testing, moving equipment, it'll take us eight hours, sir."

"Have to do a lot more than that."

General Wayland went the phone banks, "Mr. President, we'll have to get permission to cross the air space of Saudi Arabia. That'll take an extra hour."

"Tell them we're responding to their request for help." The President chuckled, "What can they do, General?"

General Wayland smiled, "Never thought having no weapons could be a military advantage."

Kate handed her phone to General Wayland and went to one of five fax machines that were coded in red.

"Sir, the fax."

The President walked to Kate, "Where can we find them?"

"According to Mr. Mehra, Tesh Dupree is a fourteen year old American girl. Her address is 905 Myrtle Street, South Detroit. Laku Rumula is a five year old boy who lives in Kanpur, India and sir; according to Mr. Mehra—he's blind."

The President whispered, "My God, does the fate of...how does he know that? Get our embassy in Calcutta. Tell them what we know, and tell them to find the boy, and let's get hold of Miss Dupree's family."

"Mr. President, HS can brief you on 'The Empty Quarter' anytime," interjected a major.

Two minutes later, the room listened as Dr. Tawfik, an Asian specialist, from HS briefed.

"The Rub al-Khali lies in the heart of Southern Arabia and is the largest sand desert in the world, 225,000 square miles. It is 500 kilometers wide and stretches 1,100 kilometers across Saudi Arabia east into Oman. The Rub al-Khali translates as 'The Empty Quarter' and for good reason. The Empty Quarter is the essence of desolation. It is dry, empty, devoid of soil, hundreds of square miles of sand characterized by giant sand dunes and in between, smaller mobile dunes. There are occasional salt flats. It rains lightly, every few years. There are no human inhabitants except for a few scattered Bedouins and most of them leave during the 140 degree heat of summer."

The President asked, "My apologies for interrupting, Doctor, but we are under the gun here. Is it possible to land a chopper in The Empty Quarter?"

"I'm not a military expert sir, but the sand would support, have to be careful of sand storms, but this time of year that's . . . yes sir, I think so."

The President stood up, "Good. We're going to have a piece of it cleared for Bio Level 4 in the next eight hours. Doctor, would a five year old boy and a fourteen year old girl be safe for a short period of time there say…a few hours?"

"Well sir, it's December which means the temperature is ranging between 100 and 110 degrees Fahrenheit. Yes sir, if they're dressed appropriately with adults who know the desert. Of course, this assumes they're very healthy children, and supplied with water. Oh, and you have to be careful if you approach or get close to the Bedouins. They have a custom of firing at you, usually a 5.45-millimeter rifle. It's not an act of aggression. It's a greeting. After they shoot, they'll shout 'Salaam Alaikum' which means *peace be with you* then they'll invite you to their tent for tea. If they don't shout after they fire best to leave."

The President smiled, "If they have a rifle they can fire, we'll make 'em rich. Dr. Tawfik, I assume you know the terrain of the 'The Empty Quarter?"

"Yes sir, been there twice."

"So, two children, one monk, two professor types and a former SEAL on a mission to communicate with visitors from outer space not to mention maybe, saving the planet, would be okay there?"

Dr. Tawfik gawked at the President and in five seconds his face changed from curiosity to disbelief to *"My God, he's serious."* He stammered, "Mr. President, the three numbers."

"The three numbers?"

"Yes sir, the three numbers in the UN security breach, 45 23 and 17. Forty five degrees longitude, 23 degrees, 17 minutes latitude puts you in the middle of the Empty Quarter, exactly where their craft are located." All eyes in the room went to Dr. Kawfik.

A lieutenant knocked softly and stuck his head in the door. "Excuse me sir, the pizza you ordered is here."

CHAPTER NINETEEN

Preparing

Two FBI agents knocked at the door of the apartment, 905 Myrtle St., South Detroit. They waited and knocked again. An African American woman in her fifties answered. The agents provided identification and started to explain. Mrs. Dupree listened, smiled and turned, "Tesh honey, you were right, they're here."

Mrs.Dupree turned back to the agents standing in the doorway, "Oh, would you look at me? Where are my manners? Come in. Come in!"

One hour later Mrs. Dupree and her daughter were on a military jet.

Five thousand miles away, in the eastern part of the worst of Kanpur's slums, two officials of the Indian government and two men from the American embassy, were being escorted by eight Kanpur police. They drove slowly through stench and poverty as far as they could. The mud street narrowed. They exited the Mercedes limo, left two policemen with the car and continued on foot through rag, wood and tin shacks amid the stares of scarecrow-like hundreds. The fourth time they stopped and asked directions an old man wheezed and pointed. A hundred dollar bill was placed in his weathered hand, more than he had earned the past year. The group continued as the old man looked at his money, and began to weep.

The men stopped at a tin shack where a dozen children played barefooted in mud, avoiding the human waste they could see. Before they could speak, an old woman appeared at the door of the shack leading a boy by the hand. The boy used a wooden stick as a cane. The boy stood silent with his face to the ground. One hour later the men and the boy were on a private jet. No one from his family accompanied him.

The Cleansing

On the U.S. Burke, Joshua T. Jones, Dr. Jason Maxwell and Dr. John Taylor received word of the stand down. They were told to eat and rest. They ate, and an hour later, were briefed on "The Empty Quarter." After the briefing they went on deck to board the CH-54 Super Stallion to fly back to Anchorage. The crews on deck stopped, fixating on the moment. Josh had seen this before. There were no salutes, no handshakes, nothing, just silence, except for the one man closest to the chopper. He whispered as Josh boarded, "God's speed."

They were airborne. This new breed of choppers had replaced the CH-53s six months after Josh left the SEALs. His BUDs training included the CH-53, and they were war machines, but the CH-54s were two generations ahead of anything in the world. They were stealth to any known radar system including the best in the U.S. arsenal. Their laser and heat seeking guidance systems had given way to GPSG (Global Positioning Satellite Guidance). The computers on the CH-54s had the capacity to vector on the longitudinal and latitudinal coordinates of enemy targets, directing missiles and Gatling cannon. Josh thought of SEALs equipped with this machine and shook his head, then half-smiled remembering impotent weapons.

The CH-54s Dampher/Chrysler engine whispered and moved in the direction of the Empty Quarter at 250 mph. Two hours after takeoff, General Wayland initiated communication from the war room. His voice filled the chopper as clearly as if he were aboard.

"Gentlemen, I hope you find your flying accommodations comfortable. Again, I apologize for the change in plans. Any questions?"

There were none.

"You'll be flown out of Anchorage in a Stealth. You'll land in Cyprus, and proceed to the 'Empty Quarter' in a CH-54. So far, contamination crews are reporting clean. Base camp equipment will be in place in two hours. You'll be arriving at 0750, four hours thirty-seven minutes from now. Colonel Matthews will meet and assist you to Biosafety Level 0. Here you will be fitted with biohazard gear, and proceed through Levels 2, 3 and 4.

The Cleansing

"Biosafety Level Four will be within four hundred meters of the craft. Here, accompanied by a crew of seven Special Forces men and three women, you will be transported to within fifty meters of the craft. Five of the ten Special Forces personnel are assigned to carry scientific gear needed for tests and monitoring. All five have the same equipment. We're replicating everything five times. They'll take readings as you approach the craft. Readings about the alien craft are normal according to Tega and Lidar probes dropped to within one hundred meters. The other five men are in charge of your security—getting you in and out.

"You and the Special Forces team will be transported in a Humvee, as I said, to within fifty meters. Here, the five with the monitoring equipment will proceed ahead of you.. Biosafety suits are outfitted with built-in communication equipment. Communication with me, and with each other, is just a matter of talking. We will be tracking your physiological measurements; pulse rate, body temperature, galvanic skin response—that sort of thing, also built into your suits. But gentlemen, the bottom line is that you will proceed toward the craft as long as our monitoring devices say it is safe to proceed. If I order abort, it is because your life is in danger. So, no heroics, no arguing, just board the Humvee. I'll be talking you through the entire operation. Oh, your code name is 'Welcome Wagon.' "

The CH-54 hovered to land. Josh, Maxwell and Taylor stared down at the desert and activity one hundred feet beneath them. Men and women entered and exited the base camp glistening in white biohazard space suits. Josh could identify SOGs, SOFs, SEALs and Marine airborne rangers. He knew their efficiency, but was surprised by the amount of equipment and personnel that had been congregated. Four pavilion shaped tents formed a line toward the alien aircraft. The larger first tent was like the head of a tadpole; its white top imprinted with black letters…"BASE CAMP – 1." The three smaller tents, also lettered on the top, CAMP - 2, CAMP - 3 and CAMP - 4, were connected to each other by twenty-five meter tent-tunnels. Camp 4 had a twenty-meter tunnel appendage in the direction of the craft.

Humvees and Bradleys were parked at attention in two compacted rows. The chopper landed and a white uniform, ignoring whispering blades, walked toward the chopper carrying a large suitcase in his right hand and with his left palm pointed in the direction of the CH-54. His voice, speaking to the pilot, came over the speaker in the chopper.

"Captain Riggs, do you read me?"

"Yes sir, loud and clear."

"Good. Gentlemen, I'm Colonel Frank Matthews. I'm in charge of this new suburban sprawl. Welcome. Hope you had a good flight. I have your base camp safety suits. Want you to put them on before you exit your craft. Our readings are fine out here...just being careful. Just slip them on over your clothes. Before your outing we'll get you outfitted with the good stuff."

Colonel Matthews entered the double sealed door of the chopper. The men pulled the suits over their clothes. Once they exited it was hot, unbearably hot. The walk to base camp was thirty meters. Like sand on tinfoil, the wind pelted gritty heat against their suits. Colonel Matthews led them. Base camp was air-conditioned from outside vents powered by generators. The entry of "Base Camp 1" was self contained and sealed. Two Lieutenants dressed like the Colonel met them. They ran a baton up the front and down the backs of the four men while watching screens extruding from their chests. The screens were attached to computer instrumentation on their backs. The two men checked each other's readings then nodded toward Colonel Matthews.

"Gentlemen, you can take off the suits. I'm sure you're getting a little toasty."

The three men removed the suits and introduced themselves. They entered the main area of the camp through the second sealed door.

"Come on in, gentlemen, even cooler in here." Colonel Matthews grinned as the men gawked at the equipment and activity. "Not bad for eight hours work. Been training for this since Sudan and the Hunta outbreak in India. Came in handy, but who the hell would've figured?"

The four men communicated agreement without speaking.

"Our AC vents have monitors checking for contaminants, and we check everything and everyone coming in. You'll be checked again by our MDs." Colonel Matthews grinned again, "Don't want you giving one of our visitors the flu."

The Cleansing

The base camp tent was divided into five sections by free standing, neck high partitions. The eyes of men and women mated with computer screens, and in animated conversation with the small speakers in front of their mouths, they pointed their fingers at monitors and searched for confirmation from each other and printouts. Colonel Matthews explained, "Well, gentlemen, as you can tell our base camp is sectioned and crowded. This area is receiving. We check everything here, personnel, equipment, or whatever comes in. Check for viruses, bacteria, bugs, fleas—you'd be surprised what takes up house-keeping in shipping crates.

"We've got a MASH unit set up to your immediate left. In the rear where you see people eating is exactly that, where you go when you get hungry. Grab a bite and go, no place to sit. The section to your right beyond these partitions coordinates air contaminant readings from the other three camps. The staff you see on the phones are responsible for communication. The ones reading from printouts are providing updates to labs all over the world."

Colonel Matthews looked to Josh, Drs. Taylor and Maxwell for approval. Their eyes gave it to him, and he continued, "The section to your far left is responsible for the surveillance of the aliens and craft. Lots of volunteers for that duty. Their craft is encircled, quarter mile radius, with the usual stuff, laser trip wires, motion sensors, electromagnetic fields and every type of video camera you can imagine. We've dropped the measuring devices within two hundred yards of 'em. Got UAVS flying all over 'em. Still getting people here to tell us what the damn things are telling us." Colonel Matthews grinned, "Just messing with you. Believe me, we've got 'em here."

The Colonel paused and measured the men, "Got a story you might find interesting. We shipped in two sheep, two goats, and two chimpanzees. Tagged 'em and had a chopper lower them in cages to within ten meters of their craft. Figured it was a quick way to check. Two hours later our observers said some sort of blue light encircled their cages and the animals were gone. Just disappeared, nothing but empty cages. Got it on disc if you want to take a look. Now here's the interesting part. Four hours later we get this call from a Swiss farmer, has a small sheep farm just outside of Bern, says he has our sheep and goats. Tracked us down from the info on the tags he took off the sheep."

The men stared at Colonel Matthews as he slowly shook his head, "Don't ask me, gentlemen. Don't ask me."

Jason asked, "And the chimp?"

"Not a word, but do you know how far Switzerland is from here? And the farmer said it took him a couple of hours to get through. How do you get..."

A first lieutenant from the second section interrupted with a phone in his hand,

"Colonel Matthews, General Wayland is on the line, sir."

Colonel Matthews took the phone and walked away from the men, "Excuse me, better get this."

Josh and the doctors surveyed the action in the room. They strained toward the monitors surveying the alien craft. Colonel Matthews returned.

"Gentlemen, it's good news and bad. The bad news is that General Wayland says you're to stand down again. He'll get back to us as soon as they can. The good news is that this gives us more time to get you ready."

CHAPTER TWENTY

Contact

The men were given physicals. Retina and palm ID were confirmed, as were blood types. A supply of their blood type had preceded them. Dr. Taylor commented on the equipment and thoroughness of the MASH staff.

One of the MDs examining the men responded, "We're as well equipped as a modern hospital. We can perform organ transplants if we have to. Not that we'll be needing to do that but if we did...we'd..."

A First Lieutenant female MD rolled her eyes and interceded, "Gentlemen, if you could step behind this curtain we'll get X-Rays. Dr. Maxwell, we'll take you first."

Jason obliged, but not before a long look at the organ transplant doctor. Three hours later they were eating sandwiches when the call came from General Wayland. A standing Colonel Matthews turned on a speaker, "Yes General, we're all ears."

"Is everyone there? Can everyone hear me?"

"Yes sir, loud and clear, and Welcome Wagon in attendance."

"Good." Wayland stated simply. "Thanks, Frank. Gentlemen, sorry for the delay, but we've had some rather extraordinary things happen in the last few hours that you'll just have to digest without a lot of detail."

Hesitation came through the line. "Gentlemen, we have good reason to believe the aliens have communicated. Their communication was through a Tibetan Monk, a blind, five-year old boy from India, and a fourteen-year-old girl from Detroit. I know this must sound...but what is important now is that,,,is that the aliens have apparently picked them for communication. Therefore, all three are on the way to join you, and should be arriving within the hour."

Josh asked, "Are you saying they will be joining us approaching the craft?"

"Yes."

Josh tasted bile, "General, you're saying that a Monk and children are going to be exposed to…to whatever's out there?"

There was silence then, "Yes, Mr. Jones, that is correct."

The war room

The President paced, "God, I hope we know what the hell we're doing."

Sarah and Gayle had not spoken for the last twenty minutes. They stood holding hands.

The President, attempting reassurance, said, "They'll be fine. They're good men, and the men with them are the best on the planet."

It was lame, and he knew it. He looked to the floor.

"I don't think we have a choice."

"I agree, Mr. President," Gayle said.

Sarah looked at her mother then the President, "So do I."

General Wayland nodded toward the station screen, "We'll have them on the monitors throughout the mission."

Josh, Drs. Taylor, and Maxwell walked through a section of the tent tunnel with Colonel Matthews to Base Camp 2, a 12' x 12' tent. They entered a seal lock door into a small chamber that led to yet another seal lock that was signed **INFECTIOUS AREA - NO UNAUTHORIZED ENTRY**. Underneath the sign was a panel encasing two red lights. The lights were labeled "LOCK" and "UNLOCK." The red light "LOCK" was on. A blue suited lieutenant sat in a glass booth over an instrument panel guarding the door. Colonel Matthews looked to the men.

"Gentlemen, I'll see you at L-4. As soon as you get your suits on, we'll check our communication."

Colonel Matthews gave a "thumbs up" to the lieutenant in the booth. The lieutenant pushed three buttons on the panel. The red light on "LOCK" went off and "UNLOCK" began flashing, synchronized with a bleating horn. The sealed door opened and Colonel Matthews left. As Josh, Maxwell and Taylor started for the entrance to Biosafety Level 1 the Lieutenant in the sealed booth stood and saluted.

They walked twenty meters through the second tent tunnel, and entered another sealed door labeled "Biosafety Level 1".

The Cleansing

Like the previous tent, it housed a lieutenant in a glass sealed booth surrounded by instruments. A wire protruded from her helmet, circled, and held a tiny speaker one inch from her mouth. Her voice filled the area.

"Gentlemen, welcome to Biosafety Level 1. Please remove everything touching the skin—clothing, watches, rings, contact lenses, everything. Your preps and ID are hanging to your left."

Josh smiled to himself. He knew the female Lieutenant was a SEAL. With new male recruits the female SEALs drew straws on who got to monitor the initial "dropping of laundry." Bets were made, and the females usually won. They checked shoes. As she watched, the men stripped and fitted themselves into lime green jumpsuits.

They left through a sealed door to a second labeled "Biosafety Level 2." The bleating horn and flashing red *"UNLOCK"* was accompanied with flashing yellow – *"YOU ARE CLEARED TO ENTER - CAUTION ULTRAVIOLET LIGHT."* They entered. The room contained another glass booth that housed two lieutenant majors. The left side of the tent room was lined with what looked like three porta-johns. Like the others, the majors wore light blue biohazard suits Josh had only heard about.

They were instructed to shed their prep suits. The ultraviolet indicated they were clean, but it didn't matter. One of the majors opened the doors to the 'porta-johns'. They were disinfecting shower stalls. Josh, Drs. Maxwell and Taylor were instructed to remain in the showers until the shower stopped. They were showered with disinfectant for four minutes, nozzles in every direction. They were handed large soft white towels in clear plastic bags. As Josh dried he noticed the meat-hooked biohazard suits hanging, slowly, very slowly twisting in the cool of the AC. The helmets were white, riveted to a mirroring pale blue visor, all attached to backpacks of oxygen and instruments, "the good stuff."

The new suits were one piece, made of a nylon alloy of spectra (a bullet proof composite), chromium and silicon fiber. The internal workings of the suits were controlled by two computers, a primary and a backup, each the size of a pack of cigarettes. They were housed in the backpack of instruments with the two canisters of oxygen. The suits were light, flexible and comfortable. The awkward, heavy cooling tubes that Josh remembered had been replaced by a miniature AC unit located at the base of the helmet. The AC cooled the chromium plastic threads that webbed the suit to exactly 80 degrees Fahrenheit.

The computer-controlled visor lens adjusted to the eyesight and provided 20-10 vision, both day and night. On command, there was binocular vision. The closing and opening of the suit was also computer controlled as was its communication and environmental measuring instruments. Physiological probes provided constant readings of the wearer. The suits were radiation and fire proof and would protect against a small caliber bullet. But their primary function was to give its occupant the ability to work in the environment of Level 4 viruses—the most deadly agents known to humankind. The suits had been tested in labs around the world. And they had been tested in the field, for AIDS in Africa, the 2014 Hunta outbreak in India, and with the chemical spill on Interstate 65, two miles inside the city limits of Indianapolis.

Josh, Maxwell and Taylor took a last breath of natural air and suited up. They had two hours of oxygen. After two hours they would be on "natural air" filtered through a unit that neutralized every biohazard on earth, but the visitors were not from earth so two hours would be their limit.

They were checked and double checked by the majors, and reminded that conversation was now communication with each other, General Wayland, Colonel Matthews and the President. Dr. Taylor was the first to test. "Whadda' we do if we have to pee?"

General Wayland's voice could be heard as clearly as if he were in the room. "Gentlemen, your communication is loud and clear and the answer to your question, Dr. Taylor, is... just let it fly."

The next sealed door read "Biosafety Level 3." The panel beneath had four lines. The first read "Staging Area," the second "Alarms Enabled," and the third "L4 Status." The fourth line was blank. A glass-boothed lieutenant major typed into the keyboard of the panel as the other monitored. The last line below "L4 Status" flashed "READY."

The Cleansing

The sealed door opened and the men entered the first compartment of Biosafety Level-4. A full major checked retina ID. Another read instruments as they passed through the last air lock to Main Level 4. The last door, across the room, was the entry to the last tunnel. The first line on the door read "**CAUTION - BIO HAZARD**," the second "**BIO SAFETY LEVEL 4**," and the last "**L4 SUIT REQUIRED FOR ENTRY**."

They didn't notice the signs because of the other four figures in the room. All were dressed in Bio - 4 suits. Two were adults and two were children. One of the adults was sitting with the smaller of the two children in his lap. Colonel Matthews, the adult standing spoke into the tiny speaker in his helmet, "Gentlemen, our second millennial single parent family."

He introduced the sitting adult and child as Mr. Jeston Mehra and Laku Rumula. The child standing was Tesh DuPree. He turned away from the men. "Mr. President, General Wayland, 'Welcome Wagon' is secured."

General Wayland answered, "Excellent. Gentlemen, Miss Dupree you're ready. When you exit L4 we will have you on visual. Colonel Matthews' men are waiting for you there with the Humvee. They'll drive you to within thirty meters of the craft. You know the drill from there. Any questions?"

There were none.

Josh stood mesmerized, "*Children about to…*"

Laku interrupted his thoughts. He climbed down from the lap of Mr. Mehra and, although blind, made his way to Josh. He wrapped his arms around his legs and held tight. Josh looked to the men about the room then gently picked him up.

General Wayland's voice interceded, "Gentlemen, we do not yet have visual and you're awfully quiet. Everything okay?"

"Yes sir, just getting acquainted with a little bonding. And sir, I've decided. I'm going," Josh responded.

The President asked, "Josh, are you sure?"

"Yes, sir I'm sure."

Josh took Laku back to Mr. Mehra, and sat him in his lap.

"General, tell Laku I'll be back soon."

Josh turned and uncovered a velcro panel on the sleeve of his left arm. He pushed the second button twice and his suit

145

automatically split open down his chest, abdomen, then legs. He removed his helmet, and stepped out of the suit, leaving it standing. Josh then removed the "long john" nylon inner suit, and stood naked. Captain McKarem retrieved a satchel sitting next to the exit door. Josh lapped the satchel over his shoulder.

"I'll be fine."

The sealed door opened, and Josh stepped into the last chamber. The door closed behind him. The tunnel stretched before him for thirty meters. The tent material was the same fabric as the L4 suits, and it felt warm on his feet. The tunnel was hot and dark as he made his way to a door labeled in phosphorous red **"DANGER - L4 BIOHAZARD - DO NOT ENTER."** When Josh was within three meters of the door it opened, and the heat and wind of the desert hit him in gritty shimmers. Six of the alien craft in two rows of three lay as bronzed Zeppelin bullets four hundred meters away.

"Bigger than I thought."

He walked out of the tent into the desert. Two thousand miles away the most sophisticated technology in the world imaged him into monitors in war rooms in a dozen countries.

CHAPTER TWENTY-ONE

The Canary

Josh's image silenced the war room in the Pentagon. The wind of the desert swirled sand dust, sculpting Josh as he walked toward the alien craft, a movie with no sound, no subtitles, incomplete, cementing fascination and fear. Gayle was hoarse with her question, "My God, what's he doing?"

Sarah answered, "He's protecting the children."

Both women looked to the President. His eyes went to the floor.

"I probably should have told you before, but we didn't think he would have to…" Sarah and Gayle responded with stares. The President continued, "Before the men left, Josh said one individual should approach the craft to be sure it was safe for everybody else. He, and HS agreed, that the first humans to be exposed to…to whatever is out there just couldn't be children and we agreed. And the only way to be absolutely sure was for someone to approach the craft without an L4 suit. If someone did and survived then it would be safe for—for anybody. Well, as safe as we could determine. Going in naked was Josh's idea. Said it was the only way to get exposure to whatever our instruments couldn't measure."

The President noted the welling in Sarah's eyes, "We have the best doctors in the world and the equipment we've moved into that desert is the most…"

The President stopped and dropped his eyes before the stares of two women.

A lieutenant at a monitor blurted, "He's our canary."

The lieutenant's eyes widened and his head jerked back to his monitor. Sarah's face drained as she squeezed her mother's hand. The President didn't look up until the monitors took them back. Josh stopped one hundred meters from the crafts, dropped the

147

satchel from his shoulder, opened it, removed four green flags and stuck one in the sand and continued.

Sarah asked, "What's the flag for?"

"He has green and red flags. If he feels okay, he sticks a green flag in the sand" answered General Wayland.

No one asked about the red flags. Fifty meters from the crafts he planted another green flag, twenty-five meters, another. The wind sand peppered his body in 98-degree heat.

He stopped within five meters of the first three craft, and planted a green flag. He moved to within a meter, and after seconds that held the breath of those watching, he reached, hesitated, and then touched the craft. The silence of the war room mirrored the silent movie on the monitor. General Wayland talked in a whisper. "Very good, Josh. Now get back here."

Josh moved down the side of the craft sliding his hand on its surface, reaching as high as he could, then as low. At the end of the craft he walked around it and disappeared behind it. Visual was lost. This had not been anticipated, and computers could not adjust satellites fast enough. A minute passed, then another. Colonel Matthews advised.

"General, our boys are on your order. Can be in there in thirty seconds."

The General didn't respond. Josh's naked figure appeared at the other end of the craft. He pointed two thumbs upward. He took the satchel from his shoulder and retrieved a bottle. He opened the top of the bottle, put the top back into the satchel, and set the bottle firmly into the sand. He walked to the last flag he had planted, retrieved it and started back to Biosafety Level 4, gathering flags as he retraced his steps.

Sarah asked, "What's in the bottle?"

"Water," the President answered.

Two minutes later Josh was back. He was met by three blue suited MDs who took blood, urine, hair, and skin samples where he stood. He was escorted to the MASH unit and X-Rayed. Vision, hearing acuity and verbal tests were followed by a series of motor skills.

The plastic sheets were cool on the table where he lay as machines and the doctors probed his body. Tests that normally took hours were done in minutes. He reentered the disinfectant

The Cleansing

shower and washed for ten minutes. Samples from the shower, the towel he used for drying, the flags and his pink body were tested again. He drank two pints of distilled water, ate fruit and yogurt laced with antibiotics and was re-tested. As he waited for the results, he soothed his stinging body with medicated lotion. The doctor carrying the results smiled through a blue shield when she entered.

Twenty minutes later Josh Jones, Drs. Maxwell and Taylor, Jeston Mehra, Tesh Dupree, and Laku Rumula exited the last tunnel, loaded into a Humvee and followed fading footprints. When they were within twenty meters, the Humvee stopped, and the men and children exited. They waited as five Special Forces made their way toward the craft checking instruments. They returned and nodded to the men and children.

Josh carried Laku, leg looped into his backpack and Jeston Mehra led Tesh by the hand. Drs. Taylor and Maxwell led the way, periodically stopping, reading instruments, and comparing then signaling the rest to follow.

The communication software included a language converter chip (LCC). Laku's chip was programmed to convert his Indian language to English and Mr. Mehra his Tibetian. Standing next to the President in the Pentagon, Gayle heard him whisper, "My God, I've put children in harm's way."

General Wayland's voice echoed, "Dr. Maxwell, Dr. Taylor, your readings look fine from here. You agree?"

There was static, then a response from Jason, "Nothing unusual, everything's clean so far. But I'm glad we're air-conditioned. It's 110 degrees out here."

General Wayland responded, "Yeah, the winter weather is rough this year. Everyone stay tight. Readings still good."

"Roger here. A little reading on actinium, but nothing abnormal, a stroll on the beach. You might get a read on the children."

"They're fine. Pulse rates up a little, like yours—mine."

Dr. Lois Palo was fluent in both English and the dialect of Indian that Laku spoke. Dr. Palo repeated the following in Indian avoiding the metallic computer conversion to a blind boy who, until today, had never been away from a shack of the worst slums on the planet.

"Laku, Tesh are you okay? Remember, you can say anything you want anytime and we can hear you. Do you feel all right?"

Both children shook their heads "yes", without verbally responding.

"I think I saw you nod yes, but it's better if you speak to us. So you're okay? You feel good?"

Both children said, "yes" softly. The crew stopped, and Jason compared his readings with Dr. Taylor's then Josh. Jason stepped toward the craft.

"Everything's clean. I'm going to approach the craft first. If my readings are still clean then the children."

General Wayland was the first to respond again, "Sounds good, Dr. Maxwell. We have a good view of you, and the craft and everything looks fine."

Leaders in countries around the world, their staff, leaders of the free world, members of their cabinets, all stood mesmerized and without knowing it—united.

The President commented, "My God, they were eating Christmas turkey forty eight hours ago. Now they're…"

Jason approached and touched the craft. He took a "strip" from his sleeve and taped it to the craft. He removed it and placed it back on his sleeve.

The President turned to Gayle and Sarah, "The way they explained it to me, that strip can get DNA samples on any element or compound on earth. The bets in the lab are two to one against."

General Wayland's voice was calm, reassuring, "Dr. Maxwell, for some reason your pulse is up a little. Other than the fact you are the second man in recorded history to touch an alien space craft, have any idea why that might be?"

Jason gave a thumb's up, "Maybe the heat? Readings still normal, and I'm fine. I think it would be a good idea to circle the craft like Josh did and get readings."

There was a moment of hesitation before General Wayland spoke, "Have to give you a negative on that. Gotta keep you folks together in case we need to hurry. See if you can check underneath the craft. Looking for some sign of propulsion."

The Cleansing

Jason dropped to his knees and attempted to look at the underbelly of the craft.

"Can't see its belly, buried in the sand. Josh was right. This craft is unbelievable. Smooth as silk, no seams, rivets, welds, nothing."

Jason looked to Josh and Taylor, "See if you guys get the same—Oh God!"

Dr. Maxwell froze. In the opposite direction of the way they had approached the craft, a figure two feet taller than Dr. Maxwell stood ten meters in front of them. It was suddenly just there. The figure stood silent, not moving, just standing as if observing. The bronze colored hooded robe on or attached covered its face and body like an angel or devil. But the robe didn't move, as if it were part of its body. The robe extended to within an inch of the ground, and the hood covered its head and no body or face was visible. The satellite viewing had been programmed to focus on the crew and children.

Gayle forced herself to breathe. The satellite responded to Dr. Maxwell keyboarding and the figure came in view on the monitors. The President moved forward and started to speak. General Wayland raised his hand toward the President, and shook his head. The Special Forces men moved toward Dr. Maxwell and General Wayland stopped them. He spoke softly, "Everyone stand still. Don't move."

The group stood motionless. Ten seconds passed. General Wayland instructed again, "Now, very slowly, very slowly everyone take one small step ba…"

As the General finished his sentence the figure began to move. The movement was a glide rather than a walk. It skimmed slowly across the desert toward Dr. Maxwell. As the figure approached someone murmured, "Sweet Jesus."

The figure approached to within a meter of Dr. Maxwell, passed him and approached Josh, Dr. Taylor, Mr. Mehra and the children. The President stepped forward, "General, we have to get them out now."

As he spoke, Tesh and Mr. Mehra began to walk toward the figure. Josh stepped between them and the figure. Laku moved in Josh's backpack. In a metallic-tinted voice his LCC relayed

151

his voice in English, "She won't hurt us. You need to let me down."

He struggled against the pack. Josh hesitated, then took Laku and gently lowered him to the sand. Laku, hands lurching forward, made his way to Tesh and Jeston Mehra. They approached to within two meters of the figure. The children and Jeston did not speak the sixty seconds they stood with the alien. After exactly one minute, the figure turned and headed toward the desert, and in seconds was out of sight. No one in the group or at the war room moved. Finally, Dr. Maxwell in a hoarse voice asked, "Is everyone all right?"

There was a long silence until Tesh responded, "We be fine."

"Mr. Mehra, Tesh, can you tell us anything?" asked Dr. Maxwell.

"No, but me and Laku and Mr. Jeston can come back in three days and ask questions if we want to," answered Tesh.

CHAPTER TWENTY-TWO

Confusion

The next hours were a blend of activity and confusion. The President and Homeland Security continued to monitor the screens in the War Room. Kate arranged on-screen satellite conference hookups with the leaders of the western world. The President explained as best he could the reason two children and a monk were selected to attempt communication.

Congress was addressed in closed session in the S407 security room of the Senate. Congressmen feigned anger and questioned leadership that would allow our armed forces to be disarmed. Wiser congressmen prevailed as anger and partisan bickering was recognized for what it was. The result of the session was a united government causing an exiting older congressman to comment on SNN, "*We stand united. Sad, that educating our children, caring for our seniors, our families, our environment do not bring about the same.*"

The Vice-President addressed the nation with instructions to buy time. His oratory was unlike that of a politician. He spoke softly and slowly, as if in conversation with his listeners. He raised issues like he was visiting with a neighbor on a front porch over a cup of coffee. He broached the serious with wit and humor then followed with the quoted words of a historian, statesman or mother. Early in his career, political opponents conceded that if voters only knew of Tom B. Stewart's oratory, he would be President. The Vice-President emphasized that there had been no conflict.

"*Communication has been established and is continuing. Armed forces have the craft that has landed in the U.S. contained and surrounded. Canadian armed force are assisting in Alaska.*"

He then lied with the conviction of Santa talking to a child, smiling about the rumor that weapons of our armed forces had been disarmed. There had been a degree of sabotage but it was being addressed. The major sabotage had occurred with public weapons. The problem seemed to be the contamination of ammunition at the manufacturing level.

The public was assured that the invaders had landed in the remotest of areas, many miles from civilian and population centers. The U.S. was working with foreign powers throughout the world on security measures. In fact, every craft that had landed was now encircled and contained by armed forces.

In the West the initial shock of the news was followed by a stunned disbelief, described by one news analyst as "paralyzed panic." Then, when no confrontation or conflict ensued, complemented by the media's inability to provide pictures, curiosity replaced shock. Tabloids offered one million dollars for a landing location, five million for a picture of a spacecraft, and ten million for a picture of an alien. They had numerous takers with grainy pictures with tabloid headlines, none accepted by reputable news.

An NBC evening news reporter getting public reaction at a shopping mall asked a six-year old girl why she thought no one had seen one of the invaders. Her answer viewed on national TV was the release needed: *"Maybe, they're just shy."*

The comment gave the psyche of millions what it needed to cope with the concept of alien invasion.

"Maybe they were vulnerable. Perhaps the whole thing was a hoax."

Media plagued the armed forces, tailing every move. Troops were decoyed to various remote places to distract media hordes. But the comment of the child said, *"maybe we're going to be alright."*

Public concern abated as the hours passed. In India and parts of South America there were reports of panic and riots, but the absence of confrontation and confirmation suggested hoax. The leaders of the world had bought a little time.

General Wayland and the President entered the Bio lab of the Pentagon's war command headquarters. Two white-coated members of Homeland Security briefed the President and General Wayland.

"Mr. President, General Wayland, you'll be happy to hear that physicals on the children, Mr. Jones and Drs. Taylor and Maxwell are clean. No effects at all and tests for contaminants on their bio suits were negative."

Two HS members pulled a curtain revealing a sealed quarantine room where the team members sat sipping water. An HS official turned to the President and General Wayland. "HS and Military Intelligence have interviewed the team members. I'm sure you're eager to talk with them. Dr. Maxwell would you like to begin?"

A weary Dr. Maxwell took a long draw from a plastic cup. He remained seated with crumpled papers in front of him. "Mr. President, General Wayland, I'm sure you're eager to hear about our encounter. As Dr. Newell stated, we've been interviewing the two children, Josh, Dr. Taylor and myself. First, we were interviewed individually, then as a group."

Jason hesitated and took another drink, "The aliens appear to be communicating with the children and Mr. Mehra. We say, *'appear to be'*, because the communication is not through sound or any form of voice, code or script that we can measure. It is extraordinary that they communicate using symbols, and are able to do so through some sort of telekinesis or telepathy."

Jason stopped as a close up video of the alien standing with the children and Mr. Mehra was imaged on a large screen on the left wall.

"You will note there's no sign of communication by voice, gestures or body language. We examined the video frame by frame, and we were not able to detect any evidence of communication other than the fact the alien stood facing the children at least, we think it was the face of the alien."

Frames flashed across the screen showing two children and Mr. Mehra standing facing an unknown. Jason continued.

"The alien stood with the children and Mr. Mehra for exactly sixty seconds. The sound you hear in the background is the desert wind. When we tried other sound frequencies or amplified, we just got louder wind. However, note the children and Mr. Mehra are standing as if listening. Mr. Mehra and the children maintain there were three messages communicated. The first is the most interesting. As you might recall, Josh was

155

carrying Laku when the alien was encountered. When the alien started toward the children Laku said, Jason stopped and Laku's voice in Hindu, filled the room.

"That translates into *'it's all right, she won't hurt us.'* When we asked Laku how he knew he was safe, he described the outward appearance of the alien in detail. He could not describe anyone or anything else at the scene. I remind you that Laku has been blind since birth. Other than communication we can't speculate on how he was able to do that. When we asked Laku how he knew about the alien and that she was a female he stated, "she told me." We asked the children and Mr. Mehra if they communicated anything to the alien. All three said they didn't know."

There was silence until Dr. Maxwell continued, "The second message communicated was that the children and Mr. Mehra could ask questions of the aliens in three days. You'll recall Tesh said that after the encounter. The children and Mr. Mehra said there were no words spoken but somehow they knew. And remember Mr. Mehra and the children speak different languages. So, it appears there is communication with the aliens by Mr. Mehra and the children.

"Also, Mr. Mehra and the children reacted differently to the alien than Josh, myself, and Dr. Taylor. There was no communication with us. At the moment the alien appeared and during the minute that followed, Josh, Dr. Taylor and I were terrified. Our physiological readings were off the charts. This was not true of the children and Mr. Mehra. They were cool as a cucumber, physiological readings like they were taking a nap. When asked why they weren't afraid they said, *'no reason to be afraid.'*

"Now to the alien. We have the appearance of the one encountered on video. We don't know whether the others are the same. If you'll note the following."

A video was played again for the group. A close up of the alien was displayed in slow motion. Dr. Maxwell spoke as the group watched, "The alien is 2.53 meters tall and stands upright. Since we know nothing of its genetics, evolution, or origin, comparisons to the human species is speculation. However, their apparent adaptation to our atmosphere suggests several things.

The Cleansing

Their height implies evolution and a nutritional base for millions of years. The alien apparently breathes our atmosphere, which implies a circulatory system and brain similar to ours. How they move like they do? We have no idea. They simply glide along the earth's surface and can accelerate at incredible speeds, about two hundred miles an hour, and—they're defying gravity. The alien has evolved from an environment radically different from ours or they have some sort of propulsion or they know how to counteract the effects of gravity.

"The robe appearance is fascinating. Using Crypt Technology we can ascertain the composition of material from video pictures with 90 percent accuracy—plus or minus. We were not able to determine the composition of the robe, and since the robe covers the entire body of the alien we have no idea of appearance. It could be the robe is their body. Also, my DNA strip showed nothing about the composition of the craft. We scanned the ground where the alien stood for DNA samples but as of ten minutes ago, nothing.

"Obviously, the aliens thrive, at least short term, in our environment. The aliens use small tubes like submarines to navigate underwater, which also suggests they breathe as we do."

Jason paused, giving the President time to ask, "So what don't we know that we need to know?"

"Well sir, as I said, their technology is very advanced—very advanced. The capabilities of their craft and navigation are remarkable. Based on their flying patterns, they have detailed knowledge of the earth's geography and terrain, which means previous visits or the ability to observe and study from wherever. The movement of craft positions ten hours ago implies communication and a plan. If they're responsible for disarming the entire planet that suggests knowledge of chemistry and physics well…it speaks for itself…oh, not to mention the *'script'* and the *'blue haze.'*

"Their communication skills are extraordinary. Somehow they have learned various, if not every language on the planet, again suggesting prior study of our species. They dictate who they want to communicate with and then do so telepathically."

Jason hesitated. "The last item may be the most important, and that is they show no outward signs of fear. The aliens

157

approached and landed on an alien planet while ignoring our aircraft and warnings. They have approached numerous life forms, including us, and didn't hesitate to move within a meter. Initially, we thought the remote landings were for protection, but we feel now they are not concerned about protection. If, in fact, they have the capability of disabling every weapon on the planet and can move and communicate as they do, what do they have to fear? Maybe the child on TV was correct. *'Maybe they're just shy.'*

"Oh, almost forgot something we found fascinating. During a teleconference an hour ago, two professors from the University of Paris made an interesting observation. Dr. Tuffe, a noted psychologist, and Dr. Ptere whose field is environmental evolution suggested the following."

He rummaged through the papers in his hand. "Here it is." Jason read aloud, *"The landings to date have been in the most pristine, unspoiled locations on the planet. If you were to document the tracts of land on this planet that are still primeval and untouched by humans, you would have the landing spots of the alien craft."*

Jason looked up from the paper, "As I stated, until Dr. Tuffe and Dr. Ptere offered their observation we believed the landings were some sort of strategy that offered the aliens safety. We can't get to them with any sizeable number of forces, and if we do it is without arms. However, Dr. Tuffe and Dr. Ptere suggested something else. I quote."

Jason again read from the paper, *"If the aliens are responsible for our disarming, why would they fear us?"*

Laying the papers aside, he continued speaking, "They believe the aliens are interested in exploration and have picked the most diverse primitive unspoiled places on the planet to do so. The fact they didn't land near any human habitat suggests that the aliens are not interested in human habitat and perhaps not too interested in us as a species. Their initial behavior implies this may be the case. Where they landed, there was no contact, no communication except with the children and Mr. Mehra.

"Drs. Tuffe and Ptere suggests, *'Our visitors may not be avoiding us, they may be ignoring us, and our disarmament is a signal for us to do the same.'*

"Mr. President your question, *'What don't we know that we need to know?'* Sir, that is our greatest concern. Where do they come from? Why are they here and most important, are they a threat? We have some at HS who don't think so. Their contention is that if they were, with their technology, we would know by now and, if they're a threat, why bother communicating with two children and a monk?"

Taking a deep breath, his chest rising in hesitation, Jason met the President's gaze. "Sir, as you might imagine, we have a lot of disagreement. However, we have agreement on the most important issue; we are in the midst of...we're experiencing perhaps the greatest event in human history. A highly intelligent alien life form has landed on our planet. We are not alone. The importance and magnitude of this is beyond anything we can articulate and we don't know yet whether this will be our demise or our salvation. We have colleagues who believe we'll know the answer in the next few hours or days.

"In view of our first encounter and what we know of the alien's superior intelligence, the absence of aggression, we implore that we continue to engage them in the same way. Mr. President, we urge you to recommend other nations do the same."

Jason gestured to a camera mounted on the right wall. "I have three videos I want to show you. The last one is the most interesting. I preface their showing by telling you there have been no reported violent crimes in the entire country in the last eight hours, and we're confirming the same in other countries."

The group was shown a surveillance video of a man starting to attack on a woman in the hallway of a hotel, then stops, apologizing profusely, *"Mom, I'm sorry'*, then runs away. The second was a mother's video of her husband starting to beat their five-year-old daughter. He stops then starts crying and begs forgiveness, *'Judy, I didn't mean it. I'm sorry, I'm sorry."* The last video showed a drunk trashing a bar; throwing chairs and tables as he yelled profanities. Police arrive and when he tries to attack them, he stops and starts sobbing, '*Dad, I'm sorry.*" The police approach, handcuff him and lead him away.

"We have other reports of such occurrences, but no explanation of how or why this is occurring. The individuals you just witnessed apologized, some wept and begged forgiveness from their mother, father, sister, brother or someone they were close too. It's as if the person they are attacking suddenly is perceived as a loved one. This state lasts about five minutes with, as yet, no traceable side effects. The last video is the most perplexing. The drunk and the aggressors in the other videos become non-violent when they tried to attack another human being. However, the police are able to approach and handcuff, which is an aggressive act toward another individual, without experiencing the same. Mr. President, General Wayland, I've talked enough. I'm sure you have questions."

Jason leaned back into his chair. The President walked to a red phone and began to punch numbers.

CHAPTER TWENTY-THREE

Calm

2:00 a.m. - The next morning

Dr. Bowman, the President's doctor ordered him to get some sleep. The President finally relented, and retired to a bunk in one of the offices of the Pentagon with orders to awake him in three hours. Dr. Maxwell and Gayle sat in the war room and swigged coffee. Three offices down, Josh and members of Homeland Security were comparing simulations with scientists around the globe. They had slept four hours in three days. They also had been ordered by physicians to rest, but while agreeing the President should sleep, they did not. Majors and colonels, glued to the monitors, rotated hourly. Gayle rubbed her eyes and stifled a yawn, "Well Dr. Jason Maxwell, at least now I know what you do."

"Well, you know what I try to do. Have Josh and Sarah gotten any sleep?"

"No, not as of fifteen minutes ago. We'll find them slumped across a computer keyboard somewhere."

"Is Sarah okay?"

"Fine. She's been working with public reaction. Says it's a mix of indifference and fascination. Says the absence of firearms and crime are bigger news than the aliens." There was a lull of weariness. Gayle reached and took Jason's hand, "How do you think this is going to turn out?"

Jason accepted Gayle's hand in both of his, "I don't know, but so far everything that has happened has been good."

"What do you mean? We have unknown *somethings* on our planet and we're helpless."

He raised Gayle's hand to his lips. "They've not harmed anyone or anything for that matter. No weapons, no violence—peace on earth. Isn't that what we've been looking for since we crawled out of the caves?"

"But why are they here?"

Squeezing her hand, Jason smiled, "Well, that's the question. Maybe they're just exploring. Maybe we..." Suddenly, he released Gayle's hand, and picked up his coffee cup, "But if the blue haze and the *'Script'* are their doing, they're here for a reason. And I believe they are."

Gayle tried to smile, "I worry about Sarah."

Jason looked at the floor, then back to Gayle, "I know."

Forty-eight hours later

The briefing started at 6:00 a.m. The President sat at the oval table in the war room with General Wayland. Dr. Maxwell briefed from his daily report as the President and General leafed with him using their copy.

"They're keeping up a good front except for Ramerez in Brazil and Yau Leng in South Korea. They've broken ranks. Told their people straight out they have no weapons. It's soon going to be impossible to stonewall. Soldiers, police and citizens with firearms know their weapons don't work and they're talking. The media is reporting a nice mixture of gossip, fear with a little truth. The riots in India, Mali, Algeria have subsided. Violent crime continues to abate. Australia, Germany and Austria are equipping their forces with cross bows."

Jason threw up his hands, "I don't know what to say about that. Oh, there's an unbelievable report coming out of Liberia—the children Liberian government forces have been kidnapping in Sierra Leone and forcing them to become soldiers are leaving in droves. Walking and trying to hitch hike home by the thousands. The government forces trying to stop them just gave up. Go into that remorse state and..."

An hour later, Dr. McLean of Homeland Security continued the briefing.

"When the elements and chemicals, potassium, nitrate, sulfur and charcoal, are mixed to make gunpowder, a molecular change renders the mixture useless as an explosive. The same is true of the hundreds of chemicals used to make the munitions of modern weapons. Cellulose nitrate, pyroxylin, melinite, cordite, trinitrotoluene, hydrogen, rocket combustibles, and even uranium, are victims of a molecular degeneration that render them useless as sources for weapons. Prior to mixing, the chemicals and elements remain in their normal molecular state, but when mixed they diffuse into a harmless mess. It's as if they mutate, like a virus adapting to drugs. We have no idea as to why or how this happens, or how to prevent it."

The chemist's voice trailed, "But we're working on it."

A police cruiser squealed to a stop in a south LA project. A medical team in white coats exited the back of the cruiser, working their way through a crowd. "Excuse me. Coming through. Need to get through here. Excuse us, please. Thank you."

They approached eight "gang-bangers." The bangers eyes glaring, carrying baseball bats and handguns, fidgeting about, avoiding facing each other. A fight over turf never developed. The medical team paid one hundred dollars for blood samples and CAT scans with portable units. Urine samples were traded for another twenty.

As the team left, the officer driving looked in the rear view mirror and chuckled. "Look at those idiots. They're still milling around each other. Maybe they can start pissing on each other's turf."

The medical team and the officer in the passenger seat looked back. A doctor asked, "Tried to fight again?"

"Oh yeah. Seen them try for hours. Drugs, prostitution, fencing is still alive and well, so they try to protect their turf. Unbelievable. Hey, is it true that Libya, North Korea and Iran are offering a hundred million for munitions that will fire?"

A medical team member answered, "Yep."

"Wonder what we're offering?"

"A billion" the doctor answered.

The President's war room now included civilian and military staff, six members of Homeland Security and Kate Dockery. The President spoke, "Appreciate your reports ladies and gentlemen. As I understand what you've told me, except for another switching by the alien craft yesterday that replicated their first movement, nothing has changed. Now, I have a decision to make. What should we do about the message of Laku, Tesh and Mr. Mehra., 'We can ask questions in three days'? Should we approach the craft with Mr. Mehra and the children again?"

Jason was the first to respond, "Mr. President, it's obvious that eventually someone will. The Australians are within two kilometers, as we speak, and forces of numerous nations are trying. The only thing that is preventing them is terrain. Within days, maybe hours someone will make it.

"The question is what then? What we know for sure is, we won't have any control over what they do. If they're aggressive or communicate something wrong, God knows what might happen. We were successful the first time, and if there was communication, it was that we are invited to return."

The President stood, walked to a window, and looked out. He spoke without turning. "I agree with you, Jason. Everyone willing to go again?"

"Yes sir. The children and Mr. Mehra are eager." The President turned as Jason continued, "Mr. President, we need to orchestrate the next meeting very carefully, script the questions the children and Mr. Mehra need to communicate. Whether or not they will be answered...and Mr. President we have to ask them the question."

"You mean: *Are they responsible for the disappearance of our violent people?*"

"Yes, sir."

The President rubbed his eyes. He'd slept five hours in three days. "Surveillance hasn't given us anything else?"

"Nothing new, sir."

"I'd appreciate it if you'd have your people go over everything one more time."

"Yes sir."

The President turned to Kate, "I need to speak to Tesh's mother."

CHAPTER TWENTY-FOUR

Tesh's Mom

In the corner of the war room, the President of the United States and Ms. Dupree sat in two chairs amidst the clamor of the most historic event in history. Ms. Dupree slowly surveyed the room. Ms. Dupree was tall, slender with silver streaked hair that gave her a look of motherly regality. Her white smile never ended and soft yet flashing eyes consumed everything. "Mr. President this is something, hmm…hm, really something."

"Yes, Ms. Dupree it is." Ms. Dupree smiled at the President as he spoke, "Ms. Dupree, I need your advice."

"Yes sir, Mr. President, I suspect you do. You need to know if I think it's all right to send my Tesh back into that desert."

The President grinned, "Ms. Dupree, you are a perceptive lady."

"And Mr. President, you are a good man to be concerned about a little girl and her mama, with all this alien stuff going on." There was a pause before Ms. Dupree took the President's hand, "Mr. President, my Tesh says she'll be just fine, and I trust that girl. She's been there once, says it's fine if she goes again, even wants to go, says it's important she goes. And Mr. President, I think I can speak for the family of Laku. Oh my, what a sweet child. I'm sure they would say the same thing. He and my Tesh have just attached to each other. They love the pizza your folks keep bringing 'em. You know that poor boy never had pizza till he came. Can't understand a word he says, but he loves that pizza."

Ms. Dupree hesitated and covered her mouth with her hand, "My lord, listen to my rambling and you with the weight of the world right on your shoulders. Mr. President, I've voted for you twice now, and neither time did I know if I was doing the right thing. How does anybody ever know about you politicians? But, I do now Mr. President. You're a good man trying to do the right thing and look at you, taking time for a little girl and her mother. The young ones and the fine folk who go with 'em, they'll be fine. So don't you worry, you just go and do what you have to do."

The President stood, "Ms. Dupree, I couldn't interest you in a cabinet post could I?"

Ms. Dupree laughed, "How much are you paying?"

CHAPTER TWENTY-FIVE

Confrontation

Twenty-three hours later the children, Josh, Drs. Taylor and Maxwell returned to the desert of the Empty Quarter. A Humvee took the crew to within fifty meters of the alien craft. Mr. Mehra took Tesh by the hand, flanked by Dr. Maxwell and Dr. Taylor, with Joshua carrying Laku. It had been agreed that SOGs would not approach the craft as they did the last time. They hadn't been invited.

Jason approached to within ten meters of the craft as the rest of the crew waited. The approach and positioning of the crew was to be as exactly as before. Jason approached the craft and circled, stopping every ten meters to check his instruments.

"Readings still normal, looks like it's going to be another stroll on the beach."

"Sounding good, Jason. A few of us in the war room got a pool on how many hours you slept last night." responded General Wayland.

"Slept like a fat baby except for the eight hours I stayed up working on my telepathy. By the way, can we really pee in these suits?"

"Only when they sneak up on you. Readings good here. You guys way cool."

"Confirm that, General."

"Okay, gentlemen, Tesh, stand in the same places as before."

The crew took the exact spots and waited. The videos would later show that exactly seventy-two hours from the last encounter an alien, of the same description, appeared out of the south and approached. And exactly as before, the children and Mr. Mehra walked away from the doctors and approached. Laku stopped and spoke. The language chip translated. "It's not her. He's different, but he's nice like her."

The Cleansing

The alien, two children and Jeston Mehra stood within a meter of each other for exactly three minutes. Then, for no apparent reason, Mr. Mehra's knees buckled and he almost fell. Tesh caught him, or he would have.

General Wayland reacted, "Mr. Mehra, what's wrong?" General Wayland again spoke, "Jason, can you tell if..."

Tesh interrupted, "He's just fine. He says *his apologies for your concern*. Says he wasn't ready for what he learned."

After speaking Mr. Mehra knelt in front of the alien for a few seconds then stood and took the hands of the children. Tesh nodded toward the alien, and spoke, "They want me to sing. Can you send us music?"

"They want you to sing?" Inquired a suitably confused General Wayland.

"Yes, can you play music?"

There was a shrug in the General's voice, "Anyone have a suggestion?"

"This could be some form of communication. Are the discs of Christmas music still somewhere in the war room?" asked Jason.

A major at one of the consoles offered, "Sir, give me about thirty seconds and I can download to the speakers we have set up in the desert. Which piece of Christmas music would she like?"

"Did you hear that, Tesh? We're going to patch through. Is Christmas music okay?" asked General Wayland.

"Yes, Christmas music will be fine. I know 'O Holy Night'."

General Wayland asked, "Do you have that one, major?"

"Yes, sir. Give me a minute."

Graduates from the most prestigious military institutions in the world scrambled to find a piece of Christmas music among assorted discs. A female lieutenant found it, and handed it to the major.

"Yes sir, we got it. Now, let me download. Sir, let the young lady know it will start playing in about twenty seconds—and counting."

Twenty seconds later the New York Philharmonic's version of 'O Holy Night filled the war room of the Pentagon and in the desert of the Empty Quarter.

General Wayland leaned to the President and whispered, "My God sir, do you realize what we're doing?"

The President glued to the monitor smiled, "Well General, if I understand correctly, we're playing, 'O Holy Night, in the war room of the most powerful nation in the history of civilization for a child who's singing to space aliens."

There was a pause before General Wayland responded, "That's the way I read it too, sir."

Because of the quality of the technology, the music was extraordinary. On the second bar the voice of Tesh Dupree joined the orchestra, and men and women of this planet and a planet or planets unknown were mesmerized by the voice of a fourteen- year-old girl from the ghettos of Detroit. As Tesh sang the words *'Fall on your knees, O hear the Angels' voices,'* four more aliens appeared, and stood with the others and the children. When Tesh finished she approached the first alien and hugged it. A collective gasp, and a "Jesus Christ" were heard around the war room. Mr. Mehra walked to Josh and spoke to him for a few seconds. Josh relayed his message into his speaker.

"Mr. Mehra says there is no reason for concern. They won't harm us. They've requested the men in the craft that brought us here to please join us."

Dr. McLean and General Wayland looked to the President who in turn pointed to General Wayland. The General asked, "Josh, can Mr. Mehra tell us why?"

Josh leaned forward and spoke with Mr. Mehra.

"Yes, they're going to answer a question he asked."

The President asked, "What question?"

"He doesn't know," responded Josh.

General Wayland offered, "Mr. President, I suggest we comply, but leave a driver in one of the Humvees and a pilot on one of the Apaches. We have to be prepared to extract."

President Meyer gestured affirmative. Wayland gave the order to exit the craft and vehicles except for one driver and one pilot. Special Forces from two Humvees, and Pilots and flight engineers from two Apache IIs and a Comanche two hundred yards away, exited their choppers and trudged through the desert to join the rest of crew. When they were twenty meters away from their craft, the Apaches and both the Humvees were suddenly engulfed in a blue crystalline light. The pilot and driver who had stayed, scrambled out. When they were clear, the blue intensified in color and the vehicles disintegrated. It was without sound, and it was instantaneous.

The aliens who had been listening to the singing of Tesh vanished back into the desert. Another "Jesus Christ" was heard from the war room. Mr. Mehra again reassured Josh. Josh immediately looked to the JSOCs who had positioned themselves between the crew and the alien craft. "Everyone remain calm. Mr. Mehra says no one is going to be harmed. Mr. President, General Wayland, Mr. Mehra says his question has been answered."

A stunned General Wayland stammered, "Josh, what the hell's going on?"

Josh spoke calmly, "Mr. Mehra says everything's fine. No one will be harmed. It's impossible now. It's important you know."

General Wayland barked orders, "A-team go to white rescue. I repeat, white rescue. Everyone to landing site Delta—now!"

General Wayland checked the instruments displaying the physiological readings of the crew. Pulse rates and body temperatures were up except for the children and Mr. Mehra. The JSOCs moved with precision. Taylor and Maxwell ran toward the choppers escorted by rangers. One had Tesh on his back. Josh sprinted with Laku in his satchel. Mr. Mehra stood and looked into the desert where the aliens had disappeared until a JSOC grabbed him. General Wayland calmly gave orders to the three Apache IIs that hovered two kilometers south.

"Delta two and three initiate white rescue. Repeat, white rescue. Full crew, no causalities. Delta four standby."

"This is Delta two, roger white rescue. Delta three?"

"This is Delta three, roger, on my way."

Two Apaches IIs broke ranks and six minutes later the crew, children and Mr. Mehra were headed for an aircraft carrier in the Gulf of Aden.

Six hours later the children, Mr. Mehra and crew were in quarantine at the Pentagon. The President, General Wayland, General Dickenson, Gayle and Kate entered the quarantine area.

The Cleansing

Drs. Maxwell and Taylor, Mr. Mehra and Josh sat behind the glassed area. The children were asleep in another quarantine area.

Drs. Maxwell and Taylor briefed the children and Mr. Mehra on the plane to Dulles. Both Maxwell and Taylor looked as if they had aged. Mr. Mehra had a slight smile. His eyes were away, weary, and glistened. Sarah and Josh touched hands through the glass. Sarah was the first to speak, "Well, at least you didn't show your butt to the world this time."

"Got in too big a hurry."

Jason and Gayle smiled at them and looked at each other. Jason looked toward the President, "Ladies and gentlemen, the physicals of the crew were replicas of the last one. Passed with flying colors. Since Tesh hugged one of the aliens her suit was examined for DNA. Nothing. However, the information that Mr. Mehra and the children have is of concern. As you know, we scripted questions for Mr. Mehra and the children to communicate to the alien or aliens. Only three of our questions were addressed. However, we have a considerable amount of other information.

"I'll begin with the first issue. Are Homo sapiens or other living species, plant or animal, on this planet in any danger?

Answer: Mr. Mehra and the children all stated the same communication, *'many species, plant and animal, including Homo sapiens, are in danger, but not from the aliens.'*

Question two: Why are they here? Answer: *'To rest upon the nature of our planet and to secure the tranquility needed for Truens.'* We have no idea the meaning of that answer. Mr. Mehra asked the alien it's meaning, and was told *'it will be known.'*

"None of the other questions were addressed before the alien asked Tesh to sing. According to Mr. Mehra and Laku, the aliens lost their ability to verbalize as they began communicating telepathically. The aliens apparently love the sounds of our planet—wind, water, brooks, ocean, birds etc. How they knew about the voice of Miss Dupree, we don't know."

Jason's mouth opened but it just as quickly closed shut when he wasn't sure what to say. He tried again. "Mr. Mehra says the most important information communicated by the alien pertains

171

to the script. I quote, *'The script is now and will remain. In three weeks, your species will adhere.'* Mr. Mehra asked what that meant.

"The answer was and again I quote, *'Armies of the planet will cease to exist.'* Mr. Mehra then asked if that meant all armies on this planet must disband.

"The answer was, and I quote, *'Yes.'* Mr. Mehra then asked what would happen to armies that refused.

"That's when Mr. Mehra was instructed to have the crew leave their craft and the JSOCs to leave the Humvees. You know what happened to the Apache and Humvee then."

Again Dr. Maxwell hesitated, "We asked Tesh why she hugged the alien, and she said *'because Laku could see him.'* "

There was silence then Dr. Maxwell continued, "We asked Mr. Mehra why he stumbled during the communication. I think it is best he answer that question."

Mr. Mehra, whose eyes focused on the table in front of him, looked up at the others. He spoke deliberately. The translator converted his words to English.

"It is important you know of our visitors. In the past I, like many others, have been deceived by those who profess to be wise, but the visitors do not deceive us. We can believe them. Their interest lies in the tranquility and preservation of our planet. They will study many species but not us. They are aware of our domination but consider us a very savage, primitive life form. This, they told me, is due to the inferiority of our evolution."

Mr. Mehra again studied the table, "We did not evolve with the capacity to genetically pass our history. They did. Therefore, we are without the ability to know and act on our history. We are condemned to repeat our ignorance."

He stopped as if anticipating questions. No one spoke. Mr. Mehra continued, "They shared with me and the children the nature of their wisdom. They inherit knowledge of their ancestry. All learning, understanding, truth, morality, belief, deeds, work, discovery—everything is passed to their offspring, and it is passed genetically."

There was shuffling around the room as intelligent men and women digested the meaning of what had just been said. The

President inquired, "Are you saying they bear children, and their children are born knowing everything that has been learned in the past by all of their species?"

Mr. Mehra spoke softly, "Yes, nothing is ever lost—nothing, and they learn cumulatively. When one learns they all learn. And that is not all. Learning is their source of life."

Silence reigned again until General Wayland asked, "Learning is their source of life? What does that mean?"

Mr. Mehra answered, "As they mature and learn, their learning is passed to all of their kind. If one is moved or in our language *'loves'* another's discoveries or wisdom, it is communicated and a bond or union is formed and new life is conceived."

"Do you know of their innate intelligence?" asked the President."

"Yes, they are far superior to humans."

"Do you know to what degree?"

"No."

The President spoke as if talking to himself, "My God, they are a race of Einsteins who for millions of years have been learning and passing on their wisdom to more Einsteins who then pass on…"

"Yes," Mr. Mehra answered.

General Dickenson cleared his throat, "Gentlemen, I know we have a lot of brain power around this table but unfortunately I'm just an old warrior, so I would appreciate if you would explain, in very simple terms, what the hell we're talking about."

Dr. Maxwell explained, his tone suggesting he was explaining to himself more than the General.

"General Dickenson, assume you had been born with an IQ of 200. Also, assume that you had been born knowing, not having to learn, but knowing everything that every human being that has ever lived has ever known and learned. And remember they too had IQs of 200. You do not have to learn how to read and write, to add, subtract, or compute quantum physics, or paint the Sistine Chapel, compose the Fifth Symphony or ride a bicycle. You already know that because you were born knowing it because some human who lived before you discovered, experienced, composed, or learned it.

"Add to that genetic formula, the motivation of knowing that the only way you are ever going to experience sex, love, or family is to take this unbelievable wisdom you have inherited and expand upon it. My God, their evolution is perfect. I understand why they consider us barbaric primitives—compared to them, we are."

Jason smiled to himself, "It makes sense. The script. They're giving us what we've been...my God, what we're faced with. Is it good or bad? For a thousand generations we've dreamed of a time of no war, no conflict, or as our alien visitors communicated 'tranquility.' I can't begin to fathom what it means. If anyone of us can, that General Dickenson, in my humble opinion, is what the hell we're talking about."

General Dickenson glared at Jason and then looked about the room, "Do the rest of you believe what Dr. Maxwell just said? No offense, doctor."

Silence met him until he broke it.

"Well, what the hell are we supposed to do?"

The President reflected, "You said they responded to three questions. What was the third?"

"Do we want them back?" answered Mr. Mehra.

Blood rushed from the President's face, "You're referring to the question, *Were they responsible for the disappearances?*"

"Yes," responded Mr. Mehra.

CHAPTER TWENTY-SIX

Don Quixote

Vice-President Stewart sat in his office. Blue-white cigar smoke slowly rose toward the ceiling, blended and languished. He ignored the random ringing of his phones and intercom until a faint knock at the door severed his thoughts. "Yes?"

An aide opened his door slightly and a tilted head appeared, "General Dickenson is here, sir."

The Vice-President waved his hand. Fifteen seconds later General Dickenson entered and again sank into burgundy leather. "Tom, I thought I was too old for this, but son-of-a-bitch, my juices are flowing—damn."

The Vice-President smiled faintly, "The President is about to disassemble the armed forces of the United States, and your juices are flowing? Not going to be able to kick much alien ass without an army, General."

"That's bull-wash and you know it. There's no way to dismantle our armed forces in three weeks. Hell, even if we try and go full bore, logistically, it can't be done. Dammit, why do I always have to ask for one of your cigars? As much nookey as I've lined up for you over the years, you'd think a man wouldn't have to ask for a damn cigar."

Stewart slid the box toward the General, "Well, General, did you know that three hours ago the United States UN ambassador communicated to her colleagues in New York that the United States is going to disarm? And our President has instructed our illustrious Secretary of State, Ms. Annabelle E. Rotter, to encourage every country on this planet to do the same. I'm curious, General. How many countries do you think will listen to our pussy President, and where does that leave men like you?"

The General gazed upward and added more smoke to the ceiling, "Good questions but the number of countries that might follow our pussy President might surprise you. First, no weapons

175

that will fire then blue lighting those Apaches and Humvees, damned impressive."

"Disarming the planet," The General, mused, blowing rings of smoke into the air. "We're talking about over three thousand years of military evolution to the tune of hundreds of trillions not to mention a billion or so lives. Do you want to gamble on those damn Vulcans having the balls to blue light every weapon in existence?" His voice grew softer. "You ready to roll the dice? Do you really want to fuck with em'? Tom, think about the power they've displayed so far. Remember what I told you about geniuses a few days ago? Hell, they're not only geniuses; they can't even get a piece of ass unless they learn something. That's motivation. Those bastards are for real."

The Vice-President looked hard at the General, "So what should we do? Disarm? Let them take the whole country? Hell, the whole damn world? Jesus Christ, what then?

"No, no, dammit, when you're in a political dogfight with an unknown, what do you do? Shit, Tom, I don't have to tell you this. You buy time, look for weaknesses, pay for sleaze. Hell, it's the same in the military."

The Vice-President grimaced at the General's cigar ashes falling on a two-thousand-dollar chair.

"So?"

"So, we send a few boys home, park the hardware but keep everything greased. Hell, let the boys plant some trees—build a road. Keeps em' on the payroll. Got to keep em' on payroll, that's crucial. Buy time until we can find a damn bullet that'll work. Oh, did I tell you the AM sound wave cannon works?

The Vice-President came out of his chair, "What? You son-of-a-bitch, how long have you known that?"

The General laughed and raised his hand. More ashes spilled.

"Don't get your whities in a knot. There's good news and bad news. Only got about fifty of the damn things. Found 'em moth-balled at Jackson. Quit making 'em when we went to lasers. And the damn things won't work on anything alive. We tried it on humans, and the boys trying to fire went limp. Tried with hundreds, couldn't do it. Whined about their mother, dad sister, hell their children. Said they saw them and couldn't fire. Then we tried targets—buildings, vehicles, no problem as long as they, now get this, as long as there was no one in the building or vehicle. Figure that one?"

"How do they know if someone is in a building?"

"Beats the hell outta me, but we tried over two hundred and somehow they knew."

The Vice-President ground out his cigar, "Are you telling me the cannon can be fired by men at anything except humans?"

"We can fire the bastards at anything that's not alive."

"Not alive? Are you saying they can fire at a vehicle if no one is in it?"

"Damn Tom, are you slow today or what? That's just what I said. They can fire the damn things at anything not alive."

The Vice-President's eyes widened, "Then they could fire at the alien craft."

"Well, we don't know that yet, but . . ."

"Any other country have em'?"

"Naw, like I said we only made the fifty ourselves. Everybody went to lasers and microwave."

"Do any of the President's groupies know?"

"No. Got those magnificent bastards in safe keeping with boys we can trust."

"What about the ones who tested them?"

"They didn't know what they were testing and when they did, we just said, *'Well, that didn't work'* and sent them back to their units."

"When can we use them?"

"You mean on the alien craft?"

"That's what I mean, General."

"Now Tom, you better think about that. Let me ask you again. Do you really want to fuck with those guys? That blue electricity, or whatever the hell it is, disarmed the planet, paralyzes people, and disintegrates weapons. And they do this when they're just showing off. Hell, they're probably responsible for all those scumbag degenerates disappearing. Imagine what they could do if they got serious or pissed. I think we should keep the little secret of the sound wave cannon on hold for the time being.

"Something else to think about, those bastards may not be here forever. Hell, what if we wake up tomorrow morning and they're gone? Thought about that one? Who's the super power then? The country that has a weapon that works—that's who."

The Vice-President leaned forward, "Can we make more of 'em?"

"Got our boys working on it. Those damned aliens may have underestimated the lengths us humans will go to find something that'll kill you."

CHAPTER TWENTY-SEVEN

Down Time

The President sat with shirt unbuttoned revealing a v-necked T-shirt, while Dr. Bowman's stethoscope searched his partially exposed chest.

Dr. Bowman appeared old and frail but razor brown eyes and a hawkish face mirrored his demeanor. His black suit and thinning sprouts of corn-silk hair were impeccable. A pocket-watch chain gated his vest in gold. He lifted the stethoscope from the President's chest then held his patient's wrist, and with a tilted head eyed his gold watch. Thirty seconds later, he returned the watch to his vest. Dr. Bowman's voice was a crisp, abrupt, New England monotone.

"Mr. President, I was your mother's physician when you were born some fifty seven years ago. Been taking care of you since. Took care of your parents too."

He hesitated, folded his arms, and looked at the President.

"Do you have complaints about the care I provided your parents?"

The President stopped buttoning his shirt, "Well, of course not Dr. Bowman, you've always..."

"Do you have complaints about the care you've received the past fifty seven years?"

The President leaned forward, "Doctor Bowman you've always been my family's physician and the service you've given us has been the most..."

"Well, Mr. President, I appreciate that and I'm willing to continue doing so, but unless you get six hours sleep in the next seven you'll have to find yourself another doctor. Won't have any part of caring for a President who dies in the office under my care. Would not reflect well on Harvard Medical. I need your decision now. Got other patients to tend."

The Cleansing

The President smiled as he continued buttoning his shirt. He picked up the phone. "Ann, yeah, he's here—have to take a nap, would you get..."

"Six hours, Mr. President."

The President cupped the phone, "And tell the others to do the same." The President hung up the phone and smiled again toward Dr. Bowman. "Doctor, just out of curiosity, how many hours sleep are ninety-year-old physicians getting these days?"

Dr. Bowman cut his eyes to the President, picked up his bag and headed for the door. "Six hours in the next seven, Mr. President."

Sleeping in six-hour shifts, via lottery, was mandated. Sarah's name came up in the first group so she retreated to one of the small rooms in the Pentagon that resembled a budget motel room. It featured olive drab walls, brown carpet and no windows. The bathroom door opened on the left as one entered, while on the right, in an open closet, hung lonely wire hangers that trailed as she passed. Beyond the bathroom and hangers the room opened and contained a single but serviceable bed. A small television, computer, and FAX were assembled on a table against the back wall. A small wooden table beside the bed was home for the telephone, a fluorescent clock and a TV remote.

Sarah ignored everything but the shower and bed. The shower was warm, the towel scratchy and with damp hair, she crawled under clean sheets and was asleep in seconds. She awoke, glanced at the clock, and it was seven hours later. She had overslept and no one had awakened her.

Guess the world still exists, she thought, noticing Josh sitting at the table, to her side, engrossed in a computer printout. He read from a small lamp shielded with a book, trying not to wake her. Sarah lay still and watched.

"How'd he get out of quarantine so soon?"

They hadn't had any time together since the landings. She had been immersed in examining the blue haze tapes, and repeating over and over to Homeland Security what she and Josh had observed. After the encounter in the Empty Quarter he, the remainder of the crew, and the children were the property of scientists and MDs.

She thought of their relationship and smiled. If she tried to explain to friends, anyone, what it had been like, they'd roll their eyes then lock her up. The blue haze, aliens, then going to meet the aliens—naked. She warned herself on their fourth date, but she wouldn't listen—hadn't listened. *Well, there was the sex.* She smiled again, remembering a date.

Late getting to his trailer, she'd gotten yet another speeding ticket. She had burst through his door to find him sitting, feet propped in his recliner, engrossed in a book.

"Well, there goes my driver's license."

Josh looked confused, "Your license?"

"Yes, my driver's license. Got my fourth ticket. Your fault, you know."

She threw the wadded up ticket at him. Josh caught the ticket with his left hand and smiled, "My fault?"

"Yes, I was hurrying to get here to see you. You're supposed to be so smart. How can I get out of this?"

"You're the UN ambassador's daughter and you're asking me how to get out of a speeding ticket?"

Sarah ruffled her hair and plopped onto the couch, "Well, you should be good for something."

Josh grinned and tossed the ticket back at her. She let it fall to the floor.

"I don't use the UN daughter thing. I don't use 'mommie' to get me out of trouble. Nothing admirable on my part. Imagine what the tabloids would do with the UN ambassador's daughter using influence to get out of speeding tickets. Might have to this time, though.. They will take away my license."

Josh didn't answer. Instead he looked back at his book and changed the subject, which he did when he considered the topic trivial. He offered the book to her.

"Interesting book. Tell me, who are your heroes?"

"My heroes?"

"Yeah."

"Sojourner Truth, Maria Burg. Yours?"

He looked up but not at her.

The Cleansing

"Cleisthenes, Wang Weilan, Lo Chou Lee.." God, Lo Chou Lee: he was so young and there's nothing in his background, his life to explain...can you imagine?"

He looked at her as if she knew exactly what he was talking about.

Later that evening, as Sarah drove to her apartment, she couldn't believe what she was doing. It was midnight and she drove past her turn-off and headed to the university mall. Here she pulled in next to Pal-Mart, to Music Land. They stayed open all night. She found Marian McPortland and bought two of her CDs. Then she headed to the university library. She spent two hours looking up Cleisthenes, Wang Weilan and Lo Chou Lee. She found Wang Weilan and Cleisthenes. Driving back to her apartment, she thought, "Why is it, every time I see him I wind up with my feet in the air, then have to go to the library to figure out something he said."

She'd watched him read long enough, "Hey, turkey butt."

Josh looked up from the printout and smiled, "Well, when your butt is as cute as mine..."

Wasn't like him to be humorous. She liked it. Liked his butt, too. "Turkey butt ugly, if you ask me."

He continued to smile, "Then why am I getting emails—lots of emails?"

"Well, if I showed my butt to the whole world on SNN, I'd..."

Josh, wide eyed, interrupted, "SNN?"

"Oh, you haven't heard about that. Oh yeah, they picked it up and showed you buck naked in prime time, over and over and have you seen the pictures they ran on the front page of '*USA TODAY?'* "

Sarah stood and wiggled her butt at Josh.

Josh swallowed, "They showed me in the Empty Quarter on *SNN?* Did they show me going and...coming?"

"Oh, yeah. What're you studying?"

"With the little fuzzy rectangle, right?" begged Josh.

Sarah wiggled her eyebrows, "What's with the printout?"

Josh looked at the pages in his hand, "Oh, just—just checking over the script. HS has theories on the four items and they make sense. Well, as much as they can make sense, except for the last one, *'reproduction of Homo sapiens will cease.'* "

Sarah swung her feet from the bed to the floor.

"Last I heard, babies are still being born."

Josh looked at the printout.

"Got people all over the country, actually, all over the world spot checking with hospitals, OBs, clinics, midwives and women are still reporting pregnancies."

He stopped and studied the top of the printout. He leaned forward and ran his finger along the top. His eyes widened and he hurriedly flipped through the papers stopping to check pages at the top. He stood up abruptly and started for the door, stopped as if remembering, and turned to Sarah.

"You get some sleep. I have to check on something."

"I just slept more than I was supposed to. What's wrong?"

"It's probably nothing, but I have to…"

Before she could respond, he was out the door.

CHAPTER TWENTY-EIGHT

Vengeance Revisited

Ishmael Zolef awoke at 5 a.m. to the sound of annoying fluorescent beeps of an alarm radio. He lay in his bed for a luxurious ten minutes relishing an infidel's day. The number of times and ways they would poison themselves. Millions rising from poisoned padded synthetic foam rubber mattresses, fumbling at a button for five more minutes, turning up contaminated heat to shower, the soap they would use, their synthetic clothing, even their cosmetics. He thought of the millions of morning medications, the presumptuous luxury of carpeting and tile. He envisioned piggish people preparing breakfasts packaged in wax coated cardboard. They would drive gas consuming cars on tires of synthetic rubber to buildings, offices and work places all constructed, heated and furnished with the same radioactive materials as their homes.

Ishmael leaned back against his pillow. "*Oil is their opiate and none of them will escape—none.*"

The tankers had been leaving Jazireh-ye Khark laden with microscopic death for two months. They arrived at the ports of the western world, Brussels, Manchester, Newfoundland, Melbourne, Galveston and Houston. Their crude pumped to the massive petroleum refineries. There, hundreds of thousands of barrels would be refined in the giant fractionating towers. Here the oil would be mixed with light, middle and heavy distillates and solvents to make hundreds of products from petroleum derivatives. Black Death, level three radioactive waste, distributed to millions in their homes, businesses, hospitals, and schools. It had taken twelve years.

Ishmael stood at his bedroom window and gazed out toward the great oil terminal of Kharg Island and whispered, "God is great."

The Cleansing

CHAPTER TWENTY-NINE

Confusion

Two weeks later

Homeland Security was meeting with the President, Vice-President, the director of the Ballistic Missile Defense Organization, Chief of Naval Operations, the Secretary of Defense, General Wayland, General Dickenson and the CIA associate director.

General Wayland was in the process of finishing his report on the military stand down.

"In conclusion, ladies and gentlemen, all operations of our military, in compliance with the President's orders, are preparing for disassembling. However, we cannot disengage two million men and women and mothball eight trillion dollars in weapons and equipment, scattered all over the globe, in three weeks. And, as I explained earlier, total disarmament is impossible. In fact, we're not sure what is meant by *'armies of the planet will cease to exist.'* If we don't have weapons that work, do we exist as an armed force? We have sixty percent of our men and women on leave until further notice. In the next seven days we will have our navy in port, scattered all over the globe, but in port. The remaining forty percent are continuing the disarmament—logistics, maintenance, moth balling, security operations, that sort of thing.

"However, there's so much in the military we cannot disassemble. Someone has to monitor satellites, communication centers, maintain security around nuclear weapons, borders, international boundaries, not to mention maintaining and securing what we're mothballing. Will this be interpreted as not disarming?"

General Dickenson asked, "What do we do with the men and women we're mustering out? Do we put them planting shrubbery and picking up trash? We need clarification on what the hell we're supposed to be doing. Communication with two children

185

and a monk—what the hell are we thinking?" He shook his head in disbelief.

"And the other issues aren't getting any better. Those in our military, civilian population, the Pentagon and Congress who are opposed to disarming are after my head. Resignations by our officers and enlisted men are coming in by the hundreds every day. I'm talking about men and women who would die for their country, and salute the flag as they did. They believe *'we're being duped.'* And the truth is, if we continue our present course, we'll be helpless in the presence of not only the aliens, but any country that finds a weapon that works."

Vice-President Stewart turned and spoke, "Mr. President, with due respect, I have to agree with General Dickenson. Consider what we're doing. First, we have no weapons that work then we disband our armed forces? What'll we do if these aliens decide they want to start disintegrating more than Apaches? What if we find weapons or ammunition that work? We won't have the forces in place to use what we find. And if another country finds a weapon that works, who's the super power then? No one has offered an explanation as to why they want us to disarm. If they are so advanced, why do they fear our military?"

An uneasy silence filled the room until the President raised a question.

"Gentlemen, we've been through this a dozen times the last two weeks. Believe me—I know the heat we're getting. General Wayland, what's the status of NATO and other countries?"

"Mr. President, most countries are disarming or putting on a good front. Their observing of the Apaches disintegrating was apparently very convincing. They're marshalling out their men and women and storing equipment. But I do emphasize *most countries*. There are exceptions. Libya, France, Australia, North Korea, Iraq and Burma have stated they are not going to disarm, and there are a number of others who have not yet begun. Guess they'll be our guinea pigs."

A major general asked, "Guinea pigs?"

General Wayland responded, "Yes. The aliens gave us three weeks to disband. What will happen to those who don't? We'll know in a week."

The Cleansing

"Jason, this is as good a time as any to bring everyone up to date on what we discussed before the meeting."

Dr. Maxwell moved in his chair.

"Yes sir, Mr. President. Gentlemen, you'll recall the third item in the script is 'discontinuance of planet destruction and extinction of species,' and Mr. Mehra told us one of the aliens communicated the same message.

Jason handed the President copies of a three-page report. He took one and passed the others on. "The details of what I am about to say are contained in the report. Summarizing, destroying rain forests has ceased—period. Clear cutting equipment won't run, fires to clear the forests are extinguished by a blue haze. It began in the rain forests of Madagascar and the Philippines and spread to rain forests in South America. We've had reports of poachers in south central Vietnam 'freezing up' trying to poach the red-shanked Douc Langur. That's an endangered Asian monkey. The same is true of hunters around the Iberian Peninsula.

"We have reports from ocean fishing trawlers off the New Zealand coast. Their trawling equipment has ceased to function. There's an endangered dolphin along that coast. Similar events are occurring in Antarctica, Russia, and Africa. It appears to be selective. Those activities that are affecting the habitat of endangered species, and I include plant species, are being terminated.

"We've had incidents in the states. The logging of redwoods has come to a halt, and the dams blocking the River Sockeye Salmon from the Pacific to Idaho's Redfish Lake where they spawn, have disappeared."

General Dickenson stood, "Did you say disappeared?"

"Yes General, I did. As of seventy-two hours ago, they were gone. Strip-mining in West Virginia and Kentucky and clear cutting in Alabama has ceased. Gentlemen, they mean it when they say the destruction of plant species and animal life will cease.

"I am happy to report that the script item *'cessation of the reproduction of Homo sapiens'* hasn't happened yet. Children are still being born, and at a normal rate," Maxwell concluded.

The President glanced around the room.

187

The Cleansing

"And what Jason just said is part of the reason I decided to comply with the alien's suggestion that we disarm, and the fact that there has been no aggression by the aliens."

"Disintegrating the Apaches was, in my opinion sir, an overt act of hostility," the Vice-President interjected. If any country on this planet did that it would be considered an act of war. Destroying our economy, the timber industry, oil refining, fishing, mining, not to mention the defense industry. Jesus! And our response is to disarm. Mr. President, with all due respect, disarming is insane."

The President answered softly, "You have a lot of folks who agree with you—but Tom, we're already disarmed. We have no weapons. And that demonstration with the Apaches I think was just a sample, a small sample of their capabilities."

"What are we going to do? Roll over and let these alien bastards take over the planet?" The Vice-President's voice rose. "Never in the history of this country have we disarmed. Mr. President, it's time somebody told you that we're at war. And the last time I checked, disarming is the same as an unconditional surrender. And sir, my legacy is not going to be presiding over the surrender of our country. No sir, not on my watch."

The room became a tomb. The President turned ashen but composed himself before he spoke, "Ladies and gentlemen, could you give us the room?"

There was a slight pause as people languished in stunned reaction then sudden movement to leave. The President and Vice-President sat alone facing each other.

"Tom, we're all under stress. I'll assume that was the reason for what you just said. But it is important for you to remember that my Presidency is my watch, not yours." The Vice-President leaned forward to speak but the President stopped him.

"I'm not finished."

The Vice-President clinched his jaw and sat back. The President took a deep breath and again collected himself. "You don't have to tell me we're in a crisis. And, I'll be the first to admit I need advice, all the advice I can get. But when you disagree with me, you will express it with respect or in private."

"Sir, I apologize," the Vice-President replied. "But what if you're wrong, like you were with Medler?" J.T. Medler had been named Secretary of Agriculture and had to resign four months later for embezzlement.

The President's look told him, without speaking that he knew he was lying. He was not sorry.

"Tom, as my Vice-President, I expect your support on final decisions."

"I understand what you expect, sir. Anything else?"

"No."

The Vice-President stood, and walked to the door.

Two minutes later, the meeting continued without the Vice-President.

General Dickenson stated cautiously, "Mr. President, we still don't know what we'll do if they become aggressive."

The President looked at the table and didn't respond.

"Mr. President, the Aussies are equipping their men with cross bows. We have flammable liquids that still work— gasoline, heating oil, kerosene, and we do have incendiaries."

"And when your men try to use them, what happens?"

There was a pause, "Well sir, they…they can't do it."

"And when the Aussies try to use their cross bows, what happens?"

"The same thing, sir.

The President looked about the room, "Are there any other questions—suggestions?"

No one spoke.

"We have one other issue. Jason, would you like to introduce our guest."

Jason stood and introduced, "Ladies and gentlemen, Dr. Weldon of Hopkins Medical Center."

Dr. Weldon, a gangly, tweedy man in his fifties, discarded his pipe, stood and in an English accent addressed the group.

"Concerning this 'melancholy' that paralyzes those attempting to be aggressive, we may have our first breakthrough, as to explanation. Mr. Joshua Jones is to be credited with uncovering the initial clue. Six months ago, an article appeared in the New England Journal of Medicine, which stated that a number of coroners and medical examiners throughout the colony had come upon an intriguing phenomenon.

189

The Cleansing

"It seems that while performing autopsies on the brain, they discovered a blue tint on the inner layers of the cerebellum and the core of the hypothalamus. As you may or may not know, those parts of the brain are instrumental in the control of emotions. Numerous labs about the world have analyzed this blue tint. It appears and I emphasize *appears*, to be some sort of protein enzyme that, as yet, has not been identified, except to say that it is the same enzyme found in water samples two weeks after the sighting of the blue haze about the globe. In excess of seven thousand brain autopsies that have been reported, all have revealed this same blue enzyme. It is important to note this includes children as well as adults."

CHAPTER THIRTY

Ramifications

Forty-eight hours later

"Sorry lady, can't go in there," The guard said, stopping her and pointing to his watch.. "Air time, twenty minutes."

Kate Dockery read his badge, noticed he was wearing a firearm, smiled, and dug in her purse for ID.

"Officer Padgett, I'm Kate Dockery and I have an appoint…"

Officer Padgett blurted, "Oh, geez, I thought I recognized . . . I'm sorry, Ms. Dockery. Didn't recognize you. Go right on in. You, uh…you need me to escort, you need me to page somebody?"

"No, but thank you. Mr. Greene is expecting me."

"Yes ma'am, it's close to air time, so you'll find him in the newsroom unless you have an appointment. Then he'll be in his office or wherever you two agreed to, uh, just…just go right on in, Ms. Dockery."

Kate hurried toward the bustle. No one paid her any attention. She saw Ted two seconds before he saw her. He smiled and approached, walked through a handshake and hugged her.

"Kate Dockery, God, you look good. How do you do it?"

Kate had known him since college. He could pass for the same age then and now. Mid-forties, paunchy, short, sidesaddle hairline, hadn't changed a bit—still a model for a TV recliner ad.

"Clean living and honest politics. How are you, Ted?"

"Clean living and honest politics? Like a former wife, no such thing. Excuse me a sec." Ted turned and yelled across the room, "Craig, I'll be in my office. Tell Prissey, when she gets back, to hold everything."

Kate followed Ted across the newsroom, down a wide busy hallway and into his large TV-lined and cluttered office. He moved a stack of newspapers off a couch.

191

The Cleansing

"Sorry. I told the crew to clean up before you, aw hell, I forgot and you know it. Coffee? Good stuff. Burn the hairs off your tongue."

Kate settled into a spot beside clutter as Ted moved his chair to the side of his desk toward her.

"Sounds good. Straight up."

Ted picked up his phone, "Two coffees. One Republican, one Democrat."

Ted hung up the phone and looked to Kate, "Love you, darling, even voted for your man but we have to run it. Won't be any surprises. Unless a civilian says something, but that's not..."

Kate interrupted, "Ted, I'm here to bring you up to date on a couple of things; not asking you to pull a thing. We went over what you sent us and think it's great. Hope you bag a Pulitzer."

Ted scratched his head with one finger as he smiled, "Well, damn, that's great. That's just great."

A knock at the door interrupted, and coffee was delivered. Both sipped and grimaced.

"But you could've told me that on the phone. Why is the Chief of Staff of the President taking the trouble to come see me?" He grinned. "Don't misunderstand, I'm honored, but geez, you guys have to be up to your buns in vulcans or whatever the hell those things are."

Kate took another drink and didn't flinch, "You're right on that, way up to our buns. That's why I'm here."

Kate set her coffee on Ted's desk, "Ever since we went into office you and I have been straight with each other, well, fairly straight. Haven't always agreed, but we've mixed politics and news reporting about as well as friends can."

"Can't argue so far."

Kate looked straight at Ted, "We need a favor."

Ted's head retreated an inch, "How big a favor?"

"A big one. As big as it gets in the news business."

Ted stood, went to the window in his office, closed the blinds and turned to Kate, "How bad is it?'

"We don't know."

"So you want to manipulate what you don't know?"

"Yes."

Ted exhaled, "As far as I know, and I've been here nearly twenty three years, we've never manipulated the news—ever."

Kate smiled. She knew that wasn't true, and so did Ted.

"I know, but you've…we've never encountered anything like this."

Ted's resistance was lame and he knew it, "Well, 9/11, stolen nuclear weapons, air carrying Ebola, Russian-Chinese border conflict, the…"

Kate moved to the edge of her chair, "Ted, nobody on this planet has any control over this. We're…" She stopped herself as Ted walked to the couch, moved more papers and sat down.

"What can you tell me?"

She cut her eyes toward the door, "Got anymore of that coffee?"

The same evening

In the town of Ten Sleep, Wyoming, just south of Big Horn, the Red Moose Bar's red and green lights spilled into the street as the juke box brayed, "Boot Scootin' Boogie." The regulars were taking advantage of the break in the weather. They'd driven miles, from cattle and horse ranches, on dirt roads lined with dirty snow to Highway 16. From there it was a straight shoot to Ten Sleep and the Red Moose.

The mat at the door was mostly ignored. Inside karaoke competed with "Boot Scootin". Players came and went at the pool table. A sign hung over the mirror behind the bar, "No Fukin Fighting." The beer was flowing, but the sawdust on the floor was still dry. It was early.

The TV went unnoticed until 8:55p.m. when Moss reminded Jess, the owner, about the SNN broadcast. Jess unplugged "Boot Scootin" and walked to the karaoke area next to the pool table.

"Hey Stu, could you folks hold it for a while. They wanna hear the broadcast."

"Which one?" Moss threw up a hand, "You want to watch *'Jolly Roger?'*"

There were two *"yeahs"* and a *"sure."* Moss pulled up a chair and stood on it.

"Okay listen up, listen up."

The bar quieted to bottle clinking and the pop of pool balls.

The Cleansing

"SNN in here."

Moss pointed to the TV closest to the bar, "'*Jolly Roger*' on the karaoke room TV."

Moss pointed toward the next room, "I'm going to adjust sound in both rooms, so don't mess with it."

A dozen customers sauntered to tables in the karaoke room. The pool playing continued.

"Hey, Jess, whadda think of these aliens?"

Jess didn't turn as he adjusted the sound for SNN.

"Well, they're good for business. Whadda you think?

"I think it's the damn government. They've figured out some chemical or something that controls people and put it in our water, and they have to have something to blame it on."

"You tried to hurt anybody lately?"

"Hell no, and I ain't going to. People are crazy to do that. Going to wind up dead or in a straight jacket. I don't care what they say there's something to all 'em psychos disappearing. Now's they's something to that."

Jess took a seat at the bar as SNN began.

"Good evening, ladies and gentlemen. I'm Morton Stillwell. Tonight we are reporting on what many believe may be the most important event in human history—alien life on planet Earth.

On December 24, craft of unknown origin landed in isolated locations on every continent on our planet. Since that day, we, the human species, have experienced changes in the very nature of what we are. Our relationships with each other and other species on the planet have been redefined. Poet Laureate, Anne Towbridge, put it directly and succinctly, *'we are no longer the dominant species, the question is, now what?'* The inability of the human species to engage in acts of violence toward each..."

The competing TV tuned to BBC blared "Welcome to Joll... ly Ro.g...er and here he is." The studio audience rambunctiously hooted, stomped and whistled. Loud applause blended with sound effects. A seven-foot orange-headed man complete with 1950s horn rimmed glasses, yellow and orange plaid suit, and matching bow tie skipped to the stage in front of the audience.

"Thank you, thank you."

The hooting and whistling continued. Jolly Roger, turned his back to the audience, dropped his pants and wiggle a naked mooning butt as the roaring welled. Jolly pulled up his pants and faced the audience.

"Thank you and shut your bloody mouths."

The noise magnified as Jolly Roger grabbed a microphone, "This is BBC. I'm Jolly Roger; who the hell are you?"

In unison the audience bellowed, "Jolly Roger's geeks and freaks."

They roared as Jolly strutted the stage, a cross between a fundamentalist preacher and a pay-for-view wrestler.

"Well, you freaks and geeks, tonight we're going to find out what it's about. We're talking aliens here. What the bloody hell's going on?"

The audience stomped and whistled their approval, "Tell it. Tell it. Tell it."

"Guess you heard we got competition tonight. I ask you—you geeks and freaks, I ask you. Can those honkers from SNN compete with Jolly Roger?"

The roaring audience was panned amid roaring 'no' and whistles. Thumbs pointed down, mid fingers up.

"Will SNN have a woman on their show who's been shagged by an alien?"

The audience roared, "No!".

"Will SNN have a bloke on their show who's pregnant by an alien?"

Again the audience bellowed, "Will SNN have…"

In the bar of the Red Moose, to the right of the SNN TV, two tables back, the conversation was muffled.

"What do you think's going on, Will?"

"Beats me, but I tell you one thing, whatever it is, it's for real. Wake up one day and the whole world's screwed up. Nell still won't come out of the house."

"Really?"

"Yeah, her brother was visiting. We had a few beers and I told him I hadn't done the freeze. He stuck his chin out. I wouldn't try 'till he called me a damn Republican. I started to take a swing and I swear to God he turned into little Jimmy. I froze like a popcicle. Scared Nell half to death. Freaked out. Still won't come out of the house. Probably shouldn't have done that."

SNN continued, "Where do they come from? Why are they here? Have they communicated? Over the next two hours, we are going to attempt to answer these and many other questions that people are asking and facing around the world. We have correspondents stationed at various international locations to provide updates on how this is affecting the day-to-day life of people about the globe. We have a panel of scientists, religious leaders, newspersons and government officials with us who will attempt to explain what all this means. To my left is Senator..."

At the bar, watching SNN, Joe Harley drew on a beer, "Think they'll tell us the truth?"

"Yeah, right. If you was a politican, would you tell the truth about this? How the hell could you? Do you really believe they're disbanding the army?"

"What about all them suicides?"

"May as well tell the truth. It's going to come out anyway."

"Damn, it's already out. No violence, no guns, you think that video was rigged? Man, I don't. Did you see the size of that son-of-a bitch?"

The sound of the TV drew the viewers back.

"Ladies and gentlemen, that is our panel. We are going to begin our discussion with their reactions on the reports of our global correspondents, following this short break."

The sound was muted and three around the table went to the restroom. Two minutes later the sound returned.

"Let's begin with Senator Bosmon. Senator, we'd like to begin by going straight to the issue. Can you bring us up to date on how much the government knows about the craft and the aliens? And, most importantly, what danger they pose?"

"Morton, I'd like to first thank you for inviting me on this panel and I assure you and the American people that I am going to be honest and forthright. This is not a time for deception and stonewalling. Now as to your question—ladies and gentlemen the landings are real and confirmed."

At the table, Hap groaned, "Well, no shit, Sherlock. Damned politicians. The sons-a-bitches land, then there's no violence, unless you want to kill yourself then we don't have any guns, people freaking out. The next thing you know, the army's disbanding and he says they're for real. Fucking politicians"
"Shut up, Hap, I wanna hear this."
Hap did and eyes and ears went back to the Senator.

"First, this is not a government conspiracy, period. Let's be very clear on that. We have pinpointed all the landing sites and, as you said earlier, Morton, they're all over the globe. What danger they pose is, frankly, yet to be determined. But to date there's been no hostility by the intruders. We've advanced troops to the Everglades and to Denali Park. Other countries are getting troops to landing sites within their borders.
"However, the landings are in the most remote, desolate areas you can imagine, sometimes hundreds of miles from human habitat. There are no roads, no access of any kind. So getting to them is going to take…"
Stillwell broke in, "Any updates on firearms and any further information on the landing in the 'Empty Quarter?' "
"We're still working on firearms, but rest assured we're not putting our troops in harm's way without the means to defend themselves. I might add that the rumor that thousands of UN troops have been killed fighting the aliens is ludicrous. The rumor that people who have engaged in violent behavior are dying is not true."
"Senator, are you saying our troops have arms that work? And what about the rumors that our armed forces are disbanding?"
"What I'm saying, Morton, is that our troops can defend themselves."
Stillwell looked into the camera, "I guess we can take that as a *'yes.'* "

The Cleansing

Stillwell turned to another member of the panel, "Dr. Pritchard, as a psychologist, how is all this affecting people in our country and around the world?"

Dr. Pritchard stopped taking notes to answer, "There are so many facets to your question, it's difficult to know where to begin. You stated earlier that this is impacting the very nature of what we are. Perhaps, it's best to address your question as a social issue."

The doctor tapped at her clipboard with a pencil then put it down, "We are not alone. We now share, not own our planet and the universe. The question of millenia has been answered. Social order, as we know it, will never be the same and it could be chaos or utopia."

"Please elaborate, Doctor."

"Well, the first issue is the contemplation of life in the absence of war and violence. The second is our lack of control."

Stillwell interjected, "You mean the aliens are in control?"

"Exactly, the social institutions of humankind, our forms of government, religion, all have an underlying premise, and that is, we are the dominant species. We determine, or define if you will, what our institutions are about. We, the human species, make the rules, determine how we live with each other and nature on this planet. Often, we don't do a very good job of that but social order is based on the fact that we are the dominant species. That is no longer true. We had no control over what has happened, and, more importantly, we have no control over what is going to happen next."

Stillwell asked, "Could you give us an example?"

"Well, religion is a good example. Religions contend their laws and beliefs come from God, but it is their followers, disciples, and believers that interpret, transcribe, and teach those beliefs. Some religious leaders claim to be divinely inspired and even if they are, they are divinely inspired human beings. The same is true of philosophy."

Back at the Red Moose, Will muttered, "Anybody know what the hell she's talking about?"

The President sprawled on a couch in the Oval Office watching SNN. He was supposed to be asleep. There were two knocks at the door. The President hesitated, then responded, "Yes?"

Dr. Maxwell entered, "Hope I'm not disturbing you?"

"No, not at all. Watching the news. Come in."

Jason entered, "Mr. President, it's true about the abortion doctors."

The President put his forefinger and thumb to closed eyes and rubbed resigination,

"Got a recording?"

"Yes, sir."

The President pointed to the player, "Don't want to miss any of this broadcast, but we've got a commercial."

Jason turned on the device, inserted the disk, and pushed "play." The film began. In the operating room the girl was in the stirrups. A nurse comforted her with inaudible words and held her hand. A doctor, entered went to the side of the girl, and talked with her for two minutes. He nodded toward the nurse who gave the girl an injection.

Jason pointed to the TV, "This is where it happens."

The doctor went to his instruments, positioned himself to begin and stopped. The film went to grainy black. Jason turned off the player and muted the sound on the TV.

"It's all over the country. From the reports we're getting, all over the world."

"The violence thing?"

"Yes sir, has to be."

The President slumped, "Just doesn't make sense. Why suicides, the worse kind of violence? Heard about the family in Des Moines?"

"Yes sir, and the one in..."

Jason didn't finish. The President focused on the silent TV, "How can a whole family, even the children?"

The President paused and looked at his hands, "Our visitors still just doing their thing?"

"Yes sir, the same. Stay within a hundred miles of their craft. Still seem to be exploring. Dr. McLain pointed out something. If they communicate telepathically with each other, as they do with the children and Mr. Mehra, what's their range? He thinks they communicate with each other, at will, anytime, anywhere they want."

"Why the bloody hell don't they do the same with us?"

"Good question. Maybe we're not capable, maybe..."

The commercial continued too long.

"And what are they doing here?"

Dr. Maxwell didn't respond.

"Anybody have any ideas on the Truen thing?"

"Got linguistics all over the globe working on it."

"I'll take that as, nothing yet."

"Yes, sir."

The President rubbed his eyes. "Your boys come up with anything on their question?"

"About our unrighteous citizens disappearing?"

"Yeah."

"Nothing new from our last report. Their quesiton implies they know about the disappearances. Might suggest they're responsible, might not."

"Yeah, but do we want them back?"

"Ten good people been working on that. Six say *'no,'* four *'yes.'* The 'no's' argument is that *'never in the history of humankind have we had peace. Now we have a world where the dark hell of violence is gone. No killing, butchering, rape, child abuse, torture, slavery—not to mention war. And to bring back all that misery would be insane.'* Hard to argue that the best thing is to return to the nightmares of human existence."

"So, what's the argument of the ones who say 'Yes'?" asked the President.

"Well, they're human beings, our kind, so to speak, and we should be the one's to deal with them. The one's who argue "yes" have one undeniable point. If we answer "yes" and the degenerates reappear then we know the aliens were responsible and that has implications to horrifying to comprehend."

There was a long silence until the President asked, "Jason, you know who has the second toughest job in the country?"

"The second toughest?"

"Yeah."

"No sir, can't say that I do."

The President rubbed his right arm, "Me."

"You, sir?"

"Yep."

"I figured you for the toughest one, Mr. President."

"No, I'm number two. My wife has the toughest."

Jason smiled, "Yes, sir. I'm not married but have a notion on where you're coming from."

"Know where she is?"

"Yes sir, she's working in therapy centers."

"Right. Started in LA, then St. Louis, then to Houston, and now she's in Charlotte. Working one on one with people. Driving security crazy. Had her on every news channel in the country, every night, working one on one with the people. Just ordinary citizens who need help. Staff says it's great for morale. People seeing the President's wife not afraid, out working. You agree?"

"Yes sir, it was HS's idea."

The President stood up, "Jason, I need a drink, and I need some good news. I'll get us a drink if you can provide the news. Brandy okay?"

"Yes sir, brandy's fine, but I'd be happy to get..." The President waved Jason off, and went to a cabinet. "I do have some good news, Mr. President."

"You've got my attention."

"Well sir, despite that tragic family, suicide rates are down and patient loads at our therapy centers decreased by thirty percent last week. There has not been an assault, a murder, a rape, or any type of violence in this country, or the world as far as we know, in the last three weeks. Oh, and the stock market was actually up a little yesterday, but I guess you know that."

The President returned to the couch, gave a brandy to Jason, turned as if to do something else, hesitated, then sat down, "After dropping forty percent in three weeks, where else could it go?"

There was silence.

"But that is good news about the suicides and the therapy centers. Why do you think that is?"

"Well, sir—time. It's been three weeks. People adjust. People are beginning to ask, 'What has really changed?' "

The Cleansing

The President stopped his drink in midair, "What has changed? What has changed? What do you mean..."

"I know. I know but how many people get up every morning and plan their day around aliens and violence? A third of our citizens are retired. The others go to their jobs, go to school, raise families. Violence is something they hope doesn't happen to them. I know it happens to too many, far too many, but for most it is something they read about, see on TV, movies, worry about. If they've been a victim and survived, it's something they try to forget or put behind them. War for the past five generations has been isolated and by some miracle we've advoided a nuclear holocaust."

"Yeah, but that's not it, Jason. The reason we haven't had total chaos is because no one has seen one. People aren't getting up every morning and finding an alien in their backyard. They're not visible. Like you just said, they're still just something on TV and in the paper. But, what if they take a notion to visit Fifth Avenue or the Beltway, or Main Street, Peoria?"

"What would happen, Mr. President?"

The President contemplated his brandy, "A President's worst nightmare?"

"Worst nightmare, sir?"

"Yeah."

"What's that, sir?"

"What you can't control. What you can't predict. A terrorist nuking New York or releasing some hellish virus in Chicago. The big quake in LA, a nuclear spill that ... "

The President paused, "Presidents pray the biggest problems they'll face are deficits, medical care, social secrutiy, the Mid-East and of course the big one, getting reelected." The President chuckled before returning to a more serious angle, "You spend your career, your life, thinking you want this job. Lie, deceive, promise, sell your soul. Justify it by telling yourself, when you get there you'll be different. If you can make it, you'll do some good. And, the truth is you can if you've got the stones. Despite all the BS, the politics, the sleaze, you can do some good. Then the nightmares hit you. You're it, you're in charge, you're responsible and what if nature or some maniac pushes a button? But God, how could anyone ever anticipate..."

The Cleansing

The President stopped and both men emptied their glasses.

"Kate called earlier, said she bought us a little time. Still think that was a good idea?"

"Yes, sir the broadcast is going like we wanted."

"The children all right?"

"Yes sir, still can't get Laku's family to join him, but he's fine. That Ms. Dupree is one fine lady. She took him in like one of her own."

The President almost smiled, "Yeah, she's a special lady. Mr. Mehra still on his vigil?"

"Yes, sir. Oh, Josh left."

"Josh left? Where'd he go?"

"Children's hospital at Chapel Hill."

"Children's hospital? Oh, that's right, he's in med school. But we'll need him next week."

"Yes, sir, he'll be back. He didn't go because he's a student. He has a niece who's a patient there."

"What?"

Jason filled in the President about Josh's niece.

"Who would have ever thought…does she need anything? Can we help?"

"She's getting excellent care, sir. The best, but it doesn't look good."

Again there was quiet.

"Think they'll communciate next week?"

"Yes sir, I do, but what, I have no idea. Got people working on it but..."

SNN interrupted Jason.

The President headed for another brandy.

"Going to be interesting meeting with Congress after this broadcast. Want to trade jobs?"

Jason shook his head, "Second toughest job in the country. Think I'll pass."

Josh stood with Sarah talking with the doctor. He held his niece, Cindy, who had locked her arms around his neck and her legs around his chest.

"We're hopeful. The swelling in her brain has receded. Almost normal. Her vision has improved. All good signs. But the neural damage, that's something that we just don't know. She's young and that helps. Her brain is still growing, maturing. In cases like this, being young is good. If she were older ... "

The doctor shrugged and Cindy whispered to Josh, "Love you, Uncle Josh."

Josh patted Cindy's back, "Love you too, Cindy."

"Can we go see mommy now?"

Josh didn't respond and Sarah offered, "Cindy, why don't you come with me. We can get an ice cream in the cafeteria."

Cindy grinned and extended her arms to Sarah. Sarah glanced at Josh.

"We girls are going ice creaming. You know where to find us."

Sarah walked away with Cindy wrapped around her. Cindy, looking over Sarah's shoulder, waved to Josh as the doctor continued, "I have to tell you Josh, the odds aren't good."

Josh looked away, "You have my number. You may not know, but I'm involved..."

The doctor chuckled, "Man, everyone knows. You're quite a celebrity around here, especially with the nurses."

"The nurses? Oh yeah, the butt thing."

"Well, it was a little more than butt. You did it up right, *'full monty.'*"

Both smiled and the doctor asked, "What's going on with all that? Got a lot of people scared to death, me included."

"Be able to tell you more after the next visit. Right now what you read and see on TV is about it." Josh shook the doctor's hand. "I appreciate all you're doing. If she needs anything, call me, okay."

"Hey, she's family. We're pestering experts all over the country. Hope you can get back in school soon."

Josh turned to leave, then turned back, "What I called you about the other day—pregnant women are still coming into the clinic?"

"Sure."

"But, I mean women who are recently pregnant, coming in for the first time."

"Yeah."

Josh started to leave again, but asked, "How far along are women, on average, when they come for their first visit?"

"Oh, it varies, one, two, three or four months. Some later, some..."

"Any as early as two or three weeks?"

"No, not often, except for single women, scared teenagers ... oh yeah, and women over forty."

"Had any of those the last three weeks."

"Well, now that you mention it, can't say that I have."

"How about the peds?"

"Can't say." The doctor shrugged.

"Think they'd mind if I ask?"

"No, but you'll have to wait for the next shift for a couple of them. Something wrong?"

Josh shook his head. "Just something we're keeping tabs on."

Sarah and Cindy returned, eating popcicles. They sat and Josh held Cindy for a long time. Cindy smiled, then dropped her popcicle as her eyes crossed. The smile left and she went limp.

Back at the Karaoke room TV, Jolly Roger had the audience roaring again.

"And here's what you blokes been waiting for, that alien seductress, Ms. Lotta Wonderful."

Lotta strutted to the stage to the sound of stripper drums. Black leather contrasted milky white complexion and blond hair to her waist. All was mini except for store-bought breasts and eight-inch heels. Lotta danced to Roger and pulled his head to her cleavage, winked at the audience, and wiggled. The audience thundered approval. Roger pulled away, adjusted his horn rims, wagged a disapproving finger, then his tongue, and buried his head in her breasts. The audience was in a frenzy as Lotta and Jolly pranced to chairs.

"Sorry, Roger, I've been that way since those aliens, well, you know."

"No, we don't know and my geeks and freaks want to know everything."

The audience chanted in cadence, "Lotta, Lotta, Lotta!"

The Cleansing

Will, watching SNN, gestured toward the bar.

"Jess, need another cold one."

Jess looked about the table, "Anybody else?"

A pitcher and four frosted mugs were delivered.

"Why don't they get to the important stuff? Like, why're they messing with us? Where are they from and how long is this going to last? You know we could be their slaves. Have you thought of that?"

"I think that was kinda what that lady psychologist was saying, Will."

Emma, the only female at the table, picked at a beer label, "Hell, it's not like they're in our backyard. Don't you think if they wanted to kick our ass, they'd have done it by now? Far as I'm concerned, what they've done is fine with me. No wars, fighting, killing people. Shit, what's wrong with that?"

"I'll tell you what's wrong with that. What's to keep em' from doing anything they want to with us?"

"How do you know they haven't? That senator's full of it. Dale's boy was with the 3rd Infantry that was sent to the Everglades. Got dysentery. Damn near died. Was in the hospital a week before they could send him home. Said there wasn't a weapon down there that worked. They weren't allowed to talk to anybody outside their company. Couldn't talk to anybody. Couldn't even call home. What's that all about?"

"Now, Candler, where the hell would they find a phone in the Everglades?"

"Well, dick head, ever heard of a cell phone?"

On SNN, Dr. Pritchard looked directly into the camera.

"Let me propose a question. If somehow, by some miracle, any one of us were given a magic wand, and if we waved it three times there would never again be violence or war. How many of us would do it? Think of what that would mean, not only no war it would mean, no murder, rape, no violence of any kind. And that is just the tip of the iceberg.

"I read an article by the sociologist Dr.Blewett just yesterday. He asked, *'what if the enormous amount of money and resources that are consumed for war, defense, and law enforcement were*

206

to become available for addressing social ills'? Imagine the progress the human species could make."

Morton interrupted, "So what's the problem, Doctor?"

"Well, there are two problems; one, we are not the ones waving the magic wand and two is more disturbing—what will the next wave of the wand bring?"

"Good point or points. So, what should we do?"

Dr. Pritchard's voice was soft and reflective, "The human species has never experienced anything like this. This will impact every aspect of our lives. No violence, yet we are defenseless. People are afraid but for the first time in our existence, not of each other. The ramifications—the question is not how this will be recorded in human history, the question is who or what will do the recording."

The same night

On the barbwired border between Albania and Kosovo, the cold mocked the down uniforms of the soldiers. Brittle snow growled under boots as they paced in step to keep warm. One of twenty patients from the mental institution remained. The other nineteen had already been loaded back on the truck. The one remaining dropped his rifle and whined.

"Might hurt em'. Don't want to. Don't want to."

The Kosovo Captain gestured toward a Corporal, "It won't work. Take him back with the others."

The Corporal retrieved the rifle and escorted the last one to the back of a truck and watched him crawl under canvas with the nineteen others. The Captain talked into a cell phone, "They tried sir, but not one would fire, I mean pull the trigger. They're worse than our regulars."

A static voice responded, "I told him this would happen. Just because they're retarded doesn't mean ... "

The static voice paused, "Who are the mental defectives here, Captain?"

"I don't know, sir. Want us to continue with the dogs?"

Resignation responded, "Yes, the dogs. How could they understand? Pray we don't find bombs."

"Sir?"

The Cleansing

There was breathing with the static, "Yes, Captain, continue with the dogs for ten minutes then take them back and you and your men get some sleep."

"Yes, sir."

For ten minutes, the Captain and his men watched pack-laden German Shepherds avoid barbwire, cross the border, and penetrate Albania for two hundred meters then return.

The same night

The gray pickup pulled to the curb in south side Chicago on Fifth. A few brick apartments stood as a refuge amidst vacant lots, abandoned buildings, and iron-gated businesses. Traffic was crisp, looking for drugs or prostitutes or both and were obliged. Black teenagers, wearing red headbands, ganged about on the other side of the street selling and directing requests. Two white men and a woman in their mid-twenties emerged from the pickup. The skinhead men and woman wore camouflage bought from *Pal-Mart* with home-made armbanded swastikas. The swastikas were backward.

All three carried Uzis. They pointed the Uzis at the black teenagers and jerked their arms, mocking fire.

"Hey, niggers, want some of this? Hey, any you mother fuckers, want some of this?"

The black teenagers locked on the yelling skinheads.

"Hey, we're talking to you, nigger. Ain't you going to do something about it?"

The three laughed and poked each other with their Uzis.

"Popcicle darkies, come on, let's see it."

"Hey, don't you apes hear too good? We'll come over there so you monkies can hear us."

The three crossed the street and faced six teenagers who responded, "Well, would you looky here, got us some honky dicks. Damn man, where you get hair cuts like that? Yo' mother quit fucking your barber? Hey bitch, what'd you bring them dick heads with you for? I told you I don't go for no watching. You suck mine like we always do—right after you do the brothers."

The skinhead female pointed her Uzi, "Like white meat, don't you, nigger? Want to lick on mine?"

208

She pulled up her shirt revealing breasts, "Bet you'd like some of this, wouldn't you, ape head?"

She took the hand of one of the skin heads and rubbed it on her breasts. The teenagers turned toward each other.

"Aw man, would you look at that. It's a family thing. They brother and sister. Now, bitch, I told you about pointing them things at me. You call them tits? Your momma, she got fine ones. She know you growed something like that, she'd whup your ass."

"Momma? Shit, her daddy got better tits than that. Hell, her brothers tell you that."

The bantering continued until the skinheads got bored, "Come on. 'Bout time for these niggers to go fuck their momma. I need a beer."

The bangers hooted and laughed, "Can't leave now. Just getting started. Ain't through yet."

One of the teenagers fell to his knees laughing and pointed across the street.

"What's so funny ape dick?"

The female skinhead looked across the street at their pickup and shrieked. It was swarmed by defecating and urinating black teenagers inside and out.

Sixty seconds later

The SNN broadcast had gone to commercial. Jolly Roger had long since broken with the tradition of scheduling commercials at the same time as other programs. If they channeled to him, he would keep them. And sixty percent of the time he was right. Audience participants were having their fifteen seconds.

"I don't care if you are knocked up by an alien, Lotta. Still love you. Will you marry me?"

Lotta smiled, "Well, you are a cute thing. Think you could handle a Lotta?"

"Oh, Lotta, I'd bust trying."

"You rich?"

"No, but I got a good job. Drive a bud truck."

"Oh, I do love my ale."

"Marry me, Lotta, and you can have all the booze and cute thing you want."

The Cleansing

Lotta stood and grabbed his crotch, "Well, cutey, you sure you want to marry a man?"

The audience whistled and jeered at the boy now richer by a thousand dollars.

The SNN commercial ended.

"But the psychological trauma, may just be the tip of the iceberg. The way this has come about has many so afraid they won't leave their homes. Many are in financial ruin because of the crashing market..."

The beer had begun to take effect at the Red Moose.

"Jeb, you been hurt by the market any?"

"Took twenty head to market last week. Got eighty cents a pound. Eighty damn cents. Ever heard of it being that low?"

Emma waved at Jeb, "Hey, I want to hear this next guy."

"Who is he?"

"Dr. Perez. He's smart."

"Where's he from?"

"I don't know. Some college. Hush, I want to hear this."

The table obliged.

"Dr. Perez, you teach sociology at the University of Montana. How are your students reacting to all this?"

Dr. Perez leaned back in his chair. His bow tie, sweater vest, and narrow glasses were professorial; however, his beard and girth garnished his appearance with a santa twinkle. "I'm pleased with their reaction. They ask a lot of questions and I think they're asking the right ones."

"What are they asking, professor?"

"They're fascinated with the obvious intelligence of our visitors. Dr. Pritchard stated they've changed our very nature. My students want to know how. And that, ladies and gentlemen, is the isssue. That is the issue."

"Please explain, professor."

Dr. Perez leaned toward the camera, "Every semester I teach a graduate seminar entitled '*Religion and Philosophy for the New Millenium.*' The first assignment is to explain the characteristics of a perfect society. These students are advanced graduate students, very sophisticated, so they roll their eyes at this sophomoric intrusion on their intellect but they indulge me ... it's the first day of class."

"I get answers you would expect: world peace, eradication of disease, poverty, absence of violence, freedom and democracy throughout the world, etc., etc. Since they're graduate students, their answers are usually well articulated, a bit better than their sophomore answers."

Dr. Perez rubbed the front of his massive girth, "Then, I give the students their next assignment. The assignment is 'Explain, in detail, the social processes required to make your "Perfect Society" a reality.' Oh, the anguish I get from that. For those that explain with religion, I remind them of the horrors of the crusades, the Dark ages, the Salem witch trials along with the past thousand years of terrorism in the Middle East and give them back their papers to rewrite. Some cop out saying the cost of solving such problems makes solution impractical or impossible. I counter with, 'in this assignment cost is no object.' If you need billions, trillions fine, you have it, and I return their papers. After a few rewrites my students learn, as we have experienced as a species for thousands of years, that defining our problems is easy, finding solutions, that's another story."

Morton Stillwell interjected, "So what's your point, professor?"

Dr. Perez looked down then at Stillwell, "We have some very intelligent people gathered here tonight. Can any of us define a system, method, model of any kind—political, religious, economic, that would solve the global problems of war, poverty, violence, pollution, disease? The point is, for the first time in our history, we have such a model. An imposed model, but nevertheless a model. My students ask, if our visitors are capable of that, and obviously they are; can they provide us a cure for cancer? For AIDS? Can they tell us how to save our environment? How to cure the mentally ill? My brightest students ask, if they can change our nature, can they teach us of our nature? Is there a God? Can they tell us our future? Of other species in the universe? Of life and death?"

Morton Stillwell asked, "Do your students think they can do those things?"

The Cleansing

Dr. Perez took off his glasses and examined them, "Well, like us, they don't know, but they've already given us world peace. Good questions, though, don't you think?"

"But don't the students fear domination, control, what they'll do next?"

"Yes, of course, but they point out that we've always been dominated and controlled. Not by aliens but by war, fear, violence, governments, disease, nature, heredity. Don't misunderstand; my students are not naïve. They are well aware this could be our undoing, but some hold out the hope that it could be our salvation."

"What do you think, Professor?"

"I agree with my students."

"And what do you tell them?"

Professor Perez smiled, "That I agree."

Stillwell looked away from Dr. Perez to the camera.

"I think this would be a good time to go to our first correspondent in the field." Stillwell turned to his panel, "Dr. Wells, as a man who opens every Senate session of our Congress with a prayer, we would like your opinion on this next report. Ladies and gentlemen, we'll return in two minutes."

Back at the Red Moose, Emma tilted her beer toward the TV, "Told you he was smart."

Joe commented as he stood up, "He's either smart or a damn fool. I gotta pee. Will, you want to shoot a round?"

Joe pointed to a vacated pool table.

"Not right now. Want to watch this."

"Ladies and gentlemen, welcome back to our report. We're going live now to correspondant Marie Pennington in northern Afghanistan."

The TV scene faded to Marie standing on a dusty sand and dirt road in a remote village ten miles north of Kabul. A few old trucks mingled with horse drawn wagons stirring dust, causing walking villagers to pull at their veils and scarfs. Marie was surrounded by a dozen women. They were dressed in black that extended from feet to head. Only their eyes could be seen peering through veiled mesh.

212

"Marie, hope you can hear us," Stillwell said. "I assume that's you. Hard to tell with your outfit. Please describe what's going on there?"

Marie pushed at her ear piece then talked into a handheld microphone.

"It is me and I can hear you just fine, Morton. I'm here north of Kabul in the village of Kauti. It is considered the stronghold of Muslim fundamentalists and has remained that way since 9/11. What has and is taking place here is quite remarkable."

Marie gestured to the women gathered about her, "As you can see, the women still wear burquas. As you know from the history of 9/11., in 1996, when the Taliban took over Madhu, the government of Afghanistan, unbelievably strict rules were instituted for women. The burqua became required dress. A woman caught in public not wearing a burqua, could be beaten or stoned to death. Women were stoned for not having a veil mesh about their face. Since 9/11 this has changed in most of Afghanistan but here in Kauti fundamentalists still rule, and women continue to wear burquas and veils. In fact, I would not be allowed here were it not for what is happening."

Marie looked to the woman on her left, "This is Tera. Her sister was killed in 1997 for driving. Her seven year old son had been hit by a truck and she was taking him to the hospital."

Marie turned to another of the women, "In 1999 Lea's mother was stoned for being seen walking with a man who was not a relative. Between 1996 and 2001 women were not allowed to work. Women were not allowed to go out in public without a male relative as an escort, and I'm talking about professional women. Professors, lawyers, doctors, and artists were confined to houses with blackened windows.

"Many women, including four of the ones you see here, had no male relatives or husbands. Since they were banned from working, they were reduced to begging in the streets. It was either beg or starve. As you might guess, depression, suicides, all sorts of mental illness among women became epidemic. No medical treatment was available because they were women. Under Taliban, men, husbands, or mobs had the right, fundamentalists say the moral obligation, to stone and kill women for the slightest offense.

The Cleansing

"This is still true is many of the rural southern and northern provinces. It is more, how shall I say, more evasive now. If a woman is beaten or disappears for some violation, no one reports it. Women still live in fear, and until recently were afraid to speak out."

"How has that changed, Marie?" asked Morton.

"Well, rather than tell you, Morton, we're going to show you, and I can assure you less than a month ago we would have been stoned for what we are about to do."

On SNN, in the presence of millions of viewers, Marie and the women took off their burquas and veils revealing attractive ladies in Western suits, dresses, and slacks. The women giggled nervously, and huddled close. Horns bellowed, and men could be heard yelling.

"Morton, a few weeks ago the women you see about me could have disappeared in the night for what we are going to do."

"Unbelievable. What are the men yelling?"

"Oh, different things, mostly whore and infidel."

"How are the religious leaders in the area reacting?"

"They believe the aliens are the devil. Many of them are saying this is the end of the world. They truly believe this. Although suicide is strictly forbidden under Taliban law it has been a daily occurrence among the fundamentalists. They believe the devil is killing their God."

Morton asked, "Do any of the women believe this? I mean do they believe the aliens are the devil?"

"Yes, some do. Many women here are very devout and believe their religious beliefs have been stolen by the devil aliens. But the overwhelming majority of women, especially the educated, feel liberated."

"Thank you, Marie. Ladies and gentlemen, that was Marie Pennington reporting live from Afghanistan. We'll get the reaction of Reverend Wells right after this break."

Thirty minutes earlier

In the Kimberly plateau, rangers of the First Austrilian Airborne had made it to the three alien craft. First Lieutenant Bridger and his men worked twenty-four hours securing the steel netting. Bridger checked, double-checked and triple-checked the netting before calling in the halftracks. It had taken a week of round-the-clock days to helicopter in sections of the two halftracks. It had taken another week to assemble.

"Sir, the craft is secure."

In the distance, diesel engines coughed then spewed the stench of power. They tracked the mountain to the rangers where they coughed again, lurched to a stop, and waited. Three-inch steel cables, secured to winches on the halftracks, were linked to the stainless steel rings of the netting. Again the lieutenant triple-checked.

"She's secure, sir."

"All right Corporal, give it a go."

Bridger pumped his right arm up and down at the drivers. First gear strained, belching gray-black diesel. Twelve hundred horse power drove bladed steel terrets ripping into the earth. With the first movement of the craft, the blue began. Silent fluorescent light encircled the halftracks. Doors flung open and four drivers jumped from the trucks and ran. Two stopped at fifty yards and looked back, one at a hundred. The last one didn't.

It lasted fifteen seconds. The trucks and netting were gone. No traces, no ashes, no smouldering, nothing. The lieutenant looked at his mesmerized men. He whispered into his communication radio, "It didn't work, sir."

There was a pause, "No, sir, the men are fine, got one we need to chase down but ..." Another pause, "We recorded it, sir. Think it best you see for yourself."

In Eastern Tennessee, four miles west of Erwin, two miles up Power Branch past Flag Pond, the SNN newsman stood in the middle of the encampment. Campfires breathed trails of gray-blue smoke about camping trailers. Men leaned on trucks as women hung out clothes with one eye on children playing in a creek.

"Morton, I'm standing in the encampment of a group that calls themselves 'Angels of the Universe.' The group numbers about seventy and claim to worship the aliens. Standing with me is their leader, Mr. David Phelps."

The Cleansing

David stood, looking at the ground. He removed his western-style hat and finger combed his blond flowing hair. He was young, in his twenties, but the gray in his blonde beard didn't show it. His shirtless overalls tried to hide a lean gaunt body, but without a shirt, it couldn't.

"Mr. Phelps, how long has your group been worshipping the aliens?"

"Well, we don't consider them aliens. We're all part of the same universe. We've been worshipping them all our lives, but didn't know it until they came."

"What exactly do you believe, and how do you practice worshipping them?"

"We believe the aliens are a manisfestation of God and we don't practice worshipping them, we live it."

"How do you do that?"

"By trying to live what they're teaching us."

"Which is?"

"Non-violence and peace." He said, his tone suggesting it should be obvious.

"What do you hope to accomplish?"

"Our hope is to be worthy of their teaching."

"Have any of your members seen or communicated with an alien?"

"No, but we will; we all will."

"Earlier we spoke with one of your followers. He said your father had seen an alien."

"Yes."

"Where was that?"

"In Antarctica."

"Is he here? Can we talk with him?"

"No," Phelps shook his head. "He's still in Antarctica."

"Did you know the aliens were coming?"

"No, but all of us have prayed for our children. No war, peace, harmony. Imagine the life they can have now."

"Do you consider yourselves a cult?"

"No, we have no rites or ceremonies. There are no rituals. What you see here are just people who share the belief that humankind should live in peace."

"Well, Morton, there you have it. A group in the hills of Eastern Tennessee who claim the aliens are gods."

"Thank you, Jim, we ..."

As the camera faded away from the camp, a small girl ran toward the cameraman and pointed a stick at him.

"Bang, bang."

David put himself between the cameraman and the girl. A chasing mother picked the little girl up. The picture and audio were back to Morton. As David Phelps and the mother holding the little girl walked back to the camp, the mother asked, "Did they notice? Do you think they noticed?"

David Phlelps looked to the sky, "Pray they didn't."

The President looked away from the TV to Jason.

"What's a good chaser for brandy?"

Jason shook his head, "Asking the wrong man, Mr. President. Not much of a drinker."

"Well, we've seen people who believe they're the devil and some who believe they're gods. Got three countries sponsoring a bill in the UN wanting to proclaim them the enemies of humankind. Gayle flew up to try to put out the fire. Earth's welcome wagon with a razor wire chaser. Heard about the fraternity at UT?"

"You're talking about the record for freezing?"

"Yeah, how many did they get?" The president curiously asked.

"Some sophmore did it over a hundred times."

"You serious? Is he all right?"

"He's fine."

"Wonder why he stopped?"

"The guy he was trying to stab got nervous." Did you hear about the experiment at Maximum Security Center in Florida?"

The President thought for a moment. "The one we built for psychos?"

"Yes, serial killers, predators, mass murderers, real stand up bunch of guys and got a few ladies in the mix, too. Houses about four hundred."

"We're running experiments on those people?" Annoyance registered in the President's voice. "First I've heard about it."

The Cleansing

"Divided them into two groups. Told members of the one group if they could stab another prisoner they'd be set free. The intended victim, also a volunteer and got special privileges for volunteering, sat in a chair, their back to the one intending to stab. They asked the sceond group of prisoners to do the same, only the intended victim was an obvious dummy."

The President swilled his last sip of brandy, "We're running experiments trying to kill someone?"

"Yes sir, afraid so."

"Since I haven't heard anything about this, let me guess. Even the psychos couldn't stab anyone."

"Correct, and the dummies?"

"I'd guess they couldn't maim the dummies either."

"Wrong on that." Jason shook his head slowly. "Got dead dummies all over the place. But that's not the interesting part. We covered the intended victims with a blanket. Couldn't tell if they were a dummy or a live human being. Told the psychos to take a shot. Care to guess."

"You're joking. What sick mind— how'd it turn out?"

"Couldn't stab the live ones but had no problem with the dummies."

"Are you sure they couldn't tell the difference?"

"Ran all sort of test—blood, urine, galvanic skin response, brain wave activity, and so forth. Been repeating the tests every day since. We're sure, sir."

The President hesitated then asked, "Did you try?"

"Took me hours to get up the nerve. Kept thinking what if I can."

"And?"

"Finally tried and got the feeling you get just before you fall asleep, and then the live one was my mother, dummy no problem and sir, I couldn't see what was under that blanket, but I could tell the difference. There's a little warmth when you come out of it, then you feel fine, exhilarated actually."

The President looked at the bottom of his empty glass, "Imagine, exhilarated because you can't harm someone. Wonder why none of those prisoners disappeared?"

218

"We think it's because they're locked up. We've got several duplicate experiments going with military and civilian volunteers."

In the Karaoke room, Jolly Roger could be heard screaming, "Watch this, you geeks and freaks. Watch this—bloody nobody on SNN going to try this. Get your sweet bod out here Honey Dew."

A black woman rivaling a panther in beauty and grace slinked onto the stage in a florescent pink bikini bottom, pasties, and western hat. Her left hand took the stogie from her mouth and flipped it toward the audience. A double-bladed axe lay across her right shoulder, draped by her right hand. Stripper drums beat to rhythmic swaying and the axe was used as a baton, spiraling red oak, flashing glints of a blade. Honey spun, then tossed the axe ten feet above her head, and caught it on its descent and kissed the blade. The crowd roared in unison, "Kill him, kill him, kill him!"

A pastie fell and in slow motion was retrieved as the camera zoomed details of its return. The music subsided. Jolly hugged Honey.

"Honey Dew, you know the rules, and they're all nice and legal."

Jolly extended a paper to Honey. A hard-breathing Honey with axe propped against a long glistening leg shook her head 'no.' Jolly protested.

"Honey, you said you could do it."

"Oh, Jolly, I can't. Love you too much."

"You promised you'd give it a go. Oh, I forgot to tell you, it's gone from a million to five million. Five million—pounds sterling if you can do it."

The audience stomped and roared approval. The camera focused on a glistening Honey. Honey grabbed the check and stuffed it into the front of her bikini bottom.

"Lay your bloody head on that chair, Jolly. You've gone too far this time."

The audience screamed, "Kill him. Kill him."

Jolly dropped to his knees and laid his head on the chair. Honey licked her thumb and pulled it across the blade of the axe.

The Cleansing

She tore her pasties away. The screaming crowd was on its feet. Guards about the stage went shoulder to shoulder. Honey rubbed the side of the axe along her breasts and straddled Jolly's face.

"Last one you'll ever see Jolly."

Jolly screamed, "Do it, you bloody bitch. Do it."

Honey pulled her right leg away from Jolly's face and with the force of a sweaty lumber jack, started to swung the axe toward Jolly's neck. Before the axe could peak, Honey froze and dropped the axe. The audience moaned and Jolly stood and pranced, twirling Honey's pasties above his head. He stopped at a bulletin board at the left corner of the stage and thumbtacked the pasties amidst numerous others.

Hap, watching in the Karaoke room, was laughing.

"Damn, that man's crazy. Hell, I'd kill him for five million dollars."

Roy swirled his can and took the last draw, "Closer to ten million. He was talking pounds but I'll be damned if I'd trust my head to a bunch of aliens."

"Now shit, you know that's fixed. No way they going to chop his head off."

"Didn't look fixed to me. But you're right; he's nuts."

In the next room, SNN returned.

"Reverend Wells, in additon to being the Senate chaplain, you minister to the First Methodist Church of Washington D. C. which has over six thousand members. What is your reaction to the report on the women in Afghanistan?

"I have mixed reactions and emotions. Imagine the tragedy of those poor women. You would think, after all that has transpired since 9/11, their occupation, the..." Reverend Wells paused, "What this demonstrates is the importance and power of religious beliefs to people all over the world and who are we to judge? What if anyone one of us had been born and raised in that environment? It's easy to condemn, harder, much harder to put yourself in someone else's soul. I'm very fortunate to be a member of the Christian faith. I count my blessings every day, as we all should do when we witness something like that."

Stillwell asked, "Do you believe the aliens are the work of the devil?"

"I don't know what to believe at this point. I pray every day along with people of my church and with, I'm sure, people throughout the world, even the fundamentalists responsible for what we just saw."

"How are the people of your congregation handling this?"

"Well, there are many who are afraid, many who need counseling. We have members asking questions I can't answer, no one can answer, but eventually, I think God will. And to be honest, we have some who don't seem to be affected at all."

"And the congressmen you minister to?"

The minister shrugged, "The same."

Stillwell looked into the camera, "Ladies and gentlemen, correspondant Dave Heckler reporting from New York."

"We're here in New York on Pennsylvania Avenue. The funeral procession of cars you see behind me is for a man who committed suicide. He left a note saying the aliens were going to destroy the earth by fire, and he couldn't stand the thoughts of being burned alive. That's the tenth suicide this week in New York that's related to the alien landings."

There was a pause as the last of the procession passed.

"You can follow along with us as…sir…sir…"

The camera crew hurried after a young businessman on a busy intersection. He opened a taxi door and was immediately approached by a camera crew.

"Sir, we're from SNN. Could we ask you a couple of questions?"

"About the aliens, right?"

"Yes, sir."

"Well, I need to be uptown in," the man stopped and looked at the reporter. "Did you say SNN?"

"Yes, sir."

The man shrugged in acceptance. "Sure, why not."

"Do you believe it's true?"

"You mean do I believe we have visitors from outer space?"

"Yes."

221

The Cleansing

"Well, I think I do. Something's going on. No firearms, no violence with the paralysis and that video. How else do you explain that?"

"How would you explain it, sir?"

"I can't, I really can't, but my wife and I aren't afraid to let my little girl, she's six, play outside now."

The film crew looked for someone else.

At the table Joe motioned for another beer.

"You all had any problems with stealing?"

"No, I think that little fiasco with Nelson got the word around."

Those about the table chuckled.

"Right smart of old Nel to record that little bastard trying to steal his pickup."

"Where the hell did Nelson get a video camera?"

"Ordered it from one of those home-shopping networks. Said he didn't even know if he was working it right."

Joe sipped his bear, "It wasn't Nelson; it was Lewellen who thought of the camcorder. Said she heard him yelling at the boy and came running out of the house screaming *take his picture, Nelson, take his picture* and hell he did. Dumb bastard tried to take the camcorder away from Nel. Nel and Lewellen duct taped his ass, called the sheriff, and ten minutes later the little shit was hauled off to jail."

There was chortling and more beer.

The camera crew stopped two college-aged girls.

"Excuse me, we're from SNN. Could you take a minute to answer a few questions about the aliens?"

"Sure."

"Do you think they're for real?"

"Yes…yes, I sure do."

"What makes you so sure?"

"Oh, I dunno know. What else could it be? You know, like, no violence, no weapons. Nobody has, well, nobody on earth has the technology to do that."

"How is it affecting your life?"

"I think like, the same as everyone's life."

222

"How so?"

"Well, people don't have to be afraid anymore. Like, no rape, child abuse, murder, nothing like that."

"Our latest SNN poll shows that 74% of the population have tried to be violent, 80% of males and 68% of the females. Have you tried?"

"I haven't, but Trish has." The girl speaking pointed to her friend.

The camera turned to Trish. "Did you do it on purpose?"

"Yes."

"How did it feel?"

"Like everyone says. Like you're warm then I saw my brother. He's ten. Didn't hurt. Tried it on her."

Both giggled.

"What about our armed forces? Do you believe our army is disbanding?"

"No. I think we'll always have an army."

"Are you afraid of what the aliens might do next?"

"Yes, at first, I was like, really afraid, but then when nothing happened, except no one could be violent, and I sorta got used to it. I'm still afraid of, like, what might happen next and what if the violence comes back? And why are they here and doing all this stuff?"

"Do you believe the government is telling us everything?"

"No, they never do."

The TV went to commercial and again was muted.

Hap groaned, "More damned commercials. The end of the fucking world and we get commercials."

"I liked those girls. Made sense. Damn government can't trust those…oh, them layoffs that's been in the paper are the truth. Ed's boy that works at that McDonnell-Douglas plant in Pasedena, he's back home drawing unemployment. Got laid off; said there was a bunch of 'em got laid off."

"Hell, think about it. If this goes on very long, we're going to be in a mess. Half the damn country's work is connected to the government and the defense industry. And this stuff about the logging and mining, there's going to be some people hurting, and it's going to be soon."

"Now, how the hell is it going to hurt you, Deke? You ain't struck a lick in years."

The table smiled and tilted cans and bottles toward the ceiling.

"Well, now, Buford you better ask your wife about that."

"Hell, Deke, who do you think told me?"

Bottoms of bottles and cans beat the table as the commercials ended.

In the oval office the President and Jason continued to watch the broadcast.

"Seen anything you didn't already know?"

"No sir, can't say that I have."

The President leaned back in his chair, "Thought I had it made."

"Sir?"

"Thought I had it made. Two terms as President of the United States. Accomplished a few things I believe the country needed. Endowments for secondary and elementary schools, alternative energy bill, population control act, genetic research ethics code. Place in history. Last two years of the second term, all downhill. Hoping to savor, put a little icing on the cake with the Technology Access Act and the space pollution control initative. Then, the circus comes to town."

"Another brandy, Mr. President? I'm pouring this time."

"Sure."

Jason poured two brandies, sat down and untied his shoes.

"I think you've had a great run, sir."

"Well, thank you, Jason. Problem is, we're still running and we have no idea where the hell we're going."

The TV crew approached a man sleeping on a park bench under cardboard and was spit on. They approached a haggard woman pushing and pulling shopping carts.

"Ma'am, would you mind giving the nation your opinion on our visitors from outer space?"

The woman had been approached from the side. She turned and brought a chorus of "Jesus" and "damn" from the bar viewers. The TV interviewer tried to muffle his response. Her face was battered and gnarled, her skin wrinkled wax paper. Her nose was distorted, flat, and purple streaked. An eye drooped from purple weight and had no eyebrow. Her lips split in crimson crevices. She glared at the camera. Her voice was a throaty whisper. "Yeah, I'll give you my opinion on the aliens. I hate 'em."

She moved her face closer to the camera. The cameraman zoomed back but too late. The commentator stammered, "Why do you hate 'em, ma'am?"

The woman spun to the commentator, "They took my man. The bastards took my man."

"They took your man?"

"Yeah, I hate 'em."

"Do you mean they abducted him or...?"

"No! No! You think I'm crazy just 'cause I'm out here in the streets? I ain't crazy."

"Then how'd they take him, ma'am?"

"He left me. He just left. Left a week ago."

"He left because of the aliens?"

"Yeah, it was their fault. Hadn't been for them, he wouldn't a left."

"How's that, ma'am?"

"Couldn't beat me. Kept trying, but he couldn't, so he left. Said if he couldn't beat me what good was I? I hate 'em. They took my man."

The old woman started to cry and walked away.

Back at the bar table, eyes came away from the TV and to each other.

"Do you believe that? Jesus!"

Emma was fixed on the TV, "Lord have mercy."

Case looked at Emma and pointed his bottle toward the TV.

"Emma, what would you do if you had a man like hers?"

"Well, you know who castrates livestock at our place. That'd be for openers."

Case tipped his bottle toward Emma, "I heard that."

On SNN, Morton asked of the panel:

The Cleansing

"Ladies, gentlemen, you heard our latest poll. Seventy-four percent of the country have tried to engage in violence and couldn't. Seventy percent did it on purpose, despite the government's urging not to do so. Any adverse reactions to date?"

An MD answered, "None so far, but we're still recommending not to do it. We don't know about long-term effects, or, for that matter, short-term effects."

"How many on this panel have experienced the freeze?" Morton asked.

There was considerable shuffling and clearing of throats. Hearing no real response, a summary of past events was outlined for the conclusion of the broadcast.

"The landing of unknown craft in the remote, desolate places on the planet is true. It is not a hoax. Landing locations have been identified and include every continent on the planet. The origin, nature, and type of the craft is still unknown as are their pilots or occupants. The rumor that these pilots or occupants are space aliens has not been verified. The flying capabilities of the craft exceed any known craft on the planet. The rumors that a number of French and Chinese planes have been shot down and thousands of NATO troops have been killed are false. The video of the encounter in the 'Empty Quarter' is authentic. The rumor of a second encounter in the 'Empty Quarter' is unconfirmed.

"The absence of violence since the landings is true and is global. Since the reported landings, there has not been one verified report of violence of any kind in our nation and around the globe. While some suggested the landings and the inability for violence are not related, most certainly think they are. The inability of people to commit violence is of unknown origin and cause.

"Civilian firearms do not work—globally. The rumor that the military has a store of firearms that work and are distributing to police and law enforcement is unconfirmed. The rumor that nuclear weapons, on a global scale, have been disabled is unconfirmed. The rumor that aliens from the craft have met with international leaders is, as of this broadcast, not true."

An announcement of a follow-up broadcast and two minutes of commercials ensued.

The Cleansing

The same evening

In the small dark viewing room of a bunker hospital, Ishmael Zolef watched the operation with two other men. One wore the white smock of a physician, the other, khaki with stripes of a military Colonel. The Colonel was dark, gaunt, erect, cheeks shallow and pitted, his left ear a massive scar that extended to his throat, eyes, one white one black. His uniform was trimmed in oiled, black leather. His boots were frosted by sand dust. One medal adorned his left breast, the star of the "Grand Cordon," his grandfathers—the "Cordon" sash over his right shoulder, the badge resting below his left hip. A leather crop dangled from his belt.

The three watched as a member of the surgical team picked up the drill. Its diamond tip emitted a piercing wail as it penetrated the skull of the male patient. The sound was unlike any Ishmael had ever heard, a screaming diamond, raping bone. Blood and bone of shaved scalp flecked the white scrubs of the team. Four holes were drilled; then a surgical saw was used to detach a fourth of the patient's skull. The procedure took less than ten minutes. The doctor laid the saw aside and looked in the direction of the viewing room. The Colonel spoke coarse and raspy into a suspended microphone, "Thank you, doctor."

The doctor and his team stripped their hands of bloody surgical gloves, tossed them in a metal container and left.

Ishmael turned to the Colonel, "We do not need this. The radiation is still active and we have already distributed a half million barrels. We do not need this."

Entranced by the exposed brain, the Colonel turned his head but not his eyes toward Ishmael. The patient's right arm twitched in unison with his right leg.

The Colonel's voice was a whisper, "What about tomorrow? Will your oil be active tomorrow? Can you assure me your oil will active tomorrow, Mr. Zolef?"

"But you are making them vegetables. It is a waste."

The Colonel gazed at the exposed brain, "They are the worst of criminals, should have been put to death long ago."

227

The Cleansing

Zolef turned to the physician standing with them, "How can you do this? You are men of healing. How is such violence even possible?"

The doctor looked down as he answered, "They do not know what they are doing. The team you saw opens the skull. The patient is then taken to the laser room. The technicians there do not know. Their laser is preprogrammed, changing one millimeter for each operation. The programmer does not know."

"Ingenious, isn't it?" the Colonel responded.

The Colonel turned and in disgust threw up a hand at the twitching patient being wheeled from the operating room, "Try him and let me know."

An orderly nodded as the Colonel turned to Ishmael, "They twitch. They all twitch. All they can do. Perhaps the next one." Ishmael shook his head. The Colonel stared at him two seconds too long. "Mr. Zolef, have I told you of the officer who betrayed us?"

"No."

"We threw him into prison after we forced him to witness the ravishing of his family. Stayed in solitary for two years. We'd forgotten him until the aliens. We bound the soldier who raped his wife and smothered his two-year-old son and threw him in solitary with the traitor. We gave the traitor a machete. Can you imagine what happened?"

Ishmael did not respond.

"The traitor rants and paces day and night and many times every day he picks up the machete and tries to kill the murderer of his family and every day he fails. Been trying to kill him for weeks. Don't you find that fascinating?"

Again Ishmael did not respond. The Colonel walked closer and gazed about the operating room. He turned abruptly.

"Our experiment is simple. Could it be the aliens are so brilliant they have forgotten or do not know of ignorance? If you do not know of your violence, if you do not know…perhaps it is the knowing that makes you impotent. And knowing comes from the brain."

The Colonel banged his forefinger to his forehead, "If we can destroy the knowing, we have warriors again and everything is ours. Everything!"

Ishmael's voice broke, "But the doctors, the violence they are directing..."

He was interrupted again, "They are ignorant, the doctors, the technicians, all of them. They believe they are part of a team performing experimental surgery on the criminally insane. And, in truth, they are. The patients are from our prisons and asylums. Ironic isn't it? We told the first team what we were doing and they couldn't do it. Envisioned their mothers, fathers, children—whined with that sickening impotent…" The Colonel tilted his head, "Ignorance—so simple. The clergy gave us the idea. Did I tell you of our savage?"

The Colonel did not wait for an answer, "Found him in one of our dungeons while forging for our experiments. Murdered thirty that we were aware of and he was perfect. No father, an insane mother who kept him locked in a cellar. Starved and beat him for years. Never saw the outside world—nothing but the cellar. The only thing in his life was a vicious mother, nothing else, yet he survived. Escaped when he was twelve, returned two hours later and beheaded the only human being he had ever known. Do you see how he's perfect? There's no love or anyone for him to envision and stop him. We found a woman the image of his mother and threw her in his dungeon. Gave him an axe. Care to speculate?"

"No."

"He couldn't do it. When he tried the woman became himself as a little boy." The Colonel paced, "God, their genius is beyond …"

Ishmael forced his eyes to the physician, "Have any of the surgeries been successful?"

The Colonel answered palming his eyes, "Not yet, but we are patient. We will find a way. They underestimate us, Mr. Zolef. They do not know of the God-like motivation that drives us to dominate."

The Colonel smiled, "Impressive that man can paint the Sistine Chapel, build the Parthenon, pyramids, become a saint, write a book, a symphony. But what is building the Parthenon to splitting the atom? It took a hundred thousand slaves a hundred years to build the pyramids. It took a million geniuses a millennium to split the atom—to develop genetic toxins. If it is

229

The Cleansing

holy for one man to paint the Sistine Chapel is it not divine for generations of thousands to create napalm that clings to human flesh? Tell the man who writes a book to make a bullet and I will grant him genius."

The Colonel clenched his fists at Zolef, "The masses do not worship for forgiveness and some eternal guarantee. It is the power of their gods they worship. Show me one of their gods you can put on a leash. They are all immortal with legions of angels or demons at their command. But tell me Mr. Zolef, what rules the world, their religions, their gods or our wars—your oil?

"They forsake their gods when our genius is needed to kill millions whose only sin is that they differ. Their hypocrisy has no bounds claiming the lack of war will divert our talent, our resources to feeding the hungry, providing sanctuary and educating their ignorant. They are the same fools who believe righteous men and their causes are the forgers of destiny. And all the while they and their offspring cover their ears to the screams of a billion war widows and orphans.

"War defines everything—who is just, unjust, righteous, what is sacred—evil. If Emperor Qin, Mao, Khan, Napoleon or Hitler had realized their dreams, who would then be the prophets, the holy men? What would be the commandments in holy books read in cathedrals?

"Half of everything that has been consumed on this planet has been for war. Yet, when the plague of peace descends upon them they fret and beat their chests at each other until they can stand it no longer. Then they seek us out for yet another war as their religions make it holy." The Colonel's voice whispered, "Einstein said it best, *'Only two things are infinite, the universe and human stupidity.'*"

The Colonel turned away, "Our genius and resources must now find the best long bow, the sharpest sword and a man to use them. So where lays God—In sanctity or power? They underestimate us, Mr. Zolef. We will find a way."

"But we can destroy the infidels with my oil."

The Colonel smiled, "Mr. Zolef, do you know what hell is?"

Ishmael whispered, "Hell is coming face to face with the devil and he's your twin."

The Colonel smiled.

CHAPTER THIRTY-ONE

Truens

The third encounter with the aliens was complete. The same crew met for exactly one minute with an alien. Laku said the alien, a female, was not one of the previous two. Mr. Mehra confirmed. Members of Homeland Security headed by Dr. Maxwell and joined by the President, were briefing outside the glass that quarantined them.

"What can you tell us Mr. Mehra?"

"I asked the questions."

"Did you get a response?"

"Yes, to some. We are in no danger, except from ourselves. They gave the same answer as last time as to why they are here, *'To rest upon the nature of our planet and to secure the tranquility needed for Truens'*. I asked how long they are going to stay. Time is not important, only tranquility. As to the other questions. Origin of the universe? Other species? Human kind? God? Such questions will be answered when we have the capacity for understanding.."

"And are they responsible the disappearances of criminals?"

"The same response. *Do we want them back?*"

"Our reproduction ceasing, any explanation?"

"*When the species we doom, thrive.*"

"But we are reproducing, so what does that mean?"

The group looked at each other.

"Why don't they communicate more? Why are they staying so isolated?"

"They are more interested in other species and the beauty of our planet. Our habitats detract, reflecting our nature. We are primitive, our habitats do not add to the beauty of the planet as do the habitats of other species."

"But don't they recognize us as the most intelligent species on the planet?"

"They recognize us as the most dominant."

"Will they help us with our problems?"

"They are."

"When can you communicate with them again?"

"In three weeks."

Tesh interrupted, "She told me how we can be better."

Jason asked, "How we can be better?"

"Yes."

"How's that, Tesh?"

"She just said, *'the best for children'.*"

"She said that, communicated that to you?"

"Yes," the girl nodded, "she did and to Laku too."

The interpreter asked Laku and he nodded.

"Mr. Mehra, was that communicated to you."

"Yes."

"Any explanation as to what that meant."

"No."

Jason looked about the other HS member, "Anyone?"

A child psychologist from Berkeley answered, "Well, if we could somehow wave that magic wand and provide the best for every child on this planet—safe home, loving parents or guardians, a good education, what would happen?" There was no response. The psychologist continued, "We can say with a great deal of certainty that about 80% of the social problems we have would disappear."

An HS member commented, "Our social problems are disappearing. That's what we have now."

"I'm talking more than violence. We still have hatred, prejudice, poverty, drugs, pollution, and crime of all sorts. More than one hundred million children live in poverty, more than one-third lives on the verge of starvation while one percent of the population owns one-half the resources. I'm talking about social ills other than violence.

"There are a few cultural examples where children were considered and treated as the most important members of the family. In the early 1900s in Tahiti, isolated tribes in Bengal in the 1800s, certain aborigine clans. In these cultures everybody doted on the children. They were loved and taught to do the same, and I mean all the children. The result was an absence, almost a total absence of what we in the West define as social ills. No violence or what we would define as crime. No theft, in fact there was an absence of infidelity, lying, deceit, jealousy. Maybe this is what our alien friends were trying to convey."

The President commented, "So what we need to do is take care of our children and eighty percent of our problems disappear?"

"Yes sir. Sounds a little preachy, but that's about it."

The HS member hesitated then stammered, "It was in your platform when you ran for President—sir."

"That alien would make a good politician" President Meyer responded, smiling, "They mentioned Truens again, did they communicate anything else about that?"

"Truens are the best part of what we are, therefore, different for each of us," answered Mr. Mehra.

"What does that mean?" asked the President.

Tesh answered, "We'll know tomorrow."

Jason looked to Tesh, "The aliens are going to tell you about the Truens tomorrow?"

"No, the Truens are coming tomorrow."

Midnight

Sarah lay very still with Josh in her room in the Pentagon. An hour passed before she asked, "Think something is going to happen tomorrow?"

"Yes."

"What time do you leave?"

"Four a.m."

"What do you think is going to happen?"

"Truens."

"Any ideas on that?"

"Got me there."

Sarah spooned to Josh's back, "What's the best of what you are?"

"Well, according to my fan mail, my butt."

Sarah pinched his butt, "Little do they know."

They lay quiet for a long time. "Seriously, what do you think they mean?"

Josh rolled over and faced Sarah, "You're being serious."

"Yes, but I reserve butt pinching for smart ass answers."

"Okay, the best of what I am? What comes to mind are Cindy, you, my mother, my sister playing as a little girl, the kids I read to when ..."

Josh paused, "Maybe Truens are memories, good memories. But is that different from the best of what you are? What comes to mind with you?"

"My father, brother, mother—living in North Carolina with them. We were so...you know, what popped in my mind when I heard what Tesh said about the Truens?"

"What?"

"When it would snow. When Adam and I were in grade school, we would literally pray for snow. There was a big hill behind our house perfect for snow sledding. I remember one December it came a big one, about twelve inches. For some reason Mom and Dad were home. Must've been during the holidays. We took sleds out after breakfast, built a big bonfire. Kids came from everywhere. We sledded till dark. We'd sled, get cold, run to the bon fire, warm up and take off again. It got late; the run was getting icy, about time to go in. Adam and dad were coming down the hill on the last run. They were flying and Mom and I were peppering them with snowballs. The look on Adam's face."

"He was scared?"

"Oh yeah, but it was a happy scared. Laughing. Dad sitting behind him grinning."

"So the best is good times with your family?"

"Yeah, I guess so, but what popped into my mind was the look on Adam's face and how lucky I've been."

At 4:00 the next morning, Josh left with Tesh, Laku, Mr. Mehra, Drs. Jason Maxwell and McLain. Four hours later they were suited and in the desert. They waited for two hours before the children were evacuated. The men waited for another ten hours. No aliens appeared. Nothing happened. All left except Mr. Mehra.

234

The Cleansing

7:00p.m. the same day

In the intensive care wing of Sunset nursing home in Tupelo Mississippi, ninety-two year old Bess Ellis lay in her bed. Her room included a bath, a closet, a bed, dresser, couch, table and chair and a suspended TV. Subconsciously, she pawed at the tubes in her nose. Her eyes opened then closed. She tried to keep them closed. 'They' left when she opened them, but she would forget.

"Wonder if he's milking yet? Got to get the kids breakfast, bus will be…make sure they wear coats, cold, wet, can't be catching something."

Sleep drifted about her, mixing past and present. Her speech slurred, "Time to get up. John, time to get up. Didn't mean to. Didn't mean to."

Her bed was wet and warm then John and the youngens were around the breakfast table. It was Saturday. No need to hurry, except for the milking. But her eyes were open, and John and the children were there with her and the glow. It was like a butterfly but glowed like a firefly.

"Mam-maw and Papaw coming for dinner."

"Can Jennifer come over and spend the night?"

At the nurse's station Nurse Bradley glanced at the next chart. The last visitor was six months ago. Meds for the day were checked. She added her initials, racked it, pulled the next tray of jello, oatmeal, toast and orange juice and headed for room 202. The door was labeled "Bess Ellis." The glow came from the bottom of the door.

"Third shift. How do they expect these poor people to sleep with the…"

She hipped opened the door and gasped. She grabbed at the tray as it fell and spilled. The butterfly light engulfed her and she was in the pickup in her mother's lap. Her dad was driving, "Glad you liked your first day of school, honey."

He reached to her, pinched her cheek, and both smiled.

Fifteen minutes earlier

The buzzer sounded, steel doors opened to "civilian on the floor" and Pat Stewart entered cellblock A of the North wing

235

death row of the Illinois State Prison at Marion. Six armed guards were waiting. The guards called Cell Block A, "Hell's Zoo." A dozen cells housed the most horrific criminals in the nation. One of the guards acknowledged her, "Ms. Stewart."

"Officer Dixon, gentlemen."

The guards were courteous and Pat knew they didn't have to be. They walked through two more guarded steel doors manned by lard-faced guards. Metal thunder slammed behind her.

"Why do you carry arms?"

"The prisoners don't know."

"Really?"

"They're not allowed any outside contact."

"No TV, newspapers, mail, nothing?"

"Nothing."

"How do you get away with ...?"

Pat didn't finish her stupid question and none of the guards answered. She had been given access to the court records of the prisoners. That was the answer. She'd been trying to get this interview for four years and the only reason it was granted was because of the freeze. Pat bit her lip. *"You're here. Don't blow it now."*

Four years and she was here and this was Jeffrey Bass. No one was allowed near Jeffrey Bass, no one. Of the twelve, he was the worst. His isolation cell was equipped with a showerhead, which came on for two minutes every morning at 6:00 a.m. Food was slid to him through a metal slit. Jeffrey Bass had been in isolation for seven years. He'd been convicted of killing sixteen people and a cellmate. What he did to his victims was so horrible the details were never made public and drove two veteran investigating officers to early retirement. He was two hours away from execution.

Fifteen minutes later Pat was completing the interview. The voice came from the slit in the solid metal door.

"So, don't you see Pat Stewart? I did it to get into heaven and here I am."

Jeffrey Bass giggled like a twelve-year old girl, "Had to do them the way I did so I could be sure. And, here I am in heaven. So don't you see, Pat Stewart, the joke's on them. They got their man and put him in heaven. The joke's on them, Pat Stewart, the joke's on them. No reason to kill me, I'm already here."

"So you consider where you are, heaven?"

"Been here seven years. No spike in seven years. Twelve if you count before here."

"Why don't you tell me about the spike?"

"Can't. Not nice to talk about hell. Might come back. He's dead. I think he's dead. I killed him. I think I killed him. How do you kill a spike, Pat Stewart? How do you kill a spike? Might come back. Can't get here though. Hell, can't get to heaven."

Bass giggled again.

"Want to say anything else about your execution?"

"You're the first I've talked with in heaven. Are you an angel? Those I did it to, some of them talked about heaven, some hell. They thought I was hell. They're wrong—spike's hell. Got their nothingness for the spike. I can even taste it. Ever taste nothingness, Pat Stewart? Got my nothingness. Got it right here and it's heaven."

He giggled again.

"We have to get him ready" said one of the six guards.

Pat turned off her recorder.

"No way I can see him? A picture would be icing."

"No way ma'am. That door never opens with civilians on the floor."

An hour later, an MD started to inject a strapped Jeffrey Bass. He stopped and stepped back.

"I can't do this. He's my brother. How did my bro....?"

Blue gold fluorescence filled the execution room.

"Jesus Christ, what the…"

Twenty minutes later Jeffery Bass was back in his cell singing.

Forty-eight hours later

"Mr. President, I think you should see this."

Dr. Maxwell again entered the oval office. The President was looking over monitoring reports from the empty desert.

"Hope you got more than I'm looking at."

"I think I have, sir."

Maxwell walked to the DVD player and put in a DVD.

"Ever heard about the International Fireworks Competition in Sweden?"

"You're talking about the countries that try to outdo each other with fireworks displays every year in Stockholm?"

"Yes sir, about seventy of them this year."

"Sure. My wife's been after me for years to go. You know some of those countries spend millions on those displays?"

"Yes sir, and you're right about the millions. We spent four million last year. Came in fifth place."

"Really? Didn't know that. Didn't they move the dates on that?"

"Yes sir, used to be in August. Moved the dates to take advantage of the New Year's holiday. It's been going on for a week. This tape is of last night's display. Recorded by an elderly couple from Gloucester."

"Gloucester, England?"

"Yes, sir. This took place in front of over two hundred thousand people."

Jason pushed the play button. The recording began. The Japanese fireworks display was in progress. Giant orange and green dragons, created by a thousand rocket bursts, lit up the sky. The dragons spit fire of white, orange, green and red. In perfect synchronization another five hundred rockets flanked the dragons with flags of the rising sun that waved blazing stripes of red and white. The sound was staccato thunder of exploding thousand dollar rockets coordinating the fire flaming tongues of the dragons. A quarter of a million observers roared and applauded approval.

"Wow, that's good" commented the President. "Going to be hard to beat that. They must have spent a fortune."

"Watch what happens next, sir."

From the east and west, as the display continued, giant butterflies appeared. They glowed with the same luminous beauty of the fireworks. They hovered then darted up, then down and lit on the backs of the dragons and stripes of the rising sun.

"How in the world did they do that?" asked the President.

"They're not part of the display, sir."

The President slowly turned his head to Jason then back to the screen.

"Notice the audience, sir."

The audience was absolutely quiet, watching with a stunned rapture. The man recording the video spoke with an English accent.

"*Martha look, what is that?*"

"*Why it's part of the fireworks, dear. No, no it can't be that. Much too beautiful for...oh my, oh dear. Do you see them, James? Do you see them?*"

"*Yes, I see them. It's all right, Martha. I see them, too. It's our children. Our babies.*"

The recording continued to display the radiant fluorescent butterflies as they danced and played among the fireworks. They flitted toward the ground then back to the sky. The fireworks burned out, but the butterflies remained and more arrived. The sky was full and the video sound was of laughing children and murmuring smiling tearful adults hugging each other.

Like the fireworks, the ten-foot butterflies were brilliant reds, blues, oranges and pinks. They played as with each other or for those watching. The sound was a pleasant hum. Someone later said it was the sound of a child smiling. The last sound on the video was the soft crying of Martha. The film went black. Both Jason and the President were quiet. Jason spoke slowly, "Do you feel it, sir?"

The President didn't answer.

"Mr. President?"

The President was locked on the TV.

"Jason, what did I just see?"

"What did you feel, sir?"

The President hesitated and forced himself to take his eyes away from the black screen. "I was with my wife when Gretchen was born. Was the most beautiful, the most—thought I would never experience anything like that again, but I just did."

"Yes, sir."

"Jason, what did I...?" The President's eyes widened at Jason, "Oh God, those were Truens."

"Yes sir, the circus has clowns."

The Cleansing

The President looked around the room. His eyes searched. He looked at the ceiling then back to Jason. "Are you going to tell me...does everyone...did everyone that saw them have the same experience?"

"Yes, sir."

"Jason, did you feel...?"

"I was home with my parents when mother got word she had been accepted to play with the New York Philharmonic."

The President cocked his head at Jason.

"I led sort of a sheltered life, sir."

Both men half smiled as Jason continued, "The people who attended the fireworks competition are reporting the same types of experience that you did, sir, only more intense. Being in their presence seems to make a difference."

"How many have you talked with?"

"Over two hundred, sir."

"When you say the same type of experience, do you mean they were all family related?"

"No, not all, sir. Everyone experienced or visualized something that had happened in their past that was extraordinary. So far, all have stated that it was the happiest time or experience of their lives."

The President paced the room, "No bad experiences."

"No sir, all were good...more than good, sir. They were just unbelievable."

"Any other sightings?"

"We have an unconfirmed report from Illinois State Prison in Marion."

"Illinois State Prison in Marion?"

"Yes sir." He paused and met the President's eyes, a question on the tip of his tongue. " You remember Jeffrey Bass?"

"The serial killer?"

"Yes, sir. Some news reporter was interviewing him before his execution and filming his execution. No one could inject him. Had three prison doctors who tried."

The President eagle-eyed Jason. Jason shrugged. "I don't know, sir. They have it on tape. Some light appeared then and I quote sir, a giant butterfly."

The President stopped pacing and sat down, "Do you have the recording?"

"It's on its way."

"My God Jason, what are these creatures? Jesus, they can control our minds, our emotions, what in God's name?"

The red phone on the President's desk rang. The President exhaled slowly. He heard the third ring and picked up the phone. "Yes?" He listened for a few seconds, "No, that'll take too long. Get him to the phone. Well, I guess you'll have to take it to him. That'll be fine. Thanks, Colonel."

The President hung up the phone. His eyes glistened.

"That was Colonel Matthews from the desert. Mr. Mehra walked into his office and said it was important he talk with me. Said he could tell us about the Truens."

"Why didn't he just put him on?"

"He walked into the office, said he had to see me and went back to the ships. They're going to take him a phone and patch him through. Want to conference in some of your people?"

"How long do we have?"

"Said they'd have him on in ten minutes."

It was Jason's turn to exhale, "We're scattered everywhere. Might be best to just record."

The President and Jason stared quietly at the floor.

The red phone rang at Command Headquarters in the Pentagon. General Dickenson answered the phone, "Yeah."

He listened then smiled, "Tom, where the hell are you?"

The Vice-President answered, "North Korea."

"North Korea? What the hell are you doing in North Korea?"

"Our President sent me to calm the natives, remember?"

"Yeah, I know but North Korea? Shouldn't you be in Europe or Asia or someplace?"

"North Korea is in Asia, General. Listen, I got news I think you'll find interesting."

"Oh? I'm all ears. Have you been keeping up with...?"

"Roswall, the North Koreans have got soldiers that can pull the trigger."

"What?"

"Your line secure?"

"Damn Tom, it's a red line." The general exclaimed. "You called it. What did you just say?"

"General, the North Koreans have soldiers who can fight. All they need is weapons."

"How'd they do that?"

"Don't have time to explain. You'll see soon enough. I've offered them a trade. A few of their soldiers for one of our stash."

There was a pause

"General, are you there?"

"Yeah, I'm here, but you know damn well we can't do that. If what you're telling me is true..."

The Vice-President interrupted again, "Roswall, it's true. Believe me, I saw them perform."

Roswall breathed into the phone, "Okay, but even if what you're saying is true you know damn well we can't send them one of our stash. If we do, we make them a super power and you're talking about North fucking Korea."

The General struggled to control his voice. The Vice-President laughed into the phone, "Not going to send them one, General. I'm not that stupid. Going to bring a half dozen of their soldiers back with me, reason I'm calling. Want you to meet me at Dulles at 3 a.m. Secure North B, and bring a van. Nobody knows about this except you, me and well...a couple of Korean Generals who'll keep their mouths shut."

"You're bringing back North Korean soldiers and nobody is to know. What in the hell are you thinking? You can't..."

"Roswall, it's all right. Trust me on this. Just be there with the van."

The General heard a click and the phone went dead.

The phone rang in the Oval Office. The President nodded to Jason and turned on the conference caller.

"Yes."

"Mr. President, Colonel Matthews. We have Mr. Mehra on the line. The wind is picking up so it's going to be touch and go with reception."

"Can hear you loud and clear, Colonel."

Colonel Matthew's muffled voice could be heard in the background.

"Mr. Mehra, the President is on the line."

"Hello, Mr. President. Thank you for allowing me to speak with you."

"The pleasure is all mine. Dr. Maxwell is with me. We understand you have some information on the Truens?"

"Mr. President, Dr. Maxwell, I know of the Truens."

The wind could be heard sanding the tent of Mr. Mehra..

"Mr. Mehra, we'd be very interested in hearing about that."

"They are creatures of another time and place. They have been brought here for their survival. A sun burned their place. The Truens can survive only where there is beauty, tranquility and peace. They evolved with an extraordinary ability. When they encounter any species they evoke the most tranquil beautiful experience of that species' life. It insures their survival. Our planet is beautiful and tranquil but because of us it is not peaceful."

The President asked, "When you say 'us,' you mean the human species?"

"Yes."

"Mr. Mehra, are you saying that we were disarmed and violence ceased for the Truens?"

"Yes."

Jason responded, "But the nature of our planet is violent. Evolution depends on the survival of the species. Animals kill. Violence is a necessity for life and survival."

Mr. Mehra's voice was almost silenced by the wind pelting his tent.

"The capacity for violence of the human species has no limits. It encompasses all species, the planet and it is without compassion or reason. Remove the violence of humans and other species and the Truens thrive. Continue the violence of humans and all will cease to exist, including us."

Jason asked, "Why then suicides?"

"There are too many of us."

"Too many of us? They want to get rid of us?"

"Not all."

"How many?"

"Until other species thrive. The aliens have found only three that prosper with our proliferation."

"What three? Dogs, cats and...?"

"No, rats, roaches and flies."

The President and Jason looked at each other.

"How do the Truens bring about the feelings and emotions when you encounter them?"

"As the aliens said, they are the best that is within us. For the aliens this is wisdom, for us, it is tranquility and peace."

Jason asked, "So, the Truens do this for their preservation?"

"Yes. It is to make their habitat as one with our species."

"Any idea how?"

"No."

There was silence again except for the wind. The President asked, "How long are they going to be here, Mr. Mehra?"

"I do not know, but our destiny lies with the Truens."

The President and Jason looked at each other as Jason asked.

"What does that mean?"

"It means the Truens must thrive."

"Or?"

"Or like them, we will not."

Silence as the President considered the words. "Does that mean we won't survive unless violence ceases?"

"Yes."

"Well, that's pretty much been taken care of," mumbled the President.

"We should pray that is true," responded Mr. Mehra.

Air Force III landed at Dulles. It taxied five hundred yards short of the terminal where General Dickenson waited with a van and a limo. One minute later, the plane door opened and in slow motion a grasshopper leg of metal steps descended to the ground. Two bodyguards exited first, then six children, all boys, followed by Vice-President Stewart. The boys were preschool age. The General, familiar with Asian children in Vietnam, estimated their age at four to five. He noticed that unlike most foreign children in a foreign environment, they weren't afraid. The Vice-President descended the steps with the boys about him. He extended his hand to the General.

"General, good to see you."

The General shook the Vice-President's hand and leaning toward his ear whispered.

"Tom, what the hell is this?"

"General, I want you to meet our educational representatives from North Korea.

These young men are in the states to attend one of our preschools for a couple of weeks. They're going to get a taste of American education from an Asian perspective. Great for international relations."

The General leaned toward the Vice-President, "Where the hell are the soldiers?"

The Vice-President smiled, "Let's get the boys in the van. We'll talk in the limo."

In the limo the General and the Vice-President sat shoulder to shoulder in the sealed back seat. The General twitched in his seat.

"Get me out here at three in the morning. I'm not one of your flunkies, Tom. My plate's pretty full these days. In case you haven't noticed, the whole fucking world is on its knees because of…"

"Don't get your Depends in a wad, Roswall. Lighten up. I brought the soldiers. It's the boys.

The General turned and faced the Vice-President, "What the hell are you talking about?

The Vice-President smiled, "Been right in front of our noses all the time. The children, they can fire weapons. Do you believe it? The damn children."

The General's eyes blinked as beads of perspiration appeared on his forehead, "Have you completely lost your fucking mind? You can't mean children—you can't use children to fire and how do you know? The North Koreans don't have any ammunition that works."

"True, they don't but the boys can pull the trigger. I saw them by the hundreds in simulations, firing away. North Korea's regulars couldn't do it. Just stood by and watched. The children don't know the difference. That's the reason they can do it. The Korean General kept talking about moral development. Kids have to be around five or six before they start to understand they can hurt somebody. Oh, they know how but it doesn't register what they're doing, even older before they understand the meaning of death. Before that it's just play. Goes all the way back to some French shrink, some Piaget or somebody. These Korean boys have been taught with guns, and they can pull the trigger, no problem. Don't know what they're doing. All we have to do is equip them with our stash."

The General gritted his teeth as he glared at the Vice-President, "Would you listen to yourself? What are you suggesting we do? Take these kids to the Empty Desert, give them our cannons and tell them, oh, it's playtime now. Fire away."

The Vice-President put his nose one-inch from the General's, "That's exactly what I propose we do. Have you got any soldiers who can do it? Hell no, you don't. But the North Koreans do, and they're training kids by the thousands. Light years ahead of us. Light years. If they had our guns, they'd rule the world and have those damn aliens under control. So, we're stealing their technology. Done all the time, General. If it works, we'll start training our own. If it doesn't, then we blame the Koreans for sending children over to attend school that have been trained to kill. Either way our ass is covered."

The General moved a half-inch closer to the Vice-President, "This is nuts. This is absolutely nuts."

The Vice-President grabbed the General by his lapels, "Dammit it, Roswall don't you go pussying out on me now. This is the only chance we've got to save the country, hell, the whole damn world. If this works, I'm President, and we rule the world. And in case you've forgotten, your job is making that happen. Now, if you can't handle that, I'll get someone who can."

The General glared at the Vice-President. His eyes lowered to the hands gripping his lapel, then slowly back to the eyes of the man gripping him. The Vice-President's fingers, being scratched by a Medal of Honor and a Purple Heart, gently released the General's lapels and fixed his eyes on the road ahead.

CHAPTER THIRTY-TWO

We're Dying

Two days later

In the "Neighbor's Clinic" of South Side LA, Dr. Spangler looked around his waiting room. It was full, and several waited outside. His medical assistant, Ms. Laila Leddy, a graduate student at UCLA, handed him three more medical charts. Dr. Spangler handed Ms. Leddy two as he took the three.

"Laila, what in the world is this?"

"Beats me. Getting worse every day."

Dr. Spangler looked at the first chart, "Same thing as the others?"

"One has the flu, but the two others, same thing. Got one that is throwing up. Dehydrated."

"Which one is that?"

"A Jimmy Gonzalez. Nice kid, going to LA Community. Pumps gas all day; goes to school at night. Oh, and by the way before you get away, want you to take a look at my hands."

"Why, what's wrong?"

Laila extended her hands to Dr. Spangler, "Same thing."

Dr. Spangler tucked the three charts under his left arm and took Laila's right hand. He examined her palms, fingers, turned her hand over. It was dotted with reddish blisters. He did the same with her left hand.

"When did these start?"

"Bout two weeks ago. Started out just like the others. Red splotchy things keep getting worse. And no, I haven't changed my diet. Not using any different detergents or soap or lotion. Still live in the same place I have for years. No new paint or wallpaper or anything like that."

"You are just like the others. Any nausea?"

"Not until yesterday morning. Threw up. But it wasn't like food poisoning. It was different. And no, I'm not pregnant. Last

I heard, you have to get laid for that. Hard to do when you're working fourteen hour days."

"Anything anywhere else? Your legs, feet?"

"No, just my hands."

Dr. Spangler smiled through a worried look, "Looks like you been putting your hands where you shouldn't."

Laila put her left hand on her hip, "Like I said, fourteen hours a day."

"Get some of those samples of Lac-Hydrin cream. Might want to use zinc oxide at night."

"Started that last week."

A nurse interrupted, "Dr. Spangler, Dr. Shapiro is on the line."

Dr. Spangler walked away, head turned to Laila, "Want to take another look later. Remind me."

"Okay. Is that Chicago?"

"Yeah, they're having the same problem. Don't forget to remind me."

Laila took the next batch of charts mirroring Dr. Spangler's worried look.

On the docks of Galveston Texas, Mario Teil, the foreman, hand signaled his crew. Mario was a giant of a man, and on the front lines getting oil from foreign tankers into the pipelines that transported the oil to the refineries. Octopus eight-inch lines crawled about the docks. They worked with precision. Hand signals communicated work started, done or needed. Each knew his job. Mario knew his men, the ones he could trust and the ones he had to watch.

The lines attached, the signal for the pumps was fists together. The hum began the sucking of the oil from the bellies of the tankers. The lines quivered with their liquid load that ended at stainless steel pipes. The refineries were hungry, always hungry. Jess looked over the dock.

"Damn, that's the fourth one today. Been seeing 'em all week. Saw half a dozen or so yesterday."

Jess pointed at two dead rats lying in a small puddle of oil. Travis, one of his crew, looks over his shoulder as he ratcheted a dripping line.

"Yeah, damn things are dying all over the place. Noticed the fish that's floating around here. They're dying faster than the rats. What you reckon is killing 'em?"

"Hell, who knows? Maybe they put poison out again. They need to keep us posted on shit like that."

"Hell, Mario, you're a teamster. You do your job, they do the thinking and the posting."

The ratcheting continued.

"Went to see Ace last night."

"Yeah! How's he doing?"

"Not worth a damn. Can't get him to quit throwing up, blisters getting worse. I didn't say anything to Thelma, but he looks awful. She said he'd lost thirty pounds. Man, he looks bad."

"That don't sound good. I'm getting some of them blisters."

Jess pulled off his gloves and looked at his hands. Travis pitched his ratchet into a toolbox, "Hell, everybody on the docks are getting 'em."

One week later

The President was in the oval office with HS members, the Vice-President, Gayle Trent, Kate Dockery and General Dickenson. Jason was briefing.

"Mr. President, I have a little to add to yesterday's meeting. The aliens just continue to explore, which is nothing new, but we have confirmed Truen appearances on every continent now, almost every country…always at random. How they travel like they do, we have no idea. They just appear, different people, ages, races, gender, places. They might appear to a child in Bangladesh or they might appear right here. If there's a pattern, we haven't been able to find it. And it's always with the same results—euphoria, happiness.

"Videos of their Bern appearance are being sold in Europe and will be on the market in the states this weekend and you know how much they've appeared on TV. The ramifications so far are good, well actually, unbelievable. Suicides are now almost non-existent. Theft that has been out of sight is a tenth of what it was before they landed. And here's something that just…I don't know. In Europe, they're starting to experiment with the videos. If you can believe this, they're using them to treat mental illness, all sorts of mental illness, depression, neurosis, social anxiety, even psychopaths.

"They're being shown in halfway houses to the homeless, alcoholics, drug addicts, in prisons to delinquents and criminals, in nursing homes to the elderly. The results so far are…"

Jason threw up his hands, "In short sir, for lack of a better word the results have been miraculous."

Everyone in the room looked at each other. The President asked, "Any negatives?"

"No sir, none."

The Vice-President slammed his fist on the table, "What do you mean none? Controlling every aspect of our lives is not a negative? The word slavery comes to mind. Think about what is going on, what they're doing to us. They land. in the blink of an eye, we're docile as lambs then we're disarmed and then they decide this is a great place for their pets. Make our planet their doghouse. Start working on our minds. Start making us feel good."

The Vice-President drew out the word "feel" as he waved his hands it the air, then continued, "The words crack addict come to mind. When are we going to wake up? Do we have to wait till we're on leashes?

The Vice-President turned to Jason, "I have a question, Dr. Maxwell. Do you or anyone at HS know the long term effects of exposure to these Truens?"

"Well, Mr. Vice-President they've only been here three weeks. We're monitoring about two hundred who have seen the Truens, and we have tested a group while they were watching the videos. To date there have been no adverse side effects. However, our subjects report an enhanced, almost euphoric sense of wellbeing, happiness, and satisfaction with life. This is supported by our tests on brain wave act..."

The Vice-President interrupted, "I'll take that as a 'no', that you or anyone in HS has a clue."

Stewart grimaced, "Ladies and gentlemen, I know I'm in the minority here, but we'd better start thinking about the 'what ifs'. What if they decide the human species is no longer needed?

What if they decide we're their slaves? What if they decide to just get rid of us?"

The Vice-President slammed his fist on the table again, "You'd better listen to me. There are a ton of 'what ifs' nobody has answered for me yet. Have they answered them for you?"

The Vice-President raked his eyes around a silent room until the President spoke.

"Tom, have you seen one of the Truen videos?"

The Vice-President smirked with a half smile, "No sir, and I don't intend..."

The Vice-President was interrupted by a knock then the abrupt entrance of Josh and Sarah. Josh was pale and out of breath as he spoke.

"Mr. President, ladies and gentlemen, our apologies for interrupting but we have something you need to know."

The President responded, "We've been worried about you two. Where in the world have you been?"

Josh looked about the room without answering. Sarah looked at Josh and stepped forward. Gayle asked, "Sarah, what's wrong?"

Sarah replied, "As best as we can determine, and we're ninety percent sure, there haven't been any pregnancies since the aliens landed."

"How could you know something like that?" asked Gayle.

Josh answered, "The script—cessation of the reproduction of Homo sapiens. It doesn't say when. We assumed this was wrong because children are still being born. Obviously, the women who are currently giving birth were pregnant before the aliens landed. I repeat, that's before the aliens landed. But, what about since they've landed? What if women are no longer getting pregnant, how would we know?"

Again there was silence around the room until Jason responded, "Oh, my God."

Josh looked at Jason and knew he got it. Jason almost whispering, "We wouldn't know."

"I'm not following. Women know when they're pregnant" responded Dickenson.

"Yes, sir General," Josh said, "but only after weeks. And, they can only be sure when they've seen a Doctor, taken a pregnancy test, missed a period."

"But women, at least women in industrialized countries, have access to tests that can tell them after only two days," responded Gayle.

"That's right, Dr. Trent. That's why Sarah and I are here. We've been working with Neurosciences and Children's Hospital at Chapel Hill. We checked over five hundred women who have been trying to get pregnant for the past sixty days or longer. Under normal circumstances, fifty-five percent would have been successful. They would be pregnant. We gave each a pregnancy test. Forty three percent of the women were pregnant."

The President asked, "Little lower than what you expected but the point is, women are getting pregnant. So what's the problem?"

Josh hesitated, then spoke, "Of the women who had been trying since the aliens landed, none were pregnant."

There was a lull that was heavy and warm until Jason asked, "What percent should it have been?"

"Thirty days and less—forty percent."

The General blinked then spoke, "But, Josh, that could be some quirk, just some luck of the draw, so to speak."

"General, you're right. That's why we had the same thing done in hospitals in Mexico City, Toronto, Belgrade and Stockholm. Over fifteen hundred women were checked in those cities with the same results."

All about the room looked blankly at Josh except the Vice-President, who hid a slight smile by dropping his head and bringing his hand to his brow. No one noticed except Josh. The President asked, "Josh, who else knows about this?"

"No one, sir."

"How about the people who ran the tests?"

"Told everyone it was routine. Masked our information by mixing in and testing women who had been trying for more than two months. Sarah and I pulled out what we were looking for. Only had one hospital, Stockholm, who asked to see the data. We sent it mixed. They might look at it the way Sarah and I did. That was three days ago and we haven't heard from them so..."

The President's voice was slow, "Josh, Sarah, good work. Dr. Maxwell, can you confirm this without it getting out."

"Yes, sir."

"How long will it take?"

"We'll need twenty-four hours."

"Let me know as soon as you can, but do not let this out."

"Yes, sir."

An HS member commented, "Sir, if this is true the panic will be ..."

The President nodded, "No one, ladies and gentlemen, no one says a word."

The Vice-President looked up and didn't' hide his smirk, "Well, any warm fuzzy feelings on this one?"

The next morning

Dr. Maxwell stood before the President, "Mr. President, it's true."

The President's eyes dropped, "One hundred percent sure?"

"Yes, sir."

"Any idea how?"

"We checked men and women. It's both, sir.

"What do you mean?"

"Well sir, the bottom line is, men are shooting blanks and women are not receptive."

The President didn't respond.

"Sir, men are sterile and women, even at the peak of ovulation, can't get pregnant. In short sir, men are sterile, women are barren."

"If men are sterile, how do you know about women?"

"Checked with sperm banks. The sperm in banks are fine. Sperm's sealed. We tracked over two thousand women who had used sperm banks over the past thirty days. Seventy percent should have been pregnant. Better results when it's done in the lab. None were."

"You run your own tests?"

"Some sir, but mostly logged into hospital and clinic data banks. Checked data over the past thirty days. We've checked every continent, almost every country. It's the same everywhere, sir."

"Are you telling me that since the aliens landed no woman on the planet has gotten pregnant?"

"Sir, we haven't checked every...yes sir, that's what I'm telling you."

The President looked away as Jason continued, "We do have a few thousand female eggs in banks that could be fertilized and implanted. But that's not enough to..."

The President interrupted, "It's only a matter of days or hours until this is out?"

"We figure about four days sir. A week tops."

The President stood up, looked around as if looking for something then sat back down.

"You know, Jason, I was beginning to have hope that this— the knowledge of these aliens, these Truens might just might be something that humankind...I was beginning to hope that we might be able to take a step forward that would surpass every..."

The President stopped and slowly shook his head. It was difficult for Jason to face him, "Yes, sir." Jason hesitated to speak, "Mr. President I hate to...Sir, there's something else you need to know."

The President looked at Jason with a brook trout glaze.

"While checking the data banks we noticed something else."

Jason hesitated.

"Jason, I'm all right. What is it?"

"There's an outbreak of radiation poisoning. It's not to the point yet where it's epidemic, but it's close. Over three thousand cases in the states so far. Sir, that's not many if we're talking about the flu, but radiation poisoning? Usually, about twenty cases per year in the whole country, normally from some lab accident. Appeared first in Galveston and LA. Started checking the large cities and found more cases, worse in Houston and Galveston. We've got people working on it trying to find the source. Checking water sources, related industries. Also, checking outside the states. But it's odd that the poisoning and sterility are occurring at the same time."

"You think they're related?"

"We don't know, sir. Over time, radiation will cause sterility in men and women. But the subjects we tested for fertility were

254

in good physical health. No traces of radiation except for three men who work in Galveston."

The President stood and turned his back to Jason. His shoulders slumped. He talked slowly, his voice hoarse, "If this impotence lasts how long would, how long do we have?"

"Well sir, it's not impotence. Sex is still alive and well. You sure you want to hear this right now, Mr. President. We can go over this later."

The President didn't answer. Jason continued, "Sir, the world's population is eight billion. We add to the population at the rate of ninety million per year; one hundred fifty million births, sixty million deaths. Assuming birth and death rates continue normally for the next eight months population won't be affected. After that ..."

Jason stopped. The President was now sitting staring as if in a stupor.

"Sir, are you sure you want..."

"What happens after eight months?"

"We'll start losing population at the rate of sixty million a year. This will continue for about ten years. Then, because of aging, the death rate will start to accelerate. In fifteen years, it will be one hundred million per year, in twenty years, one hundred fifty million. Then the acceleration doubles every two years."

"How long do we have as a species if this ..." The President stopped and looked at Jason.

"We have about fifty years. Children born over the next eight months won't be able to reproduce and we haven't factored in..."

Again Jason stopped.

"You haven't factored in what?"

"Well sir, as the population declines and ages, disease, famine, catastrophes will become commonplace. People will be too old to work, produce, maintain social structure, care for themselves. Social order will diminish then cease to exist. No food, medicine, psychologically, people will—sir, we have fifty years, maybe less."

The President looked at Jason, "You're telling me that you've tested children and as adults; they're not going to be able to have babies?"

255

"Yes, sir."

The President buried his head in his hands, "I had doubts but always hope...always hope, but for this..."

He turned to Jason, "I don't know what to do."

"Mr. President, in three days the children and Mr. Mehra meet with the aliens again. Maybe ..."

Jason didn't finish. The President's eyes rolled back into his head and he slumped to the floor. Jason grabbed the phone on the President's desk and screamed, "Code blue. Code blue."

One hundred and twenty seconds later, hooked to an IV, the President was in a screaming ambulance, convoyed by black limos.

CHAPTER THIRTY-THREE

Confrontation

Ten hours later

Dr. Bowman stood in the situation room of the White House and faced Vice-President Tom S. Stewart, Josh, Jason and General Dickenson.

"The President is going to be fine. He has collapsed from exhaustion. Just needs rest.

I tried to tell him, but you know the President. Going to keep him, if I can, for another twenty-four hours. If anything changes, I'll let you know, but like I said, he's fine."

The Vice-President acknowledged, "Thank you, doctor."

Bowman left. The Vice-President looked to Jason and Josh, "Should have seen this coming. I feel responsible, but we have to move on. Josh, Dr. Maxwell, until the President gets on his feet I'm going to rely on you. I know you two are more on the pulse of what's going on than I am. First things first, get me up to date on this radiation poisoning."

Jason answered, "Mr. Vice-President, we have over eight thousand confirmed cases in the US. All are reported in large metropolitan areas, Atlanta, Chicago, New York, LA, Detroit. Half of the cases are in the Galveston and Houston areas. We have fifteen thousand cases confirmed outside the US, mostly in the west, London, Paris, Berlin, Sidney. But there are cases in Tokyo, Helsinki, Lisbon—I have a list."

Jason laid a paper on the President's desk. The Vice-President picked it up and read as Jason continued, "You'll note that the poisoning is concentrated in large cities in the Western hemisphere. Whatever is causing this is very selective. Really complicates tracing the source."

The Vice-President asked, "What about no pregnancies?"

"Nothing new on that sir, other than we've confirmed with over ten thousand women now."

The Cleansing

The Vice-President laid down Jason's report, "Dr. Maxwell, can we lay this on the aliens?"

"I don't know, sir. We're running tests. Taking brain cell tissue from cadavers that are tinted blue, running tests on animals to see if it makes them sterile. So far, nothing. Doesn't affect them at all."

"And humans?"

"Well sir, we can't experiment on humans that way."

The Vice-President looked at General Dickenson, "Might have to and soon."

No one responded.

"What about tomorrow's meeting with the aliens?"

"We'll be leaving at 4 a.m." responded Jason.

The Vice-President's voice softened, "Dr. Maxwell, Jason, I might be all wrong about our visitors. I watched a tape of the Truens." The Vice-President looked away, "Unbelievable." He looked back at Jason, "But I think you'll agree with me, we're in trouble and need answers. Do you mind if General Dickenson and I tag along tomorrow?"

Maxwell hesitated, not anticipating the question, "You mean actually go into the desert?"

"Yep, like to get a close look. We might see something or there might be communication you've haven't picked up on. Same people have made the trek every time. Maybe an addition to the lineup would help."

Maxwell slowly nodded, "Yes, sir."

"Good. The General and I will leave a little early. Get suited. Don't want to hold you up."

"I'll ride with you and the General, sir. Help you out with the suits, fill you in on what to expect," responded Josh.

The Vice-President responded too quickly, "Appreciate it, Mr. Jones, but that won't be—Oh, what the hell, you're right. We'll leave at 0300. That way Jason, you and your kids won't have to wait."

Ten minutes later, General Dickenson and the Vice-President sat alone in the Oval Office. "Tom, you sure you want to do this?"

"Don't think we have any choice, General."

"Why'd you let that boy come with us?"

"That boy is smart. If I'd said no, he'd smell something. He won't be any trouble. In fact, it's good he's coming with us."

The General pulled on his cigar, "But if something goes wrong. Damn it, this could be..."

"Don't start, Roswall. Everything is going wrong. Can't be much worse than the extinction of the human race."

They sat and starred straight ahead.

"Did you really watch one of those Truen tapes?"

The Vice-President rolled his eyes.

8p.m. the same day

Josh, Sarah, Maxwell, and Gayle acknowledged security as they passed through metal detectors at DC Medical. They took the elevator to the secured fourth floor. In the elevator Sarah asked, "Why all the security?"

Her mother smiled, "Hard to break old habits."

They exited the elevator, cleared more security, knocked at room 444 and peeped in. Annabelle, Kate and Dr. Bowman were there. The President, elevated in his bed, motioned for them to come in, "Well, the gang's all here."

Gayle walked to the bed and took his hand, "How are you, Mr. President?"

"Fine now. What you have to do around here to get a little attention."

"Don't let him kid you. After Kate and I got here, we had to wait twenty minutes for him to wake up," quipped Annabelle.

The President grinned, "I'm all right. Just got a little tired. Everything set for tomorrow?"

"Yes sir, guess you heard we're going to have company," answered Jason.

"No, haven't heard about that."

"The Vice-President and General Dickenson are going with us."

The President raised his eyebrows, "Oh, really. Why's that?"

"Said this was an important meeting. Felt they might be able to contribute."

The President poked at the pillow behind his head, "Well, hope they're right about that. Anybody else joining you?"

"No sir, not that we know of."

"The children ready?"

"They're always ready and eager."

"Got the questions down pat?"

"Yes sir, they know what to ask, or think," A shrug, "or whatever."

"Hope so. We sure need some answers."

Dr. Bowman stepped forward, "Ladies and gentlemen, unless there's something urgent, the President's wife and daughter will be here in a about a half hour and he does need to rest. I trust you understand."

As they started to leave the President spoke, "Josh, Jason could I see you for a minute?"

The others left the room and waited in the hall.

At 6:30 a.m. Josh, the Vice-President and General Dickenson exited the Super Stallion and were greated by Colonel Matthews. Contamination checks were brief and the men were escorted through the tadpole tents.

"Mr. Vice-President, General Dickenson, a lot has changed since Josh's first trip. We've brought in more equipment which, so far, has been a waste. Still can't keep up with 'em. They're too fast or too something. Haven't found a thing that can latch on to 'em. The good news is that we've had no bad readings. No radiation, no contaminants, nothing. So what we've done is to gradually move our tent tunnel closer. We're within twenty yards. They don't seem to mind, but twenty yards is close enough. Any of you gentlemen seen one of those Truens yet?"

"No," answered Josh.

"No one here either."

The red flashing and buzzer signaled the men had entered the change tent.

"Since we're so close now we don't have to use the Humvees. Just walk to the last tent exit and you're there. The MASH unit is there now. That'll be good for those six Korean boys. They've been checked out by the Docs and they're waiting..."

Josh interrupted, "Six Korean boys?"

The Colonel looked at Josh then at the Vice-President. The Vice-President fixed on Josh, "Yeah, forgot to mention my boys to you. State department diplomacy thing. North Korean government sent six boys to experience our preschools. Wanted to know, if while they were here, they could get a close up view of the craft. Record it, have something to take home as a souvenir. A little touristy, but great for diplomacy. I wanted to clear it with the President, but with his condition, didn't want to bother him. I sent them on ahead last night. Hope they weren't any trouble, Colonel."

"Oh no, your men took care of everything. They were a little sleepy. But, if I were only five years old and traveled all night, I'd be sleepy too."

Josh startled, "Five years old?"

"That's correct, Mr. Jones. Five year olds are typically preschoolers."

"Sir, I'm not sure putting five year olds in the desert is a good idea?"

The Vice-President smiled, "Oh, I understand your concern, Mr. Jones, but the North Koreans insisted. And, we've been trying for forty years to get a foot in the door with them. It'll be fine, just going to give them a little peek, shoot a souvenir video, and send them home. Oh, that Laku boy from India, how old is he? Four, five?"

Stewart, not waiting for an answer, turned to Colonel Matthews, "Like I said earlier Colonel, we're going in first. Get the boys a kodak moment and get out. Don't want to be in the way when the doctors and the other kids arrive. So, if we can expediate things, I'd appreciate it."

"Yes sir, Mr. Vice-President. The boys are ready and waiting at Medical. We don't use the bio-hazard suits anymore, but if you'd like, we'll get you fitted."

"No, the issue's fine."

The Vice-President turned to Josh, "Josh, no need for you to bother yourself with our little expedition. General Dickenson has his men with the boys. They can escort us. So, if you'd rather stay and wait on Dr. Maxwell and the children that would be fine."

"I appreciate that, Mr. Vice-President, but I'll go with you. Wait there for Dr. Maxwell. Gives me a little extra time to get some readings."

The Cleansing

The Vice-President looked at Josh for a few long seconds, "Okay, that's fine." He glanced at his watch, "Let's get cracking. Don't want to keep our boys waiting."

Ten minutes later Josh, the Vice-President and the General were at the last exit tent. Six Korean boys waited with four of General Dickenson's men. All were in fatigues and stood at attention. Two large handled satchels lay beside two of the four men. Colonel Matthews spoke, "Wow, look at those kids. Where'd they learn that?"

The Vice-President responded as he walked and stood between them, the Colonel and Josh, "Korean discipline, Colonel, Korean discipline. Start teaching them when they're two." The Vice-President turned to the men standing at attention, "Let's move out."

Josh stepped toward the canvased red marked exit, "I'll go first. Check out everything. Will signal you when it's time to exit the tent." The younger man looked at the Vice-President, "Just going to step outside, let the children see the craft and that's it, right?"

"That's it. We're going to take the time to shoot a little video. So lead the way Mr. Jones."

Josh looked about the tent. No one moved. He started for the exit, stopped and pointed, "What's in the satchels?"

The Vice-President glanced at General Dickenson. The General hesitated. Stewart answered, "Video equipment."

Josh took his eyes away from the satchels and looked at the Vice-President, "I'll signal you."

Josh pushed the canvas exit flap open and walked into the desert. The Vice-President turned to Colonel Matthews, "Thank you, Colonel. No need to bother you anymore than we have. We can take it from here."

"Yes, sir."

The Colonel turned and walked back down the tent tunnel. The Vice-President walked to the exit flap and opened it enough to see Josh taking readings, working his way toward the alien craft. The Vice-President turned to one of the General's men standing beside the six Korean boys, who had yet to move, "He's only fifteen yards out, so don't make any noise setting up the equipment. Don't want to interfer with him getting his readings. Okay, we don't have much time."

The soldier saluted, "Yes, sir."

Two of the soldiers picked up satchels and exited the flap leading into the desert. Once into the desert, the first soldier unzipped a satchel, retrieved video equipment, and began to prong it into the desert sand. The second one waited. Inside the tent the Vice-President signaled General Dickenson. The General motioned to another of his men standing beside the Korean boys, "It's time."

"Yes, sir."

The soldier turned to the Korean boys and said "Play" in Korean.

Expressionless and emotionless the boys started to march single file toward the exit.

General Dickenson yelled, "Wait."

He dropped to his knees and took one of the last boys by his shoulders and looked into his eyes. He let the boy go and did the same to the next one. Without getting up he looked at the Vice-President, "Damn you, Tom, these boys are drugged. What in the hell are you trying to pull?"

The Vice-President spoke very calmly, "Just a little medication that gives them stamina. Keeps them awake. We're down to the short hairs, Roswall, move your ass."

The Vice-President's eyes darted to the remaining soldiers escorting the boys. The exit flap opened from the outside, "Sir, video and toys are in place."

The boys exited the tent. The General scrambled to his knees and followed. Outside the tent, ignoring the wind and sand, with military precision, two of the children went to the video equipment and four went to the two sound wave cannon that had been pulled from the second satchel, tripoded and lasered in on the craft. Fifteen yards ahead, Josh faced the craft taking readings. The Vice-President started to grab the General by the shoulder, but was stopped by a voice coming from behind him.

"Tom, we'll take it from here."

The Vice-President turned. The President, Colonel Matthews, and ten SOGs stood behind him. The Vice-President stumbled backward a step. He looked at General Dickenson then stammered, "Mr. President, what are you doin...?"

It was too late. The hum/thump of sound wave cannon vibrated in the desert. The sound echoed off the alien craft within two feet of Josh. Josh turned and saw boys firing the cannon. Gray came over him. He slumped backward. His mind said 'parate quieto, las minas' but his voice didn't.

He started toward the boys and a thump hit his chest. He smashed back into the craft, fell into the sand and quivered. The thumping continued, kicking sand about Josh and hitting the craft. Another blast hit Josh, picking him off the sand and smashing him again into the craft. General Dickenson screamed "no". He ran toward Josh as SOGs sprinted toward the cannon. A blast hit the General in the back and he staggered forward falling over Josh's body. Three more blasts hit him. Each picked up his body six inches. One of SOGs reached the children screaming "no" and kicked over one of the sound cannons.

Two of the Korean boys stood up from kneeling positions, looked around and started to cry. The other four looked about confused and frightened. The Vice-President screamed "play" in Korean and started for the cannon. Three of the SOGs with the President pushed him to the sand and shielded his body with theirs. Five others, including General Dickenson's men went for the videos and cannon. The cannons had been set on automatic and spun in the sand continuing to fire. A SOG was hit in the leg and screamed as he fell. Another was hit diving on one of the cannons. Another took a direct hit in the face. Then the blue came. The blue encircled the cannon and in three seconds they were gone. A SOG yelled, "Who's hit? Who's hit?"

President Meyer struggled to get up, "Dammit, let me up."

Colonel Matthews barked into his wrist, "Area X. Area X. Four men down. Four men down. Medical swat teams now."

There was a crackled frantic response, "Yes, sir! We read! Yes, sir!"

The Colonel pointed to the children, "Get them out of here. Move! Move!"

Three SOG's responded, grabbing a boy under each arm, and sprinted down the tent. As Colonel Matthews ran toward Josh and General Dickenson he pointed toward the two SOGs who had been hit and yelled, "These men—now!"

Colonel Matthews reached Josh and General Dickenson and knelt. Someone knelt beside him. He glanced and saw it was the President. General Dickenson was on his back lying in the sand beside Josh. Blood oozed from his eyes, ears and mouth. His voice was a gargled whisper, "Mr. President, Mr. President."

"I'm here, General. I'm here. Don't try to talk, the medical team is ... "

The General struggled to talk. The President glanced at Colonel Matthews attending Josh, then leaned close to the General, "I know, General, I know, save your stren…"

The General's garbled voice interrupted the President, "Love my country. Served her sixty years. Didn't mean…"

The General's eyes tried to focus, then closed. He pulled at the President's sleeve. "Mr. President you have to…Marge. You have to tell her I…"

"General, your country will honor what you did today. Shielding one of her fine sons. You're an honor to your country and you have the word of your President that's what Mrs. Dickenson will know."

The General's eyes opened to the President. His right hand moved toward his forehead. It made it to the bridge of his nose before it dropped. The President leaned closer and returned the salute. The corners of the General's mouth moved as his eyes turned white. The President heard a voice behind him, "Mr. President, we need to get in there."

The President turned. The medical teams had arrived. One minute later Josh, the General, and two SOGs were on stretchers about to be moved. A blanket covered the face of the General and one of the SOGs. As the medical teams lifted the stretchers one of the SOGs froze and said very softly, "Don't anyone move."

All eyes followed his. Twenty yards to the left of the craft stood an alien. It swayed back and forth and a low pitched hum could be heard above the wind. It was joined by another then another, and all swayed and the hum became louder. Then they were gone.

The Cleansing

Inside the MASH tent medical teams swarmed over Josh and the injured SOG. The SOG groaned, "Dammit, I'm fine. Take care of him."

"Sir, your leg is shattered, and he is being taken care of. You have to be still."

Colonel Matthews heard the conversation as he walked through the area, "Consider that an order, soldier."

The SOG came to attention while lying flat, "Yes, sir."

The Colonel leaned toward the head Physician tending Josh, "I'll be in security. If anything..."

The physician took a quick glance at the Colonel. The Colonel looked at a quivering Josh, "Keep me posted."

The physician didn't look up, "Yes, sir."

One minute later, Colonel Matthews entered the tent with the white letters "SECURITY" on the entrance flap. The President and Jason Maxwell were standing with four SOGs. Sitting in a chair beside them was the Vice-President.

The President spoke, "Colonel Matthews, I'd appreciate it if you'd have one of your medical people take a look at our former Vice-President. Then I'd appreciate it if you'd arrange to get him transported out of here."

The Vice-President sat with his head slumped forward toward the floor as Colonel Matthews responded, "Yes, sir, it'll be my privilege, sir."

The Colonel motioned toward the SOGs and two of them took Stewart by his arms, "Time to go, sir."

As he rose and was being led out he stopped and looked at the President.

"You're making a big mistake."

The President put his nose to within an inch of Stewart's face, "You're responsible for the death of two of my country's soldiers. You're responsible for the injuries of two more. You put children entrusted to you in harm's way. God knows what else you've done, firing on their craft. And, you did it on my watch as my Vice-President."

The President backed away and looked down, "You're right Tom. I did make a mistake with you. But, the biggest one was waiting too long to correct it."

The President nodded toward the two SOGs holding the former Vice-President by the arms, "Get him the hell out of here."

The SOGs started Stewart down the tent tunnel. The President asked Colonel Matthews, "Those Korean boys all right?"

"Yes, sir, left five minutes ago. A couple of them were still crying. They really thought they were playing. God, I can't imagine how you could train children to…they're fine, sir. Want us to transport them back to North Korea?"

"No, Colonel. Best we stick to our agreement. I think those boys will benefit by a little preschooling in America."

"Yes, sir."

"How's Josh and the other soldier? What's his name?"

"Captain Townsend, sir. Won't know for a while. I appreciate you calling the family of Lieutenant Cook. I know they appreciated it too."

The President looked away, "Hoped I'd never have to do that again." The President turned to Jason. "Jason, I think we should abort. God only knows what this has caused with the aliens."

"I thought so too, sir, until I talked with Mr. Mehra. He said we should go ahead."

"What do you think?" asked the President.

"Well sir, the problems with no answers are still there."

The President raked fingers through his hair, "Yeah, and we may've just caused a another big one. Have any idea what the swaying and humming was all about?"

"No, sir."

"Might be some sort of warning."

"Yes, sir, could be."

The President walked across the tent, stopped, and looked to the floor, "Okay, let's go ahead. And, Colonel I'd appreciate it if you'd check on Josh and Captain Townsend, I need to call Ms. Dickenson and Sarah Trent."

Thirty minutes later, the President was pacing in the Medical tent. Colonel Matthews stood sipping coffee. A doctor emerged from the operating room, "Mr. President, I'm Doctor Emlinger.

Just finished with Captain Townsend. He's fine. His leg is going to be in a cast for a while but he's going to be fine."

"No permanent damage to his leg?"

"We expect a full recovery."

"That's good. That's great. What about Josh?"

"Well sir, they're still working on him. The internal damage is pretty bad but Dr. Woo, who's heading up the team, is the best. Have to wait and see what he says."

"Thank you, doctor."

"Yes, sir. And Mr. President, Josh is a strong young man, but one more hit and, well sir, General Dickenson saved his life."

One hour later, the President and Colonel Matthews pulled themselves away from the monitor viewing Jason, Dr. Taylor, Laku, Tesh and Mr. Mehra in the desert. The President spoke, "My God."

Colonel Matthews did not respond. A Lieutenant Major in whites appeared.

"Mr. President sorry to interrupt. I'm Dr. Woo."

The President turned to Dr. Woo but didn't see him. He looked back pointed at the monitor, "My God. Did you see that?"

Dr. Woo looked at Colonel Matthews, then back to the President, "No sir, I just got out of surgery with Mr. Jones. Should I come back later?"

The President focused, "Oh sorry, Dr. Woo, I'm...you didn't see that?"

"No, sir."

Colonel Matthews asked, "How's Josh?"

"We have him stabilized. There was internal hemorrhaging and bleeding. The bleeding is under control, but the damage to his organs? We're not sure. Those sound waves do terrible things. His liver is of the most concern. Good thing we could treat him here. If we'd had to fly him out—he's a young man, Mr. President. We'll do all we can."

"Thank you, Doctor."

Dr. Woo turned and walked back into the operating room. Colonel Matthews said to the President, "We can talk with them now if you want."

The President followed the Colonel to the quarantine tent. Jason, Laku, Tesh and Mr. Mehra sat behind clear plastic sheeting. The President asked, "What can you tell us?"

Mr. Mehra responded, "I can tell you I saw a Truen die in the arms of an alien, and as it died the alien said we should take care of our children and they have our answer."

"Died because of what happened with the cannon?" asked the President.

"Yes."

"What did they mean *'they have our answer?'* Are we in any danger from that?"

"Well sir, they've only asked us one question."

"What question? Oh, God!"

"Yes, Mr. President."

The tent was quiet until Tesh stepped forward, "When the Truen died I learned a lot."

"What did you learn, Tesh?" whispered the President.

"They shouldn't die. They should never die. They are too perfect to die. When they live we can see the beauty in ourselves. When they die we see all the terrible things we've done. They should never die, Mr. President. We need to be careful."

"Why's that, Tesh?"

"Cause we can kill them."

Mr. Mehra bowed his head and began to weep.

"No answers on the radiation poisoning or women not getting pregnant?" asked the President.

Mr. Mehra looked up, "We will thrive when other species thrive."

No one responded until Laku said something. All looked to his interpreter.

"He wants to know what a hundred thousand means?"

"A hundred thousand?"

The interpreter said something to Laku and Laku responded. The interpreter looked at Laku for a time before turning to the President, "When the Truen died, Laku said he saw children starving, and he doesn't know what a hundred thousand children starving to death every day means."

269

The Cleansing

Four hours later

The Stallion chopper landed and Gayle and Sarah Trent exited. They were met by the President and Jason.

Sarah spoke as the President hugged her, "How is he?"

"They have him stabilized. So far, so good, but you need to know. The wound is bad."

"Can I…we see him?"

"Sarah, he's sedated. He won't know…of course you can see him."

Josh lay motionless under a canopy of clear sheeting. Tubes extended from his nose and mouth. A draining tube came from his side stopping in a half full clear plastic bottle. Intravenous needles were embedded in veins of both arms. His breathing was rhythmic and metallic. When Sarah saw him she muffled a cry with her hand. She walked to his bed, dropped her head into her hands and cried softly. Gayle, the President and Jason glanced at each other and stepped outside.

"Mr. President, we're a little short on space here, so use my office. I need to check on a few things. You folks want something to eat? Coffee?"

Colonel Matthews offered his tent office to the President, Gayle and Jason.

"Thank you, Colonel. Coffee sounds great," said the President.

"Guess we need to get back," the President said. "I'm sure Sarah will want to stay."

Gayle nodded. There was a pause until the President spoke, "I'm going to ask General Wayland to take temporary command of the Joint Chiefs."

"Good choice, sir. Will be well received in the UN," agreed Gayle.

There was another pause. Jason offered, "I'll have the Colonel get our chopper ready."

CHAPTER THIRTY-FOUR

Resignation

Twenty-four hours later, Sarah Trent startled awake up in her chair. She looked at Josh. His eyes were open looking at her. Tears came with a short breath as she slipped her hand under the plastic sheets and took his. She felt a gentle squeeze.

"When are you going to learn to quit messing with kids?" His eyes widened. She smiled softly as she wiped tears from her cheek, "I have something for you."

She took her hand from his and retrieved the brief case beside her chair, opened it and pulled out a large brown envelope. Stamped *"CONFIDENTIAL"* in large three-inch red letters. She slid the enveloped under the plastic onto Josh's bed.

"It's the SEAL report on *'Code Israel.'* "

She took his hand again, "Josh, you didn't hit any of the children, you didn't hit any of their parents or their teachers."

His eyes glistened as he looked at her then the envelope.

"I know what you're thinking. Would I have brought you the envelope if you had?" She reached and touched his face, "No, I wouldn't have."

Almost imperceptibly, he smiled.

Fifteen minutes later

Gayle hung up the phone and hugged Jason, "That was Sarah. He is awake. She talked to him. Doctors have upgraded him to serious."

"That's great. Oh, that is great."

Gayle smiled agreement, "She gave him the report."

"Think they'll ever know?" asked Jason.

"Well, he found out about Lo Chou Lee."

Jason's eyes widened at Gayle. "He knows that Lo Chou Lee was the driver of the tank in Tiananmen Square?"

"Yes, mentioned to Sarah that he was one of his heroes."

Gayle walked to the fireplace and threw in a large brown envelope stamped CONFIDENTIAL. They watched it burn.

One hour later - the Oval Office

"Still no pregnancies sir, and radiation poisoning has been documented in every major western city in the hemisphere. A few cases are being reported in smaller cities and it's beginning to affect plant and animal life."

President Meyer gripped the bridge of his nose. "And cities outside the Western Hemisphere?"

"Not yet, sir." Jason shook his head, sorry he didn't have anything good to offer.

"And no leads?"

"No, sir. But it is coming from somewhere and is still coming. Readings are getting worse every day."

"Tell me."

"Sir, radiation is measured in RAD's, which means *'roentgen absorbed dose.'* A RAD denotes the amount of absorbed dose of ionizing radiation per mass..." Jason caught the puzzled expression of the President. "Sir, a typical chest X-ray releases approximately .05 RADs. A one-megaton atomic bomb releases a thousand RADs and kills one hundred percent of all life twenty seven hundred yards in every direction. In the worst areas, since the outbreak, the number of RADs has been increasing. It's like a giant X-ray machine has been turned on and we can't find it to turn it off."

"How bad is it?"

"We're getting readings around Galveston and Houston ranging between forty and fifty RADs. As you go inland, it dissipates, but it is increasing in our major cities, in fact, in all our cities. The more dense the population, the worse it is."

"How is it affecting people?" The President looked and felt far older than he had been only weeks ago before Christmas.

"In the worse cases—blisters, nausea, vomiting. However, sir, the problem is the radiation is getting worse. It's increasing by ten to twelve RADs a day."

"How long do we have?"

"Sir, one hundred RADs causes severe vomiting, hair loss, sterility, bleeding."

"And if it goes higher?"

"If the radiation levels get to one hundred and fifty we'll have millions of deaths."

The President began to pace, noticed what he was doing and sat back down at his desk, "Medical teams?"

"Spreading out all over the country, sir...but..."

"But?"

"In a few days, there's not going be enough medical anything."

"Can we ask for help from the countries not affected?"

"Already have. Got hundreds of teams flying in, but it's only a matter of time until this spreads. It's in the air, sir. And that means it spreads with the wind, weather, air currents..." Jason threw up his hands.

"If we could find the source and cut if off?"

"If we can cut if off in the next forty eight hours, we'll have about a thousand deaths, a half million very sick people, a lot of dead plants and animals, contaminated water and food supplies, but we could recover. Take some time but we could recover." Jason hesitated, "Sir, I do have a bit of good news."

"I'm listening."

"Truens are still appearing at random and with the same results."

The President looked at Gayle and Jason, "If they're going to kill us with radiation why Truens? And, for that matter, why sterilize us before killing us with radiation?"

"Got our second team working on that, sir"

"Second team?"

"Yes sir," Jason nodded, "got the first team working on the source of the radiation."

"Better get all your teams working on that."

"Yes, sir."

A Major burst into the room. "Mr. President, we know where the radiation is coming from."

CHAPTER THIRTY-FIVE

Our Fate

Twelve hours later, Josh sat up in bed, immersed in computer printouts on radiation poisoning from Homeland Security. Sarah sat in a chair beside him, an elongated printout six inches from her nose. She looked up, "You should be resting you know. HS has people all over this, and their insides don't look like spaghetti."

Josh thought aloud without taking his eyes off a report, "It's coming from petroleum products, so it has to be coming from a refinery or the oil. Checked the oil, everything's clean, that leaves the refineries. How in the world, they've checked every refinery we have—twice."

Sarah looked at Josh wide-eyed, "Wait a minute. Where's that printout where they checked the tankers?"

Josh picked up the printout to his left and handed it to Sarah. "They checked twenty tankers and the oil was clean. What're you looking for?"

"Did they randomly check?"

"Yes," Josh answered.

"Did they check where the tankers were from?" she insisted.

"You mean which country?"

Sarah ran her finger over the figures on the printout, "Yes."

Josh laid down his report and leaned toward Sarah, "Sit on the bed so I can take a look."

Sitting on the edge of the bed, she passed the printout back to Josh, "You call out the countries."

Josh took the report and squinted at the numbers, "Okay, they're number coded."

Sarah leaned to the report and pointed, "Lower left are the numbers with country."

"Okay, Saudi Arabia, Libya, Saudi Arabia again…"

"Slow down," she complained.

"Sorry, got two Saudi Arabias and one Libya."

"Already have them. Go ahead."

"Russia, Iraq, Saudi Arabia—going too fast?"

"A little. That was Russia, Iraq and Saudi Arabia?"

"Yes. The next two are Egypt then Iraq again…"

Three minutes later Josh leaned toward Sarah, "Who wasn't checked?"

"Mexico, Iran and India."

"We get tankers from Mexico?"

"A few from their wells in the Gulf" Josh responded.

"Where else do tankers come from?"

"I think that's it. It has to be from one of those three."

Josh and Sarah looked at each other. Josh nudged Sarah with his elbow, "And I'm supposed to be the smart one. Oh, that hurt." Josh lay back on his bed as he pointed to the phone.

"Call the red line."

Five minutes later Sarah hung up the phone, "Had to patch me through to Jason. He's in Galveston. They caught on two hours ago. Got crews back on the way to the docks. But, it's going to be at least four hours. They're covered up closing down stations, recalling gas, heating oil…God, what a mess. They're trucking in clean gas for emergency vehicles, police; heating oil is the problem. They're distributing electric heaters but it's gonna take weeks."

Josh gazed at Sarah until she asked, "What's wrong?"

"We don't have weeks and the problem is, the contamination is still coming."

"Well, they're doing everything they can. They'll stop it at the docks. Banned driving, they've got a headlock on the country. What else…?"

Josh swung his feet over the side of the bed and grimaced. Sarah stood up. "What do you think you're doing?"

"The satellites" he exclaimed, surprising Sarah. "We've got control of them right here. They can tell us where it's coming from."

Sarah pointed at the bed, "What're you talking about? And you lie back down, right now."

Josh thought aloud, "The KH-13s can detect radiation sources—hot spots. The ones focused on the aliens, we can realign them from here. Should start with Iran. Don't think it's India or Mexico."

"Okay, fine.'' Sarah pointed at the bed. "I'll get Colonel Matthews. He can do whatever. You just lie down.

Three minutes later, Josh and Sarah had explained to Colonel Matthews. Colonel Matthews rubbed his chin, "You're telling me the radiation is coming from oil?"

Josh answered, "Yes, and they've checked and rechecked our refineries. Found nothing. When they checked oil in the Alaskan and Mexican pipelines, same thing. So, they started on the tankers that come into Galveston and Houston and again nothing. But they only checked twenty tankers, and none of the tankers were from India, Mexico or Iran. They caught the mistake and are on their way to the docks. But, it's going to take four hours or longer. Colonel, we don't have the luxury of *four hours or longer.'* The KH-13s can tell us in thirty minutes or less."

The Colonel looked hard at Josh, "I hear what you're saying, but I can't take the KHs off those alien ships. Strict orders, I'd have to call the President, then…"

"If that is what you have to do then do it. But sir, if this contamination continues for another forty-eight hours it won't matter," interrupted Josh.

"But, they're already recalling gas and not letting people drive; they're on top of it."

"Colonel, contaminated oil is being mass produced some-where, and it looks like it's Iran. It's still coming to every western port in our hemisphere, and Europe. We can stop it before it gets to our refineries, but what if the sources of the contamination spread? Who is next to start sending radioactive oil? Libya, Iraq, Saudi Arabia? And finding the source is only ten percent of the problem. The other ninety percent is the technology that makes it possible."

"But, Middle Eastern countries aren't going to send us contaminated oil.'' Matthews shook his head. "They need our money as much as we need their oil."

"Some country already is," a frustrated Josh responded, "and what if the technology can be used to contaminate drinking water, food supplies, the atmosphere?"

Colonel Matthews stared at Josh. Josh continued, "Assume, in the next four hours, they find out its Iran. It'll take them a minimum of seventy-two hours to get a force transported and in place to take out the source, if we can take it out without weapons.

"Colonel here, with the KHs, we can find out if it's Iran in less than thirty minutes and have boots on the ground in Iran in the next three hours. If a job needs to be done, we can do it from here and with the time constraints we may be the only ones who can."

The Colonel stepped back and looked away, "You're asking me to send forces from here, that are assigned to guard the world against space aliens to a foreign country to...to..."

"Yes sir, to save the world."

"Assuming you're right—we don't have the forces here."

"Sir, you have two hundred SOGS, SEALS and marine airborne. I'll need twenty. We'll take a Stallion. It has stealth. At night, we can land a kilometer from Kharg Island. That's Iran's major export refinery, and if they're the source, that's where they're doing it. We can find it and take it out."

Sarah shrieked, "Why do you say 'we' Josh? You can't go, there's no way you can, what makes you think you even have too?"

"I speak Arabic and Kurdish. If there's someone else here who can then...otherwise, I have to go and I'll be fine."

The Colonel fixed on Josh for a full ten seconds, "This is...how do you know you could take out, whatever, without weapons?"

"I don't sir, but we have to try."

Colonel Matthews paced, "We could ship in one of those sound wave cannons. Damn, why didn't we keep them here?"

"That would take eight hours. We don't have time, sir and we don't have a choice."

The Colonel grimaced, "Okay, but let's be sure of what we're doing, if that's possible. We'll take a peek with the KHs. If we find anything I'll call the President."

"Yes, sir."

The Cleansing

Fifteen minutes later Colonel Matthews hung up the phone. He looked at Sarah.

"He agrees we should do it—and do it from here. Mr. Jones, we'll leave in fifteen minutes. You're sure about going? We could..."

"Yes sir, I'm sure." Their eyes locked until Matthew looked away.

"Okay, Dr. Woo will be here in a sec. I'll see you at the Stallion."

Colonel Matthews took an uneasy glance at Sarah and left. Sarah helped Josh dress, buttoning an Iranian military shirt.

"You're crazy, you know that. You're crazy. What are you trying to do, kill yourself?"

"I'll be fine. Just going to take a ride, walk a bit and come back. Woo is going. I'll be fine."

"Sure, you'll be fine. Can't even dress yourself. What can Dr. Woo do out there if you start bleeding?"

Josh put his forefinger to Sarah's lips, "We have to have someone who can communicate. Sarah, this has to be done and who knows, maybe I'll get lucky and not run into any kids."

Sarah turns away. Moments passed before she turned back, "Try not to show off your butt."

"Full coverage at 11:00."

Two minutes later, Dr. Woo entered with a tray and avoided looking at Sarah. She noticed. He sat the tray on the table beside Josh's bed. He picked up a syringe, raised it to eye level and pushed until a drop appeared at the end.

"This first shot will help with the pain. The next one, internal bleeding, thickens the blood."

He administered the first shot, retrieved a larger syringe from the tray and asked Josh to drop his pants. Sarah shook her head, "I knew it. I knew it. Where's SNN?"

Dr. Woo picked up his tray to leave, "See you at the chopper."

He turned and motioned to Sarah. She and Dr. Woo walked to the flap of the tent. He whispered, "I'm not going to lie to you. He shouldn't do this. But I'll be there, and I won't let him

278

out of my sight, and I'm taking lots of syringes. He's stubborn and he's strong. I'll do my best to get him back in one piece."

Sarah glanced toward Josh, "It's not one piece I'm worried about. It's how the all the pieces fit together."

Dr. Woo half-smiled and left. Sarah went back into the tent. Josh was standing at the edge of his bed. He took a step.

"See, I'm fine, drugs working already. Should've had this stuff in Siberia and Quito."

Sarah moved to his bed and hugged him, "You're really going to do this?" Josh kissed Sarah on the forehead and started to leave. Sarah stopped him. "Since you're determined to kill yourself, I have an idea on how you can take out the source of the radiation once you get there."

Fifteen minutes later, ten SEALS and ten SOGs, Josh, Colonel Matthews and Dr. Woo, sat in a CH-54. The CH-54s whispering complimented the darkness, and at 325 miles per hour headed toward one of the largest oil exporting stations in the world—the Jazireh-ye Khark terminal on Kharg Island. The Colonel briefed.

"Gentlemen, listen up. The SOG team will be transported to rendezvous position, one kilometer west of the target. You have the coordinates. From there they will advance on the objective. Captain Trey and his SEAL team will be dropped in the gulf a half-kilometer from the beach. From there they will advance on target.

"Communication will begin at 0200. The SOG team will initiate communication every five minutes until teams intersect or situation dictates. If the SOG team fails to neutralize the target, SEAL teams will advance and carry out mission. All operations cease at 0500 and teams will return to Stallion rendezvous position. We will depart at exactly 0530. Any questions?"

There were none.

"Gentlemen, you know the drill. We're under their radar, they're not expecting company and their security is lax. Put on your makeup and contacts. Check each other. You should look like Iranians close up.

The Cleansing

"Gentlemen, I repeat. When you encounter the enemy engage your weapons immediately and proceed. Do not talk or approach, engage and proceed. Is that clear?"

There was a chorus of "yes, sir."

"Good, check your equipment and Captain Trey, keep your weapons dry. I want all four working when you hit the beach."

"Yes, sir."

Colonel Matthews sat down beside Josh, "How you holding up?"

"Fine. Dr. Woo knows his drugs."

"He's the best. Been on many of these?"

"My share, but none like this."

The Colonel chuckled, "I heard that. Sure you don't want to go with your SEAL buddies? The doctor could give you another shot. Swimming might be just what you need."

"Think I'll pass on the tad-poling. A stroll on the beach will do just fine."

There was quiet until Colonel Matthews asked, "Wonder how they let the radiation slip through?"

"Don't check oil at the ports—too eager to get it to refineries."

"No, I mean the aliens. They neutralized everything we have, weapons, nukes, everything. How'd they let radioactive oil slip by?"

"Thought about that one myself. Maybe whatever they used didn't penetrate the oil. Maybe they made a mistake. Could be they're not perfect."

The Colonel shook his head, "I don't know if I want to agree with you on that." He started to turn away but looked back, "You sure you're all right?"

"I'm fine, Colonel, thanks."

"Good, I'm going to check out our weapons. Want those things working. That Sarah Trent is a smart young lady."

As the Colonel worked his way toward the front of the chopper, Josh doubled over. Dr. Woo moved to his side and administered a shot.

Ninety minutes later the chopper landed. The lights of tankers and the refinery could be seen in the distance. Colonel Matthews faced his men.

"Follow your orders and complete your objective. Captain Tray, we'll see you and your men back here at 0500 or sooner."

"Yes, sir."

Ten SOGs, Josh, Dr. Woo and Colonel Matthews exited and advanced toward the refinery. The CH hovered, and then headed silently out to sea. Colonel Matthews patted Josh on the head, the signal that Josh would be the only one to speak for the rest of the mission. Josh whispered in Arabic, "Check."

Four jackets shielded four pieces of equipment and a push of a button turned them on. There was a lapse of ten seconds and the buttons were pushed again, turning them off. Four SOGs gave Josh a "thumbs up."

Josh whispered into a small speaker on his wrist, "Weapons working, sir."

They moved with precision. Josh struggled to stay ahead. He stopped and two more shots were administered. Only one encounter, a rigger and a woman writhing in passion under a blanket. They quieted under their blanket as the SOGs passed, pretending not to notice.

The team moved to within three hundred yards and checked coordinates. The SEALs should have beached one minute ago, two hundred yards behind them. Josh checked his watch: 0200. In Arabic he spoke into the speaker, two of the eight Arabic words taught to the SEALs prior the mission.

"Clear, zero."

Two words in Arabic responded, "Clear, one."

The SEALs had beached, were advancing but had lost one of their weapons. Josh and the SOGs turned inland. In the next fifty yards, they would be among workers, noise, trucks, forklifts, and the giant pipelines that fed the tankers. Strings of poles with tin umbrella lights exposed them. Josh stopped and nodded toward a SOG. The SOG pulled clipboards from a satchel and distributed. They advanced, stopped intermittently, pointed to pipes and wrote on their clipboards.

Colonel Matthews saw it first. The small block building that perched on the largest of the pipelines. The pipeline entered the side and exited the other, like a train through a tunnel, only the train didn't move. It had no windows and was odd, out of place. Two-inch lines snaked from the building to the other pipelines. Colonel Matthews checked coordinates. This was the building.

They were among workers accustomed to Iranian soldiers. It was the midnight shift. They were tired and they were working. The SOGs were ignored. Two months ago the place was swarming with guards and dogs. Josh thought, "*It's too easy.*"

They approached the chain length fence gate that breached the refinery. The gate was open and two midnight shift guards sat in their metal hut, lights on, reading an Arabic newspaper. The SOGs approached and didn't hesitate as they walked through the gate. One of the guards looked up. Josh waved his clipboard at them as he continued walking. One guard nodded and went back to his paper.

They were within fifty yards of the block building. Josh bent double. Two SOGs held him up as Dr. Woo administered another shot. The other SOGs stood close shielding, pointing to pipes.

The SOGs moved slower, one on either side of Josh. They were within twenty yards of the building. It was surrounded by chain link fencing and manned by six armed guards. The gate was locked. Josh and two SOGs approached first. Two of the six guards met him at the gate. Josh spoke in Arabic. "I'm Major Ashid. Call the other men here, now." Without waiting for an answer, Josh motioned to the other four guards. "Come here, now. Important."

The guards looked at each other and hesitated. Josh raised his voice. "I don't like repeating myself. Come here, now! That's an order."

The four joined the other two at the gate, and faced Josh and the SOGs. Josh motioned to the SOG on his left. The SOG dropped his clipboard then pulled a thin monitor from his vest. He pointed it in the direction of the Iraqi guards and pushed a small button on the right side of the screen. The screen began displaying Truens from the fireworks competition in Stockholm. The Iraqi guards watched for twenty seconds, and one by one dropped their impotent rifles in the sand. Two SOGs moved ten yards to the right of the guards, dropped to their knees, and began cutting at the fence with wire cutters.

Josh spoke."We're here to save the children. Please open the gate." Without hesitation, one of the guards pulled a monitor control from a clip on his belt and pointed it at the fence. The monitor clicked and the gate slid open. The SOGs entered.

Two of the Iranians stepped toward Josh and one asked, "How can we help?"

Josh reached forward and put his right hand on the shoulder of the Iranian. "Do you know how to stop it?"

"No, only Zolef knows that."

"Where is Zolef?"

The Iranian guard pointed to the cinderblock shed. As Josh turned a guard grabbed his arm, "You must cut the small line. It is the alarm."

The guard pointed to two conduit lines coming from the bottom of the shed. Josh shook the hand of the guard and pointed to a SOG. The Iraqi soldier shook his head. "No, we will do it. You go. Knock once. Say you have food. It is time for them to eat."

Josh and the guard's eyes locked for a second. Josh turned to the iron steps that led up to the door of the shed. Four SOGs followed him. The others waited with Colonel Matthews who whispered as the Iraqi guards cut the line, "My God."

At the top of the steps, Josh motioned to the SOGs. Two turned on their monitors. Josh knocked once on the metal door.

"I have your food."

There was a pause, then metal unlocking at the door. The door opened and a guard was face to face with a monitor displaying Truens. The guard stood mesmerized. A SOG eased the door open. Another Iraqi guard fixed on the monitor. Zolef and his assistant sat facing a wall of instruments and computer screens, their backs to Josh and the SOGs. The assistant turned and faced a SOG monitor. He gasped. Zolef heard the gasp and without turning reached forward and pulled a red handle downward. Nothing happened. He moved the handle back and forth. He moved his hand slowly back to his side.

"You cut the line."

"Your guards did," answered Josh.

Zolef still did not turn, "The traitors cannot help you. You can't stop it. It's not here."

"I know, but you have the codes. We can't stop it, but you can."

"My guards cannot be traitors. I know. I picked them. They had families like mine. Did you kill them?"

"No."

"Then how?"

"Truens."

Zolef started to turn but stopped, "You speak of the angels of the sky?"

"Yes."

Zolef 's assistant turned to him, "You must see, Zolef. You must see." He pointed toward the monitor. Zolef didn't move.

"My family is dead, my father, mother, my wife and my children. You killed them. And it was for oil. Oil! When you kill like that do you enjoy it or do you delude yourself with remorse?"

"How was your family killed?" asked Josh.

Zolef laughed and almost turned, "You are from the West?"

"Yes."

"You are American?"

"Yes."

Zolef voice was hoarse, "I was going to study at one of your universities, The University of Indiana. Imagine, I was going to study in the country whose technology developed the missile that murdered my family. You know of the AGM-130?"

Josh's whispered, "Yes."

Zolef continued to face the wall of instruments, "You called the *'Holy War,' 'Desert Storm.'*"

Josh did not respond.

"Why does the West not know that technology created for destruction can never be made to discriminate? Why do you delude yourselves? How can you not know that children, families…?"

Josh remained quiet.

"What is your name?"

"Joshua T. Jones."

"Your rank?"

284

"I'm a civilian."

"What is your former rank?"

"Lieutenant."

"Lieutenant Jones, do you know why you kill? I know why I kill."

"Why?"

Zolef's voice retreated, "In the Holy War your media reported collateral damage as hundreds of thousands of our people died. Your media reported that an AGM-130 missile strayed off its intended target and slammed into a roadway on the outskirts of Baghdad. They did not say the explosion engulfed a car killing my family. What is the truth, collateral damage or the death of a family?'

"The death of a family," rasped Josh.

Zolef put his hands on the table in front of him, "If our families do not live, if our children do not live, then why do we and to what end? What do you become when you kill families and children?"

Josh flinched and his head dropped. The room spun and turned gray. "Stand still the mines. That's why I'm here to save…" He began to tremble and doubled over. He coughed and spit blood. A SOG went to the door and motioned to Dr. Woo. Josh dropped to one knee and spoke. "I've wanted to kill, and I've killed children. I'm here to save you from that, but you have to do it, I can't."

"Do not insult me. Do not lie. You brought Truens."

Josh struggled to speak, "To show you why."

"They cannot bring back my family."

Josh coughed blood again as Dr. Woo administered a shot, "Josh, we have to get you ba…"

Josh interrupted and looked to Zolef, "If you have the power to save them, they are your family."

Zolef looked down and hesitated, "You do not speak as a killer."

There was silence. Zolef half turned, "If I look at the Truens what will I see?"

"Those you love."

The Cleansing

Josh thudded to the floor causing Zolef to turn. A SOG focused a monitor on Zolef. Zolef froze. Dr. Woo bent over Josh then looked to a SOG.

"He's hemorrhaging. He's going to die. I can't save him."

Zolef moved his eyes away from the monitor to Josh. He walked to the SOG holding the monitor and reached for it. The SOG hesitated then handed it to him. Zolef walked to Josh, and kneeled down beside him. He put the monitor to Josh's face.

"You must watch while I do the codes."

Josh eyes closed and he coughed more blood.

Zolef screamed, "Open your eyes."

Josh did. Zolef put the screen in Josh's face, stood and went to the control panel. He turned and screamed again, "Do not close your eyes."

Zolef went to a keyboard and began to code. Two dial arrows on the wall panel went from red to blue. Zolef sat for ten seconds before turning to Josh.

"It's done."

Josh's eyes moved from the monitor to Zolef, "Can it happen again?"

"I will destroy the data banks and the code."

Josh tried to smile before his eyes rolled to white. Dr. Woo motioned to the SOGs.

"We have to get him back—now. He's not going to make it."

Four minutes later, Josh lay on a stretcher made from lampposts and jackets. Dr. Woo spoke, "Let's go."

Zolef picked up the monitor and laid it on Josh's chest, "Don't turn it off."

Two SOGs picked up Josh. When they went out the door they found the building surrounded by Iranian soldiers and workers all viewing two monitors placed on the top step. A path was cleared and two Iranian trucks awaited the SOGs. Josh was loaded and they were about to leave. Colonel Matthews climbing in the back of the truck spoke into his wrist.

"Transmission, code E. Repeat, code E. Pipes clean. Repeat, pipes clean."

A crackled voice responded, "Roger, clean pipes. Going home. Out."

Zolef approached Colonel Matthews and saluted. The salute was returned. In broken English Zolef asked, "Can take two with you?"

Colonel Matthews didn't hesitate, "Yes."

Colonel Matthews held the back flap of the truck open for Zolef. Zolef shook his head.

"I need an hour."

Colonel Matthews handed his clipboard to Zolef. He turned to the second page and pointed, "Rendezvous coordinates. We'll wait."

Again Zolef saluted. The truck drove away. Forty-five minutes later the SOGs and SEALs waited in the Stallion chopper. Dr. Woo working with Josh spoke. "Colonel, we need to get him…"

Colonel Matthews interrupted, "Here he comes."

A military truck approached. It stopped ten meters from the stallion. Zolef got out of the driver's side. He walked around the truck and opened the passenger door. An older man exited, and assisted a second who walked with a crutch. Both were in rags of a uniform. They made their way to the Stallion. Colonel Matthews jumped from the open door of the Stallion. Zolef spoke.

"These men would like to go home, Colonel."

Colonel Matthews faced two graying old men. The one held the other with his left arm and saluted with his right. He spoke in a labored whisper with an Australian accent.

"Sergeant Riggs, Captain Dowd, reporting for duty, sir."

Colonel Matthews stood looking at the men then to Zolef.

Zolef stepped forward. "Have your doctor care for his leg. I shot him, and take care of your man who thinks he is a killer. He has found a better way to fight wars."

Colonel Matthews forced his eyes away from the two men and turned to the chopper. "Let's get these men loaded."

Two SOGs exited and helped the two men aboard. Once aboard one of the men started to weep, "Thomas, we're going home. We're going home."

He hugged his companion. They wept together. Colonel Matthews turned to Zolef and gestured for him to board, "Time to go."

The Cleansing

Zolef shook his head, "I have code to destroy. Maybe your next trip." He reached for the hand of Colonel Matthews, "May you and your family be blessed."

The Stallion left. Zolef stood on the beach watching.

"God is great."

Twelve hours later

In the Empty Quarter one of the two lieutenants monitoring the screen images of the alien craft jumped forward in his chair.

"Holy shit!"

The other lieutenant pushed the blue button beside her computer. Blue lights flashed throughout the tadpole tents in concert with belching horns. Fifteen seconds later, Colonel Matthews was at the screens with the lieutenants. Staring at the screen, he punched on his hand phone. "Get the President."

He turned to give orders. Sarah was standing at the entrance of the tent. She asked then looked to the monitors. "What's happening? Oh, God."

She turned to run and bumped into Mr. Mehra coming into the tent. Mr. Mehra addressed Colonel Matthews, "I need to speak with the President."

He sat down and Sarah sprinted to the MASH tent. The blue lights flashed in the tent absent the horn. She sat beside him and took his hand. He lay still, eyes closed.

"Josh, the craft are taking off. They're leaving."

There was no response.

Ten minutes later. The Oval office

"That's confirmed. Are you sure?"

The President hung up the phone and looked at Jason.

"They've left the Kimberly Plateau. What's left?"

Jason, on his knees, put a blue pin on the Kimberly Plateau. He stood and surveyed a blue-pinned-studded map on the floor and pointed. The Pamirs in Asia."

Jason looked up at the President, "The Pamirs is the only place left, sir."

"How do we confirm…"

The phone rang. The President answered and listened.

"You sure?"

He exhaled and hung up the phone, "They've left the Pamirs."
Jason and the President stared at the map, then each other.
"Could they just be changing places again?" The President asked.
"Maybe, but they always changed places a few at a time. They've never all left like this."
The President went for the phone, "Damn, I forgot Mr. Mehra."

Ten minutes later - The Oval Office
"Finally got through. Mr. Mehra, can you hear me. Good. I'm sorry for the delay. Been kinda busy here. What can you tell us?"
The President listened for five minutes without saying a word then hung up the phone. He looked at Jason and Gayle, "They're gone, but they'll be back."
"When?" asked Jason.
"He doesn't know, but it'll be a while."
The President stood and dropped his head and rested his hands on his desk.
"Mr. President, what's wrong?" asked Gayle.
The President looked up at Gayle, "They left the Truens."
Jason looked at Gayle then back to the President, "The Truens are still here?"
"Yes."
"Why? What…?"
"The Truens are here to thrive and reproduce."
"And they can only do that in a non-violent environment," responded Jason.
The President half smiled, "Yes."
There was a pause.
"We have angels among us that have to thrive. Think we're up to it?"
Gayle looked at Jason, then the President, "Are you saying we're capable of violence now?"
"Soon. Very soon," responded the President.
"And if the Truens don't thrive?" asked Gayle.
"Their fate is ours," answered the President.
"What about the radiation?" Jason asked.

The Cleansing

"Not of their doing."

"What about our reproduction?"

"When other species thrive."

Two days later

Laku tugged at the skirt of Ms. Dupree.

"Yes, Laku?"

"I want to go home now."

Thirty days later

Dr. Maxwell walked to the three electron microscopes.

"Slides in?"

"Yes, sir."

Maxwell looked in one of the microscopes, then the other, and then the other. He repeated this twice.

"Good work. What do the projections say?"

"Violence capacity in a year, reproduction in five, plus or minus a month or so."

"And you checked brain tissue at all ages?"

"Yes sir, age, gender, race in twenty different countries. The blue tint is dissipating."

"Have you crunched the numbers?"

"Yes sir. We used six years because of the plus or minus, and the nine months after the five years it will take for babies to start being born. The world population will decrease by a billion five—two billion tops. Aging will be a factor. We just don't know how much, but we're talking close to a fourth of the world's population."

The technician hesitated, "Really going to mess with the world economy. We've never had a shrinking of consumption and expansion. But, we're getting the figures to get..."

"What clued you?" asked Maxwell.

"Well sir, you'll recall when the aliens first entered the earth's atmosphere our planes intercepted, and although the planes couldn't fire, the pilots could pull the trigger. Just hours later, they or no one else could. We wondered why. Started checking brain tissue and sure enough, in those few hours there was a difference. Darker tissue. God, those aliens were precise. At any rate, we thought maybe the darker the tissue the more effective it was. Checked it over time since they'd landed, and sure enough it's getting lighter. We're back in business."

Jason looked at the slides again, "Is a billion and a half enough for other species to thrive?"

"The elderly are much less violent, sir."

"Think taking care of our children will finally sink in?"

Two weeks later - the slums, Moti Jheel, Calcutta

Jeston Mehra sat in the Mirmal Hrdiay Home for Dying Destitutes with the girl in his lap. The child was only a foot tall with the head the size of a thumb. Contorted clawed arms and legs wrapped toward her body. A blind boy with a cane stood beside them. Jeston's left arm hugged the child in his lap. His right arm held the blind boy close. "Trina, I'd like you to meet Laku. Laku this is Trina."

Jeston hugged both tighter. Trina spoke, "Hello, Laku."

"Hello, Trina," answered Laku.

Jeston laughed as he pulled a plastic bottle from his coat pocket. "I have soap bubbles."

Trina and Laku smiled as Laku's hands lurched forward.

"Wait Laku. We're not blowing yet." Jeston opened the bottle and seconds later he was holding the stem for Trina. She struggled to blow as she giggled. Laku's lurching hands popped bubbles as he laughed.

Outside a beggar saw the glow surround the home. The beggar smiled.

It was Christmas and the gathering at the Trent family home in Chapel Hill was in full swing. Sarah's spoon banged her glass.

"Listen up everybody. Got a surprise, hush up for a second." The crowd stopped conversation and laughter and looked to Sarah. "Want everybody to watch this. She turned and walked five steps to the wheelchair of Josh and rolled him to the middle of the room.

"Okay JJ, you're on."

Josh looked at Gayle standing with the President and Jason, "What're we going to do with her?"

Gayle smiled and raised her drink at Josh, "Only easy day was yesterday."

The Cleansing

Josh smiled and braced his hands on the arms of his wheelchair. He strained and stood. The crowd responded with noise and applause. He took a few steps and high fived Sarah. He heard a squeal and turned.

"Uncle Josh." Cindy ran toward him with arms outstretched, a Spaniel trailing after her. Josh carefully dropped to his knees. She hugged him as he winced. "I love you, Uncle Josh."

"Love you too, Cindy."

Laku, on crutches, came from the side and joined the hug. He looked at Josh. "You took too long."

"Sorry Laku, won't happen again."

Standing by the Christmas tree, Gayle took a sip of apple cider.

"Always liked happy endings."

The President answered, "Hope you're right about that. Oh, and on a happy Christmas note, all the contaminated gas has been accounted for. It's history."

Jason said as they clinked glasses, "Guess we'll know in about six months."

The President, Jason and Gayle looked at each other and nodded, but forgot to touch glasses.

The next day

He sat in the tree and grunted, "Climb on you forever."

The giggle of the college girls hushed him. He was high in the tree and they didn't notice him as they stopped and adjusted their backpacks.

He watched as they followed the trail. He hugged the tree and started to climb down.

"Need to get you rooted."

A fluttering sounded over his left shoulder as a golden blue light covered him. He turned then smiled.

292

OTHER TITLES by FIRESIDE PUBLICATIONS

- THE FURAX CONNECTION by Stephen L. Kanne
- THE FIND by James J. Valko
- BLESSED: My Battle With Brain Disease by Mary J. Stevens
- ENGLEHARDT by Gisela Englehardt
- THE COST OF JUSTICE by Mike Gedgoudas
- TEXAS JUSTICE by Judith Groudine Finkel
- LOVE TAG by Peter Shianna
- THE LONG NIGHT MOON by Elizabeth Towles
- AN AGENT SPEAKS: A Primer for Unpublished Writers by Joan West
- THE CRYSTAL ANGEL by Olivia Claire High
- BEYOND FOREVER: Experiences From Past Lives by Taylor Shaye

For more information or to order any of the above books, please visit www.firesidepubs.com or contact:

Fireside Publications
1004 San Felipe Lane
Lady Lake, Florida 32159

To contact the author, please email: beneller@verizon.net